SHOLOM ALEICHEM

OLD COUNTRY TALES

SELECTED AND TRANSLATED,
WITH AN INTRODUCTION BY

Curt Leviant

A PARAGON BOOK

Paragon Books
are published by
G. P. Putnam's Sons
200 Madison Avenue
New York, New York 10016

Library of Congress Cataloging in Publication Data

Rabinowitz, Shalom, 1859–1916.
  Old country tales

  (A Paragon book)
  I. Leviant, Curt, 1932-   II. Title.
PZ3.R113Om   1979   [PJ5129.R2]   839'.09'33
79-13846
ISBN 0-399-50394-3

First Paragon Printing, 1979
Printed in the United States of America

For my wife
ERIKA LEAH LEVIANT

C.L.

ACKNOWLEDGMENTS

For their kind assistance in explaining some of Sholom Aleichem's rarer terms and idioms, I would like to thank the following people: Dina Abramowicz, librarian of the YIVO Institute for Jewish Research; Jacob Birnbaum, staff member of the *Great Yiddish Dictionary;* Henry Altman of the *Jewish Day—Morning Journal;* and Monia Dusawicki.

As in my previous volume of Sholom Aleichem translations, *Stories and Satires,* my heartfelt gratitude is once again extended to my parents, Jacques and Fenia Leviant, whom I always consulted whenever I encountered any difficult Yiddish words, especially those of Russian origin, and to whom I owe my early appreciation for Hebrew and Yiddish. I am also deeply grateful to my wife, Erika, whose keen critical acumen in the untiring reading, checking and proofreading of the entire manuscript was a constant source of aid.

Thanks, too, are due to Shimon Gewirtz, Eliezer Silverman and Art Sorotkin for their careful proofreading and helpful comments on parts of the manuscript; to B. Z. Goldberg, one of our leading Yiddish columnists, and his wife, Marie Goldberg, Sholom Aleichem's daughter, for their kind cooperation; and to Sybil Wyner for typing the manuscript.

It is a pleasure to render thanks, too, to Charles Dwoskin, of G. P. Putnam's Sons, whose enthusiastic reception of my suggestion for a fiftieth anniversary Sholom Aleichem volume sparked the production of this book.

Any list of acknowledgments would be incomplete without a final word of gratitude to Sholom Aleichem, for whom this collection is a posthumous gift of loving appreciation.

C.L.

CONTENTS

INTRODUCTION

In the year 1966 the world commemorated the fiftieth anniversary of the death of the beloved Yiddish humorist, Sholom Aleichem. A culture hero among his own people, Sholom Aleichem's fame deservedly spread beyond Jewry during his own lifetime and since. His works have by now been translated into virtually every European and Slavic language, and even into Chinese, Japanese and Esperanto. This wide distribution—actually many millions of copies of his works have been printed—confirms Sholom Aleichem's universal appeal. America's awareness of Sholom Aleichem in particular and of Yiddish literature in general has come rather late, but the last two decades have seen a remarkable renaissance of interest. Various translations into English, mass circulation via paperback editions, and the acclaimed musical *Fiddler on the Roof*, based on the Tevye stories, have made Sholom Aleichem a part of the American cultural scene.

Sholom Rabinowitz (his pen name was Sholom Aleichem, a traditional Hebrew and Yiddish greeting) was born in 1859 in a small village in Russia's Ukraine, where he received both a traditional Hebrew and secular Russian education. Although he undertook various occupations—tutor, crown rabbi (employed by the regime to keep records of birth and death), publisher, stockbroker, businessman—his first love was always writing. Sholom Aleichem was able to write any place, day or night, while eating or resting. Often, while strolling with family or friends, he could be seen gesturing, his lips moving silently as though testing a forthcoming dialogue or scene. Writing was the driving force in his life and accounts for his prodigious output—the standard edition of his works totals twenty-eight volumes and many more are as yet unpublished.

By the turn of the century, he had already come to be regarded as a classic writer and was earning a living solely from his pen. Later, he also toured European cities, giving highly successful readings from his works. After a brief visit in 1906–1907, Sholom Aleichem returned to settle in the United States in December, 1914, and supported himself and his family by contributing to the Yiddish press and stage. On May 13, 1916, he died of tuberculosis at the age of fifty-seven, mourned by the more than one hundred fifty thousand Jews who attended his funeral and by the entire Jewish world.

Although Sholom Aleichem's name is now synonymous with humor, he began his career as a Hebrew satirist, in imitation of Mendele Mocher Seforim (1836–1917), and achieved a fine reputation as a Hebrew novelist; in fact, his first "work," composed when he was fifteen, was a Hebrew version of *Robinson Crusoe*. Throughout his lifetime Sholom Aleichem never neglected Hebrew: he corresponded with his relatives in Hebrew and hoped someday to translate his own works into the sacred tongue.

Sholom Aleichem's career in Yiddish began in 1883 with the publication of his first story. He heeded the call of his friend Mordecai Spector that Yiddish writers turn from exotic topics and famous figures and devote their attention to an unsentimental depiction of the three million neglected shtetl (small village) Jews. Soon Sholom Aleichem made this sphere his very own and became, in his own words, "the watchman of Jewish provincial life."

Despite his writing about the folk, it would be fatuous to say that Sholom Aleichem was a naïve folk writer, a primitive, untutored genius. Wherever simplicity and folksiness appear, it is the diligent creation of a conscious artist thoroughly aware of literary form and tradition, and knowledgeable not only in classical Jewish sources and contemporary Yiddish and Hebrew literature, but also in the mainstream of Russian and West European literature. Always concerned with the ideological questions and esthetic problems of his time, Sholom Aleichem was a trenchant critic of Yiddish and Russian literature. He had a deep appreciation of the latter and was influenced by such varied authors as Turgenev, Ostorovsky, Shtchedrin and Chekhov, and, by his own admission, Cervantes, Heine, Swift, Dickens and Thackeray. (Interestingly enough, some of Sholom Aleichem's influence may be noted in Ilf and Petrov, joint authors of what are considered *the* comic Soviet novels, and in the *Odessa Tales* of Isaac Babel, who was an editor of the Russian translations of Sholom Aleichem's stories.)

But the actual sources of Sholom Aleichem's writing go far beyond foreign literary models and extend into Jewish culture. Sholom Aleichem's humor, for example, did not spring forth full grown. There was a quasi-literary precedent for it in some of the popular Yiddish pamphlets, whose often banal clowning had no pretension to high literary standards. In his autobiography, Sholom Aleichem tells of one pamphlet his father read to a group of friends. The uproarious laughter made the young Sholom Aleichem envy the witty author, whose story contained some of the linguistic playfulness and penchant for joking common to village Jews in Sholom Aleichem's region.

These pamphlets showed Sholom Aleichem that Yiddish writers need not perpetually maintain a didactic or satiric front. Although the writing was unpolished, they did make use of a host of (albeit rudimentary) comic devices: outlandish names, humorous dialogue, puns, interplay of Hebrew and Yiddish words, distorted quotations from classical sources (an art which Tevye would later develop), broad physical description and invented comic situations. Evidently inspired by these varied devices, Sholom Aleichem, after continuous experimentation, refinement and invention, made them an organic part of his style.

In his own day, Sholom Aleichem's brand of literary humor was actually revolutionary. Prior to his advent, Yiddish and Hebrew literature had been basically serious. It was one of Sholom Aleichem's great innovations to introduce into high-level imaginative writing the playful and ironic humor of the Jews which had hitherto been a part of the oral folk heritage. But the sources for Sholom Aleichem's humor are more diverse than these nonliterary popular pamphlets. Sholom Aleichem also learned from his serious Yiddish predecessors whose writings did contain some humorous scenes. The Russian masters taught him about the comic grotesque. But more than any individual's literary creation, Sholom Aleichem utilized folklore—the heritage of an entire people: folk humor, anecdotes, riddles, quips, sayings and tricks of Talmud Torah youngsters, the early comic Purim plays, Hasidic tales (see "The Village of Habne"), the folk tradition of parodying sacred verses from the Bible and phrases from the Midrash and Talmud, and finally the folk speech itself, from the drayman's language to the curses of the shrew. All these are the varied roots which, blended with his genius for the comic, his powers of observation and his excellent memory, blossomed into the unique style of Sholom Aleichem.

In their introduction to *A Treasury of Yiddish Stories,* Irving Howe and Eliezer Greenberg cite what they call "an extreme comparison. . . . Yiddish [at the end of the nineteenth century] found itself for a moment in the position of creative youthfulness that the English enjoyed during the Elizabethan age." From the point of view of linguistic richness, the comparison is not that farfetched when applied to Sholom Aleichem. In its diversity, inventiveness, and range of expression his language might very well be said to be Shakespearean.

Sholom Aleichem's use of high and low diction, his coinages, his dialectal subtlety, his puns and word plays, his comic use of Hebrew suffixes for Yiddish verbs, his interplay of Yiddish, Aramaic, Hebrew and Slavic words (all languages with which his readers were familiar), his use of classical Hebrew texts, folk expressions and imaginative and highly improbable epithets—all point to a complete mastery of the Yiddish language as a tool for the creation of a great literature. For there can be no great literature without a language commensurate to the widest range of nuances of thought and feeling.

The language of the folk could easily be juxtaposed (and Sholom Aleichem often did this for comic purposes) with a lofty Hebrew verse from the Bible, a quote from the Talmud, a truncated phrase from the Prayerbook, a line from a renowned exegete. All these were religio-literary shorthand which prompted a host of associations in the reader's mind (no footnotes needed), and all smoothly blended into, and without shocks of dislocation were comfortably absorbed by, Yiddish. As with the Hebrew phrases, so with the polysyllabic technical and other terms from Western languages—these too could easily be placed next to tender and pithy folk sayings. Yiddish, a fusion language like English, accommodated all the so seemingly incongruous linguistic groupings and in the course of its nearly one-thousand-year history became rich and highly suggestive.

Just as a reader of Mark Twain could detect the many dialects which the American author authentically reproduced, a Yiddish reader could appreciate Sholom Aleichem's keen ear for the various differences within Yiddish. Even to an undiscriminating reader the Yiddish of Sholom Aleichem's New York Jews bears no resemblance to that of European Jews; nor is the Yiddish of big city and shtetl Jews the same. Not only are the modes of expression of various regions carefully reproduced, but within the shtetl, too, the people of varying social and intellectual levels speak differently: the servants, the workingmen (including the jargon of all sorts of trades), the middle class, the rabbi, the secularly educated, the children.

A reader of Yiddish who is also attuned to the ironic modes of Western literature and the rich possibilities inherent in the interplay of various linguistic layers must marvel at the achievement of Sholom Aleichem's prose: its scope, texture, adaptability and originality are at once a perfect mirror of the language of the people and the artistic expression of it.

There are those who cling to the idea that the shtetl was one warm and happy place—a latter-day Paradise. That this is a myth should be obvious to anyone reading the works of Sholom Aleichem. Certainly there were moments of warmth, beauty and joy, and a perhaps irreplaceable feeling of communality, but there was also poverty, hunger, insecurity, and pogroms. Sholom Aleichem, then, is no chronicler of a romanticized shtetl, but a thoroughgoing realist with an almost all-encompassing vision of Jewish life.

True to his credo that fiction should "depict events which are realistic, possible and plausible," Sholom Aleichem's world—it actually ranges beyond the shtetl into town and city, and even abroad to America—contains not only the good-humored and wise Tevye, the lovable orphan Mottel, and the kindly plain people, but also revolutionaries, cardsharps, informers, rogues, thieves—even adulterers and Jewish white slavers are hinted at. In other words, his re-creation of Jewish civilization describes a complete human comedy, whose members represent various segments of the moral spectrum.

Unlike some of the Yiddish writers who followed him, Sholom Aleichem does not accent either the darker side of life or its erotic aspects, as they have traditionally been explored in Western literature, or as Isaac Bashevis Singer has been dealing with them in his works. Sholom Aleichem does not close his eyes to white slavers or pogroms, but he never focuses on the inherent brutal facts directly. A kindly man himself, for Sholom Aleichem human nature is essentially sound. Even the peasants, would-be pogromists in "Tevye Reads the Psalms," are misguided, but not basically evil. As for the Jews, their antipathy to violence may be summed up by one line in "The Great Panic of the Little People": "Far be it from a Kasrilevkite to shed blood. Just point out a nicked finger in the distance and he falls into a dead faint."

"My muse does not wear a black veil on her face. My muse is poor, but cheerful," wrote Sholom Aleichem. Perhaps this is why acts of violence are always reported indirectly. We hear of them, but we never see them. Reading Sholom Aleichem one never experiences the impact, the terror of a pogrom as one does in the tales of the Yiddish writer Lamed Shapiro, or the Soviet-Jewish writer Isaac Babel. "The world is in a miserable state," Sholom Aleichem once wrote in a letter, "and just on spite we ought not to cry about it. And if you want to know the truth, that's the source of my perpetually good mood, my humor. Just on spite, I'm not going to cry. Just to spite them there's going to be laughter."

Sholom Aleichem began his career in sharp reaction to the cheap writing which flooded the Yiddish literary market. The salacious dime-novel brand of romantic fiction was widespread among the Jews, especially women readers. By taking stock themes from popular European literature—the cowboy western, or the soap opera might be a proper modern analogy —and judaizing them slightly, the authors of these potboilers caught the fancy of East European Jewish readers. Sholom Aleichem felt that this type of lowbrow literature was poisoning the readers' sensibilities and aspired to raise the literary level of Yiddish.

He succeeded admirably. He created a little kingdom and peopled it with hundreds of subjects, rich and poor, religious and free-thinking, gentile and Jew. Not only did Sholom Aleichem describe all types of people, but he also chronicled for posterity the complete rhythm of Jewish life: birth and death, childhood and old age, feasting and fasting, holidays and weekdays, synagogue, home and marketplace. Which is why someone once said that if all records of Jewish shtetl life were to disappear, it could easily be reconstructed from Sholom Aleichem's works alone.

Sholom Aleichem loved the shtetl and knew all aspects of its society. His sensitivity to social stratification, for instance, may be seen in his children's story, "The Flag." In his description of the festival of Simkhas Torah, Sholom Aleichem shows that the Torah circuits begin in the more prestigious synagogues, and conclude in the basement prayer-room annex of the Butchers' Synagogue, the nethermost rung of the social ladder, where the narrator's father is the assistant sexton, low man on the religious functionaries' totem pole. There is added poignancy in the fact that the observer of the social order is Kopel, an eight-year-old boy, experiencing poverty and perpetual hunger, and acutely aware of the shtetl facts of life. But Sholom Aleichem does not devote his attention only to one group. After depicting a poor boy's conflict with a cruel rich boy in "The Flag," in "Visiting with King Ahasuerus" he tells a story from the angle of vision of a sweet-tempered lonely rich boy. Here Sholom Aleichem juxtaposes the silver candelabra, the private tutor, the command performance of the Purim players, the lavish cuisine (meat and white bread daily!) of the rich house, with the hungry orphan, Feivel, the naked children, and the shack of the poor Purim player. Nevertheless, the young heroes of both stories are not that far apart: each lad yearns for the small joys and freedom of childhood. For each the grass is al-

ways greener elsewhere: the rich boy envies the freedom of
the poor, and the poor boy the toys and candy of the rich.

In the shtetl, a person's worth was not judged exclusively
by his wealth or social standing. Moral stature, piety and
learning were idealized; and the latter was an important
factor in social mobility. Most respected of all in the shtetl
was a figure like the aged Reb Yozifl, the frail and saintly
rabbi of Kasrilevke, poor in possessions but rich in wisdom.
Another beloved person was Old Dodi, hero of "David, King
of Israel," whose sole concern was collecting clothes and food
for unfortunate Jews languishing in prison. Many such kind-
hearted figures can be found in Sholom Aleichem's works.
Those graced with learning and piety are never denigrated
by the shtetl; they are always venerated, for they have
achieved some of the ideals for which the shtetl strived.

But all of Sholom Aleichem's characters are by no means
cut from the same holy vestments. He not only pictures a
society where piety and adherence to religious values is the
norm, but also pokes gentle fun at those on the fringe of
traditional Jewish life, tempted and won over by foreign
ways. In "A White Bird," a monologue where Sholom Aleichem exercises a two-pronged irony, he depicts a social order
where the wife flirts with another man because her husband
always plays cards, frequents nightclubs of shady reputation
and keeps a mistress. All this is a far cry from the old-time
Kasrilevke. Broken are the traditional ties. Religion here has
lapsed into superstition. Only the externals of Judaism remain—various foods and folk beliefs devoid of moral/ethical
significance. It is no accident, then, that the sole religious
value accented by the heroine of "A White Bird" is the Yom
Kippur Eve Sacrificial Ceremony—a ritual which has been
criticized by many Jewish authorities as being superstitious
and pagan.

But even toward negative characters such as assimilated
Jews, pious frauds, the selfish rich, a thief or a suspected
arsonist, Sholom Aleichem bears no malice. His Jewish
crooks have no underworld mentality; many of these shli-
mazls are still objects of affection. In line with the Midrashic
statement that God was always on the side of the oppressed,
Sholom Aleichem's sympathies, too, were always with the

underdog: his kindly pen could not, or would not, create wicked people.

Sholom Aleichem's characters, however, are not either black or white. Although in the monologues some rascals bare their souls, they often have some redeeming virtue. If the first impression is a bad one, the author, through characterization as subtle and enigmatic as the human personality, gradually introduces statements which make the reader change his mind about the speaker. For instance, even though there is strong suspicion against the narrator in "Burnt Out," the reader feels a measure of sympathy for him. After all, he *is* the object of the town's wrath, there is no real evidence against him, and he does not dream of revenge. Although the hero damns his fellow villagers in speech, his dream of triumph is to invite all his enemies to his daughter's wedding, drink to each one's health and give the biggest donations for the synagogue and for the poor—certainly a most desirable expression of vendetta.

Another type of tale favored by Sholom Aleichem was the railroad story. The railroad provided him with a perfect vehicle for many stories outside the realm of the shtetl. After their initial skepticism at the existence of the railroad, the Kasrilevkites made up for lost time and took it over as if it were their own. For the Jews the train became an extension of Kasrilevke, a shtetl on wheels. There they slept, ate, prayed, played cards, and, above all, spoke and exchanged stories—and even managed to get to their destinations. Since its physical confines are limited and suspenseful adventures can be plotted with the timetable in mind, the train is an ideal setting for a tale. These unique time-space possibilities are fully exploited by Sholom Aleichem, and are often the decisive point in the story. Moreover, since in the casual meetings aboard a train human relationships quickly blossom and fade, people can reveal themselves with greater candor and without fear that the shtetl may eye them askance on the morrow.

In a society where everything is Jewish, not only do gentiles like Hapke ("The Great Panic of the Little People") speak Yiddish, and behave like Jewish women, but even animals (see "Methuselah") assume Jewish traits. And where the people are imbued with Jewish values, it is perfectly natural for the author's images to reflect this totality. Hence the dome of the sky looks like a skullcap, the forests whisper prayers, a bird sings like a cantor, and shadows are as long as the Jewish exile.

A story in which the Jewish image becomes the overriding figure is "The Song of Songs," one of the most lyrically beautiful and tender love stories in Jewish literature. Even early in his career Sholom Aleichem realized the difficulties that a Jewish writer faced in writing a romance. In the preface to his early novel, *Stempenyu* (1886), he writes, "I began to realize by how much and in what way a Jewish novel must differ from all other novels. The truth is that the circumstances under which the Jew falls in love and declares his passion are altogether different from the circumstances which control the lives of all other men." These remarks may also be applied to "The Song of Songs." The title, as well as the imagery, reflect Israel's biblical classic which tradition has interpreted on a pure spiritual plane as the love song between God and the people of Israel. Whether or not one subscribes to this interpretation is irrelevant. The fact is that in the Song of Songs the Jews have seen beyond eros into the holiness of love. And this is the theme of Sholom Aleichem's story.

In the absence of a firm tradition of romantic love, literary or otherwise, the shtetl lovers resort to the most obvious literary source, the Song of Songs, for declarations of love. And so, for this Jewish love story, Sholom Aleichem chose *the* traditional archetype—traditional in both the religious and literary sense—and perfectly blended theme, content and imagery.

Although Sholom Aleichem has been called a man without didactic intentions, in his satires—those stories where he leaves the tender humorous mode and switches not only key but instrument—he pokes fun at certain people and institutions, and is as scathing as was his avowed literary grandfather, Mendele. In one satire, "The Little Redheaded Jews," he takes to task the shtetl Jews who scorn the Herzl in their midst and pay no heed to his impassioned speech for Zion. Here and in his nonfictional pamphlets, Sholom Aleichem reiterated the theme that Jewish civilization on alien soil cannot continue. A member of the Lovers of Zion movement which preceded Herzl's brand of political Zionism, Sholom Aleichem correctly prognosticated the coming disaster in store for Jews living in an area where the regime and the native population were antagonistic to them. Fifty years later most of European Jewry and its institutions were destroyed by the Germans and cooperative indigenous populations.

But even a writer who eschewed didacticism could not divorce himself from it. For one great quality of Yiddish literature—and this quality is closely linked with the concept of the book in Jewish tradition—is its moral fervor. There was no art for art's sake, and no literary artist wrote mere entertainments. Literature, rather, was part of the continuous dialogue between teacher and taught which harked back in an almost unbroken line to the towering morality of the prophetic tradition.

Sholom Aleichem viewed a society he knew intimately not through rose-colored lenses, but through spectacles of love. Hence he was able faithfully to depict—and castigate—his fellow Jews. But unlike many modern writers, he was not alienated from his society, but identified with it. For in his day there was no great gap between the artist and his public. Both got to know each other quite well. All classes read Sholom Aleichem: rich and poor, young and old, maid and mistress, religious and free-thinking, assimilated and thoroughly Jewish, intellectual and poorly educated. Each group found something in Sholom Aleichem, for he wrote about them and understood them all.

And in time—so great was his popularity—Sholom Aleichem became an extraliterary figure, a living legend, a part of Jewish life, an institution. For this pre-eminence there are many reasons: among them are his readability, inventiveness and scope; his rich gallery of vivid characters; his re-creation of an entire civilization; his magnificent transformation of folk sources into art; his style and humor; his forging of a literary language from the folk smithy of the Yiddish soul.

But beyond all this is Sholom Aleichem's vision. In depicting the hopes, joys, woes and indomitable spirit of his characters, he expresses the collective consciousness of the Jewish people. And this is why it is not hard to understand why a Jew once came up to Sholom Aleichem in Warsaw, took his hand and kissed it, saying: "You are our consolation. You have sweetened for us the bitterness of Exile."

CURT LEVIANT

OLD COUNTRY TALES

Tevye the Dairyman

Tevye, Sholom Aleichem's greatest creation, is one of the most memorable characters in modern literature. Gentle, compassionate, wise, Tevye has a forgiving nature and a great capacity for humor and self-irony. In fact, many have seen in him an alter ego for the kindly Sholom Aleichem himself. Nine loosely related but thematically unified stories, describing the adventures of Tevye and his daughters, make up the volume called Tevye the Dairyman. *The first Tevye story was written in 1895; others followed, one every few years. They not only reflect the growing artistic maturity of Sholom Aleichem, but also the swiftly changing social conditions. "Tevye Reads the Psalms," the last of the Tevye series, shows his resiliency and wit in handling a band of peasants determined to have a pogrom. It was written between 1914 and 1916, the last years of Sholom Aleichem's life.*

TEVYE READS THE PSALMS

No doubt you remember, Mister Sholom Aleichem, that I once gave you a rundown of the weekly biblical portion "Get Thee Out" and supplemented it with about three dozen commentaries. I told you how Esau (the peasant, that is) squared his accounts with his brother Jacob (me) and how he revenged the sale of that ancient birthright by driving Jacob out of town, bag and baggage, kith and kin and bedding, too, as was only right and proper. They put to rack and ruin all my belongings, demolished my entire little shred of poverty and even did in my poor horse, the mere mention of whom still brings tears to my eyes. After all, on Tisha B'Av we read in Lamentations, *For all these things I weep*—so surely the poor creature deserves a tear.

But never mind. I'm willing to forget the whole thing. Because if you really think about it, it's the same old story. Am I more of a privileged character in the eyes of God than the rest of my brethren whom the peasants are booting out of their sacred villages, and cutting off, rooting up, routing out and mowing down every place where there's even a hint of a Jew? Like the prayer, *Be mindful of us*—they're mindful that not a trace of us shall remain. Ah me, but why should I complain to God? Look at all the other exiled village Jews who like stray sheep are wandering up and down God's creation with their wives and little ones. They don't know where they'll bed down for the night, they don't have a place to lay their heads, and they're perpetually in a quiver lest they see in the distance the gleam of a constable's button or any other approaching plague. It's just like the Bible says,

The Lord will set a people against thee—the peasant, of course.

But Tevye is no ignoramus. Unlike other village Jews, he understands the Psalms, he's no stranger to the Midrash and, with God's help, he can even manage to scratch out a chapter of the Pentateuch with Rashi's commentary. But what of it? Expect the peasant to be set store by all this, as is only right and proper, and take his cap off for such a Jew, or give me a great big thank-you? Yet, when you come right down to it, it's nothing to be ashamed of, and it's certainly no drawback. I mean, that like other decent folk I'm not blind to the little letters, thank God. I get the meaning of a biblical verse, can find my way in and out of the text. As the Ethics of the Fathers puts it, *Know how to reply*—in other words, you're in good shape if you have all the answers.

Do you think, Mister Sholom Aleichem, that I'm pulling all this out of my sleeve? or that I want to give myself a pat on the back for my great knowledge and learning? Pardon me, but that could be said only by someone who doesn't know Tevye. Tevye's not in the habit of talking through his hat and, as you well know, he's never been a common braggart. Tevye only likes to talk about things he himself has seen; that is, something he personally has experienced. If you'll just sit down for a little while, Mister Sholom Aleichem, you'll hear a fine story. You'll learn how handy it is for a man not to be just a dumb hunk of flesh and fowl, but to have an inkling into higher realms and know how to spice his talk with biblical verses, even though they're only from our ancient Book of Psalms.

To make a long story short, if memory serves me, this happened quite some time ago, ages ago, I'm afraid, during the days of revolution and constitution, when with free spirit and unfettered hands the peasant mobs tore loose over Jewish towns and villages and made a point of wrecking all Jewish property. Just like the Prayerbook says: *He smashes the foe and humbles the arrogant*—in other words, he smashes windows and tears up featherbeds. I think I've already told you that such things don't surprise me. They don't even scare me because I feel it's simply a case of either/or: If it's destined, decreed up on high, why who am I to be an exception among all Jews? After all, we read in Ethics of the Fathers, *All of Israel has a share*—in the pogroms, of course. On the other hand, perhaps all this is only a quick epidemic, heaven help us, a passing tornado, so surely there's no reason to lose heart. The storm will blow itself out, the skies will brighten and, like the Prayerbook has it, *Renew our days as of old*—in other words, the good old times will come again.

But, like the saying goes, once a peasant, always a peasant. How true! The entire mob tramped in from the village, as I once told you, I believe, and brought me glad tidings. They'd come to do to me what they were doing to all other Jews. That is, they'd come to fulfill the sacred precept of Smite the Jew. So right off I naturally let fly with a round of abuse. I pleaded and asked questions as only Tevye can. Can it really be? How and why and wherefore? And anyway, what sort of mean trick was it to pounce upon a man, said I, in the middle of the day and rip the feathers out of his pillows?

But nothing doing! Plead till you're blue in the face. I saw that I was wasting my time. They were as stubborn as mules, that gang of peasants. They just had to do it, they said, for the sake of appearances. They had to satisfy the authorities. They were afraid, they said, lest some official, or some other minor plague would happen to come by—that's why the local gang wanted to show the authorities that here they were no different. That they weren't the sort who would skip a Jew, just like that, without a hint of a pogrom. For otherwise, they wouldn't be able to look the authorities straight in the eye. Therefore, they said, the local gang decided that they would have to do something to me. They just had to.

Then, at the very last minute, I got an idea.

"Know what?" I told them. "If the local gang has so decreed, then there's nothing more to say. After all, what can be higher than the local gang? Yet, when you get to thinking, actually there *is* something even higher than the local gang?"

"Well, tell us, what *can* be higher?"

"God," I said. "I don't mean my God and I don't mean your God. I mean, *Our God and the God of our forefathers*—in other words, the God of us all. The one who created me and you and—forgive the proximity—the entire local gang. That's who I mean. So that's who we'll have to turn to to find

out if he's ordered you to harm me. Conceivably, that's
exactly what he wants. But, on the other hand, chances are
just as good that he absolutely disapproves. So how do we find
out? We'll have to cast lots. Now look, here's a copy of God's
own book, the Book of Psalms. You all know that book. We
call it *Tehillim*, Psalms. You call it the Psalter. And this
Holy Psalter will be our judge, our Justice of the Peace, so to
speak. This book, then, will decide whether you're to beat me
or not."

Openmouthed, they exchanged glances, and then Ivan
Poperille, the village chief, stepped forward and said:

"Would you mind telling us just how the Holy Psalter will
decide for us?"

"If you give me your word of honor, Ivan," said I, "and
shake hands that the gang will abide by the Psalter's decision,
then I'll show you how it can be done."

So Ivan stretched out his hand and said, "A promise is a
promise."

"In that case, fine and dandy," I said. "Now I'll open a
page in the Book of Psalms at random, and the first word that
I see I'll read out loud. All you have to do is take the trouble
of repeating that word after me. If any one of you standing
here will be able to pronounce the word I hit upon, it will be
a heavenly sign that you are ordered to do with Tevye as you
see fit. But if you cannot pronounce the word, why then it's a
sign from God that he forbids you to harm Tevye. Agreed?"

Ivan, the village chief, exchanged glances with the gang
and said, "All right."

"That's fair and square," I said, opening the book of
Psalms before them. "All right. Now here's the word: 'Cataracts.' Let's see if you can pronounce 'Cataracts'?"

They looked at one another, at me and then asked me to
repeat the word.

"I'll go along with that. I'll even repeat it three times.
Cataracts, Cataracts, Cataracts."

"No, Tevel, don't say 'ca-ca-ca,' " they said. "Say it plain,
slow, and clear."

"Agreed! I'll say it plain, slow, and clear: 'Ca-ta-racts.'
Happy now?"

So the mob thought awhile and then set to work, each

according to his own ability. One said, "Cats attack." Another muttered, "Cats and rack." A third kept repeating, "Catch a rat." Now why did he say that? Was he perhaps thinking of Naftoli-Gershon the limper's cat who once had caught a rat in his house in Anatevke?

"You know what, fellows?" I said, seeing that this could go on forever, "I see that this job is not easier said than done. It seems that 'cataracts' is too tough a nut to crack. So I'll give you another word also taken from our book of Psalms. Here goes!—'Indignation.' "

Once more the same merry-go-round began. One of them said, "In the station." Another exclaimed, "Dig your nation." A third spat out, "Confound it, constipation, the devil take you."

In brief, they apparently realized that there was no getting around Tevye, so the village chief, Ivan, upped and said:

"Here's the long and short of it, Tevel. We don't have anything against you personally. You're a Yid, it's true, but not a bad sort. Yet one thing's got nothing to do with the other. We've got to beat you up, anyway. That's what our local gang has decided. So we'll just have to smash a few of your windows. If worse comes to worse, you can smash your windows yourself, just to shut them up, damn their hides. For if by some chance the authorities ride by, they can see for themselves that we haven't passed you up. Otherwise, we're liable to get into hot water on account of you. And now, Tevel, heat up the samovar and treat us to some tea and of course half a jug of whiskey for the gang. We'll each have a shot and drink to your health, for you're a clever Jew, one of God's own people."

As I live and breathe, these were his very words, just as I'm repeating them to you now, so help me God.

Well, now I ask you, Mister Sholom Aleichem, for after all, you're a Jewish writer: Isn't Tevye right when he says that we've got a great God and that as long as a man's alive he mustn't give in to despair, especially a Jew, and especially a Jew who's no stranger to our good friends, the little letters in small print? For when you get down to it, it's just like we say in the prayer, *Happy are they who dwell*—in other words, happy are they who dwell among books and know a thing or two. And no matter how much we rack our brains, and no matter how much we attempt hifalutin explanations, we have to admit that we Jews are basically the finest and the smartest people in the world. Like the prophet says: *Who is like Israel thy people, a nation on the earth*—in other words, there's no comparison! A gentile is a gentile, and a Jew, after all, is a Jew. Like you yourself say in your stories—you've got to be born a Jew.

Happy are you, O Israel—in other words, I'm lucky, I was born Jewish, so that I could know the taste of Exile and of tramping around all over the globe among the nations. Like the Torah says, *They journeyed and then encamped*—in other words, one day here, the next day there. For ever since I got the true meaning of the weekly biblical portion "Get Thee Out" knocked into me—remember that long story I once told you?—I've been constantly on the move. I haven't found a single place where I can stop and say, "Here, Tevye, is where you'll settle without cares." But Tevye asks no questions. If he's told to move on, he moves on.

Today we met on the train, Mister Sholom Aleichem. Tomorrow this same train can take us to Yehupetz. A year later it can cast us in Odessa, Warsaw, perhaps even in America. Unless of course the Almighty takes a good look around and suddenly decides: "You know what, children? I think it's high time for the Messiah." Oh, how I wish he'd pull a nasty trick like that on us, that ancient God of ours. Meanwhile, live and be well, have a good trip, and send my best to all our fellow Jews. Tell them not to worry, for our ancient God still lives.

Romance

The Song of Songs *is a four-part novella, of which the following story—like the others, this too can be read independently—is the concluding section. Previous parts of the work describe the growth of Shimek and Buzie (although approximately the same age, Shimek is actually Buzie's uncle), and the development of their young affection. Throughout the novella, Sholom Aleichem symphonically repeats key passages, such as the thumbnail sketch of Buzie, and verses from the biblical Song of Songs, which provides chief metaphors for the story. His theme and setting, too, reflect the ancient love poem: we see not the cramped, mundane village, but sky and wood, stream and flowering fields at the height of spring. A product of Sholom Aleichem's most creative period,* The Song of Songs *is one of the most tender and enchanting love stories in Yiddish literature.*

FINAL PAGES FROM
THE SONG OF SONGS

And there was evening, and there was morning—an uncommonly lovely spring morning, the kind that comes during the seven weeks between Passover and Shevuos.

I was among the first to rise that summery day. Dawn was just breaking. A cool, gentle night wind still breezed in the air. Soon the bright warmth-caressing sun would begin its journey across the blue sky. My small sleepy village was just waking from its sweet slumbers. Imperceptibly, as though with angels' wings, the silent earth was astir.

Fully awake now, my first thought was:

Buzie!

Again Buzie?

Yes, once and again, Buzie. Again and yet again, Buzie. Over and over again, Buzie. For writing about Buzie makes me so happy that I shall never grow tired of telling you stories about her and presenting once again a thumbnail sketch of her. The reader who is already familiar with Buzie will no doubt excuse the digression; but the one who is not should read with care, for it is essential that he know who Buzie is.

2

I once had a brother named Benny. He drowned in the river. He left an orphaned daughter. She was called Buzie. Short for Esther-Libe: Libuzie—Buzie. And she was as beautiful as the Shulamite of the Song of Songs. We grew up like brother and sister. We loved each other like brother and sister. That's who Buzie is.

Years passed. I went away from home against the will of my parents. I disregarded their wishes, refused to follow their ways, pursued my own path instead, and went to seek a secular education. Once before Passover I got a letter from my father:

"Congratulations! Buzie has become engaged and will be married the Sabbath after Shevuos. We expect you home for Passover."

I returned the good wishes and hurried home for Passover.

Buzie was in full bloom. She was beautiful, lovelier than ever. And in my memory there blossomed the Buzie of old, the Shulamite of the Song of Songs. A storm raged within me and a fire was kindled in my heart—a fire directed at no one but myself. At myself and my boyish dreams, so foolish and golden, for the sake of which I had left my parents, disregarded their wishes and went to seek a secular education. Thus I forfeited happiness. Because of my neglect Buzie became someone else's bride and not my own.

That Buzie was near and dear to me ever since she had been a baby was true enough. But when I came home and saw Buzie, I realized that I loved her.

I loved her with that holy flaming passion which is so beautifully described in the Song of Songs: *Strong as death is love, severe as the grave is jealousy, its flashes are flashes of fire, a flame of the Lord.*

3

I was mistaken. I was not the first to rise that morning. My mother had risen even earlier. Already dressed, she was busily preparing breakfast and brewing tea.

"Father is still sleeping. So is the little one." That's how she referred to Buzie. "What do you want to drink, Shimek?"

It made no difference to me. I would drink whatever she gave me. My mother poured me a glass of tea and served it with her beautiful white hands. No one else had such lovely white hands as my mother. She sat down opposite me and talked softly so that my father would not hear. Indeed, it was my father she spoke of. He wasn't getting any younger. He was getting older and weaker. He was coughing. He coughed mostly in the morning, when he rose. Sometimes he would wake during the night and cough all night long. At times, during the day, too. She tried to convince him to go to the doctor—but he refused. An obstinate man. His stubbornness was unbearable. Not that she wanted to talk ill of anyone, God forbid. It's just that—well, since the subject had come up, she was talking.

Thus my mother softly talked to me about my father. She also talked about Buzie and her eyes glittered. While pouring me another glass of tea she asked what I thought about Buzie. Knock wood, she had grown like a tree, right? The wedding would take place the Sabbath after Shevuos. God willing, that's when she'd be married. What an excellent match! An intelligent young man. From a fine family. Rich, too. With a beautiful, well-ordered house. Buzie had fallen into a bed of clover.

"Nevertheless," my mother continued, "you should have seen how much effort it took—it's Buzie I'm talking about— before we finally got her consent to think of a match. But now, thank God, she's happy. Ecstatic! What letters they write to each other! Every single day!" My mother's face shone and her eyes sparkled. "What gloom if a day goes by without a letter! But that's how they feel now. But before? Dear Lord! By the time we were privileged to hear the word 'yes' from her, the lifeblood almost went out of us. Buzie— there's another hardheaded one for you. She's like the rest of her family. They don't give an inch. . . . Not that I want to talk ill of anyone. It's just that—well since the subject has come up, I'm talking."

We heard my father coughing in his room and at once my mother disappeared.

4

Who is she that appears like the dawn, as beautiful as the moon, as bright as the sun?

It was Buzie, who had just come out of her room.

I took a good look at Buzie and could have sworn that one

of two things had happened: she had either been crying or hadn't slept a wink that night.

My mother was right. Buzie had grown like a tree, blossomed like a rose. But that morning her eyes, her beautiful Song of Songs eyes, were misty. A thin veil seemed to cover her face. Buzie was altogether an enigma for me. A painful enigma. There were many things I wanted to know. Why hadn't Buzie slept that night? Whom she had seen in her dream? Was it me, the beloved guest whom she had awaited so long and who had rushed in so unexpectedly? Or had she seen someone else in her dream? The one whom my parents had forced upon her against her will? Buzie was an enigma, a painful enigma. *A garden inclosed is my sister, my bride—a garden inclosed, a sealed fountain.*

5

Buzie was an enigma for me. A painful enigma. Her mood changed several times a day. Just like the weather on a cloudy summer day. First hot, then cold. The sun peeps out from behind the clouds and everything becomes beautiful. Along comes another cloud and everything turns dark and gloomy.

Every day Buzie received a letter from a certain "someone." And every day she answered it. I knew quite well who that "someone" was, but I did not ask her. I did not talk to Buzie about him. I felt that he was an intruder, an interloper. Yet Buzie herself talked about him. But wasn't she overdoing it? The few moments we spent together she talked about him and praised him. Praised him to the skies. Wasn't she going overboard with her praises?

"Do you want to know about him?" she said, lowering her eyes. "He's a wonderful man, simply wonderful. And he's kind. Yes. He's a very kind man. But," and here she raised her eyes and smiled at me, "he's not fit to be compared to you. How can he possibly measure up to you?"

What did Buzie mean by this? Did she want to console me? Or was she making fun of me? No. Buzie was neither consoling me nor making fun of me. Buzie was unburdening her heart.

It was as clear as day.

After drinking tea, Buzie and my mother went to the
kitchen to eat breakfast, and my father and I began our
morning prayers. I rushed through the service. When I
finished, my father, wrapped in his prayer shawl and phylacteries, still stood facing the wall and praising God. Suddenly
Buzie came into the room, parasol in hand, and called to
me:

"Come!"

"Where?"

"To the outskirts of town. Let's take a walk. It's such a
beautiful day."

My father turned his head and looked at her over his silver-
rimmed glasses.

"Just for a little while, Papa," Buzie said as she drew on
her gloves. "Not for long. We'll be back soon. Mama knows
we're going. Well, Shimek? Are you coming?"

The finest music, the most beautiful symphony, could not
have sounded as lovely as those words. In them I heard an
echo of the Song of Songs: *Come my beloved, let us go out to
the field. Let us lodge in the villages. Let us take an early
stroll in the vineyards. Let us see if the vines have budded, if
the pomegranates have flowered.*

Intoxicated with joy, I followed Buzie. I felt I was walking
on air. What was the matter with Buzie? This was the first
time since I had come home that she had invited me for a
walk. What was bothering Buzie?

6

Buzie was right. It was a beautiful day. An uncommonly
lovely day.

One could appreciate a summery day like this in my little
village only by removing oneself from the straits and the
crush to God's big, wide, and beautiful world. The meadow
before us, clad in its green mantle and adorned with the gems
of its rainbow-colored field flowers, was bordered on one side
with a silvery stream and on the other with a small but dense
wood. The stream looked like the silver collar of a new azure-
threaded prayer shawl, while the wood looked like a thick
mop of occasionally windblown curly hair.

Buzie wore a blue baize dress, light as a breeze, transparent as air and sky. Her parasol was ribbed with green and her gloves were lavender. Her attire was as bright and rainbow-colored as the field flowers.

"This is the last time that I had to ask Mama's permission. I wanted to say good-bye to the town, its outskirts, and its cemetery. I wanted to have one last look at the mills, the stream, and the bridge. And for the sake of this, Mama consented. They have to give in to a bride. A bride gets everything she wants. . . . What do you say to that, Shimek?"

Shimek did not say a word. Shimek only listened. It seemed to me that Buzie was unusually gay today. Unnaturally so. She laughed as though she had to. But perhaps I only fancied it.

"Do you remember, Buzie, when we were here last?"

I reminded her. It was long ago. Many years had passed. The two of us had gone to gather greens for Shevuos.

"Remember the last time we followed this same path, passed these mills, and crossed the bridge over the stream? But it was different then, Buzie. Then we ran like young gazelles, we jumped like the deer over the mountains of spices. But now?"

"But now?" said Buzie, bending down to pick some flowers.

"Now we're walking primly, as is only fitting for such sedate people like us. . . . Remember, Buzie, when we were here last?"

"It was the Eve of Shevuos," Buzie replied and presented me with a bouquet of sweet-smelling flowers.

"Is this for me, Buzie?"

"For you, Shimek," she said, looking at me with her beautiful blue Song of Songs eyes. And her glance penetrated right into my heart.

7

The village was far behind us. We were already at the bridge. There I gave her my hand. (The first time since I had come home.)

Hand in hand we crossed the bridge. The wooden boards swung back and forth. Beneath us the water streamed. It tumbled and twisted and gurgled so softly on its downhill path that I could hear the knocking of Buzie's heart, which was so near, so near to me. (The first time since I had come home.)

I sensed that Buzie was gradually moving closer and closer. I breathed the familiar scent of her beautiful hair. I felt the tender smoothness of her exquisite hand and the warmth of her body. And I imagined that I could hear her saying the words of the Song of Songs: *I am my beloved's and my beloved is mine.*

I fancied that a new luster, an added charm, had come over sun and sky, field, stream and wood. What a shame, what a terrible shame that the bridge was so short. In another minute we would be on the other side of the bridge, on the meadow. And a moment later her delicate, smooth and exquisite hand slipped out of mine—and sun and sky, field, stream and wood were stripped of their luster and charm.

"It's strange," Buzie said, and at that moment her beautiful blue Song of Songs eyes became pensive and deep as the sky. "It's strange, but every time I pass a body of water, no matter how small, I see my father, and each time . . ."

"You're talking nonsense," I quickly interrupted.

Buzie was lost in thought for a moment.

"Nonsense?" she laughed. "You're right. I *am* talking nonsense. Because I'm a little fool. A foolish little girl. Isn't that so? Tell me the truth, Shimek. I want you to tell me the truth."

Buzie laughed, threw back her head, and displayed her charming pearl-white teeth. Her face shone in the sunlight, and all the colors of the field sparkled in her beautiful blue eyes, in her pensive Song of Songs eyes.

8

In vain. I could not get her to agree that she wasn't such a fool, that she wasn't a fool at all. Buzie knew that there were people more foolish than she. Buzie knew it. But compared

to me, she said, she was a little fool. Imagine! She believed in
dreams.

"What do you say, Shimek? Don't you? I do. Just yesterday
I dreamt that my father had come to me from the other
world. He was smartly dressed and held a cane in his hand.
He was so friendly, spoke so sweetly to me. 'I'm going to be at
the wedding,' he said, twirling his cane. Well, what do you
say to that, Shimek?"

"Buzie, one must not take stock in dreams. Dreams are all
nonsense."

"Nonsense, you say?"

Buzie fell into a momentary reverie. She began running in
the rainbow-colored field, then stopped.

Buzie herself looked like a flower. Like a rainbow-colored
flower in that rainbow-colored field which extended endlessly
about us into the distance. Buzie was sprinkled with yellow
petals and dappled with scarlet shoots. The dome of the blue
skycap was over her head, the silvery stream at her feet. From
all sides the scents of many pungent spices converged upon
us. I was enchanted. I was intoxicated.

Buzie, herself enchanted, stood in the rainbow-colored
field and looked at me wistfully, her eyes as deep as the forest.

What was she thinking of now? What were her beautiful
blue eyes, her pensive Song of Songs eyes, saying now?

I am a rose of Sharon, a lily of the valley.

That's what her eyes told me. And it seemed to me that
never before had Buzie been the authentic Shulamite of
the Song of Songs as she was today.

9

Buzie looked like a flower, like the rose of Sharon. Like a lily
was she, the lily of the valley, in that rainbow-colored field,
which extended endlessly about us into the distance. She was
sprinkled with yellow petals and dappled with scarlet shoots.
The dome of the blue skycap was over her head, the silvery
stream at her feet. From all sides the scents of many pungent
spices converged upon us. I was enchanted. I was intoxicated. . . .

Buzie walked along and I followed her. Her walk was

quick and nimble. She moved swift as a gazelle in the
rainbow-colored field, which extended endlessly about us
into the distance. Her face shone in the bright sun and all the
colors of the field sparkled in her beautiful blue eyes, her
pensive Song of Songs eyes. Never before had Buzie been the
authentic Shulamite of the Song of Songs as she was today.

"Buzie, do you remember this field?"

"Once upon a time it belonged to you."

"And this hill?"

"Your hill. Once it was all yours. Everything was yours,"
said Buzie with a quick smile on her pretty lips. And yet, I
felt she was laughing at me as she had years ago.

"Let's sit down?" she said.

"Let's sit down."

I sat down on the slope of the hill and made room for her.
Buzie sat opposite me.

"Right here, remember, Buzie? I once told you how I—"

But Buzie took the words right out of my mouth:

"How you can lift yourself up by pronouncing the holy
Name of God and fly like an eagle right up to the clouds,
above the clouds, over fields and forests, mountains and
valleys, over seas and deserts, until you come to the other side
of the Hills of Darkness to the Crystal Palace. There your
enchanted princess has waited for seven years," Buzie
laughed, "until you would finally have pity on her and come
flying to rescue her and free her."

Wait. Buzie was inordinately gay today. Unnaturally gay.
She laughed as though she had to. It was high time to have an
earnest, sober talk with her. Time to open up my heart, to
reveal my inmost soul to her. And I expressed my thought in
the language of the Song of Songs: *"When the day grows
cool*—when this blissful day is over—*and the shadows flee.
. . .',*

10

All the time that I had been at home I had not even told
Buzie a fraction of what I poured forth that morning. I laid
bare my heart to her, revealed my inmost soul, told her the
real reason for my coming home.

Had it not been for my father's congratulatory letter with the four words: "The Sabbath after Shevuos . . ." I would not have seen this downhill-flowing stream nor the little forest which greened close by.

And I swore to her by the stream and by the forest, by the lovely blue sky mantle above us and by the golden sun which sparkled in her eyes, I swore by everything that was bright and beautiful and holy—I swore that I returned only because of her, only because of her. For I loved her—finally the word tore out of me.

"I love you, Buzie, do you hear me, I love you with that holy flaming passion described in the Song of Songs: *Strong as death is love, severe as the grave is jealousy, its flashes are flashes of fire, a flame of the Lord.* Buzie, what's the matter? Are you crying? Oh my goodness, Buzie!"

11

Buzie was weeping.

Buzie wept and the entire world became garbed in gloom. The sun ceased to shine. The stream to flow. The forest to green. The insects to fly. The birds to sing.

Buzie wept. She hid her face in her hands. Her shoulders trembled. And her weeping grew more frantic from moment to moment.

So would weep a child who sensed that he had lost his parents.

So would weep a devoted mother whose child had died.

So would weep a girl who mourned the lover who had deserted her.

So would weep a person who blamed himself for letting his world of happiness slip through his fingers.

In vain was all my consolation. Wasted were all the metaphors from the Song of Songs which I had addressed to her. Buzie refused to be comforted. Buzie refused to hear my metaphors from the Song of Songs. Too late. Too late had I remembered her. Too late had I become aware that someone named Buzie existed—a Buzie who had a heart which yearned and a soul which longed for another sphere. Did I by any chance remember the letters that she once had written to me?

But—she faltered—how would I remember such foolishness? Shouldn't she have realized long ago that our paths were different? That she couldn't measure up to me. How could a provincial Jewish girl like her measure up to me? She now realized how great was her folly in pestering me with her childish letters, her silly insinuations that Mama and Papa were longing for me. No! She should have realized that she couldn't measure up to me. How could a provincial Jewish girl like her be compared to me? She should have foreseen that since I had disobeyed my parents, disregarded their wishes, refused to follow their ways but pursued my own instead, I would surely travel far and become so high and mighty that I wouldn't want to see anyone or know anyone.

"No one, except you Buzie."

"No—no one. No one. No one at all. You'd see no one, listen to no one, forget everyone."

"Everyone, except you, Buzie."

"No. Everyone. Everyone. Everyone!"

12

Buzie stopped weeping—and everything came to life anew. The sun shone as before. The stream flowed. The forest greened. The insects flew. The birds sang.

Buzie stopped weeping and her eyes, her beautiful Song of Songs eyes, were dry. Her tears dried like drops of dew beneath a burning sun.

And suddenly she began to justify her crying spell. Now she saw how silly she had been. Why all the tears? Did she have any reason to cry? Did she lack anything? Others in her place would feel overjoyed, ecstatic. Her eyes, her beautiful blue Song of Songs eyes, blazed. I had never before seen such fire in Buzie's eyes. Red spots apppeared on her cheeks, her beautiful rosy cheeks. Never before had I seen Buzie so inflamed and ablaze. I wanted to take her hand, and I said to her in the language of the Song of Songs:

"*Behold, you are beautiful my love.* How lovely you are, Buzie, when your cheeks are burning and your eyes shoot flames."

In vain, Buzie paid no mind to my Song of Songs. Buzie

had her own Song of Songs. She did not stop praising "some-one"—praising him to the skies.

"*My beloved is dazzling and ruddy*," she said to me. "My fiancé is fine and handsome. *Distinguished among ten-thousand*. Better than many, many others. Perhaps he's not as learned as some, but he makes up for it with kindness, loyal devotion and love. You ought to see the letters he writes to me. Oh, what letters they are!"

"*You have ravished my heart*," I continued, as though I hadn't heard a word she said. "*You have ravished my heart, my sister, my bride*. You have captured my heart, my sister, the bride-to-be."

And she replied: "*His mouth is most sweet and he is altogether lovely*. You ought to see the letters he writes to me. Oh, what letters they are!"

The tone of her voice rang uncommonly strange. The voice I heard—at least so it seemed to me—wanted to overcome, outshout, another voice, the one deep within her.

It was as clear as day to me.

13

Suddenly Buzie rose from the sweet-smelling grass, brushed herself, smoothed down her dress, and put her hands behind her back. She stood in front of me and looked at me from top to toe.

At that moment Buzie was proud and beautiful, magnificently beautiful—more beautiful than ever before.

I hardly dared utter it, but I felt that were I to designate Buzie as the Shulamite of the Song of Songs it would be a great honor for the original Shulamite of old.

Could it be that this was the end of our conversation? I, too, rose and approached Buzie.

"*Return, return oh Shulamite*—come back to me, Buzie," I continued my Song of Songs imagery and took her by the hand. "Return to me, Buzie. Return to me while there is yet time. I have another word, just one more word to say to you."

In vain, in vain. Buzie did not want to hear the one word I wanted to tell her. We had spoken enough, she said. We had told each other enough—perhaps more than we should have. Enough. Enough. The time was late.

"Look how late it is," Buzie said, pointing to the sky and the sun, whose kindly golden beams bathed her in light from head to foot. And a new color came over Buzie, the lily of the valley, the rose of Sharon. She was now golden in the rainbow-colored field which extended endlessly about us.

"Let's go home," she said, urging me on. "Home. Home. It's high time, Shimek. High time. Mama and Papa won't know what to think. Come. Let's go home."

And in her last phrase I heard the voice of long, long ago echoing with the language of the Song of Songs:

"Make haste, my beloved, and be like a gazelle or a young deer upon the mountains of spices."

14

Days passed. Weeks flew by. The beloved holiday of Shevuos arrived. The Sabbath after Shevuos came and went. So did another Sabbath and yet another. And I still remained a guest in my village.

What was I doing here? Nothing. Absolutely nothing. My parents thought that I had repented, turned over a new leaf, regretted the fact that I had disregarded their wishes, refused to follow their ways, but pursued my own instead. And they were pleased, they were very happy.

And I? What was I doing here? What did I seek here? Nothing. Absolutely nothing. Every day I walked alone beyond the outskirts of town. Past the mill. Past the bridge. To that rainbow-colored field which extended endlessly, bordered by a silvery stream on one side and a small but dense wood on the other. The stream looked like the silver collar of a new azure-threaded prayer shawl. The wood looked like a thick mop of occasionally windblown curly hair.

There, on the hillside, I sat down alone. On the same slope where the two of us had recently sat—Buzie, the lily of the valley, the rose of Sharon, and I. On that same slope where once, many years ago, the two of us, Buzie and I, ran like young gazelles and leaped like deer upon the mountains of spices. There where the most treasured memories of my eternally lost youth and happiness lie hidden—there I could sit alone for hours on end, bewailing and bemoaning my unforgettable Shulamite from my Song of Songs romance.

15

And what happened to the Shulamite of my Song of Songs romance? What happened to Buzie? How did it end?

Don't press me to tell you the end of my romance. An ending, even the very best, always contains a note of sadness. But a beginning, even the very worst, is better than the finest ending. Therefore, it is much easier and far more pleasant to tell you the story from the beginning, once and twice and even one hundred times. And in the same fashion as always:

I once had a brother named Benny. He drowned in the river. He left an orphaned daughter. She was called Buzie. Short for Esther-Libe: Libuzi—Buzie. And she was as beautiful as the Shulamite of the Song of Songs. We grew up like brother and sister. We loved each other like brother and sister.

And so on.

A beginning, even the very worst, is better than the finest ending.

And so, let this beginning also be the epilogue to my hapless romance, a true story which I have taken the liberty to call—The Song of Songs.

Jewish Children

Sholom Aleichem's rise to fame in Yiddish literature came with a children's story, "The Penknife," in 1887; eventually, he wrote many more, all of which are collected in his two-volume Stories for Jewish Children. *The essence of Jewish childhood is nowhere else so authentically captured as it is in Sholom Aleichem. He possessed the great empathy, imagination and insight needed to portray the world from the child's point of view and to re-create its fun and frustrations. Literary skill aside, his own nature, too, served him well. Sholom Aleichem deeply loved children and, magically capable of becoming one of them, would spend hours playing in their midst. On the one hand, the children of Sholom Aleichem's stories are frank, irrepressible, bursting with life; on the other, they are reality-rooted and often learn that the burden of the adult world comes sooner than expected.*

VISITING WITH KING AHASUERUS

Do you know who I was jealous of when I was a little boy?
Ahasuerus.

No, not the biblical King Ahasuerus who reigned from India to Ethiopia, over one hundred and seven and twenty provinces. I mean Koppel the tailor and his golden crown—well, actually his paper hat—and his long gilded broomstick scepter.

I was green with envy over Mordecai, the King's vizier (Levi the shoemaker), and his gaberdine worn inside out and his tufted flaxen beard.

I even envied Queen Vashti (Mottel the joiner), who wore a dress over his gaberdine and tied a kerchief over his beard in order to look like a woman. And, believe me, Queen Esther (Oyzer the assistant sexton) rigged out in a green apron, and Haman (Yoske the teacher's helper) with the shards on his head, were no less worthy.

But most of all I was jealous of Feivel the orphan who would don a red shirt and masquerade as Joseph the Righteous for the troupe's performance of *The Sale of Joseph*. When his brothers would rip off his red shirt and cast him into the lion's den, Joseph (Feivel, that is) would fall upon his knees, fold his hands, and conjure the evil beasts to have no dominion over him, singing a plaintive song whose words touched you to the quick:

> Snakes and Scorpions,
> Hear my plea!
> Do ... not ... harm ... me.

For don't you see
For don't you see
Who I am?
I am Joseph the Righteous
Isaac's grandson,
Jacob's son,
Jacob's son.

Although Joseph the Righteous was an orphan, a poor lad who bedded down in the smallest synagogue and thrived on catch-as-catch-can, and although I was the grandson of the wealthy Reb Meir, I would gladly have changed places with him just for the sake of that one day of Purim.

From the crack of dawn on the glorious day of Purim, I kept an eye out for the troupe of strolling players who went from house to house, always followed by a gang of barefoot kids running in the snow. Why couldn't I be a member of the gang? Because! I was forbidden to join them because I came from a rich and prominent family. Because I was Reb Meir's grandson! So I was trapped like a dog, stuck in the house all day long, and was later obliged to go with the grown-ups to Reb Meir's Purim banquet.

While on our way to Grandfather's house, I spotted the gang.

"Why are you twisting and squirming like a broken corkscrew?" my father asked.

"Knock wood, you're quite a young fellow now. Can't you get a move on?" said Mama. "God willing, the Sabbath before Passover you'll be eight years old, may you live to be one hundred and twenty."

"Oh, no! Don't disturb him now. He's seen the comedians," cried my elder brother Moishele, himself anxious to stop and feast his eyes on the players.

"Go on. Get a move on," said my tutor, Reb Itzi, my personal Angel of Death, poking me from behind.

I looked down at the mud and kept pace with the others, immersed in sad and melancholy thoughts: Always with the grown-ups. Ever with my tutor night and day. Sabbath and holidays. All I see is Reb Itzi's red nose, may it shrivel up.

2

Grandpa Meir was the richest man in town. He lived like a monarch. He had an enormous living room graced with a huge silver chandelier that hung from the ceiling. The large, heavy silver candelabrum on the table and the many other smaller silver candlesticks cast their light into every corner. They were displayed by Grandma Nekhome only twice a year: during the Passover Seder and the Purim banquet.

At the head of the table, on a large chair bedecked with greens, sat Grandpa Meir himself. A small man with a thin beard, he had a slightly bent nose, silvery hair and black eyes which sparkled youthfully. He wore a long silken gaberdine with a plaited belt and a wide-brimmed fur-trimmed hat. Before him was the mighty and awesome braided Purim-loaf (a piece of which had already been sliced off), sprinkled with saffron seeds and studded with raisins.

At the center of the table sat Grandma Nekhome, a tall, handsome woman, decked out in a gold-colored silk dress adorned with little apples. Her headdress was dotted with diamonds and other gems, and she wore a string of expensive pearls on her neck. Next to her stood a huge oblong platter filled with hot, aromatic, sweet and peppered fish, stewed in onions, raisins, and all sorts of spices. The two edges of Grandma's beautiful kerchief peeped out behind her ears. Her rings and diamond earrings sparkled and shimmered. She beamed and smiled as she distributed the fish.

The uncles and aunts sat around the table, as did the children, boys and girls who were named after the same grandparents, uncles and aunts. First came Uncle Tsodek and Aunt Tsviya with their three boys, Moishele, Hershele and Velvele, and their two girls, Sorele and Feigele. Next was Uncle Naftoli and Aunt Dvoirele with their four boys, Moishele, Hershele, Velvele and Notele, and their three girls, Sorele, Feigele and Rokhele. Then came Uncle Avrohom and Aunt Sossi with their five boys, Moishele, Hershele, Velvele, Notele and Yenkele, and their four girls, Sorele, Feigele, Rokhele and Taibele. What's more, Uncle Berish and Aunt

Esterl had six boys and five girls; Uncle Binyomin and Aunt Leya had seven boys and six girls; and Uncle Kalman and Aunt Itel had eight sons and—all with the same names.

But enough of the family census. Some don't like to count heads, though, on account of the evil eye. Once, for the fun of it, Grandpa wanted to see how many people were sitting around the table, so he took a silver goblet in his hand and began to not-count (so as to avert the evil eye): not-one, not-two, not-three . . . not-seven. But Grandma tore the goblet out of his hand and made him stop counting.

"A pox on all our foes," she shouted. "What are you counting for? There's plenty of plates to go around, knock wood!"

Now that everyone had gathered for the banquet, Grandpa himself assigned the places. Grandpa Meir liked everything to be neat, clean and sparkling; but above all he liked order. And, indeed, everything worked out.

The uncles sat in one row, the aunts in another. The small fry were seated in such a fashion that no two brothers or sisters had adjoining seats—for close kin can't get along. That's why one Moishele was seated next to his second cousin Hershele, and another Hershele sat alongside of a distantly related Moishele. And so it went down the line. The same held true for the girls: Sorele was with one Feigele, and another Feigele was with a Rokhele; a second Rokhele was with a Rivkele, and so forth.

Only I wasn't lucky enough to have a partner. So I was seated next to my own personal Angel of Death, my tutor, Reb Itzi. I considered Reb Itzi not only a tutor and teacher, but a mentor, guide and governess all rolled into one, whose purpose was to instill in me the ways of good manners and all the social graces.

"When you sit at the table," my governess, Reb Itzi, expounded, "you're supposed to sit like a gentleman. Look straight ahead, hold your hands beneath the table and don't talk while you eat. And when you eat noodle soup take noodles and soup in equal proportions. Sip the soup, put down the spoon and wipe your lips; then take another sip of soup, put down the spoon once more and wipe your lips again. Do not slurp one spoonful after another like a peasant."

Reb Itzi sat down next to me and recited the blessing over the bread. Then, while removing a red handkerchief from his breast pocket, he showered my plate with shreds of tobacco and began to blow his nose. It was an unnatural squeal, sounding like a ram's horn at the peak of a long and mighty blast. Nevertheless, he still managed to watch me out of the corner of his eye to see if I was sitting like a gentleman.

After his first glass of wine, Grandpa, who had a pleasant voice, began to sing, tapping out the rhythm with his fingers:

"The Jews of Shushan shouted for joy . . ."

". . . when they saw Mordecai robed in purple," the rest of the table chimed in, caterwauling in a hodgepodge of voices rising in pitch. My tutor, Reb Itzi, whose musical talents were meager—he had a voice like a screech owl—also sang along. That is, he held his mouth open, closed his eyes, yet still managed to peek at me with half an eye to see whether I was sitting like a gentleman. He tilted his head and banged his middle finger on the table. In brief, he showed Grandpa that he, too, was part of the group.

And when it came to *Blessed is Mordecai and cursed is Haman,* everyone promptly blessed Mordecai and cursed Haman—dear Lord, may one tenth of what we wished him come true!

3

"The Purim players have arrived!" announced Tankhum, the domestic servant, who wore a red gaberdine and addressed everyone (with the exception of Grandma and Grandpa) in familiar fashion.

Hearing the good news, the small fry jumped up. In a flash we left the table and surrounded King Ahasuerus, who was already wearing his golden crown.

"Happy holiday!" the troupe cried merrily as they formed two rows. King Ahasuerus sat on his golden throne and Memukhen (Khaim the coachman) hopped up to him on one leg and sang a German ditty:

MEMUKHEN: Memukhen, that's me of the Persian court.
A young man am I, a youthful sort.
Upon one leg, you see, I hop,
My lovely singing none can stop.

AHASUERUS: Tell me, Memukhen, my loyal slave,
Why have you come to rant and rave?

MEMUKHEN: Let his highness notice how
To Haman no one wants to bow.

AHASUERUS: (*angrily*) Who dares defy the special orders
Which I've set up within my borders?

MEMUKHEN: A Sabbath keeper, a cursed Jew
Whose cloak is black and hardly new.
Jew-boys he'd always circumcise
Folks like that are no great prize.

AHASUERUS: Then bring the Jew right here to me
We'll hang him on the highest tree.

MEMUKHEN: Enter, enter, hurry now
Mordecai-Mondrish, take a bow.

Mordecai, wearing a tufted beard, entered and began to vindicate himself before King Ahasuerus. He told the king who his noble ancestors were:

"The three great Fathers, each a Patriarch—
And all the Torah precepts are my Noah's Ark."

Then he continued:

"Oh woe that Haman has become
The biggest windbag of your kingdom."

"Are you Joseph the Righteous?" I asked Feivel the orphan. He leaned against the wall, a weary and mournful expression on his face.

"Joseph the Righteous," said Feivel.

"Are you going to perform?"

"If they tell me to perform, I'll perform," said Feivel. Then he bent down and whispered into my ear: "How about getting me a hunk of that Purim-loaf, huh?"

"If they catch me, they'll have a fit," I whispered back.

"Well, then just nab a piece so no one sees," he said, his eyes gleaming.

"Nab? You actually want me to steal it?"

"Is that what you call stealing?" he said.

"What then do you call it," I said, "borrowing?"

"I'm starving," he said quietly, devouring the Purim-loaf with his eyes. "I haven't had a thing to eat all day."

While everyone's attention was on the players, I slowly sidled up to the table, stretched out my hand, tore off a hunk of the white loaf, and slipped it into his hand. Joseph the Righteous deftly lowered the piece of bread into his pocket and squeezed my hand.

"You are a good boy. God bless you with the best of everything."

4

"Perhaps you also want to see *The Sale of Joseph?*" said King Ahasuerus, as he removed his golden crown and donned a plain hat.

"That's quite enough," said Grandpa. He gave King Ahasuerus a silver coin and ordered his servant, Tankhum, to sweep up the mess that the comedians had made. During the commotion, while the chairs were being rearranged, and everyone was returning to his seat, I managed to slip out for a minute and accompany the players.

"Come," said Joseph the Righteous, taking me by the hand. "Listen here. You're a top-notch lad and I like you. So come with me."

"Whereto?" I said, my heart throbbing.

"To King Ahasuerus," he replied. "There's no more performances tonight. Now we're going to King Ahasuerus' Purim banquet."

Joseph the Righteous took my hand and we jumped over a mudhole.

Gradually night fell and the mud became deeper and deeper. I imagined I had sprouted wings which carried me aloft. In another minute I'd begin to fly through the air.

"I'm afraid," I said to Joseph the Righteous, holding on to his hand.

"What are you afraid of, silly?" he said, chewing the piece of Purim-loaf I had given him. "There's going to be a banquet. You'll hear us sing. . . . Boy, this is some Purim-loaf! Tastes great. Melts in your mouth like butter. I can't see how folks can look at such a gem of a white-loaf and not gobble it up."

"Some gem!" I said proudly. "At our place we eat white-loaf even on weekdays."

"You mean you *always* eat white bread?" said Joseph the Righteous, licking his lips. "How about meat?"

"Every single day," I said.

"Every single day?" He swallowed. "Me, I eat meat once a week, on the Sabbath. Well, actually, not every single Sabbath, because I can't find a rich householder to invite me every Sabbath. And if with God's help you're stuck with a pauper for Sabbath, why you get a dish of troubles at mealtime and plagues for dessert."

"What do you mean by plagues for dessert?" I asked.

"Don't you know what it means to lunch on plagues? That means you feast on your heartaches," he tried to explain. "When there's nothing to eat, you nibble your cares away. Me, I live on what I'm given. Oyzer the sexton, bless him, supports me, sometimes with a piece of bread, sometimes with a potato. Oyzer is a wonderful man, he's got a gem of a soul. Do you know him? He's the one who played Queen Esther."

"Where's your father?" I asked him.

"I don't have a father."

"Then where's your mother?"

"I don't have a mother."

"Grandma? Grandpa?"

"I don't have any grandparents."

"How about aunts or uncles?"

"I have no aunts or uncles."

"A brother or a sister?"

"I don't have a brother or a sister. I'm an orphan. I haven't got a soul in the world."

I quickly glanced at his face and then at the moon; both, it seemed, were of one color. I moved closer to him and, nimbly moving our legs, we both hurried after the gang of players.

5

"Here's where King Ahasuerus lives," said Joseph the Righteous, and we entered a small dark house with an earthen floor.

"Freyda-Etel dear, come over here. Heard what I said? Get out of bed!" King Ahasuerus yelled at his wife, a sick asthmatic woman who when seized with a coughing fit held one hand to her head and the other to her heart. Since during the day speaking in rhyme had become second nature to the troupe, they were hard put to talk in prose.

"Right now my only wish is to grab a piece of spicy fish," said Memukhen. "We've got enough of Purim-loaf to even choke a famished oaf, and three-cornered jam-filled Purim-cakes to jam in till your belly aches. Pastries and dainties is what Purim's for, and bottles of liquor, drinks galore. Mordecai, come, untie your sack or I'll treat you to a well-placed whack."

"Rather than see the punches fly, this sack I gladly shall untie," said Mordecai as he unpacked his bag.

"At the food you're all ready to have a go," said Vashti, "but it seems you've forgotten about the dough."

To which Haman replied, "Vashti isn't drunk on rice. He knows that money's the finest merchandise."

And so on it went, everyone replying in doggerel of course.

However, when the time came for dividing the tips, they stopped speaking in rhyme. They talked plainly and simply, as most normal people do about money matters. As usual, the lion's share went to King Ahasuerus, a time-honored, annual procedure. But when it came to distributing the money to the rest of the troupe, the wool began to fly. Memukhen asked why Vashti should get more than he, if he had to sweat more than anybody and hop around on one leg.

"It's me who has to speak hifalutin. It's me who has to grind out rhymes and be flowery of speech and shout my head off. And no sooner is the cash about to be divvied up than Vashti becomes a senior partner! Why? Because he's buddy-buddy with King Ahasuerus—a tailor and a joiner are always in cahoots."

"Pipe down," King Ahasuerus bawled. "You two-bit carter, you unbridled horse-pusher, you greasy yokel, you plaster of Paris harness, you broken-down axle. How dare you speak up to King Ahasuerus? Another word out of you and I'll knock all your teeth down your throat, and then you can put that in your pipe and smoke it."

Memukhen quieted down. Everyone stood in awe of King Ahasuerus, the master of the house and the troupe's entre-preneur. But Mordecai and all the others grumbled silently. Only Queen Esther was happy. He dropped the few coins he had received into his pocket and cracked a joke. The group promptly cheered up and, in high spirits once more, began to speak in rhyme.

"May the measly few coins we bring to our wives be the rich men's portion the rest of their lives," said Memukhen.

I sized up King Ahasuerus' quarters. In the middle of the room stood a large table, covered with a dark coarse cloth. At one side was a workbench with tools, and on the other, a wooden bed piled almost to the ceiling with pillows. Oppo-site the oven was a cot upon which a black tomcat dozed with its feet folded under. From the top of the oven a few pairs of black, gray, and blue eyes peeped down.

"Get down here, you little rascals," Joseph the Righteous told them, beckoning with his hand. Without waiting for a second invitation they scrambled down, one at a time, wear-ing tattered shirts which didn't extend beyond their belly buttons. Joseph the Righteous was apparently quite at home there, for the naked children came up to him like little lambs and bent their curly heads for him to pat.

"Are you hungry?" said Joseph the Righteous. "Soon we're going to eat. We've brought you all sorts of goodies."

He catalogued the treats which were brought home and the little lambs looked at one another, drooling, swallowing, and licking their lips. Joseph the Righteous patted their curly heads, swallowed and licked his lips, too. They anxiously awaited the start of the meal so they could begin to eat. Soon God answered their prayers, for King Ahasuerus took a bottle, poured himself some whiskey, and downed the first cup in honor of the "sacred" festival of Purim. All the others followed suit. Then everyone, grown-ups and small fry alike, sat down to the table—everyone except Freyda-Etel, who was busy at the stove. Even the black tomcat jumped up, yawned, stretched its back and walked up to the table, in the hope that it, too, might have a snack.

Joseph the Righteous, the naked, curly-haired little lambs, and I all sat down on a long rickety bench, which wobbled from side to side. The small fry laughed at the hippety-hop bench as though it were the funniest thing in the world. Just then the troupe noticed me and began to wonder: Who's this? We don't seem to know him!

"Who's this little peanut?" asked King Ahasuerus.

Joseph the Righteous told them who I was and how I came to be here. Apparently everyone was pleased, for they came up to me, one by one, slapped my back, pinched my cheek, and addressed a rhymed quip at me. Then the banquet began. First Freyda-Etel served peppered fish and potatoes. Although they weren't seasoned with all sorts of spices like at Grandpa's house, they were quite tasty, nevertheless. The only trouble was they were full of bones. But what I liked most of all was that everyone ate from one plate. It was lots of fun to see all the forks landing in one dish. After the fish, the troupe once again took a bit of liquor. They toasted one another and became merry in a different fashion. They got up from the table, joined hands and began to dance and sing:

> We all are
> What we are,
> And Jews are
> What we are.
> We all have
> What we have:
> And troubles are
> What we have.

"Sing me another," shouted Mordecai. "Come on, let me hear another song."

At which the troupe began to sing and dance and clap their hands:

> Man must know
> How to delight
> Before his God,
> His sacred light.
> Joy in moderation,
> For his holy nation.
> For God, the King,
> Living and great,
> Next year in Jerusalem
> We shall gladly wait.

"Well, what do you say? Some good time we're having, right?" said Joseph the Righteous. Having stilled his hunger, he became a new man. He took a drop of whiskey, gave me some too, and dragged me into the dance. I didn't quite know why I should be so merry, but nevertheless I suddenly felt very good. I felt I was deliriously happy. My happiness knew no bounds. But suddenly—

6

Suddenly the door burst open and I saw my father and my tutor, Reb Itzi. My heart sank within me. I haven't the faintest idea what went through my father's mind when he saw me dancing in a circle among the whole troupe of players. But I saw that he remained rooted in his place.

His glance went from me, to the players, to my tutor, Reb Itzi. And this procedure of look-'em-over was followed in turn by Reb Itzi, me, and finally the players. Everyone was dumbstruck. Then Memukhen stepped forward and said in rhyme, as was his custom:

"Why stand there in such dismay? Isn't today a holiday? Do you know, pals, what I think, let's all have a nice big drink. And as a chaser, a hunk of cake, to chase any trouble and any ache."

Memukhen offered a glass of whiskey and a piece of pastry to my father. Father pushed him aside without a word. But Memukhen, not easily rebuffed, said:

"Mister rich man, Reb Asher, the son of Reb Meir, don't you think I'm an excellent player? No, you say, then *I'll* have a cup. Let's say Amen and bottom's up!"

Memukhen drained his whiskey glass and began to sing:

> The pauper is a gay buffoon,
> The rich man is a souse.
> The pauper sings a merry tune,
> The rich man is a louse.

"Hey, Mordecai, speak up! Propose a blessing for the rich men of town and have a drink in their honor."

Mordecai poured himself a drink and began to bless the rich men, using the traditional Torah-blessing melody:

"Bless ye one and all, with Satan take a fall. May demons greet you and big worms eat you. Devils fret you and God forget you. Like Lot be drunk, smell like a skunk. May your mangy mouths be bitter, and imps impede you by the litter."

"Why don't you speak up, Reb Asher?" said Reb Itzi, the tutor, taking a sniff of tobacco and snapping his fingers in the air.

"Can't you see they're all intoxicated?" said my father, smoldering with anger. He grabbed my hand so tightly that it hurt. All three of us left King Ahasuerus' house without so much as a by-your-leave. Once outside, my father stopped, took one look at me, and briskly slapped me twice.

"That's just a prelude," he said. "Once we get home, your tutor will really give it to you. Now listen here, Reb Itzi, I'm turning him over to you, and I want you to whip the daylights out of him. Till he's black and blue. A boy going on nine! Let him remember what it is to run off with the Purim players, those low-down, low-class, third-rate clowns, those down-at-the-heel tramps. Let him remember what it means to ruin everyone's holiday."

Not a tear came out of me, but I felt my cheek flaming. My heart was heavy as a stone. I didn't even think of the trouncing Reb Itzi was going to give me once we would get home.

My thoughts were elsewhere, with King Ahasuerus and Joseph the Righteous, with the naked little curly-haired lambs. The troupe's little song kept buzzing in my ear:

> Man must know
> How to delight
> Before his God,
> His sacred light.
> Joy in moderation,
> For his holy nation.
> For God, the King
> Living and great,
> Next year in Jerusalem
> We shall gladly wait.

THE HOLIDAY KIDDUSH

1

[My Nickname—Meager Talents—What'll Become of Me?]

My gang of pals never called me anything but Ivan Ignoramus. Was it because I refused to study? Well, that wasn't the
only reason. Truth is, I *didn't* want to study. Who *does?* Did
they dub me Ivan on account of my wooden head? Maybe.
Truth is, I *was* a numbskull. Nothing penetrated, my teacher
complained. I had to work my head to the bone before I
understood *anything*. But on the other hand, my memory,
knock wood, was pretty weak, too. I couldn't remember a
blessed thing. In one ear, out the other. The jabs, blows and
smacks that were pummeled into me—I can't even recall
them! My poor father ate his heart out in vain. And in vain
were my poor mother's tears. Absolutely nothing sank in.

"Thunderations, Ivan Ignoramus," my classmates yelled,
"what'll become of you?"

"Thunderations, pals, what *will* become of me?"

2

*[My Father's Joy—My Engagement—My In-Laws' Pedigree—
My Fiancée's Attributes—My Journey]*

Sometimes I saw my father happy. At the Purim feast, for
instance. Or while dancing with the Torah on Simkhas
Torah. And at various celebrations, as well. But during the
Eve of Passover I'm now going to tell you about his joy knew

no bounds. What was the big occasion? I'd become engaged. Congratulations and lots of luck!

Who was the father-in-law? Don't ask! Some in-law! First of all, what a family! Have you ever heard of the Horenshteins of Radomishl? Or the Zusmans of Ostreh? Or the Tcherno-bilskys of Shpoleh? Well, he was their commission agent! Not now, but he *used* to be. Once upon a time. Before he had his big fight with them. At present my future father-in-law was an independent merchant. Not a fabulous one to be sure, but a merchant, nonetheless. He was even offering a dowry. Not much, though. My father was giving twice as much. But in turn they were giving me a bride.

And what a bride! I myself hadn't met her. Hadn't even seen her. But those who had, like my parents and my older sister and her husband, couldn't stop raving about her. Mama declared she was beautiful. My sister said she wasn't as beautiful as she was intelligent. My brother-in-law insisted that she wasn't as intelligent as she was good-natured. Her face was kindness itself. My father said that whatever she was I wasn't worthy of her. Worthy or not, the main thing was that she would be mine, thought I. And I yearned for Passover like a pious Jew yearned for the Messiah. For I'd heard it said that I was going to spend the Passover holiday as a guest of my future in-laws.

3

[A Complicated Kiddush—The Prayer of Separation as a Bonus]

I was to be a guest of my in-laws and not, God forbid, of my bride-to-be. So said my parents. What I thought of this is my business. And as long as I was still under their wing, I had to submit and obey all their instructions. What sort? The sort you'd expect from parents. To be on my best behavior, to stand and sit and eat properly and not talk any nonsense.

"In brief," said Father, "you're not to let them get wind of the fact that you're an Ivan Ignoramus. . . . Say, wait a minute! Do you have a working acquaintance with the holi-day Kiddush?"

It turned out that I did not. I didn't even know it at all.

How should I know it? Remember it from last year? Who's got the head for tough Hebrew like that? And especially since this year the second night of Passover fell on a Saturday night. Which made it doubly disastrous! For on that night one had to recite not only the Kiddush over the wine but the Prayer of Separation as well. No need telling you that the Passover Kiddush alone was enough of a plague. Smack in the middle you had to choose one of four different Hebrew phrases. Try and remember to pick the right one for Passover —"Our Festival of Freedom." And if that wasn't enough, why you've got as a bonus the tricky Prayer of Separation. Listen to this:

> . . . *Blessed art thou, Lord our God, King of the universe, who hast made a distinction between the sacred and the profane, between light and darkness, between Israel and the nations, between the holiness of the Sabbath and the holiness of the festival; the seventh day above the six working days hast thou exalted; distinguished and exalted thy people Israel hast thou with thy holiness.*

There you have "exalted" followed immediately by "distinguished and exalted." Some piece of work, eh?

"Never mind. You'll learn it," said Father. "You're not a baby. Anyway, you still have three weeks till Passover."

4

[The Teacher Studies the Holiday Kiddush with Me—A Free Hand—Distinguished and Exalted]

But Father wasn't too keen on banking only on my abilities. So he told me to get hold of the Hebrew teacher. What in the world for? He wanted to ask him to study the Holiday Kiddush and the Prayer of Separation with me. So that I'd get to know it backwards.

"And don't treat this oaf with kid gloves," snapped Father, "even though he's my son. Cut him to ribbons for all I care, but I want him to know that Kiddush."

That's all that teacher needed was license for a free hand. Although the entire three weeks were spent on the Kiddush, at least I can proudly say that I had it down pat. But only the Kiddush. The Prayer of Separation still tripped me up. I mean, the Prayer of Separation itself went like a song. But only up to a certain point. Up to the first "exalted." At that point things went haywire. The man who thought up that prayer apparently had nothing else to do. So he popped in the word "exalted," and right at its heels, "distinguished and exalted." Would it have been any skin off his back if he had only used either "distinguished" or "exalted"? One or the other: if "distinguished," then not "exalted"; if "exalted," then not "distinguished." Why cause trouble? But when I asked the teacher, I got a whack on the face.

His standard reply!

5

[*80 Miles per Hour—The 250th "Distinguished and Exalted"*]

"How's the Kiddush coming along?" Father asked me just as I was about to leave before the holiday. "Do you know it by heart?"

"Like I know my name."

"All right. Let's hear it."

I recited it. I rode on greased rails, like an express, eighty miles per hour. But when it came to *Thou hast made a distinction between the sacred and the profane,* the express slowed down and took its time. "Thou hast made a distinction between the sanctity of the Sabbath and the sanctity of the holiday. The seventh day above the six working days hast thou exalted; exalted and distinguished . . ."

"Not 'exalted and distinguished,' you Ivan Ignoramus, but 'distinguished and exalted.' I want you to repeat 'distinguished and exalted' two hundred and fifty times."

I wandered around the house like a lunatic, softly muttering "distinguished and exalted" until my eyes grew bleary and my head began to spin. At my wit's end, I sank into the sofa, more dead than alive.

"What's with you?" asked Mama.

"Nothing," I said. "Distinguished and exalted. Exalted and distinguished."

"Did I hear 'and distinguished' again?" asked Father, catching the last part of the phrase. "Where did you get 'and distinguished' from, you Ivan Ignoramus?"

"Don't you think it's high time to put a stop to this?" said Mama, God bless her. "You're going to get him so confused with these distinguished and exalted phrases of yours that the poor child won't know if he's coming or going."

Mama, may she live and be well, had liberated me from bondage. But the phrase "and distinguished" took hold of me and gave me no peace. No matter what I said or thought the phrase "and distinguished" swam before my eyes.

6

[I Use the Horses for a Sign—A Fright—My Fiancée's Green Jacket]

I sat in the coach on my way to my fiancée's house (my parents insisted I was going to the in-laws) and willy-nilly I rehearsed the Kiddush by heart. When I came to the point where the words read "exalted; distinguished and exalted," I made a sign for myself. Since the horse on the left looked like such a noble steed, I labeled him "exalted." And since the horse on the right kept throwing up his head in such a proud manner, I labeled him "distinguished." The key was left-right-left. "Exalted; distinguished and exalted." And so it burned itself into my memory. First "exalted," then "distinguished and exalted." Excellent! I figured there was no force on earth which could knock that pattern out of my mind.

I arrived safely at my fiancée's house (my parents insisted I was going to the in-laws) on Friday afternoon, the Eve of Passover. I hardly had a chance to take a good look at my fiancée, for everyone was rushing off to the synagogue. What a tumult! Everything was topsy-turvy. The madcap pace of Passover Eve! During the turmoil I managed to get a quick glance at my fiancée. Not bad. Not at all ugly. Whether she was intelligent or not, I couldn't say. And as far as I could tell, her face wasn't "kindness itself," as my brother-in-law put it. If a cluster of little pimples scattered all over one's face was a sign of kindness then she should have been a saint!

I also thought it would be a good idea for her to give her hair a good combing and not leave it disheveled like an old witch. What's more, it wouldn't hurt her a bit if she would get rid of that green silk jacket of hers—green was by no means her color. And how come she blushed so furiously at the drop of a hat? She'd have to learn to stop that. Just wait till I'd get to know her better. Meanwhile, my future father-in-law came and took me to the synagogue.

7

*[My Father-in-law in the Synagogue—A Cold Welcome—
The Kiddush for Passover—Grinds to a Halt]*

What can I say about my father-in-law? Besides being in such a dither preparing for the sacred festival, his future son-in-law had come for the holiday and he had to bring him to the synagogue and show off his catch to the community. And this was no trifle, you know. In fact, his hair wasn't even dry from his trip to the communal bathhouse. The back of his neck was still red from the scissors' trim. His suit crackled with newness. His new boots shone and smelled of cowhide. In the synagogue he had one of the best seats. All the way up front. Everyone came up to him to wish him a happy holiday. Me they gave a limp hand and a cold welcome. For when a Jew greeted you, he only offered you the tip of two chilly fingers. Quickly, on the run.

We came home wishing one and all a broad, cheerful "Happy Holiday" and forthwith sat down to begin the Seder. The bride responded to the greetings and immediately blushed, red as a ripe watermelon. My mother-in-law beamed, decked out with an assortment of gems, looking like God's grandma. The First Seder passed uneventfully, for the Friday night Kiddush is a snap. But then came Saturday night and the Second Seder. My father-in-law chanted the long Kiddush in a resounding bell-like tone, and then signaled to his son-in-law to get up—begging his pardon for the inconvenience—and chant the Kiddush, too, as is customary. I rose, took the winecup in hand and dispatched the courier-express. Loud and pretty. On tune. Quick as a flash. Till I came to the tricky Hebrew phrases. Smack into the swamp. Then I slowed up, literally crawling along.

"Thou hast made a distinction . . . between the sanctity of the Sabbath . . . and the sanctity of the holiday . . . The seventh . . . day . . . above . . . the six . . . working . . . days . . . hast . . . thou . . . exalted—"

At once I thought of the horses, the one on the left, exalted; the one on the right, distinguished; but, forgetting which was which, I sang:

"Extinguished and desalted thy people Israel . . . desalted and distinguished thy people . . . extinguished and exalted thy . . ."

8

[Homeward Bound—Disengaged—Extinguished and Desalted Makes Its Mark]

It was early in the morning of the third day of Passover, the first day of the half-holidays. My fiancée was still asleep. But my father-in-law, wearing a silk morning gown and tattered slippers, sat sweating over a letter he was composing to my father. Next to him sat his wife puffed up like a turkey. I, the son-in-law, had already packed my things in a suitcase, all set for the return trip.

"Here," said my father-in-law, handing me a sealed letter. "Regards to your father. Give him this note and have a nice trip home."

While riding on the wagon, I was curious to see what my father-in-law had written to my father and why they had sent me packing so soon. When I opened the envelope, out fell the marriage contract and the note. In the letter my ex-father-in-law begged my father's pardon and declared:

"Don't be angry, but the match is off for several reasons. May the Almighty send your son his destined mate and my daughter hers. . . . As for the dowry and the presents to both groom and bride—everything will be divided. The groom's gifts will be given to the groom, and the bride's gifts to the bride. Everything will be settled, fair and square, calmly and peacefully and we'll part best of friends. And in so doing there will be harmony and understanding among all Jews and let us say, Amen . . ."

Luckily, he didn't say a word about my fine Kiddush, God bless him. But hold on! As soon as I set foot in the house my father promptly greeted me with a couple of smacks.

"Extinguished and desalted, huh? Where did you dig that up all of a sudden, you apostate? I'll give you extinguished and desalted!"

So that was it? How did he find out so quickly? And do you think it was only him? The whole town knew of it. And I no longer was called Ivan Ignoramus. I got a new nickname. Henceforth I was known as "Extinguished and Desalted."

Now at least I consider the whole thing one big joke. But boy, how I cried my eyes out that Passover!

THE FLAG

Children, I'm going to tell you a story about a flag: How a poor boy like me got a flag for Simkhas Torah, how hard I came by it, and how I was destined easily to lose it.

When I was a small boy like you I was called "Topele Tottrow"—that is, "Kopele Cock-crow." Why? Because first of all I had a thin squeaky voice, like a young rooster who has just begun crowing, and secondly I could not pronounce "k" or "g." And as if on spite, my father was named Kalman, my mother Gitl, my Talmud Torah teacher Gershon the Chicken-gullet from Galaganyevka—and I was known as Kopel, Gitl-Kalman's son.

"Sonny! What's your name?"

"Who me? Topel, Ditel-Talman's son."

"Louder."

"Topel, Ditel-Talman's son."

"Still can't hear you."

I yell out loud: "To-pel . . . Di-tel . . . Tal-man's son."

"And who's your teacher?"

"My teacher? Dershon the Chitten-dullet from Daladanyevta."

And everyone burst out laughing.

Everyone laughed—and I cried.

I cried not because people laughed, but because they beat me. Everyone under the sun thought it a good deed to beat me: my father, my mother, my sisters, my teacher, my classmates. They all tried to get me to talk properly.

My teacher once depressed my tongue with a stick and ordered everyone in the class to shout down my throat in the hope it would act as a medicine. But before they had a chance

73

to carry this out, Reb Zyama the joiner, my teacher's neighbor, intervened and said:

"Why are you tormenting this poor child? What has he done? Just give him to me for a minute and I'll have him talking properly in no time."

Reb Zyama then beckoned to me, held my chin and said: "Look me in the eye, my boy, and repeat after me, word for word. A kid can't catch a cat."

I looked him in the eye and repeated after him, word for word: "A tid tan't tatch a tat."

"Not like that," said Reb Zyama. "Just watch my lips and say: In the beginning God created the heaven and the earth."

I watched his lips and said: "In the bedinnind Dod treated the heaven and the earth."

"No, silly one!" said Reb Zyama. "Don't say Dod, say God! God! God!"

"Dod! Dod! Dod!"

Reb Zyama threw up his hands. "You know what I've just discovered? It's a waste of time and effort. Even black magic won't help him. He's a hopeless case."

2

In those days, owning a flag for Simkhas Torah—I mean a flag in the full sense of the word: a lit candle in an apple and the apple on the flag—was such bliss, such joy, I hardly dared dream about it. There were other treats a-plenty to dream about! Why, there were some boys in school who had money for penknives, purses and little canes. There were those who ate candy and cracked nuts every single day. Not to mention bagels and pancakes! My goodness, there were even those who ate white-loaf not only on Sabbath, but on weekdays as well. What luck!

Oh, children, I've never ever tasted white-loaf on weekdays. I was happy if I had my fill of black bread, for we were—God spare you such a bitter lot—a bunch of impoverished paupers, despite the fact that everyone in the family worked his fingers to the bone: Father, may he rest in peace, was the assistant sexton of the basement prayer-room annex of the Butchers' Synagogue; Mother, God rest her soul, was an expert at baking honey cakes; and my sisters mended socks. Believe me, I never once had the feeling of being full. There wasn't a meal which I couldn't have begun all over again.

I'm not even talking about having a kopeck in your pocket, a kopeck to call your very own. Of that I never even dreamed. But fancy this! I, Kopel Cock-crow, suddenly became rich and got forty-four kopecks to do with as I pleased.

You think a miracle happened? That some rich man's loss was my gain? Well, you've guessed wrong. Or perhaps you suspect that I simply nabbed or swiped them from some charity box? God forbid! I swear I earned them honestly and decently. I worked like a horse for them with my own two . . . feet.

This happened during Purim. Father sent me to distribute the Purim sweet-platters among the members of the basement prayer-room annex of the Butchers' Synagogue. One of my older sisters usually had this job, but now that I was getting bigger my father said it was high time for me to make myself useful. So I went from house to house carrying a saucer and some fruit-cuts which I distributed among the members of the basement prayer-room annex of the Butchers' Synagogue. I slogged through the cold slippery muck with my bare feet and changed the small coins I was given into a forty-kopeck silver piece—and I still had four kopecks left over.

3

Having come by such a fortune, I strolled about wondering what to do with so much money, knock wood.

Then suddenly my Good Impulse and my Bad Impulse appeared and began to torment me.

Said the Bad Impulse: "Why hold on to those few kopecks, you dummy? Buy yourself something. Buy sweet poppy-seed squares. Pironditchky's stall has real delicious ones. Or buy yourself some good fruit-cuts sprinkled with honey crumbs. Or at least a frozen apple. And you'll be as happy as can be."

"What? Tater to my belly?" I said. "Then in one day I'll eat up all my money. No sir!"

"Right you are," said my Good Impulse. "It'd be much

nicer to lend those few kopecks to your mother. She can certainly put them to good use."

"Some brain you are!" I said. "Then it's as dood as lost. How will she ever repay me?"

"She works her fingers to the bone, poor thing," said the Good Impulse, "and pays for your schooling."

"What do you care about schooling?" interrupted the Bad Impulse. "You'd be better off buying yourself a red polka-dotted whistle, a sharp two-blade penknife in a brass box, or a purse with a neat little lock."

"What'll you keep in the purse," asked the Good Impulse, "your poverty?"

"Buttons!" said the Bad Impulse. "You'll stuff your purse with buttons. Everyone will think it's money and then all the kids'll be jealous of you."

"What good'll that do you?" said the Good Impulse. "Listen to me. Distribute the money among the poor. Give it to charity and you'll get credit for a pious deed. Some of the paupers are starving, poor souls."

"Paupers?" The Bad Impulse turned to me. "You yourself are a pauper's son. You yourself are always hungry. Everybody's always generous with the next fellow's cash. Why didn't anyone ever give *you* anything when you were broke?"

4

One time the Bad Impulse nearly got the best of me. At school I had a friend—Yulik, a rich man's son. His pockets were always full of goodies. But he hated sharing them with anyone. You could stretch out and croak in front of him and he still wouldn't give you a whiff. One day Yulik began worming his way into my good graces. He buddied up to me, all smiles. Became a bosom pal.

"You know what?" he said to me. "I swear you're a good kid. You hate to beg like the others. I like you for that alone. They're always saying, 'Gimme a piece! Gimme a hunk!' I can't stand the sight of those grubbers. . . . Want a piece of candy?"

"A piece of tandy?" I said. "Why not?"

"How about cracking a couple of nuts?"

"Nuts? Sure!" I said. "I'd love to trat a touple of nuts."

Yulik put his hand into his pocket. I thought he was getting ready to give me the treats. Instead, he said: "I'll also give you some jam and three more nuts if you swap with me. Would you like to swap?"

"Swap!" I said. "Swap what?"

"I'll also give you my penknife," he said. "You know my white knife, don't you? It's the best there is. There's none better to be had."

What a question! Did I know Yulik's knife? Who didn't? I'd been envious of it long enough. How often had I seen it in my dreams!

"Well, but what about me?" I said. "What do you want *me* to div *you*?"

"You," said he, "give me that silver forty-kopeck piece."

"Do it," said my Bad Impulse. "It's a dream of a knife. All the kids'll be green with envy."

I was about to take out the coin, but caught myself at the last minute.

"You're some wise duy," I said. "For forty topets I tan buy a brand-new knife."

"Like mine?" said Yulik. "Nonsense! Wait a minute. You know what? I'll throw in half a dozen pure-bone buttons."

"For money," I said, "one tan buy ten thousand dozen bone buttons."

"And aren't candy and nuts worth money? I swear I'll give them to you any time—all you got to do is ask. Here, I've also got an iron nail. See? I'll give it to you free. See what sort of nail this is?"

"What do I need nails for?"

"It'll come in handy, silly," Yulik said. "You can nail it down wherever you like. You can dig little holes with it."

"Why do I have to did little holes for?"

"I'll let you use my prayerbook."

"Why do I have to use other people's prayerboots for?"

"I'll let you try on my Sabbath hat."

"Why do I have to try on other people's hats for?"

"So you refuse, huh? Then take this," he said and punched me in the ribs. "The nerve of the little beggar. I give him so many things: a knife, buttons, candies and nuts, a nail, a

prayerbook and a try-on of my hat. And he refuses them all.
There's a beggarly belly for you. No matter how much you
stuff it, it isn't enough. Just because he's got a silver forty-
kopeck piece he thinks he's a big shot. Just you wait, Topele
Tot-trow, if you ever come to me for anything, you'll regret
it to your dying day. . . . Nekhemya! Here! Take this nail.
It's yours as a present."

And Yulik gave the nail to Nekhemya (a poor lame boy)
and broke off his friendship with me.

5

Actually, why did I hold on to the money? That's a good
question.

First of all, I saved it for the Lag B'Omer party, when all
the kids would bring something to school. Some would bring
money, others food or goodies. But I was the only one who
would bring his daily breakfast: a piece of bread and garlic.
My face would burn with shame. Although I was always
invited to the party along with everyone else, I had the
feeling that it was out of pity and I didn't feel the joy of the
holiday. But now, I thought, I can thumb my nose at all of
you for, thank God, I possess ready cash. If a rich boy like
Yulik chipped in a quarter of a ruble, then I certainly could
throw in a kopeck, for what am I compared to him? A
nobody! And five kopecks would *surely* be enough. But,
actually, I planned on giving ten—let them know who Kopel
Cock-crow is!

So I laid aside ten kopecks for the Lag B'Omer party and
saved the rest for later.

Later, during the summertime when everything was green
and fruits appeared in Pironditchky's stall, the Bad Impulse
returned: "See! Green gooseberries! And look at those bright
red currants!"

"Dreen fruit," I said, "sets your teeth on edge."

"Make the blessing over new fruit," said the Good Impulse. "It's a pious deed to do that."

"There's plenty of time for that blessind," I said. "The
summer's lond enough. There still will be lots of cherries and
plums, apples and pears, melons and watermelons. I thint I'll

be better off savind the money for Simkhas Torah and buy myself a flad."

And I stuck to my decision.

6

Sukkos finally came, thank God, and I bought myself a large, yellow, two-sided flag. Painted on one side were two beasts with catlike faces—lions, really, with open mouths. Their long tongues were decorated with some sort of whistles, apparently rams' horns, for the biblical phrase *With trumpets and ram's horn* was printed next to the lions, and beneath them were the lines: *The flag of the Tribe of Judah,* and *The flag of the Tribe of Ephraim.*

And that was only one side of the flag. The reverse side was even prettier, for it had true-to-life portraits of Moses and Aaron. Moses wore a large vizor on his forehead and Aaron had a golden hoop over his yellow shock of hair. Between Moses and Aaron stood a host of Jews, crammed in tight against one another and holding Torah Scrolls in their hands. They all looked alike, as though one mother had borne them. All wore the same long gaberdines belted below their hips, and the same socks and shoes. And they all seemed to step forward and sing: "Be joyous and merry on Simkhas Torah."

Since I now had a flag, my next step was to get a stick for it. For this, the man to see was Reb Zyama the joiner, the very same Reb Zyama who once had tried to teach me to talk properly.

"Well, what's the good word, Topele Tot-trow?"

"A stit for the flad."

"What do you mean—a stit?"

"A stit," I said, "from a hunt of wood. So I tan tarry it."

Reb Zyama kept on making fun of me until I burst into tears. Then he softened up, cast aside all his work, took a piece of wood, whittled it once, twice—and it was finished.

Now all I needed was an apple and a candle. A candle made of wax, of course, and not tallow—for if tallow dripped on the apple, the apple was ruined and couldn't be eaten. But wax didn't matter—wax was kosher.

When it came to wax, I had more of it than any other kid.

In fact, if anyone wanted a bit of wax, who did he come to? Me! For after all, my father was the assistant sexton of the basement prayer-room annex of the Butchers' Synagogue—and whatever remained of the Yom Kippur memorial candles belonged to him. That was his income. He melted them and turned them into Hanuka candles, Saturday night Havdala candles, and plain wax tapers. Whatever was left over from the latter he gave to me. That was *my* income.

In short, I had everything I needed.

7

On the night of Shemini Atzeres I attached the flag to the stick, stuck a red apple on the tip, put a lit candle atop the apple, and then set out for the synagogue for the Torah circuits. I was in high spirits, feeling like a happy prince, an incomparable child of royalty.

I imagined that I was already in the synagogue, sitting next to the eastern wall with all the rich children. The lights were kindled. My flag was the most beautiful. My apple redder than all the rest. My candle the biggest of all.

The synagogue was packed, the heat unbearable. Many women and girls came to kiss the Torah. Reb Melekh the cantor, his prayer shawl outspread, led the procession of householders like a field marshal. His metallic voice quavered as he sang: "Hel-per of the poor and weak, sa-a-ve us!"

The women and girls pressed forward to kiss the Torah Scrolls and shrilled into his face: "Live and be well till next year at this time."

"The same to you and yours," Reb Melekh replied.

But before the Torah procession reached the basement prayer-room annex of the Butchers' Synagogue—the place where I prayed—it had to pass many other synagogues and houses of study: the Cold Synagogue, the Lithuanians' Synagogue, the various tailors' synagogues, the Great House of Study, the Smaller House of Study, the Old House of Study, the First Prayer House, the Prayer House of the Hasidim, the

Prayer House of the Misnagdim,* the New Synagogue, and the Yellow Prayer House. Finally they came to the Butchers' Synagogue, and only then did they come down to the basement prayer-room annex.

Now all these above-mentioned synagogues, houses of study and prayer houses were not scattered helter-skelter over town like in the big city of Yehupetz. That was one wonderful thing about Kasrilevke. In our town all the synagogues were located in one section of the same street—practically in one courtyard, known as the synagogue courtyard.

In fact, our entire synagogue courtyard could have been considered one big house of worship. Summertime, when the windows are open, a passerby heard so many different prayers wafting down he didn't know what to do first: to stop and raise his heels three times for "Thrice-holy is the Lord of Hosts," to bow down for "Bless the Lord," or to answer "Amen" to a Mourner's Prayer. At one and the same time the passerby could hear various parts of the service. While one worshipper said, "Then Moses sang," and another shouted, "Hear O Israel," a third suddenly chimed in with a Talmud chant: "When a generalization requires a specification, or when a specification requires a generalization . . . ," a fourth intoned, "Glorified and sanctified be God's great name," and a fifth intruded with, "Hallelujah, Praise ye the Lord," sung to a completely different tune.

Our synagogue courtyard had two different faces: one for weekdays and one for Sabbath and holidays. During the week it was a marketplace for Jewish books, prayer shawls, ritual fringes and *mezuzos,* rotten apples, unripe little pears, sunflower seeds and beans, poppy-seed squares, bagels and sugar cookies. Goats, chewing their cud and waggling their beards, sunned themselves as though on a private estate. But comes the Sabbath and holidays—gone is the marketplace and gone are the goats. Jews, God grant them good health, gathered in little circles and began talking and wagging their tongues, discussing local and worldwide events of recent and ancient vintage. Children and schoolboys milled about. Talmud Torah youngsters of various classes ran, leaped about and

---

* Misnagdim—those who opposed the Hasidim. [Tr.]

weaved in and out of groups of people like fish in water. Sabbath was God's gift to them—they were free as birds. They compared new jackets to see whose was longer, and holiday hats to see whose was larger; they even measured sidecurls with their fingers to see whose was shorter. Meanwhile, one youngster was slapped, another pinched, a third jabbed. And as usual, one slap, pinch and jab led to another. The place seethed with life and merriment.

But liveliest of all was the eighth day of Sukkos, the night of Shemini Atzeres just before the Torah circuits began, when the children of all the Talmud Torahs gathered with their flags. They grouped according to grades—the older ones here, the younger ones there. Everyone sized up everyone else's flag. Whose stick was longer? Whose apple redder? Whose candle was made of tallow and whose of wax? They twitted, ribbed one another, jibed, cracked jokes, giggled, and played tricks. If Yankel blew out Moishe's candle, the latter would in turn sneak up and take a bite of Yankel's apple. So Yankel made some nasty comment about Moishe's ancestors and kicked him in the pants, besides. Finally, everyone separated and went to his synagogue.

8

"Congratulations! Lookee here! Topele Tot-trow's got a flag. A fat big welcome, Mister Jew—you're looking well, and nuts to you."

That's how the gang greeted me when I entered the synagogue courtyard holding my flag.

I took stock of all the other flags, then looked back at my own. What a contrast! Theirs weren't even fit to hold a candle to mine. Let's begin with the flag itself. Nobody else's flag was so well fixed on a stick. On no one's could both sides clearly be seen. Nobody even had such a round, even, finely lathed stick. Nobody had such a smooth red apple. Nobody else's candle was such a striking success—for who had as much wax as me? For who else was slapped and cuffed when my father found me under the bench in the synagogue foyer collecting pieces of wax from the melted-down Yom Kippur memorial candles? I compared my flag with all the others before me—and my chest swelled with pride. I imagined that I was growing taller and taller, bigger and wider. I felt light on my feet. I felt like laughing, shouting, screaming, dancing for joy.

"Come on, lemme have a look," rich Yulik said in amazement as he stood next to me. He examined my flag, I examined his. There's a flag for you, I thought. Some stick. Bent like a bagel. I saw that he was furious, but I pretended not to notice and busily studied my shoelaces.

"Kopel," he said. "Where did you get such a fine stick?"

"What did you say?" I asked, looking up.

"Where did you find such a cute little stick?"

"Why do you ast?" I said. "Want to swap it for your nail?"

Yulik got the dig. Eyes gleaming, he sniffed, put his hands into his pockets and went away. I watched him, beaming with ever increasing joy. He called Nekhemya (the lame boy), whispered something to him, and winked in my direction. I noticed this but pretended not to. A moment later Nekhemya limped up to me, holding Yulik's flag with the bent stick.

"Gimme a light," he said. "Mine went out."

"This isn't your flad, is it?" I asked, holding my candle to his. "You tan't fool me. I know very well whose flad it is."

But before I had a chance to blink, Nekhemya touched his lit candle to my flag and gave the light right back to me. My flag flamed, sputtered and—wwwsht—no more flag.

Had a stone fallen from the sky and struck my head; had a wild beast attempted to devour me; had a corpse dressed in a tattered shroud sought to choke me—my fright would not have been as great as it was when I saw my naked stick and the burnt-out flag.

From deep down within me, I cried: "Woe is me, my flad, my flad, my flad."

I burst into tears. Everything became dark. The stick, the apple and the candle fell from my hand and I began to wander about aimlessly. I walked on without direction, the hot and bitter tears streaming out of my eyes. I wrung my hands and bemoaned my flag, as one does a dead man. I came home, alone, without a flag. I found a dark corner and sat down, my head between my knees, and wept softly so that no one would notice. And I asked God a question:

"Is it fair? O Eternal Lord! Did I deserve it? Why did you do this to me?"

Epilogue

Children, you know that all stories either have sad or happy endings.

For the most part, Jewish stories have sad endings. According to one of our proverbs a Jew, especially a poor one, is not destined to have pleasure. Much can be said about this. When you grow up, you'll understand. But, meanwhile, I must tell you that the story you just heard did not end just there. That flag caused me much anguish and I took sick, burning with fever. I saw extraordinary sights—fiery-tongued dragons and serpents and wild beasts in the shape of men. I heard the wild, unnatural calls of cats and vipers. I tossed and turned, ranted deliriously, had one foot in the grave. They had no hopes for my life. In the basement prayer-room annex of the Butchers' Synagogue they even began reciting Psalms. I was at death's door.

But since today is the eve of a holiday, and on a holiday—especially on Simkhas Torah—we have to be merry and gay, I'd like to end the story of my flag on a happy note.

First of all, thank heaven, as you can see, I recovered.

Second of all, for your information, the following year my flag was even nicer, my stick more beautiful, my apple redder. In fact, I sat way up by the eastern wall with all the other rich men's children. The lights burned. My flag sparkled. Jews danced around the synagogue with the Torah. Reb Melekh the cantor, his prayer shawl outspread, led the procession like a field marshal. His metallic voice quavered as he sang out: "Hel-per of the poor and weak, sa-a-ve us!" An endless stream of women and girls pressed forward to kiss the Torah and shrilled into his face: "Live and be well till next year at this time." And Reb Melekh replied, "The same to you and yours."

Dear children—and the same to you and yours!

From Kasrilevke

The core of Sholom Aleichem's world and the provenance of many of his stories is Kasrilevke, the shtetl which epitomizes all the small villages in Jewish creation and is, incidentally, the fictional representation of the village in which Sholom Aleichem himself grew up. Since Kasrilevke represents tradition as well as transition, it may be considered a state of mind as well as a fixed place. And like states of mind, Kasrilevke is perpetually changing.

In "The Great Panic of the Little People," Kasrilevke is a village suddenly aroused by a threat to its physical safety. A tender humor pervades the story; most of its characters, even the two gentile domestics, are lovingly drawn. Although Makar is a villain, the author does not demolish him. After all, what can one expect from a Russian goy? The scorn is directed elsewhere. In the midst of the humorous mode, Sholom Aleichem the satirist suddenly appears with his vitriolic sketch of the rich sycophant, Mordecai-Nossen.

A different view of Kasrilevke is found in "Methuselah—A Jewish Horse." Sholom Aleichem wrote several stories about animals that, exposed to an almost total Jewish environment, assume the traits of the people they associate with. In writing "Methuselah," Sholom Aleichem surely had in mind Mendele Mocher Seforim's allegorical novel, The Nag, wherein a suffering horse represents the oppressed people of Israel. But *although Methuselah can represent the Jewish people—there is always the tendency to relate animal stories to human significance—Sholom Aleichem's storytelling ability goes beyond cold allegory and becomes primarily a tale of an abused and pathetic old horse.*

METHUSELAH—A JEWISH HORSE

Methuselah—that's the name he was given in Kasrilevke because he was as old as the hills, and hadn't a tooth in his mouth, except for a couple of stumps with which he barely managed to chew the rare morsels that came his way. He was tall and scrawny and most of his hide had shed. His back was a wreck, and his sight was failing: one eye was blind, the other inflamed. He had spindly legs, protruding hips, sunken flanks, a mournfully drooping lower lip, and a somewhat hairless scraggly tail. There, in a nutshell, is a portrait of Methuselah.

In his old age Methuselah carried the water casks of Kasriel, the Kasrilevke water-carrier. By nature Methuselah was a gentle horse, but during his lifetime he had been worked to the bone, poor devil. After having trudged around in the clayey Kasrilevke mud from dawn to dusk and provided Kasrilevke with a full day's supply of water, Methuselah was content to be unharnessed from the casks and eat a bit of straw and some slops, which Kasriel gave him with the same tender devotion that a favorite guest would be served a platter of fish or a bowl of dumplings. Methuselah would look forward to the slops as something of a treat, for there he would always find a piece of soaked bread, some groats, and similar soft delicacies for which teeth were not a prerequisite. Throughout the day Kasriel's wife saved bits of food. Whatever came into her hands she threw into the slop pail—thinking, let the poor thing have a snack. As for Methuselah, once he had had his fill, he turned his face toward the cask and, pardon the expression, his rear end to Kasriel's wife, as though to say: "Thanks a lot for the nectar and ambrosia."

Then, his drooping lip sagging even further, he shut his one good eye and let himself sink into deep, horsey thoughts.

2

But don't think that Methuselah was such a pitiful creature all his life. Once upon a time when he was still a young colt trotting after his mother's wagon, he had aspirations of becoming a first-rate stallion. Connoisseurs of horseflesh predicted that he would develop into an extraordinary animal. "You'll see," they said. "Some day he'll be harnessed to a coach along with the finest and noblest steeds."

But when this colt grew up, they slapped a bridle on him and, with all due respect, led him to the fair, where he was placed among a pack of horses and driven back and forth perhaps fifty times. Prospective buyers constantly looked into Methuselah's mouth, raised his feet, and inspected his hoofs until, finally, one of them bought him.

And that was the beginning of Methuselah's Cain-like existence, his career of wandering from place to place. His owners kept swapping him for other horses; he dragged half-ton loads and more; he plodded through knee-high mud and felt an incessant stream of lashes and blows upon all parts of his body, especially his flanks, head, and legs.

3

For a while he pulled a mail wagon—there was a bell right over his ear which clanged without letup: ding-dong, ding-dong—and ran like mad back and forth over one route. Then he was sold to a common workingman, strong as an ox, who used Methuselah for all sorts of arduous tasks. He plowed and sowed, hauled a huge wagon laden with grain, a barrel of water, a heap of refuse, and performed other such menial workhorse chores which he was completely unaccustomed to. He then fell into the clutches of a gypsy, at whose hands he was miserably mistreated. To his dying day Methuselah would remember the dirty tricks his new master played on him to get him to run faster. In time the gypsy sold him to a horse farm, from which he was shortly removed by a Meze-pevka drayman.

This drayman had a heavy iron-ribbed wagon, adorned with lots of little bells, and covered with a strange-looking thatched canopy. The drayman laced into Methuselah un-ceasingly with sticks and whips, just as if his hide were made of leather and not of flesh and blood, and his sides of iron and not of bone. Poor soul, ofttimes Methuselah just barely managed to hobble along. While his calves were pinched by unseen tongs and a ball of iron settled in his knotted stomach, his cruel master shouted "Giddyap," whipping and poking him as though he deserved it.

Luckily, once a week the drayman gave Methuselah a day off on which he could simply stand around and chew and not do a blessed thing. Methuselah would often ruminate upon this, but he lacked the horse sense to comprehend the reason for the one day on which he would not have to budge from his stall. Why couldn't it be like this all the time? he would think, pricking up his ears, shutting one eye and winking at his two harness cronies.

4

After leaving the drayman and his wagon, Methuselah was hitched to a threshing machine, where he worked like a horse. Deafened by the roar, he turned in circles, plagued by the doses of dust and chaff which seeped into his nose, mouth, and eyes.

Where's this merry-go-round headed for? he would often ask himself, anxious to stop for a minute. Who's big idea was it to keep turning in one spot?

But he wasn't given too much time for meditation. Behind him stood a taskmaster who perpetually flicked a whip at him—swish, swish, swish. You wild animal, Methuselah thought, casting a quick sidelong glance at the man holding the whip, I'd just like to see you tied to this wheel and whipped to turn round and round without rhyme or reason.

Understandably enough, this constant turning in the dust made him a cripple, poor devil; he lost the sight of one eye, the other was always inflamed; what's more, his legs, too,

became a bit shaky. Said defects caused all his horsepower to
fizzle out. Not worth a rap now, he was once again led to the
fair in the hope that he could be palmed off on some sucker.
He was spruced up and combed down. His scraggly tail was
bound under; his hoofs were polished with grease. But it did
no good whatsoever; the public could not be fooled. Despite
the torments he suffered in being made to act young and
coltish, and hold his head proud and high, Methuselah went
his own sweet way. He lowered his head with great humility,
he stuck out his scrawny legs, he displayed his droopy nether
lip, he even let drop a tear or two.

For Methuselah there were no buyers. Actually, two men
were interested, but they didn't even bother, looking into his
mouth; they merely ran their hands over his chin, spat in
disgust and stalked away. One other man expressed interest,
though not in Methuselah himself, but in his hide. However,
the hide dealer was unable to come to terms with the seller.
He proved that the nag wasn't worth the trouble: transport-
ing him, killing him and flaying him would cost more than
the hide was worth.

But Methuselah was evidently destined for a comfortable
old age, for one day along came Kasriel out of the blue and
brought him to Kasrilevke.

5

Until he had come across Methuselah, Kasriel the water-
carrier, a broad-boned man with a splayed nose and a hairy
face, had been his own beast of burden. Without much ado,
he would harness himself daily to his water barrels and carry
them all over town. But no matter how much Kasriel suffered
all his life he never envied anyone at all. However, when he
would see a man driving a horse, he would stop and stare for
a long time at the hoofprints. His sole wish was that with
God's help he would someday own a horse. But despite
diligent saving he couldn't quite amass enough money to buy
one. Nevertheless, he did not let one fair pass by without
wandering about the horse stalls, just looking around,
window-shopping. One day, seeing a hopeless, pathetic-

looking and miserable nag standing at the fair without a bridle and not tied to anything, Kasriel stopped dead in his tracks. His heart told him that this horse was a fair match for his purse.

And so it was. There was no need for extensive haggling. Kasriel took the horse and rushed home, overjoyed. When he arrived, he knocked on the door. His wife ran out, frightened.

"My goodness, what is it?"

"I bought it. So help me, I bought it."

The couple did not know where to put the horse. Had they not been ashamed of their neighbors they would have brought the horse into the house. Straightaway they managed to find some straw and hay; and as Methuselah ate, the delighted couple could not take their eyes off him.

The neighbors, too, gathered to look at the amazing bargain which Kasriel had brought home from the fair. Everyone ridiculed the horse, poked fun at him. As usual, they cracked all sorts of jokes and jibes.

"This isn't even a horse," someone sneered, "but an ass."

"An ass?" jeered another. "It's a pussycat!"

"A puzzycat?" twitted a third. "It's a mere spirit. Make sure you guard it from a strong wind for, heaven forbid, it might be blown away!"

"How old do you think it is?" someone asked.

"Older than Kasriel and his wife put together."

"He's as old as Methuselah."

"Methuselah!"

And ever since then the name Methuselah has stuck.

6

The nickname notwithstanding, Methuselah was never so well off (even in his colthood) as he was with Kasriel the water-carrier. First of all, the work was a joke. Period. Carrying a water barrel and whoaing at every door was some tough job! And the master, why he was a gem of a man. He never even touched him, never shouted, merely held a whip for the sake of appearances. And the food, it was out of this world. True, he never laid eyes on oats—but what good were oats if

he had nothing to chew them with? The slops and soaked
bread provided by Kasriel's wife were much better. But the
slops were no match for the service. Seeing Kasriel's wife
standing with folded arms, joyously watching Methuselah
eating, knock wood, was certainly a sight.

Come nighttime a straw bed was prepared for him in the
yard. Occasionally, Kasriel or his wife came out to check if he
had been horsenapped, God forbid. And early in the morning,
when God himself was still asleep, Kasriel was already tend-
ing to his horse. He carefully harnessed him to the water
barrel, sat down and rode to the river, singing a strange
melody all along the way:

"*Happy is the man who has not gone* . . . in other words,
happy is he who has not gone by foot." But after filling the
barrel to the brim, Kasriel walked back with Methuselah, not
singing this time, merely plodding along in the mud with his
horse and twirling his whip. "Come now, Methuselah, git—
get a move on."

Methuselah dragged one foot from the mud, shook his
head, scrutinized Kasriel with his one good eye, and thought:
I've never in my life had such a peculiar creature for a
master. Suddenly the horse decided to plant his hind legs in
the mud and, just for the fun of it, stopped short, as though
to say: "All right, let's see what happens next?"

Seeing that the horse had suddenly halted, Kasriel began
puttering around the barrel, inspecting the wheels, the axles,
the thongs. Methuselah, meanwhile, turned his head to Kasriel, moved his lips in a faint horselaugh, and thought: What
an ass this water-carrier is. The dummox hasn't even got an
ounce of horse sense.

7

There is no such thing as perpetual joy. The bliss of Methuselah's old age in the company of Kasriel and his wife was
marred by the anguish, afflictions and insults he suffered at
the hands of Kasriel's children, the neighbor's children and
children all over.

From the very first minute that Methuselah was brought

into the village the small fry spotted him and immediately felt—not dislike, God forbid; in fact, they rather took a fancy to him. But this affection was Methuselah's undoing. If only they had liked him less and pitied him more.

First of all, when no one was looking, Kasriel's sons, barefoot little Talmud Torah kids, conducted experiments to see if Methuselah had feelings like a human being. So they forthwith tapped his hide with a stick—nothing. They tickled his feet—still nothing. A cuff on the ear—a feeble reaction. Only after they had tried poking a straw into the cataract of his blind eye were they convinced that he, too, had feelings, for he blinked and moved his head, as if to say: "No, not this, this I don't care for at all." Thereupon, they removed a long twig from a broom and shoved it all the way up his nose. Methuselah reared, pranced, and snorted. Then Kasriel came running, shouting blue murder:

"Beat it, you little scoundrels. Why are you fooling around with the horse? Back to school, rascals."

And the pack of scamps took to their heels and scampered off to the Talmud Torah.

8

In the Talmud Torah there was a certain Ruvele, a high-spirited young lad, heaven help us, an incomparable mischief-maker. His own mother said of him: "Such brats are a thorn, better not born." His specialty was getting into everybody's hair. There was no attic or cellar he hadn't been in. His greatest thrill was chasing chickens, geese or ducks, scaring goats, torturing cats, beating dogs, and even walloping pigs.

The whacks Ruvele got from his mother, the hidings from his teacher, and the blows from perfect strangers were all in vain. The curses hurled his way rolled off him like water off a duck's back. One would think that the beatings did some good, for Ruvele would shed real hot tears. But no sooner did you turn away than he would stick out his tongue and screw up his face. And he had just the pair of cheeks for tricks like that—they were huge as dumplings. Ruvele was always healthy and perpetually merry. The fact that his mother was a poor widow who worked herself to death and paid a full ruble per term for his schooling did not concern him in the least.

When Kasriel's children told Ruvele that their father had brought home from the fair a horse named Methuselah, he leaped up on the school bench, wiped his nose with both hands and bellowed:

"Fellas, we got ourselves a fiddle bow!"

It should be noted that from childhood on Ruvele adored musicians, went wild over a fiddle, and was in seventh heaven when he heard one being played. Moreover, he had a pretty voice and knew all the melodies by heart. His only thought was that, God willing, when he would grow up, he would buy a fiddle and play it day and night. But meanwhile he made his own little fiddle out of a piece of wood, with thread in place of strings, for which he was soundly thrashed by his mother.

"So you're gonna grow up and be a fiddler, huh? May I not live to see the day!"

Evening time, when Khaim-Khone the Talmud Torah teacher dismissed the children, they all went to bid welcome to Kasriel the water-carrier's horse. The first one to express his opinion was Ruvele:

"The nag's a remarkable beast. His tail is full of strings. And if you don't believe me, just watch."

Ruvele sneaked behind Methuselah and began plucking hairs from his tail. As long as Ruvele plucked the hairs one by one, Methuselah stood still, as though to say: "So what! A hair off my tail is no skin off my back! What's one hair more or less?" But when Ruvele bore down and began tearing out entire clusters of hair, Methuselah bristled, thinking: Give a swine a finger and he takes a hand. And without deliberating at great length Methuselah kicked Ruvele smack in the teeth with his hind leg and broke his lip in two.

"You had it coming—may lightning strike me! Serves you right—plagues upon me! Don't go creeping where you don't belong—oh woe is me!"

So said Ruvele's mother, Yente the gossip, weeping and wringing her hands as she applied cold compresses to his split lip. Then, leaving no stone unturned, she ran to Khiyene the barber-surgeon's wife.

9

Thank heaven that Ruvele was the sort of youngster whose wounds, like a dog's, healed quickly. In less than no time, the lip was whole again, looking as though nothing had ever happened to it. Then Ruvele promptly had another bright idea: what great fun it would be to take a ride on Methuselah's back. He and all the Talmud Torah kids. At one and the same time. But when and how could such a stunt be executed without anyone's knowledge? Ruvele concluded that the only right time was Sabbath afternoon, when everyone had eaten and was fast asleep, a time when anyone could simply meander into town and walk off with all of Kasrilevke, lock, stock and barrel. There was even one Talmud Torah lad who dared speak up against the plan:

"Since when does a Jew ride on the Sabbath?"

To which Ruvele replied: "You ass! Call that riding? That's what I call playing!"

On Sabbath afternoon, when everyone including Kasriel and his wife had eaten and lain down to nap, the gang quietly stole into the water-carrier's courtyard. Ruvele undertook to make Methuselah as elegant as possible. First of all he plaited his mane and made a few braids adorned with little straws. Then he crowned him with a paper dunce cap which was tied down around his neck. And finally he hung an old broom on his rump to make his wispy tail appear longer and more attractive. Now the gang began climbing over each other onto Methuselah's back. Whoever managed to grab a good seat remained there. Meanwhile, the others, hoping to find a spot later, chased after the horse, loudly urging him to shake a leg and get a move on. Parodying a verse from the Book of Esther, they sang:

"So shall be done to the steed whom Ruvele delights in honoring."

Methuselah, however, was in no great mood for trotting. He shuffled along, step by plodding step, for first of all, he had plenty of time, and second of all, today was a day of rest. But Ruvele did not cease driving the horse; he poked, prodded and pushed him, screaming at his pals at the top of his lungs:

"The devil take your fathers' fathers, how about giving me a hand?"

Nevertheless, Methuselah lumbered along, thinking: The little scalawags are playing around. Well, let them have some fun.

But when the gang started pestering him, goading him on with jabs and jolts, his pace quickened and the broom banged his legs. Which prompted him to move into a trot. Which made the broom bang his legs all the more. So Methuselah began to buck and jump. This pleased the gang and Ruvele hopped along, yelling: "Hippety-hop, hippety-hop." Methuselah kept this up until all the riders had fallen off, one by one, like matza balls. And only when Methuselah had thrown them all off and sensed that he was free did he begin to run like a madman, galloping swiftly until he had gone past the mills and beyond the town limits.

Seeing a peculiar-looking horse with a paper dunce cap, the gentile shepherd lads gave chase. They teased him, threw sticks, and set the dogs on him. The hounds didn't wait for a second invitation and took after him, snapping and biting. Some of them grabbed him by the haunches; others latched onto his throat. Methuselah began to gasp and wheeze. But the dogs did not desist until he had gasped his last.

10

The next morning the gang was given their comeuppance. In addition to bloody noses and bruised foreheads from the falls, they were trounced at home and whipped by Khaim-Khone at school. Ruvele, of course, was taken to task more severely than all the others, for when the others were drubbed, they at least sniveled; Ruvele, on the contrary, only laughed. So they laced into him all the more; but the more he was pummeled the more he laughed; and the more he laughed the more he was pummeled. Finally, Khaim-Khone the teacher himself burst out laughing and, following his example, so did all the other pupils. Such an uproar of giggling developed that neighbors and passersby—men and women, boys and girls—gathered.

"What's up? What's the big joke? What's everyone laughing about?"

But no one could answer the question because they were all doubled over with laughter—laughter so infectious that newcomers were also caught up in the swell and began giggling, too; this, in turn, caused the first group to go into hysterics once more; which prompted further salvos of laughter on the part of the newcomers—in a word, everyone held his sides, convulsed with laughter.

Only two people did not laugh: the water-carrier and his wife. A child who dies, God forbid, could not have been mourned nearly as much as Kasriel and his wife mourned and wept over their great loss, their poor old horse, Methuselah.

THE GREAT PANIC OF
THE LITTLE PEOPLE

1

[Wherein the Author Confides in His Readers]

Heaven has apparently decreed that Kasrilevke's Jews are destined to have more woes than anyone else in the world. Wheresoever there was calamity, misfortune, troubles and misery, trials and tribulations, they sought to sympathize, taking each affliction to heart more than anyone the world over. Of course, Kasrilevke's anguish over the Dreyfus affair should surprise no one. After all, Dreyfus was one of their own, a member of the family, so to speak. Like they say: Blood is thicker than water.

But by what stretch of the imagination could you reasonably account for the Kasrilevkites' involvement with the Boers, whom the English conquered and wiped out? In Kasrilevke that war, too, caused a hullabaloo. Oh my, plenty of blood was spilled over that Boer War in the Kasrilevke synagogue. But wait a minute! Don't be alarmed! Do you really think *blood* was actually shed? God forbid! Far be it from a Kasrilevkite to shed blood. Just point out a nicked finger in the distance and he falls into a dead faint. So when I say "blood" I mean something entirely different. I mean pain, heartache, and humiliation. Then why all the fuss? Simply because people have different opinions. If Srulik says one thing, Shmulik says just the reverse.

For instance, if Srulik sides with the Boers and takes up their grievances by saying: "It isn't fair! What have the

English got against those poor devils? They mind their own business and just want to be left in peace to work the earth"— Shmulik immediately ups and defends England and proves that the English are the most cultured people on earth.

"Pipe down, you bastard," someone yells. "I don't give a hoot about culture if they chop people up like cabbages."

"And I don't give a hoot about you, you big fat dope."

"And you're an imbecile, but you're built like a jackass."

To make a long story short—a few punches, witnesses, documents, depositions, a justice of the peace, and the concomitant plagues. At first glance you might wonder why these poor beggars, these poverty-stricken creatures, these penniless, down-at-the-heel paupers, should care about a land stuck away the deuce-knows-where in Africa?

Moreover, please tell me, my dear Kasrilevkites, why you have to break your heads over Serbia, where in the middle of one fine night some officers killed the Czar and his wife and chucked them out the window? I know you'll counter by asking if it's fair to attack a man while he's asleep and do him in. That's what you'd expect of wild savages. In turn, I'll ask you another question. Why should all these things worry you more than anyone else? Don't you have anything else to worry about? Have you already married off and provided for all your children? What sort of habit is it, I ask you, to stick your nose into every pot? Believe me, the world will get along very nicely without you, and everyone will undoubtedly manage to take care of himself.

The author begs his reader's pardon for addressing such cutting remarks to his fellow Kasrilevkites. But please understand, dear friends, that I myself am a Kasrilevkite. Born and bred in Kasrilevke, I was educated in its Talmud Torahs and schools and was even married there. But then I set my little ship adrift in the great and tempestuous sea of life whose waves are high as houses. And despite the fact that one is perpetually in a tumult and on the go, I have never ever forgotten either my beloved home town Kasrilevke, may it thrive and prosper to ripe old age, or my dear brethren, the Kasrilevke Jews, may they be fruitful and multiply. Whenever we experience violence, disaster or calamity *here,* far away from Kasrilevke, I immediately ask myself: What's happening *there*, in my home town?

For your information, no matter how small, forlorn, and castaway Kasrilevke may be, it is connected to the rest of the world by a sort of wire which if tapped at one end delivers a message at the other. Let me put it another way. Kasrilevke can be compared to an unborn child, tied to its mother's umbilical cord, that feels everything the mother feels. The mother's pain is the child's pain and vice versa. The only thing that puzzles me is why Kasrilevke feels the troubles and woes of the entire world, while absolutely no one cares about Kasrilevke, or sympathizes with its afflictions. Kasrilevke is a kind of stepchild of the world. The first to react to a misfortune, Kasrilevke scurries about more than anyone else and goes without sleep till it practically knocks at death's door.

Yet—oh blast those anti-Semites!—should this stepchild itself fall ill and collapse in a corner, burning feverishly like an oven, wasting away for lack of food, and thirsting for lack of water, you may be sure that not a soul would even cast a glance in its direction.

2

[A Short Letter and a Big Hullabaloo]

After such an introduction, everyone will readily be able to appreciate the tumult in Kasrilevke at the conclusion of that sweet Passover episode—God spare us a like repetition. Even before the Yiddish newspaper reached Zaydl (the only subscriber in town) and before anyone had heard the news, a certain *shokhet* received a letter from his son-in-law. This letter is herewith transcribed word for word in the writer's own style, and translated from Hebrew into the vernacular for everyone to understand:

"Peace to my beloved and scholarly father-in-law, whose name resounds to the four corners of the earth, and to my dear and beloved mother-in-law, wise, honest, and pious, may your names shine forth the world over, and peace to your household and to all Israel, Amen.

"With trembling hands and quaking knees do I write these

words to you. Know that the *weather* here has undergone a severe change. No pen can possibly describe it. All I can say is that, God be praised, all of us are alive and well. The hail and the tempest that struck this place just scared us a bit, but, thank God, the storm has passed and we're no longer afraid of anyone. My wife, children and I beg you not to worry for, glory to God, we are all well. Be sure to write us immediately a lengthy detailed letter, telling us what's new with you, how the *weather* is, and if you're all in good health."

Sages and savants have of long noted that the Jews are incomparable at the art of reading between the lines. Show them a finger—and they'll know what you're driving at. Mention a word—and they'll reply with two more. They recognize neither conundrums, riddles, nor enigmatic questions.

The afore-mentioned letter went from hand to hand. The Kasrilevkites talked only of the *shokhet's* son-in-law. And the weather report spread like wildfire through town. They told one another dreadful stories, embellished with all the horrible details, as though they themselves had witnessed the pogrom. Their faces reflected the gloom and bitter melancholy within them. At once they were bereft of joy, seemingly forever. Their one bit of hope and consolation was that perhaps it was either all imagined or an out-and-out lie. Who could tell! The *shokhet's* son-in-law was a young writer-intellectual, a fine Hebrew prose stylist. Perhaps his infatuation with rhetoric had led him to the devil-knows-where? It was sheer hyperbole and nothing else. And in order to cheer their spirits and drive gloom away the villagers told each other merry tales about the modern young intellectuals and their flowery style—tales which, at another time, would have prompted fits of hysterical laughter. The only hitch was that no one laughed now. No one was in the mood for humor. An uncommon dejection settled over them all. Everyone privately pondered the awful thing that must have happened over *there*. And then the people converged upon Zeidel.

Our old friend Zeidel had just come from the post office with his newspaper. His face was dark as night. Excited and apprehensive, he was furious at the whole wide world. Only then did the Kasrilevkites realize that the reports were really true.

"Fortunately, a nasty business like that can't come to pass in Kasrilevke," they all consoled themselves. "Such a calamity can't possibly happen here."

Nevertheless, in their hearts they brooded—who knows? Great winds can turn a tiny spark into a hellish conflagration. And the Kasrilevke Jews cautiously took stock of their relations with their neighbors—the "other people."

3

*[Describes Fyodor, the Gentile-for-the-Sabbath,
in Particular, and Other Gentiles, in General]*

If Fyodor, the gentile who extinguished the lights in Kasrilevke on Friday nights; Pockmarked Hapke, the woman who whitewashed the houses and milked everyone's goats; and other such non-Jews could be labeled the "other people," we must conclude that Kasrilevke had absolutely no cause for alarm. The Jews could easily have remained in their village until the advent of the Messiah, for since time immemorial they had fared well with these "other people"; so well, in fact, that one might even have thought it couldn't be any better.

Fyodor knew beyond doubt that though he was the sole native aristocrat of Kasrilevke, he nevertheless had to heat up the ovens for the Jews on the Sabbath, extinguish the lights, empty the slops, and perform other such menial tasks which had become second nature to him over the years. And if you think he had hard feelings toward the Jews because of this, you're mistaken. He knew, to be sure, who he was and who the Jews were: the entire world couldn't be made up of generals only; there had to be some plain foot soldiers as well. As a matter of fact, perhaps a few of the generals—that is, some Kasrilevke Jews—would gladly have changed places with Fyodor, the plain foot soldier. But on the other hand, generals were necessary, too. With foot soldiers alone the world could not exist. And so both sides were content: the generals of Kasrilevke were happy that someone catered to them on the Sabbath; and the plain foot soldier was pleased that he had someone to cater to—for this work enabled him to snatch a piece of Sabbath-loaf here and get a glass of whiskey there. On Sabbath after the Kiddush folks said to him, "Come on over here, Fyodor dear. Have a drink," adding in Yiddish, "and break a leg!" Fyodor removed his cap, held his glass with two fingers, bowed, and wished everybody a hearty and prosperous year.

"Here's to you," he said. He drained the glass at one shot and screwed up his face, positively contorting it, as though he had never before tasted such a bitter brew.

"Dammit a hundred demons and a blasted witch! That's as strong as hell."

"Here! Have some of this," they said in Russian, offering Fyodor a hunk of the soft white Sabbath-loaf, then adding in Yiddish, "and a pack of plagues upon your bones."

But heaven forbid your thinking that the Kasrilevke Jews meant those vehement curses which they rained down upon Fyodor's head. They wouldn't have exchanged an honest peasant like Fyodor for a pot of gold. Even if money were strewn about he wouldn't touch it. He would work for you like a pack of devils: heat the oven, spill the slops, hold the goat until Hapke had finished milking it, bring in the firewood, fill the water barrel, scour the pots like a devoted housewife, and, if need be, rock the cradle, too. No one surpassed Fyodor in putting a baby to sleep. No one could amuse a child as well; he'd clack his tongue, whistle, and snap his fingers; he'd gabble and gurgle, snort like a pig, and go through many other such antics. That's why the children of Kasrilevke, in love with Fyodor's bristly chin and coarse prickly coat, refused to leave his arms.

However, this did not please the Kasrilevke housewives. For they thought that when the kids were hungry and there was nothing to eat, Fyodor was liable to dip into his bag and come up with a piece of bread or something else, heaven forbid, and stuff them with God-knows-what kind of forbidden concoctions. But they were mistaken. Fyodor would never have dreamed of doing any such thing. He knew full well that the foods the Jews ate, he could eat, but the foods that he ate, they could *not* eat.

Why so? Well, that was no concern of his. Why, for instance, was he permitted to blow out the candle—really such an easy task—or touch the candlesticks, or carry the prayerbook to the synagogue, and perform other simple chores on the Sabbath? And why were all these things forbidden to them? Such matters were not open to question; each person had to follow his own path. And if on occasion Fyodor could not restrain himself and laughed at the dry Passover matza by saying: "Very crunchy, dammit a hundred demons and a blasted witch!"—he was given short shrift with: "And is your hog any better, you pig!" Which made Fyodor hold his tongue.

However, Fyodor was silent only when he was sober. But when he became so drunk that he forgot his own name—a rare occurrence for Fyodor—brother, watch out! Danger ahead! On those occasions, he would smite his chest, weep bitterly and bellow:

"What do you want from me? Why do you keep sucking my blood and eating my flesh? I'm going to turn Kasrilevke upside down. Yids, anti-Christ Yids, dammit a hundred demons and a blasted witch." He would continue shouting and raising a fuss until he fell asleep. After a good long snooze he would get up, return to the Jews, and once more be the same old honest and even-tempered "Fyodor-dear," as though nothing at all had happened.

"And where's your boots?" they asked him in Russian, adding in Yiddish, "A pack of blisters on your puss." Then they began preaching to him, raining a bunch of Yiddish curses on him, as usual.

"What do you think you're doing, you great big oaf? Just wait and see, you're going to croak somewhere! You'll drop dead beneath some fence, damn your hide, may you be the atonement for all Israel, dear God!"

Fyodor looked on silently, scratching the back of his head. He knew quite well that they were right and he wrong. He looked down at his bare feet and wondered how in the world he could have sold his boots—"Dammit a hundred demons and a blasted witch." That's the sort of creature Fyodor was.

The rest of the peasants in Kasrilevke were also in constant contact with the Jews. They knew that since time immemorial the Jews were destined to be storekeepers, merchants, and middlemen. For no one could do business or bamboozle you like the Jews, a people created for this very purpose. Or as the peasants put it:

"Business deals—that's what the Jews were made for."

The peasants and the Jews often met at the marketplace. They knew one another's names and respected one another. Hritzko called Hershke a gypper and Hershke called Hritzko a chiseler. But it was all done good-naturedly and they had it out right well. Both went to the rabbi, Reb Yozifl, who, unfamiliar with their slang, always compromised. "Split it in half!" he would say, content that there be no desecration of God's name.

4

[Hapke of the Jewish Soul—Makar the Anti-Semite]

Until now we have described gentiles of the male species. Now let us devote some space to Pockmarked Hapke. Hapke talked Yiddish as though it was her mother tongue; however, she had a special knack for mixing up typically Jewish expressions. For instance, she would say, "A joyous holi-danish," "May he rest in pieces," "mazel-tub," "happy Pass-under," "Yom-kippered herrings," and the like. In fact, behind Fyodor's back she always called him a good-for-nothing goy-ter.

Hapke had become so attached to the Kasrilevke women that occasionally, forgetting who she was, they ordered her to perform tasks which were properly the role of Jewish women only. She went to the rabbi with a question concerning ritual, helped to salt the meat, koshered the chickens, brought in the Passover dishes, and did other chores in which she was more punctilious than her Jewish mistresses. She feared mixing meat and dairy dishes like the plague, and scrupulously avoided contact with bread and leaven products during Passover. She ate matza, grated horseradish with gusto and, like other Jewish women, considered it a rare delight.

For a long time the Kasrilevke constable refused to believe that Hapke wasn't Jewish. But then, involved in a rather shameful affair, she was caught and about to be exiled to some far-off place. Fortunately for her someone else was implicated—the municipal clerk, Makar Khalodne, a notorious Jew-hater, a Jew-baiter of the first rank, one of the most educated and virulent anti-Semites in Kasrilevke. If not for their tender feelings for Hapke, the Jews of Kasrilevke could have taken revenge upon their Haman. But since Makar's downfall would have ruined Hapke, the Jewish witnesses retracted and told the examining magistrate that their previous testimony was so much barking at the moon. So the whole business was quashed. One would think that subsequently Makar should have made up with the Jews and become their best pal; however, owing to some caprice of nature, just the opposite happened: he became a more vehement bigot, a fiercer Jew-baiter, a greater anti-Semite than ever before.

It may be said that from childhood on, Makar suffered at the hands of the Jews. At first, his deep-rooted hatred was directed only at the Kasrilevke Jews; and later, at all Jews. When he was still a barefoot boy, driving his father's geese to pasture, he would often meet Jewish children coming from Talmud Torah, and, instead of saying "Good morning" he would mimic their Yiddish and their gestures, intending no insult, God forbid, but merely joking good-naturedly.

But these descendants of the gentle Patriarch Jacob, timid and innocent Jewish children who studied the Torah with Rashi's commentary, were indeed insulted by Makar's antics. They countered with a Yiddish ditty, whose words Makar did not understand. But he could guess from the lilt of the tune and the snickers of the children that he was the butt of their song and it galled him. Makar, indeed, had guessed correctly. This was the song the children sang:

> We eat nuts.
> Damn your guts.
> See our sled?
> You drop dead.
> Pant and rave.
> Dig your grave.

Silly children. First of all, the situation was exactly the reverse. It was Makar who munched on nuts and had a sled, not they. Secondly, how come ten Jewish children plucked up the courage to pick a fight with Makar? After all, Makar had a fair pair of paws which could match wits with the ten brainiest, most sharp-witted Talmud Torah youngsters. In fact, after that ditty Makar taught them a lesson, alluding to the literal meaning of the biblical verse they learned in school: *The voice is the voice of Jacob, but the hands are the hands of Esau.*

Later, when Makar studied at the parish school he was always running into the Jewish children. During the summer he met them in the field behind the village, and during the winter while they played on the ice. Each time some sort of brawl ensued between the two sides. When he called them "damn Yids"—which was actually a commonplace term like "rascal"—they called him "swine." To their incessant jests he responded with blows; he frequently interpreted another scriptural passage by demonstrating how the Philistines chased the Israelites—he and his friends pursuing the Jewish lads with sticks and stones, and hoots, jeers and catcalls:

"Hike, hike, cursed kike. Skid, skid, confounded Yid."

5

[How an Anti-Semite Becomes a Philosopher]

Makar never got beyond the parish school. He was an orphan, God help us, who had inherited a small house and a bit of a garden. Since he was literate, he plunged into civil service; he sharpened his pen, developed a fine handwriting, and was soon appointed the assistant to the village clerk. Subsequently, he worked his way up the municipal ladder to secretary, finally becoming the Grand Panjandrum himself, a position which enabled him to have frequent contact with the Kasrilevke Jews and to gain thorough familiarity with them.

The initial run-ins that Makar had with the Jews weren't too serious. Both sides were content with hurling insinuations, sharp abuse and satiric digs at each other.

"Oy vey, Abie-Ikey," said Makar to the Jews, "where's your noodle pudding?"

"Your honor!" the Jews replied with mock deference, simultaneously hinting by a vigorous scratch of the head and a fillip at the collar that he still had lice.

Occasionally, a sly innuendo is far worse than a direct slur of one's father; at times a jibe can be a thousand times more painful than a blow. And at the art of the jibe the Kasrilev-kites are the most roguish practitioners on earth. It is common knowledge that a Kasrilevkite would walk ten miles, lose a day's work, and practically risk life and limb—all for the sake of one good jibe. If a Kasrilevke pauper, a charity case, a door-to-door beggar was turned away empty-handed, he only asked for the opportunity to tell a story. And when his story was done, he was more often than not given his comeuppance: he opened the door, headfirst—yet he felt that for the the sake of getting off a sharp riposte it was well worth it.

That's the sort of folk my Kasrilevkites are, and if you think they can be made to reform, or that I'm ashamed of them, you're dead wrong.

But let's get back to our friend Makar, whom the Kasrilev-kites had unwittingly made a dangerous enemy. They had forgotten the biblical injunction: Watch out for a little trouble-makar. They thought that Makar would always be a mere village clerk in the municipality. They forgot that he was relatively wellborn and was hankering after rank and position. It was incredible! Before they had a chance to turn around, Makar had already grown up, tall and strong. He sported a pair of thick black moustaches and wore a red band and a golden button on his official cap. No sooner had he affixed that button than he straightened up, stuck out his paunch, and became taller and heftier than ever. What's more, he even became broad-shouldered. It wasn't at all the same Makar. In fact, now known as Makar Pavlovitch, he henceforth became buddy-buddy with the veterinarian, the medic, the postmaster, and with all the other big shots in town.

Makar's good footing with the postmaster was the most

advantageous of his contacts. For him the post office was an education center. There he imbibed all his information from *The Flag*, the only Russian newspaper that came to the village. Naturally, the first to read the paper was the postmaster himself, who passed it on to Makar Pavlovitch. Only then was it sent to the subscriber, a petty nobleman from Zlodievke, a village not far from Kasrilevke. The postmaster said that reading the paper a few days late wouldn't hurt the nobleman a bit, the devil take him, for he played cards day and night, anyway, and duped all his neighbors out of their last penny.

Since Makar replenished his supply of news weekly, he always had something to talk about. Of course, *The Flag* was a noted Jewish paper; that is, it took Jewish interests to heart. Its editors were constantly concerned about the welfare of the Jews and explored ways to be rid of them—for their own good, naturally. And this gave Makar a wonderful opportunity to become perfectly grounded in all aspects of Jewish behavior. With the good Lord's help, *The Flag* made Makar a top-notch specialist in Jewish affairs, a mastermind of Talmud, the Code of Law, and the entire range of Jewish customs and ceremonies, such as—usury, deception, flimflam, and especially, the use of Christian blood for matzas. All these things caught the fancy of our philosopher Makar to the extent that he sought this information from the horse's mouth, as it were—the Kasrilevke Jews themselves. Although Makar hated them like a Jew hates pork, with a few he was on tolerably good terms. One might even say that some of his best friends were Jews.

6

[Mordecai-Nossen and His Wife Teme-Beyle]

One of Makar's oldest friends in Kasrilevke was Mordecai-Nossen, a man so wealthy and prominent he could have put a dozen rich householders into his side pocket.

The opulent Mordecai-Nossen, like all other men of means, held the town under his thumb and did with it as he wished. For he was the tax agent, the synagogue trustee, the communal leader, the town's big wheel. In a word, he was everything: he was the Rich Man in Town.

But if you really want to descend to particulars, you might well ask: What did his wealth consist of? The answer to this question no one knew. If you would collar a Kasrilevkite, for instance, and ask him: "Listen here, how much money does this Mordecai-Nossen really have?"—the villager would stop, tug at his beard, shake his head, and chant in a mournful singsong:

"Mordecai-Nossen? I wish I had half of what he owes! What am I saying half? I'd be happy with one percent! Don't underestimate Mordecai-Nossen. He's loaded."

"What do you mean loaded? For example, how much is he worth?"

"Worth? It's a nonsensical question. No one's ever counted his money."

"Then how much is Mordecai-Nossen good for?"

"Mordecai-Nossen? First of all, he has a house of his own."

"Plus?"

"Plus his own private courtyard."

"Plus what else?"

"Plus a few goats."

"Plus?"

"What about his shop? Some neat shop!"

"Plus what?"

"Not to mention his tax collecting."

"Plus?"

"My, my, you certainly are an impulsive plusser. Do you begrudge this surplus wealth to a fellow Jew? What do you want him to do, open up a bank? Throw money away and ride around in a gold-plated coach?"

The Kasrilevkite would then depart in a huff, and rightly so! For could a man aspire higher than Mordecai-Nossen? He was *the* rich man, *the* foremost citizen, *the* communal leader. Who was the trustee of the Burial Brotherhood? Mordecai-Nossen. Who was the most influential man in town? Mordecai-Nossen. Who had all the power? Mordecai-Nossen. Who arranged a fine Saturday night dinner for the town's seven leading grandees? Mordecai-Nossen. Who had pull with the authorities? In brief, Mordecai-Nossen and nobody but.

Mordecai-Nossen, you understand, knew exactly how to deal with the outside world, knew precisely how to conduct himself with the authorities. Every Friday night his house guest for the fish course was the police chief. The Kasrilevke police chief was a great lover of Jewish fish. Each time he ate them he simply could not find enough words of praise. How excellently the Jews prepared fish! How tasty they were! Sweet as sugar! he said, actually licking his fingers.

"There's nothing better than Yid fish with horseradish," he said suddenly with his own peculiar intonation. Apparently the compliment pleased both host and hostess, for they both beamed, grinning from ear to ear, and, due to the heat of excitement and pleasure, actually broke into a sweat. Mordecai-Nossen then tried to convince his guest that the Jews had something even better than fish and horseradish. But his guest was skeptical.

"What, for instance?"

"I'll tell you what—"

And Mordecai-Nossen looked for something that was even better than fish and horseradish, but he was afraid to utter the words "honeyed carrot *tsimess*." For what if the police chief decided to wait for the main course? He needed his guest like a hole in the head. Should he say noodle pudding and risk having to open up the oven and serve the course being saved for the Sabbath afternoon dinner? With a Jewish noodle pudding anything could happen!

So Mordecai-Nossen responded with a little laugh: "Ha-ha," to which the guest retorted: "Ha-ha-ha."

And Mordecai-Nossen, delighted that his guest was in good spirits, replied: "Ha-ha, ha-ha." The guest jabbed his elbow into his host's side and cast a sly smile at the hostess—and both man and wife fell into raptures.

Suddenly the police chief jumped up, wiped his hands and mouth on the snow-white tablecloth, buttoned all his buttons, and said without the slightest trace of humor:

"Well, duty calls!"

Mordecai-Nossen and Teme-Beyle rose in honor of their guest. They accompanied him to the door, their fawning gaze reminiscent of a sniffing dog looking up at his master. They bowed and scraped and begged him: "Don't forget now, be sure to come next Friday night."

"In a lead coffin," the hostess hissed at her guest once the door had slammed, furious at her husband for spending all his time—day and night, weekdays and Sabbaths—with the authorities. Mordecai-Nossen listened to her outburst, but remained silent, as though he had a mouthful of pebbles. Mordecai-Nossen was a queer sort of fellow, indeed.

And now the author of this story simply must digress for a moment to present portraits of this couple and introduce them to one and all.

Mordecai-Nossen was a tall, thin, desiccated man with long hands and a perpetually wrinkled brow. Because of his drooping, jowly cheeks, his forever somber face, barely covered with a thin crop of beard, seemed square like a Chinaman's. Since his lips were constantly pressed tight and his mouth set a bit awry, he always appeared to be concealing a secret. A man of few words, Mordecai-Nossen never raised his voice. But when he came in contact with the government authorities, he turned a complete about-face. The wrinkles disappeared from his forehead, his face began to shine, his lips unpursed, his mouth straightened, and he became talkative—Mordecai-Nossen underwent a complete transformation! And do you know why he bustled about so much at the authorities? Only for the sake of honor and self-aggrandizement. In case a Kasrilevkite ever needed a favor, he would have to approach Mordecai-Nossen with his petition and say: "After all, Reb Mordecai-Nossen, who else but you has so much pull with the authorities?" The word "pull" would compensate Mordecai-Nossen for all the humiliation, trouble, and expense. Mordecai-Nossen was a queer fish, indeed.

Mordecai-Nossen's wife, squat and plump Madame Teme-Beyle, was built like a brass pestle or a potbellied samovar on which stood a pointed little teapot. Although roly-poly below, her head was small and angular. This paunchy samovar was always boiling, seething and fuming, angry at her husband, vexed with the servants, infuriated with the Kasrilevke goats, mad at the Kasrilevke women, and all riled up at the world at large. Luckily, though, all of them turned a deaf ear

to her ranting. They took no more heed of her than Haman
does the Purim rattle-clacker. Her husband was eternally
preoccupied with communal affairs and with the authorities;
the maid, out of sheer spite, always burned the groats,
charred the potatoes, and scorched the milk; the Kasrilevke
goats made her frantic by jumping up on the roof and
devouring the thatching, one straw at a time; the Kasrilevke
market women exasperated her at the fish stall and the meat
stand; the women in the synagogue and even (forgive the
proximity) in the bathhouse. . . . Frankly, no one could
stand Teme-Beyle. And perhaps with good reason. After all,
the entire community was not demented.

Now that we've become acquainted with this couple, I
think that we can safely proceed to the other individuals with
whom the wealthy Mordecai-Nossen so diligently rubbed
elbows.

7

[Mister Big Shot at the Rich Man's Store and Home]

Another frequenter at Mordecai-Nossen's was our old friend,
Makar Pavlovitch. He wasn't a house guest, but often
dropped in to Mordecai-Nossen's textile shop which, for your
information, was the first of its kind in Kasrilevke. Besides
rep, lustrine and sailcloth, calico and madapollam, one could
buy worsted, tricot, cheviot, velvet, satin, and muslin—in
short, everything one's heart desired—"modeled after the
latest samples, which can't even be gotten in the big city,
Yehupetz." So said Mordecai-Nossen, his wife, and all the
salesmen. And just you try to contradict them! All the
moneyed folk of Kasrilevke and the surrounding region were
Mordecai-Nossen's customers. Most were Christians and they
trusted Mordedai-Nossen to a T. No sooner did Mordecai-
Nossen say "my word of honor" than they stopped bargaining. But all of Teme-Beyle's sacred oaths and solemn pledges
were just so much water down the drain. They had implicit
faith only in Mordecai-Nossen's "word of honor." And no
questions asked, for that's the way it was.

Makar, a customer of long standing, was one of those to whom Mordecai-Nossen now extended credit. Makar had even shopped at Mordecai-Nossen's when he was known merely as Makar, not as Makar Pavlovitch, and when Mordecai-Nossen wouldn't trust him for as much as a spool of thread. In those days Mordecai-Nossen wasn't ashamed of telling Makar quite frankly:

"No money, no goods."

Later, when Makar became a big wheel in the municipality, Mordecai-Nossen opened an account for him—but naturally, in exchange for a note or an IOU. Mordecai-Nossen would cast a little smile toward Makar and say: "Don't you see, dear sir, there can be no ill feelings when your note is in my pocket." Still later, when Makar donned the official golden button and administrative cape, Mordecai-Nossen extended unlimited credit.

When Makar came into the textile shop now, Mordecai-Nossen brought him a chair, and greeted him with the title "Your Honor." Makar Pavlovitch made himself quite at home, crossed his legs, smoked a cigarette and chatted amiably, addressing the shopkeeper with chummy familiarity: "Hey, listen here, Mordecai-Nos." Mordecai-Nossen stood before him with fake deference and sham respect, thinking: Where did you breeze in from, Mister Big Shot? And said big shot delivered a little discourse concerning Jews, Jewish business, finagling and flimflam, ending each remark with a high-pitched laugh and a peculiar cough which thoroughly nauseated Mordecai-Nossen. Mordecai-Nossen's blood boiled, but he restrained himself and smiled. Had he been able to see his cloying, artificial grin in a mirror, that, too, would have sickened him.

Mordecai-Nossen usually didn't give a damn about the topic of Mister Big Shot's soliloquys, for Makar's blather went in one ear and out the other. But now the more Makar talked the more he touched upon points which Mordecai-Nossen could not tolerate hearing. For example, Makar asked such absurdities as: Was it true that every Sabbath in the synagogue the Jews called down curses upon the heads of all other peoples? Do they spit at churches? Were they obliged to pour the slop pail after a Christian departing from a Jew? He also asked other questions which amounted to a heap of rubbish.

In order to escape from Makar's clutches, Mordecai-Nossen tried to throw him off by drawing him into a conversation about the town council, the meat tax, even the Holy Synod. But no luck. Under no circumstances did Makar let himself be hoodwinked. Once and for all he demanded of Mordecai-Nossen:

"Why don't you admit the truth?"

Mordecai-Nossen tried to play along with the gentile and asked: "Where did Your Honor study such laws?"

Makar looked him full in the face. Suddenly he had a brainstorm. He'd catch Mordecai-Nossen unawares, and pin him, as it were, to the wall.

"Well, what about the blood?"

"What blood?"

"Come, come—you know! Passover . . . matza. . . . How about it?"

In turn, Mordecai-Nossen, too, had a bright idea. With a mawkish snicker he lightly slapped His Honor on the back and surreptitiously stroked his cape. "His Honor is a great clown, ha-ha-ha," he said obsequiously. But once His Honor had picked himself up and was gone, Mordecai-Nossen threw a quick compliment after him: "That Big Shot's got a one-track mind. One could hardly say that he was evilhearted, God forbid. He's just a plain son of a bitch."

Once, on a Sabbath, Mordecai-Nossen sat at home studying *The Ethics of the Fathers*. Suddenly the door opened and in traipsed Makar. At first our rich man was somewhat alarmed. He wondered why Mister Big Shot had suddenly come to see him after his nap? Then Mordecai-Nossen put on a friendly face and, smiling, asked Makar to be seated. Mordecai-Nossen took off his Sabbath hat, remaining in his skullcap.

"Listen here, Teme-Beyle," he shouted to his wife. "How about a snack?"

Makar waved his hand. "Don't bother. I've come to you on another matter. It's a secret. Just between you and me."

Hearing the word "secret," Mordecai-Nossen jumped up, intending to bolt the door. But Makar stayed his hand.

"Don't bother. It's not the sort of secret you have to lock

doors for. I just wanted to ask you something. After all, you're a clever man, honest and forthright. If I get the truth from anyone, it'll be from you."

Mordecai-Nossen stroked his earlocks majestically, thrilled with the compliment. His eyes brimmed with delight. He was transported with joy. His only regret was that no one else was there to hear Makar's flattering remark.

"You've probably heard about what happened to the girl," Makar said, looking him straight in the eye like an investigator. Mordecai-Nossen pricked up his ears like a rabbit.

"Which girl?"

"The girl the Jews killed and whose blood they drew off and hid for Passover."

At first Mordecai-Nossen emitted his tiny laugh: "Ha-ha-ha." But then his face blanched and turned green.

"That's a monstrous lie." Mordecai-Nossen's eyes blazed. He shook his head and his earlocks waggled to and fro.

"What's that? It's all over the papers," Makar retorted, still staring relentlessly at Mordecai-Nossen.

"The papers are lying their heads off," screamed Mordecai-Nossen.

"The papers say that the matter has been taken up officially," Makar said icily. "I myself read that there's an official report on it."

"A bunch of damned lies," Mordecai-Nossen interrupted, his skullcap askew on his head and his earlocks a-flutter.

"What's a damned lie?" Makar asked, purple with rage. "What I've said? or what's in the report?"

"Everything's a damned lie. Everything. Everything is an out-and-out lie. There's not a shred of truth in it."

Mordecai-Nossen twitched with fury. His hands, face, eyes, earlocks—every part of him was quivering. Never having seen Mordecai-Nossen so incensed, Makar deduced that there was ample reason for the Jew's agitation. Apparently, then, the matter was true. For if not, why was he in such a dither? Why did he tremble and shake so? The nerve of the Jew, branding black-on-white facts as out-and-out lies. Smoldering, Makar stood up, donned his official cap and said:

"These words'll cost you dear!"

No sooner did he make a move for the door than Mordecai-

Nossen jumped up and ran after him, regretting the whole exchange. He wanted to apologize and bring him back.

"Sir . . . Your Honor . . . Makar Pavlovitch . . . Makar Pavlovitch!"

But it was a fruitless attempt. Makar Pavlovitch was already far and away on the other side of the door. Mordecai-Nossen was frantic with heartache and chagrin, for he had said a few words too many, the devil take it. And as though on spite, Teme-Beyle now approached and began nagging him to tell her what the Big Shot had been doing here, why he had departed so quickly, and why he had slammed the door.

"Go ask him yourself!" snapped Mordecai-Nossen.

"Why, just look who's having a bit of a fit! On which side of the bed did you get up this morning? Been having any nightmares?"

Mordecai-Nossen thundered, "Pipe down, you cabbage head," so resoundingly that his wife nearly passed out. He himself was startled at his own voice, as was the maid, a swarthy Lithuanian, who dashed in from the kitchen, more dead than alive.

"Blast you," she said. "You scared the living daylights out of me."

At which Teme-Beyle pounced on the maid with two fists flying. Mordecai-Nossen, in turn, rushed at both of them. The upshot of this was a juicy scandal not even worth describing.

8

[Kasrilevke Makes Haste for the Road]

Thereafter, Kasrilevke experienced a period of troubles, suffering, and unwarranted fears. No one knew what prompted Makar to become a more rabid anti-Semite; no one realized why he wasn't seen in the rich man's shop. The rich man himself, apparently ashamed of the incident, tried to hush it up. He didn't breathe a word of it to a soul. On the other hand, Makar went as far as he could go. He constantly provoked the Kasrilevke Jews with new threats. He said they wouldn't lord it over the town for long. Soon they would be repaid in full measure. Makar appropriated *The Flag*'s complaints and grievances lock, stock and barrel: Why should a people who did not plow, sow or reap amass so many possessions? They never lifted a finger, yet they ate in full measure. They didn't deserve to have it so easy!

Makar's shameful affair with Hapke occurred at the same time; this incident proved to be a momentary stumbling block for Makar, and, as previously mentioned, almost cast him headlong into misfortune. But although Makar, praise the good Lord, had come through that episode unscathed, he nevertheless started to antagonize the Kasrilevke Jews, insinuating that they would soon be taught a lesson.

At that time, too, the letter the *shokhet* had received from his son-in-law was passed from hand to hand. And Zaydl's newspaper, confirming the Jews' fears, added fuel to the fire. Stories made the rounds, one more hair-raising than the next. It was rumored that Kasrilevke would soon witness a fine hullabaloo.

Whence did this all stem? Who first gave wings to the rumor? To this very day no one knows, and no one will ever know. At some future time when the historian of Kasrilevke Jewry comes to this period and examines all its documents and papers, he will most assuredly remain lost in thought and, pen in hand, muse about bygone events.

No one knew how it happened and where it originated, but a report circulated in town that three villages were on the march against Kasrilevke. In the course of one morning the people of Kasrilevke got up as one and began bundling their children, their bedding, and their assorted rags. Packing the entire hoard of Kasrilevke poverty, they attempted to escape the approaching flames and made preparations for the journey. Whereto? Wherever their noses would lead them. Mothers picked up their little ones, pressed them to their breasts, and tearfully kissed, hugged, and fondled them as though, God forbid, someone was about to take them away. As though anyone needed them!

In Kasrilevke one store after another closed. The Jewish villagers looked at, and hid from, one another. People rushed and dashed about, assuming that the sooner they left, the better. That morning Fyodor was nearly torn to pieces. Everyone dragged him home to help with the packing. Everyone secretly slipped him little bribes—here a chicken wing, there a few kopecks. Never before was Fyodor such a celebrity, never before did he rake in so much cash. So glutted was he with money that he spat in disgust, shouted, "Dammit a hundred demons and a blasted witch," and followed his feet to the usual place to drink a few glasses in honor of the departing Kasrilevke householders. Having had his fill, he began to get worked up. He flailed about with his fists and roared that it was high time that Kasrilevke was rid of the Jews. But as ill luck would have it, guess who was passing by at that very moment? Makar and the postmaster! When they heard Fyodor fulminating against the Jews, the two stopped dead in their tracks. They noticed the Jews busily packing, getting ready for the road. Thoroughly mystified, they both stared openmouthed at the Jews, wondering where were they hurrying to.

The fact that the two officials were ogling them caused the Jews to panic even more. They left off bundling. To hell with the belongings. Life! Life was much dearer! So they began renting any available means of transportation—wagons, teams of oxen, horses. And they took to the road in the nick of time, double-quick and lickety-split, their haste nearly matching that of their ancestors' departure from Egypt.

Heading the column, naturally, were the Kasrilevke draymen, flying swift as eagles with their large and small half-covered wagons. In those vehicles sat the town grandee, Reb Mordecai-Nossen, and his entire family, as well as the households of other rich villagers. Next in line came the hired wagons with gentile drivers, loaded with women, children, and sick people. Following them were the least affluent Kasrilevkites, popularly known as the salt of the earth. They had to traipse along, alas, heel and toe, stepping along right smartly, afraid to look back, lest they see someone giving chase to invite them back, God forbid.

A stillness fell over Kasrilevke. The village had become deserted, forlorn as a graveyard. Not a soul remained. The only living beings left in Kasrilevke were the goats—the sum total of Jewish wealth in Kasrilevke—Pockmarked Hapke, the bathkeeper and his wife, and of course—a thousand pardons for mentioning him in the same breath—the venerable rabbi, Reb Yozifl.

To each one of these living creatures a separate chapter will be devoted.

9

[Which Indulges in a Bit of Philosophy]

Biologists and other keen students of nature have demonstrated that nothing is useless, wasted, or dead. For instance, after a tree grows, blossoms and bears fruit, it may be chopped down and used for fuel. Yet scholars say the tree is not dead at all. It has merely been broken down into its component parts. The fruit provided nourishment, the blossoms sweet aroma, the wood heat. And as the tree lived and died and returned to the earth, so do we. On our graves grows grass, which enables the nibbling goat to give milk to a baby. Sustained by the milk, the baby grows up, lives and dies, and so the cycle continues ad infinitum.

No doubt you're anxious to know where all this is leading to. Well, it's leading right up to the old scattered graves of the ancient Kasrilevke cemetery. The graves, the goats and the Kasrilevke Jews all formed part of an immeasurably ancient chain, a chain to which, no doubt, countless links will be added in future years.

If you want to know how long Kasrilevke has been a Jewish town, don't look for historical archives—none exist. Just take the trouble to go to Kasrilevke's ancient cemetery. Study the old graves with their simple markers of wood and stone, faded gray tombstones which have in reverence been bent over for ages. On all sides appeared barely legible letters worn smooth by time: *Here lies a Jew, the rabbi and saint.* . . . *Here lies a pious woman, the modest and wise.* . . . Although the year was often indistinct, the graves were undoubtedly very old. Many stones had already crumbled away and many graves were completely grass-covered.

The goats—the perpetually undernourished Kasrilevke

goats—hopped over the broken fence, and, after grazing, brought home udders full of milk, from which the poor Kasrilevke children gained sustenance and strength. There was no knowing what the goats fed on. Perhaps they bore within themselves the soul of someone near and dear. There was no knowing what a close bond existed between the old Kasrilevke cemetery, the grazing goats, and, with all due deference to their honor, the Kasrilevke Jews. Indeed, this entire inquiry was prompted by the sight of the goats on the day the fleeing Kasrilevke Jews abandoned their sole treasure to the mercy of God.

It was after Passover. The snow had already melted and tiny blades of grass (where man let them flourish) were stretching toward the sun, making God's earth green and bright. But Kasrilevke—alas and alack—wasn't the place for fresh grass and aromatic trees. Among Kasrilevke's many desirable and distinctive characteristics were mud, muck, sand, and fetid, oppressive and stifling air. On the day of the Great Panic my imagination carried me to the cemetery, the only place in Kasrilevke blessed with grass. Meditating upon the whole flock of forlorn and orphaned goats, I felt a pang in my heart, both for the goats and for the little Jewish children who had gone without milk that day. The poor goats stood there chewing their cud and wagging their beards, looking ever so foolish as they ruminated wistfully. I imagined them saying: "Uncle, can you perhaps tell us where the deuce our masters and mistresses have taken off to?"

But let us now turn from the dead to the quick—the three souls who had remained behind in the village after the Great Panic. I'm referring, of course, to the bathkeeper and his wife, and their ward, the frail old rabbi, Reb Yozifl.

10

[Concerning the Rabbi, Reb Yozifl]

One of my most beloved characters, Reb Yozifl, the rabbi and mentor of Kasrilevke, has often been mentioned in my stories (none, by the way, fabricated or concocted). However, since I have been remiss to my readers and unjust to him in not depicting him in full as he deserves to be, I shall at least attempt to make amends here and now.

Old Reb Yozifl had been ailing and feeble for many years. Though broken in body, his soul was hale, whole, and pure. And, indeed, into this frail body God had set a permanently youthful soul, which He instructed to have long life until He Himself would recall it to Paradise.

Paradise, beyond a shadow of a doubt! For hell, the torments of the grave, and all the other delights which await us after death, our Reb Yozifl had already experienced, praise God, right here on earth. The Eternal had bestowed upon Reb Yozifl every heartache and plague, distress and misfortune, trial and tribulation. Apparently wanting to test His loyal servant, the Lord generously showered a series of woes upon Reb Yozifl, just as a bride is showered with rice. First God took his children, one after the other, but, naturally, not before tormenting them in full measure. Next He took his wife, the saintly Frume-Teme, who had tended him like a devoted mother. Then He bent Reb Yozifl's body a bit closer to the earth, blessed him with a varied assortment of ailments in his old age, and left him stranded—poor, lonely and feeble. And so that the rabbi might taste the authentic flavor of Gehenna, God inspired the Kasrilevkites with the bright idea of crowning a young man as the new rabbi and of farming out old Reb Yozifl—begging his pardon—to the bathhouse couple with whom he would spend the few remaining years of his life. Surely the latter incident should have given Reb Yozifl sufficient cause to complain against God, to sin like Job who, after patiently bearing his afflictions, finally cursed the day he was born.

But our Reb Yozifl was not that sort of man. Reflection and reasoning had taught him many things. He concluded that there were two possible reasons for all his woes. One was that his life of tribulation was a test imposed by the Holy One: he would suffer in this foolish sinful world so that in the hereafter he would be blessed with a double portion of his just reward. The only other reason was that he deserved everything, if not for his own sins, then perhaps for those of his wayward brethren, the children of Israel, who, responsible for one another, had to suffer for one another—just as an entire Workmen's Association was held responsible if one of its members was caught stealing.

So thought Reb Yozifl, who in his entire lifetime had not let one word of complaint pass his lips. With a philosophic smile, he forsook and completely renounced worldly pleasures. Hence, he won the unmitigated love of the Kasrilev-kites. For although Reb Yozifl was no longer their rabbi, and emoluments which had been his were taken by his successor, Reb Yozifl was nevertheless still held in awe, and retained his title and his place of honor at the synagogue, as well. The only trouble was that titles alone could not buy bread and butter. The body made its meager demands, and the rabbi was content if there was a bit of something to keep body and soul together.

The Kasrilevkites then had an inspiration. Since the Kasrilevke bathhouse was a communal undertaking, the villagers decided that the bath should be the rabbi's home and its revenue his income. Of course, the worthy rabbi would not live in the bathhouse itself, but next to it in the bathkeeper's little alcove, which contained a spare room. *There* Reb Yozifl would live and study.

Study? Well, figuratively. For how could Reb Yozifl study if, God save us, his sight was failing and he was barely able to distinguish light from dark? Yet there was no reason to despair! A scholar, no matter how aged, always found something to do. If he had trouble reading, he studied by heart: he prayed, recited Psalms, or simply meditated.

And surely there was much to meditate about. Reb Yozifl contemplated the world and its just Creator, all of whose deeds were just, and also His people Israel, whom God chastised like a beloved child. The rabbi thought of the other nations and of all the earth's creatures, from the huge elephant to the tiniest mite and the smallest worm which the Almighty generously sustained. He realized that from all this a simple lesson could be learned. If the Good Lord provided for mite and worm, He would surely provide for a human being, especially a Jew.

So ran Reb Yozifl's train of thought and he was pleased with God and His world, and with himself and his musings, to which he more than once gave voice. Like other places,

Kasrilevke, too, had its assortment of half-baked scholars, pundits, and brains who, in their attempt to poke fun, loved to ask foolish questions of the old rabbi.

"A mite, you say? I believe you also mentioned a worm. Well, Rabbi, please explain one thing. If God is so great and good and compassionate that He even feeds the smallest worm, well then why doesn't He feed His Kasrilevke Jews? Are we tinier than mites, smaller than worms?"

"Oh, what children you are." The old man smiled. "Let me tell you a parable concerning a king. Imagine that the king has invited you to a feast in his palatial hall. When you come to the vestibule and see that it isn't as roomy or bright as you had expected it to be, you turn around and go back. The same is true here. Just consider this. The little bit of pain, woe, and humiliation we suffer here in this crowded vestibule cannot be compared to the great palace of the World to Come, with its golden walls, silver floors, and diamond bricks. There life is eternal. There righteous souls are given a place of honor. There they dwell in comfort and bask in the splendor of the Divine Presence. There God Himself attends to them. He gives them the finest wine in golden cups and upon golden platters serves them the Messianic repast consisting of the Leviathan and the Wild Ox."

Reb Yozifl's closing words—namely: wine, Leviathan, and Wild Ox—were added as a bonus for the common people who usually turned a deaf ear to the Divine Presence and other spiritual matters. For a simple Jew had to have a plain piece of fish and a hunk of roast meat—a rare dish, indeed, in Kasrilevke; one to be had only on an occasional Sabbath and holiday. Everyone in Kasrilevke loved the old rabbi for his sweet and tender words, especially the common folk. But he was loved most of all by the bathkeeper and his wife, that famous couple who managed Kasrilevke's communal bath. To them, therefore, we dedicate the following chapter.

11

[Adam and Eve in the Garden of Eden]

Shmaye and Fishel the correspondents (they submitted articles to all the newspapers, but no one ever printed them) asserted that the Kasrilevke baths were a Paradise right here on earth. If their statement was true, then the names that Kasrilevke wags had given Berke the bathkeeper and his wife, Eve, shouldn't strike one as farfetched. Berke was dubbed Old Man Adam, and his wife, Mother Eve.

These nicknames were of doubtful origin. Since Eve was the real name of the bathkeeper's wife, perhaps the only appropriate name for her husband could have been Adam. This was done either because the noted couple had been isolated for so many years and lived, as it were, in the Garden of Eden; or because the men and women of Kasrilevke had the privilege of seeing the bathkeepers in the same costume which Adam and Eve had worn in the Garden of Eden before eating the forbidden fruit. Whatever the reason, we must admit that once Kasrilevke wags bestowed a monicker it stuck—like a legal name. Like a suit, the nickname was made to order: measured, cut, hand-sewn and pressed—now wear it well!

Everyone realized that neither of the two could have had any other name. What other tag could have been given to a couple who spent every day, year in, year out, removed from the village, far from the famous Kasrilevke muck? They lived at the foot of the mountain, by the riverbank where tall green willows bent into the water and where during the summer the frogs' croaking could drive one to distraction. As the place was truly a Garden of Eden, so the bathhouse couple were truly Adam and Eve in the paradise of Eden, made for each other at the time of Creation.

Adam, an ex-soldier, was a strapping broad-boned man with powerful arms. His beard was elf-locked, his wadded gaberdine shiny, and his boots perpetually bound up with rope. Eve was tall and hefty, in the pink of health. She had a dark, gleaming, pockmarked face and kindly gray eyes. Her head was covered with a checked kerchief, and she always wore a hitched-up skirt and a pair of oversized men's boots which covered her brawny legs.

The only thing this couple knew was the bathhouse, which they were either heating, cleaning, or repairing. They were never idle, except at night when all the fires were extinguished. Then Adam and Eve would sit down over a pot of potatoes, in the wintertime by the oven, in the summer outside the house. No one in Kasrilevke was more content than they, and no one had such a steady source of income. Moreover, they paid no rent at all and never lacked customers—for no matter how poor the town, a Jew had to have a bathhouse.

Yet, to tell the truth, it wasn't a gold mine. Adam and Eve could neither save money nor buy houses. For, alas, how much could a Kasrilevke Jew pay for his Friday afternoon bath? And think of the piles of wood the bathhouse consumed, especially since the boiler was old, the stones crumbling, the walls cracking, and the ceiling leaking. Every sizzling drop which fell scalded the naked skin of a Kasrilevkite who scampered away, shrieking like the damned being raked over red-hot coals. Furious with the bathkeeper, the people cursed him up and down, but Old Man Adam didn't give a rap. He went on his merry way, pouring water on the hot stones and grumbling into his beard: "Did you ever? They use a bathhouse built in the year one and they expect it not to leak."

Old Man Adam single-handedly kept the old bathhouse in a state of repair. He plugged up the holes in the wall, patched the roof, and supported it with a beam; he even cleaned the women's ritual bath to prevent the Kasrilevke jesters from cracking jokes or spreading false rumors about frogs croaking there.

Old Man Adam rose early, when God Himself was still asleep, and dragged one barrel of water after another from the river, accompanying his work by the chanting of Psalms he knew by heart. His voice echoed from the bath and was carried by the wind to the other side of the river.

The alcove adjoining the bath was still pitch dark. Eve sat over a sputtering wick mending Reb Yozifl's underlinen, which she herself had laundered the night before. She patched holes and sewed buttons wherever necessary so that the rabbi would have something to wear when he awoke.

The rabbi asleep? Well, it could hardly be called sleeping, for it seemed that poor Reb Yozifl had just arisen for his midnight devotions; and now, unseen by anyone, he rose again, washed his hands, and began to praise his Creator. Eve did not know exactly what he said—but listening to him was sheer delight. Each word touched her heart and bathed all her limbs with joy. She rose without a sound, tiptoed softly to the kneading trough, and began preparing the dough for the Sabbath loaves.

"Cock-a-doodle-doo!" crowed the white red-winged rooster, jumping from the crossbeams to the threshold, proud that he had generously wakened everyone for work.

"To the devil with you," said Eve, chasing him with a barrage of insults. "Scoot. Beat it. A chicken pox upon you. All you know is cock-a-doodle-doo—whether we want to hear it or not. Just you wait. Let me fatten you up a bit and then off to the *shokhet* with you. Then you'll have a merry cock-a-doodle-doo. Then there'll be a real to-do, a real cock-a-doodle-doo."

But Eve's harangue to the pert and cocky rooster was superfluous. For the rabbi was awake. He had already performed his ritual ablutions and begun his morning devotions. Eve did not know exactly what he said—but listening to him was a sheer delight. Each word touched her heart and bathed all her limbs with joy. With great awe she brought him a pitcher of tasty, steaming-hot chicory, as sweet-smelling as Paradise itself.

12

[Reb Yozifl's Blissful Old Age]

The suggestion that old Reb Yozifl should be supported by the communal bath was one of those bright ideas which only Kasrilevke was capable of. Actually, according to agreement, Old Man Adam was also required to heat the synagogue with wood provided at his own expense. Nevertheless, he let the worshippers freeze all winter long. His constant excuses were: icy weather, wet wood, thick fogs, and other such flimsy pretexts.

But Adam was told that if he would tend to Reb Yozifl in his declining years, the community would overlook his obligation of heating the synagogue. Were the demands of an old rabbi, alas, so great? Especially an old rabbi like Reb Yozifl, who even in his prime had been content with everything. The rabbi's wife, Frume-Teme, may she rest in peace, used to say that Reb Yozifl never uttered a word of complaint. For instance, if given hot coals for supper, he would eat them; he would burn his tongue, but eat them he would. That's how pampered a man he used to be. So imagine how easy it would be now, in his old age! The only drawback was that he'd be a bit cramped for space.

However, Old Man Adam had an idea: he and Eve would sleep in the bathhouse, and the rabbi could have the alcove. Both were under one roof, anyway. The bathhouse had another advantage—it was warm during the winter, just like the biblical Garden of Eden. But truth to say, winter's blessing became summer's bane. For the heat, both in the bath and the living quarters, was unbearable. The only other alternative was sleeping at the riverfront, itself a Paradise. During the summer it was more delightful to sleep outdoors than in—yet this convenience also had a drawback: the frogs' croaking made sleep impossible. But, frankly, was sleeping in the house any better? No, for frogs by the dozens invaded the house, too—often leaping smack into Eve's face, either from the bed, the kneading trough, or the oven.

To make a long story short, Reb Yozifl was housed in the alcove, and Adam and Eve moved into the Garden of Eden—the bathhouse, that is. They tended to the rabbi's needs and provided him with food and drink. In time they became very attached to him and loved him as though he were their own flesh and blood.

Reb Yozifl called them his children and they aptly called him their rabbi, for they had not heard so much Torah wisdom in their entire lifetime as they heard from old Reb Yozifl in one day. They considered everything they heard original and new. In their eyes the rabbi was like a traveler from distant lands who told exotic tales which defied the imagination. Openmouthed and hearts knocking, the couple would sit by the stove-couch in the winter and outdoors in the summer, gazing at the rabbi and listening to his discourses on spiritual matters. He talked about God, angels and people, he spoke of earthly and celestial beings, he discussed the sun and moon, the stars and spheres. As they sat outside

the bathhouse on bright warm summer evenings, Adam and
Eve would often feel that the old man with the bent back,
small white beard, and kindly eyes was himself a spirit. Any
moment now he would rise, hover in the air, soar off, and
vanish among the spheres. The couple felt that they, too,
were being drawn higher and higher toward the threadlike
clouds, the tiny stars, and the abode of wandering, restless
souls.

Surely Adam and Eve in the Garden of Eden were the
happiest couple on earth. And living with them in their
Garden of Eden, Kasrilevke's rabbi, Reb Yozifl, had the most
blissful old age imaginable.

13

[Reb Yozifl Gets Angry for the First Time in His Life]

Heaven and earth have sworn that nothing is imperishable.
Constant happiness is nonexistent. There is an accusing
Angel, better known as Satan, who pokes his nose in everyone's affairs, peeks over our shoulders and watches us like a
hawk lest—heaven forbid—we forget the Almighty. Well, this
very same Satan meddled into the affairs of the above-
mentioned Garden of Eden and nearly succeeded in driving
out Adam and Eve, as well as poor lonely old Reb Yozifl.
Satan came close to separating the beloved group and permanently destroying their little nest of happiness. It happened
one day when Eve came home from the marketplace. She
had wanted to buy fish, but there were none. And there were
no potatoes or onions, either. In fact, there wasn't a living
soul in the marketplace. Assuming that she had arrived too
early, Eve waited awhile; but by midmorning she saw that
there wasn't so much as a stray dog in the marketplace:
wherever she looked Jews scurried about, packing, getting
ready to depart.

What was up? They were running away.

Whereto? Anywhere.

By the time Eve had gone home and told the news to Old
Man Adam and by the time he passed this on to Reb Yozifl,
half the fleeing village had already passed the cemetery.

At first Reb Yozifl didn't want to believe it. Running away? What do you mean, running away? Then he picked up his bamboo cane with its bent brass handle (the cane itself was as old as the rabbi's tenure in Kasrilevke) and took the pains to walk into town. There he still managed to find a few Jews making preparations for the journey. He stopped them and with a smile gently admonished them.

A few of the remaining Jews heard him out and sighed piteously.

"Of course you're absolutely right, Reb Yozifl, but why don't you come with us anyway? Take our advice, Rabbi, and ride with us. And the quicker the better."

"Ride? Whereto? What for? Because of whom?"

But all his words were for naught, for soon these remaining Jews, too, were on their way.

When Reb Yozifl returned to the Garden of Eden he found the bathkeepers, Adam and Eve, deeply distressed, at the point of tears.

"Why are you so upset, children?" he said.

"Good heavens, Rabbi! Don't you know what's going on? Hapke was just here."

"Which Hapke?"

"The gentile woman who puts out the Sabbath lights. What horrible, hair-raising stories she told us!"

Interrupting each other frequently, Adam and Eve began to relate Hapke's version of the goings-on in the world. Leaning on his cane and listening attentively, Reb Yozifl reflected but did not reply. He raised his head and looked about; then, placing his old bamboo cane at his side, he removed his hat, remaining only in his skullcap.

"Now hear *me* out, children," he told Adam and Eve, "and listen to what *I* have to say. Everything you've just told me is absolute nonsense. It's not worth a broken copper. Know that the Guardian of Israel slumbers not. In other words, God doesn't fall asleep on the job. Now listen to this story about a king. Once upon a time there was a king . . ."

"King? What king? Better listen to what Hapke said," Old Man Adam interjected. He immediately regretted his boorish remark, but it was to late to withdraw his words. Reb Yozifl turned away from Adam, donned his prayer shawl and phylacteries, took a sacred book and, with the bamboo cane at his side, seated himself at the head of the table like a king during wartime, armed from head to toe, with a proud and defiant look which seemed to say:

"Now! I just dare anyone to set foot over here."

Reb Yozifl's face radiated such strength and composure that both Adam and Eve changed their mind. The situation was not so terrible, they thought. They, too, would have someone to rely on.

14

[Two Villages in Flight—The End of the Tale]

The refugees made for the road to Mazepevke, a town near Yehupetz. The first place they stopped was a Jewish village named Kozodoievke [Goat-town], known, as its name implied, for its famous goats. Kozodoievke goats were not milked like Kasrilevke goats; moreover, they were distinguished from the latter by horns—that is, by their *lack* of horns. Instead of horns the Kozodoievke goats had on their forehead a queer thingamajig which resembled—forgive the comparison—the head phylactery. Furthermore, they were by nature quite bovine and far more asinine than the Kasrilevke goats. If you met a Kozodoievke goat in the middle of the road, showed it a bit of straw, and said, "Koz, koz, koz," it would straightaway stop and spread its legs, all set to be milked.

In like manner, the Jews of Kozodoievke did not resemble those of Kasrilevke. They were the same Jews, of course; they had the same bellies and souls; they even shared the same shred of poverty. The only difference between them was a prayer in the morning service. The Kasrilevke Jews recited "Blessed be he who spoke" *before* "Give thanks to the Lord," whereas the Kozodoievke Jews, on the contrary, reversed the procedure. What possible difference could it make whether one or the other was recited first? After all, both were prayers to God. But don't you dare suggest such a simple explanation. For in the good old days when both the Kasrilevke and the Kozodoievke Jews were well off, and the only troubles they had were headaches, the incident concerning the priority of "Blessed be he" and "Give thanks" led to a bloody altercation.

Kozodoievke Jews would frequently come to pray in the Kasrilevke synagogue. At the very moment when the cantor, wrapped in his prayer shawl, stood before the pulpit and swayed back and forth singing "Give thanks to the Lord," a Kozodoievke Jew would sound out an octave higher with "Blessed be he who spoke and created the world."

On the other hand, when a Kasrilevke Jew came to the Kozodoievke synagogue and saw the cantor standing rapt in holy devotion with eyes closed and hand upraised, chanting "Blessed be he who spoke," why just then the Kasrilevke Jew would rend the air with a falsetto "Give thanks to the Lord, call upon his name, make known among the people his de-ee-ee-ee-eeeeds."

The "Give thanks" alone didn't gall the Kozodoievke Jews as much as the "deeds" the Kasrilevkite stretched out for a good half mile. Look, they said, if you feel like saying your "Give thanks," say it and be done with it. But for goodness sake what point is there in stretching out your "de-ee-ee-eeeds"? Obviously, you're doing it for spite. And since you're such a spiteful wretch, you deserve to be beaten black and blue. And so they laced into him that day for all they were worth.

This beating instigated a bitter feud between the two villages which lingered on for years. It began with a few blows and ended up with all sorts of false denunciations, as well as a continuous display of boorishness, intrigue, and mutual recriminations. The two communities monopolized everyone's attention. Perfect strangers butted into their lawsuits, made fun of their Jewish customs and childish ways, and labeled them fanatics. In a word, it was a nasty, revolting affair.

Indeed, those foolish but happy years were long gone and only God knows if they'll ever return. The villages now had bigger problems than "Give thanks" and "Blessed be he." Nevertheless, although there was no logical reason for it, the hatred between the Jews of Kasrilevke and Kozodoievke remained.

Similarly, there was no logical reason for the following: Upon seeing a Jew, why should a young gentile lad in Kasrilevke forthwith whip off his cap, put it between his teeth, then wave it back and forth, singing: "Yid, Yid, nasty kid . . ."? On the other hand, try to be a smartie and explain why a Jew talking about a peasant in Yiddish should throw in a barrelful of hifalutin Hebrew words to make it hard for the gentile to understand:

"Give the uncircumcised one a beaker of vintage—but don't exceed the brim—and a slice of staff of life, for he hasn't partaken of nourishment today. Remunerate him with two gold pieces and bid him sally forth, but scrutinize him assiduously so that he doesn't appropriate anything."

Since such ways can only be felt but not explained rationally, let's return to the Jews of Kasrilevke and Kozodoievke. There are moments in the lifetime of a man when one must forgive and forget—blot everything out as though it had never been. And a good thing it is, too! For if this were not done, the world would burst at the seams. Our sages rightly decreed that on the eve of the Day of Atonement everyone should forgive his fellow man.

The same thing happened to the feud between the Jews of Kasrilevke and Kozodoievke. During the Great Panic their enmity vanished into thin air. They bumped into each other smack in the middle of the road, where a one-time Jewish inn called The Oak had once been located (it had to close because of the state monopoly, and neither complaints nor protests availed).

When Kasrilevke and Kozodoievke met, they stopped and held the following conversation:

KASRILEVKE: Where are you off to, fellow Jews?

KOZODOIEVKE: Where are *you* off to?

KASRILEVKE: Who, us? We're just traveling . . . . On business.

KOZODOIEVKE: What? An entire community on the move for business?

KASRILEVKE: What about you? Aren't you an entire community?

KOZODOIEVKE: With us it's a different matter. We're not traveling, we're running.

KASRILEVKE: How do you know *we're* not running?

KOZODOIEVKE: Now you're talking. Where are you running to?

KASRILEVKE: Where are *you* running to?

KOZODOIEVKE: Who, us? We're running . . . in your direction.

KASRILEVKE: And we . . . in yours.

KOZODOIEVKE: What will you do at our place?

KASRILEVKE: Same thing you're going to do at ours.

KOZODOIEVKE: Did you ever? Then why do you have to run in our direction and we in yours?

KASRILEVKE: Apparently so that we can change places.

KOZODOIEVKE: Joking aside, better tell us why you're running.

KASRILEVKE: First you tell us why you're. . . .

And then and there, when the two groups of Jews conversed in the field and cast sidelong glances at each other, they first realized what they had done and how foolish they had been.

"Did you ever see such a thing? Running helter-skelter! Beating a retreat! Why are we running? Where are we running to? May their noses run!"

Everyone began wiping his eyes, weeping and moaning.

"Oh my, the things we've lived to see."

Then they began to confer, chat, babble. They talked themselves hoarse. They unburdened their hearts, shook hands, and politely bade each other good-bye. They kissed each other amicably like true pals, like in-laws after signing the marriage contract, or like man and wife remarrying after a divorce. They heaped curses upon all their enemies. They hoped for a happy ending to this miserable affair and with bitter laughs answered "Amen." And then they signaled the gentile drivers—begging their pardon—to kindly turn the horses around.

The two communities returned to their respective villages: the Kasrilevkites to Kasrilevke and the Kozodoievkites to Kozodoievke. Like birds, each to his nest, they silently stole back into their houses and silently resumed their daily tasks.

For many years thereafter they recounted and retold down

to the last detail the story of the Great Panic which had come over them. And in order to apprise our children's children and later generations of this event, we have undertaken to chronicle this grand epic in plain and simple Yiddish. Now that it is published, may it remain a memorial for all time!

Monologues

Sholom Aleichem's monologues, influenced to a degree by Chekhov, are ostensibly "told" to the author by an acquaintance he has met. Although the story is narrated from the point of view of the speaker, added characters and dialogue give the monologue perspective, flexibility of characterization and greater depth. Because of this, in "A Predestined Disaster," for instance, the reader's attitude to the seeming benevolence of the narrator and the supposed prodigality of Dani undergoes several changes. Many of Sholom Aleichem's monologues were written in the years after 1904 and all appear in the volume of his collected works entitled Monologues.

GITL PURISHKEVITCH

Just look here and see how they've gathered round me, as though I were some freak of nature. Break it up, folks. Beat it! Head for home. You won't see no comedies and you won't hear no fairy tales about castles in the sky. They told me that there's a writer chap here named Sholom Ilikem. Is that you himself, the Sholom Ilikem that writes? Well, just keep on writing, mister. I hope you never get writer's cramps, but you ought to write this whole town up and down. Believe you me, they well deserve it. Particularly the rich folk, God's own aristocrats, who have no doubts but that the whole world was made specially for them. *We've* got to sweat and slave until we're blue in the face, but they, by greasing palms, buy their way out of every plague and every decree, and, to top it off, they laugh at a poor widow that makes a living from Wissotsky's tea.

I deliver Wissotsky's tea to all the householders is what I do, and they pay me out in installments. So that's how I eke out my daily bread for myself and my only son, which they wanted to take away from me through no fault of mine. You'd do well to lend an ear, mister, and listen to the sort of things that can happen here. It seems to me that ever since the world was made there hasn't been one instance where they've taken away a one-and-only only son—he's my only means of support in my old age—from a widowed mother that owes everything she is to God and then Wissotsky. In fact, I can well boast that it's only because of God and Wissotsky that I'm still among the living. But you call that living? Dying a bit each day is called living, too.

For what can you make out of tea, alas, what with today's

competition? Wherever you look there's a poor man tramping from door to door peddling tea. So you have it out with him. If the fellow knocks off ten kopecks from the price, I knock off fifteen. And if he goes down fifteen, I go down twenty. But there's a limit. I'm not Wissotsky, you know. It's a sad business, believe you me. All I can look forward to in my old age is my supporter, my Moishe. That's all I have is a bit of an only son—ah me—the only inheritance my husband left me.

But I can't complain. He's a good boy, sound as an apple, handsome and plain as can be. He's got all the virtues, but learning he didn't like. What am I saying—didn't like? Beat him, smash him to smithereens, but still he refused to study. "What's going to be with you, Moishe," says I, "if you say no to reading, writing and praying? You'll only be fit to be a dogcatcher!"

But go talk to the wall. My next move was to get him to learn a trade. So I apprenticed him to a tailor with the express condition that he be taught the trade. But just like you don't see a needle and thread now, so he never saw a needle and thread then. Day and night he either walked the floor with the tailor's baby or peeled potatoes or emptied the slops pail. Heating up the iron—why, that was a rare privilege! So I took him away from the tailor and brought him to a shoemaker. There I met up with a first-rate cutthroat, a murderer, an assassin. If everything wasn't just so-so, he didn't think twice about throwing a hammer at your skull and knocking your brains out. So I took him away from the shoemaker and brought him to a bookbinder, a bungler who didn't make a living and never so much as laid eyes on a piece of work. So I took him away from that bungling bookbinder and brought him to a watchmaker. But *he* was an even bigger bungler. He not only didn't fix watches, he crippled them. At least that's what everyone in town said. So why should I let him make my son a cripple? So I took him away from the watchmaker and brought him to a lacemaker and asked him to teach my son to be a manipulator—of lace needles, that is. I apprenticed my boy for two years. That is, I agreed that for two years he'd manipulate for him for nothing, and the third year, when he'd be an expert at manipulating, he'd get some pay.

And this time, glory to God, I hit upon a fine working-man who didn't even mind a drink or two. He taught my son to manipulate in less time than I'm talking to you. The work agreed with him and within half a year my Moishe became a perfect lacemaker. But what good did it do me if he had to work free for him for two years running? But since I had signed him up there was no undoing it. With the good Lord's help those two years flew by. Flew? Well, just figuratively. Having survived those two years is proof enough that I'm made of iron. So I survived—think that's the end of it? Now I had to go find him a steady job or individual assignments. But where in the world do you find work for a lacemaker? You think it's something a drunkard loses and a sober man finds? And me, I'm one woman, all alone, peddling my pound of tea from door to door, the competition's great and I've even got a bankruptcy to boot. One of the house-holders who had taken three and a half pounds of tea on credit suddenly disappeared one night. He simply plucked up his roots and was gone—off to America, some said. You could have knocked me over with a feather.

I thought that the whole world had collapsed on me. It's nothing to sneeze at, you know—three and half pounds of tea at two rubles twenty per pound. And I have to keep mum about it, for if Wissotsky ever finds out I've had a little mishap, it could hurt my credit. So what does God do?

"Gitl, you crying?" he says. "Just wait till you *really* start crying. The draft's headed your way!"

Draft? What draft? He's a one-and-only child, an only son to his widowed mother that owes everything she is to God and then Wissotsky. Has such a thing ever been heard of? Is there no God? Where's your sense of justice? But when the cards say trouble, you can go knock your head against the wall! It turned out that my Moishe was the exact same age as the three sons of our rich man's three daughters, may three well-placed boils prevent them from being able to stand, lie and sit.

"Gitl," I was told, "see to it that your Moishe doesn't become the scapegoat for our rich man's three grandsons."

Ha-ha, are you kidding? My boy is a one-and-only only son, supporter of his poor widowed mother that owes everything she is to God and then Wissotsky, while the grandfather was a grandee, rich and loaded, a millionaire. Unless, God forbid, there was no God! But money talks! They examined the rich man's grandsons, one by one. The first was declared unfit. So was the second.

You can imagine how rotten I felt. For if they sent the third one packing, too, God forbid, then my Moishe's goose was cooked. And as ill luck would have it, my Moishe happened to be fit as a fiddle, knock wood, a strapping youngster without the slightest defect. In a nutshell—a he-man. The rich man's grandsons were in fine fettle, too—but the doctor rejected them. As soon as he laid eyes on a rich man's son he said, "Unfit"—and go do him something. But you think I'd keep still? So I went to the chairman of the draft board and told him:

"Kind sir, they've already turned thumbs down on two of the rich man's sweetie pies. If God forbid they turn their thumbs down once more, it's liable to come to my Moishe, and my Moishe, for your information, is a one-and-only only son, a provider for his poor mother's old age."

So he became hot under the collar and with murder in his eye ordered me to be thrown out of the office. And my fears came true. No sooner did they bring the third of the rich man's darlings through the door of the examination room than the doctor already declared him unfit. Then in they dragged my Moishe. No sooner was he declared fit and sworn in than they shouted, "Left-right, left-right"—right to the far-off Kharkov province and kiss your gaberdine good-bye! I was thunderstruck. Do you think I'd take this sitting down? So I went back to the chairman of the draft board and raised the roof:

"Rich men's kids you reject, huh, and a bit of an only son of a widowed mother that owes everything she is to God and then Wissotsky. . . . Is there no God? Where's your sense of justice?"

Of course he ordered his underlings to throw the Yid woman out. But this Yid woman didn't sit on her hands and straightaway set out for the regional governor. I fell at his feet and said:

"Your Excellency. Here's the story. Three of the rich man's grandsons were turned down, and my Moishe, my provider for my old age, the one-and-only only son of a poor widow that owes everything she is to God and then Wissotsky. . . . Is there no God? Where's your sense of justice?"

The governor heard me out and told me to submit it in writing.

"Your Excellency," I said. "Why do you need it in writing? I'm telling it to you now loud and clear, black on white. Send someone, let them ask around, and you'll see that everything I'm telling you is the God's honest truth."

So he said once more: "Put it in writing. In writing."

"Your Excellency," I said, "I'm not the sort of woman that's fit for writing, and tattling on others isn't my line of work. I'm just telling you what hurts me. They reject the rich, but poor only-sons they take away. Tell me, is there no God? Where's your sense of justice?"

"Thunderations!" he said. "What does this Jewess want of me?"

"She wants the truth to out," I said, "and her provider returned to her. That and nothing else. Heaven and earth have sworn that truth shall rise like oil over water."

Then he got angry, that governor did, and ordered the Yid woman kicked out. But even then the Yid woman didn't twiddle her thumbs. She straight off sold everything she had and set out to seek the truth right in Petersburg itself. For that's where the Minister of War, the Minister of Internal Affairs and even the Holy Synod are located. And if I had to get hold of the Czar himself, don't you think I could have found him? When it comes to the truth I could even reach God himself.

So here's what happened. As soon as I came to Petersburg I was caught up in the merry-go-round of residence rights and the threat of being kicked out. I told them I wasn't afraid of being kicked out. I didn't fear a soul besides God and the Czar. For I was going for the truth. But meanwhile, I had to eat, too. I couldn't let my soul seep out of my body, could I? So what did I do? I wasn't in the habit of asking for handouts.

So I had a bright idea. After all, Petersburg is no village. There were Jews all over town, thank God, and surely Wissotsky's tea was better known in Petersburg than anywhere else. All the officers drank Wissotsky's tea. And since I had dealings with draft boards and officers, I began to deliver tea to their homes. I let them pay out in installments and—thank God and then Wissotsky—I not only made enough to cover my bitter daily bread but was even able to spare a ruble or two to send to my Moishe in the regiment. The only thing that plagued me was residence rights. With residence rights in Petersburg I would have been a queen. But since I had troubles instead of residence rights, I was as miserable as death itself.

Things got to the point where they were about to chase me out of Petersburg, and by foot, too, along with the transported convicts, just as God has bidden it. But just then the good Lord sent me a nice lady that wrote for the newspapers, may the Almighty give her a nice long life, dear sweet God! She was an angel, not a woman. Besides rescuing me from all my troubles, she also introduced me to Pergament. No doubt you've heard of him. He was one of those who spoke in the Duma.* The sweetest, finest man I ever met—may a bright Paradise be his. What he didn't do for me! He gave me one letter of introduction after another to the sort of people who you needed special tickets to even lay eyes on. So they heard me out and the first one sent me to a second, the second to a third and I kept going higher and higher until I was in the Duma itself.

I began going to the Duma almost every day. Sometimes even twice a day. I listened to all the speeches in the Duma. All of them spoke there, but Pergament topped them all. When he got up to speak, I tell you, he could move a stone wall to tears. Nothing to sneeze at, that Pergament. That's why he had enemies in the Duma, I don't have to tell you. You should have seen those enemies. And the hecklers! They used to attack him like a pack of dogs and raise such a row that I could hardly sit still in my gallery seat—that's where I always sat, you know.

---

* The Russian Parliament. [Tr.]

When I think of Pergament, tears come to my eyes. You'll never know what a pearl, what a gem of a man he was. That he was an angel, it goes without saying. He canceled all his appointments and stopped everything he was doing just to listen to me and ask me what my Moishe was writing.

And what do you think he wrote? My Moishe wrote me that, thank God, his soldiering wasn't coming along too badly at all. The authorities were pleased with him. The only hitch was that his sergeant was giving him trouble. That peasant was pestering Moishe to death to lend him money. Moishe swore to him that he had nothing, but the sergeant didn't believe him. He said that all Jews have money—may he have a fever plus Pharaoh's plagues! There's a sergeant for you! So he laughed, I mean Pergament did. How he loved to laugh and crack jokes. Once when I came to his office he told me to have a seat and, as usual, asked me how things were going with me in Petersburg.

"I wish it on all converts the way things are going with me."

He laughed so hard he almost fell out of his chair. "You don't seem to know that I myself am a convert to Christianity."

"Converts like you we should have by the dozens," I said. "May all punishment intended for you go straight to all the other converts instead."

So he laughed even more. Would you expect a man like that to suddenly up and die! And so unexpectedly, too! How shall I put it, my dear friend? I know it isn't right to say it, but it seems to me that I didn't shed as many tears on my husband's grave, may he rest in peace, as I did on the day they told me that Pergament had died. I wept over him as though he were my own son. I can tell you that after Pergament died I became completely disgusted with Petersburg and with the Duma and with the whole wide world. Had Pergament been around, everything would've been different. Nuselovitch and Friedman were quite nice fellows, why deny it? But Nuselovitch and Friedman weren't Pergament. When I came crying to Nuselovitch or Friedman they told me they couldn't help me—they couldn't go against the law.

"Show me the law," I said, "which says that a high and mighty millionaire's three little bastards are supposed to be turned down one after the other so that in their stead my one-and-only only son should be drafted, the sole provider for a poor widow that owes everything she is to God and then Wissotsky. . . . Come on, show me that law! There's a Duma, with so many people in it, knock wood, and all of them rant and rave and insult one another. Why isn't there at least one man to stand up for a poor widow that owes everything she is to God and then Wissotsky? Aha! Button-lipped, huh? For the likes of you we need an anti-Semite like Purishkevitch,* a Jewish Purishkevitch all our own. He'd teach you a lesson, book, chapter and verse! It's been three years now that I'm traipsing about in Petersburg, in and out of the Duma—has even one person tried to open his mouth about the murder committed in taking away from a poor mother that owes everything she is to God and then Wissotsky her bit of a one-and-only hope, her provider for her old age?"

All in all, only once in all that time did one chap, some nobleman from Bessarabia, get up and make a speech about military obligations. Hearing "military obligations," my heart leaped with joy. Thank goodness, I declared. After all this woe they're finally getting at the truth. It's high time, too. But what was the rub? They talked such nonsense I felt my bile rising. I thought surely my storming and fussing before the Ministers, the Minister of War and the Minister of Internal Affairs, was the cause of this. But the upshot was—a lot of hot air. Listen to the nobleman's bright idea:

"We ought to institute a special conscription for Jews," he said, "to be known as a cash conscription."

Did you ever?

"Jews should be able to buy their way out of the draft," he said. "If you don't want to serve—then pay up!"

If that's the case, then the upshot was another victory for the rich, may they burn in a slow fire! Which means that the poor kids will have to serve, including only sons. Is there no

---

* V. M. Purishkevitch, whose name appears in several of Sholom Aleichem's stories, was a notorious anti-Semite and rightist rabble-rouser. Although a member of the 1907 Duma, he clamored for its dissolution and caused constant uproars during the Duma sessions. [Tr.]

God? Where's your sense of justice? So here's what happened.
God performed a miracle and there was such a tumult, such
chaos, you'd have thought that everyone had gone berserk.
Purishkevitch, naturally, was at it with more zest than all the
others. This evil, rotten monster, may his memory be blotted
out, wanted to bring proof and witnesses that no Jews served
in the army. None whatsoever. There wasn't a single Jew in
the service. That was too much for me. I felt a sudden twinge
in my heart and I jumped up. What? My one-and-only means
of support has already served more than three years and has
even been decorated and now up pipes that pipsqueak
Purishkevitch and spouts such twaddle to all the ministers
and to the world at large. Expect me to keep still? So I called
out from the gallery and screamed loud enough for the entire
Duma to hear:

"What about Moishe?"

You want to know what happened? Nothing! With all due
respect I was kicked out of the Duma and taken to the police
station. They even threatened to send me home on foot with
a convoy of transported convicts, just as God has bidden it. So
I told them I wasn't afraid of being sent home that way. I
didn't fear a soul besides God and the Czar. For I was after
the truth. I've got a share in the Duma same as you, I said.
You talk about conscription with your mouths, I said, while
my son is actually serving the Czar, even though he's a one-
and-only only son.

In a word, I didn't let them off lightly. It's just their luck
that I didn't remain in Petersburg over Passover, when that
turmoil began in the Duma about blood—that Jews use blood
for Passover. I'd have shown them who really spilled blood,
we or they. But it was their miserable good fortune that I
came home for Passover, for I'd been given notice from the
Ministry of War that my Moishe had been released and was
being sent home. It was even said that the chairman, the
doctor and the entire draft board would have hell to pay.
They were all under indictment. There had been an investigation, you see, and it turned out that they had a private
factory for white rejection slips. Jew and Christian alike—
whosoever had God in his heart and a ruble in his pocket—

was declared unfit. And, alas, the children of the poor, one-and-only only sons, had to go and serve. Now it was over and done with. No more privileged characters. No more of these dandy deals. Everyone would be equal now. Anarchy was dead.

Well, I ask you, Mister Sholom Ilikem, you're a man that writes—you tell *me,* do I deserve having people laugh at me and poke fun at me, having everyone's tongue wagging about me? Look, if you want to laugh, laugh till you burst, but why am I stuck with the name Purishkevitch, blast him? They call me "Gitl Purishkevitch" is what they call me. At least they ought to say—no comparison intended! This town's made up of wags, numbskulls and loafers. Tell me, haven't they all deserved being written up, down and across? In fact, why *don't* you write them up, Mister Sholom Ilikem? Write them up so that the whole world will know about them. Write it all down so that not a single one of them will escape being written up.

A PREDESTINED DISASTER

Listen, if disaster is predestined, then it catches up with you even at home. Even if you had one-and-twenty sets of brains you couldn't avoid it. Look at me and you're looking at a man who's as cool as a cucumber. I don't rush about. I don't hustle and bustle. I hate communal affairs. Offer me a synagogue trusteeship, ask me to be a godfather or carry the first Torah on Simkhas Torah, give me this that or the other things—and I run the other way.

To make a long story short, here's what happened in our village. One day a Jew called Menashe the Clunk died. An absolute simpleton—hence the nickname. He could scarcely say his prayers, couldn't distinguish one Hebrew letter from another, knew nothing of reading, writing, this that or the other thing. He was a dunce, may he forgive me, but as honest as the day is long. His word was as good as gold. He considered the next fellow's money as sacrosanct. But stingy! For a kopeck he'd let both his eyes be plucked out. All his life he saved, saved, saved. And smack in the middle of his saving—he dropped dead. Well, what can you do? Dead is dead.

When Menashe died they came to me with a request: Whereas Menashe has passed on and left quite a bundle of rubles, as well as uncollected accounts, possessions, houses, this that and the other thing; and whereas there was no one to settle his affairs—his widow was a simple Jewish woman, and her five kids, unfortunately, were still tots—they wanted me to be their guardian, warden, steward.

So naturally, I didn't want any part of a stew like that. What did I need it for? But then the merry-go-round began.

After all, folks said, you're the only one in town, you're this that and the other thing. It's a sin to throw away such a fortune! What'll become of the kids, those poor little things? Four boys and a girl? What do you care? they told me. Accept, and then you and the widow will be their joint legal guardians.

Have some pity, I replied. What do you want from me? What do I know about a stewardship? I haven't got the faintest idea whether you eat it or sail it. So they started all over again. After all! You've got to be considerate. It's a good deed! It's this that and the other thing.

To make a long story short, I couldn't refuse and along with the widow became a stew, I mean a steward, a legal guardian. And thank the Lord, now that I had boarded that stewardship, I began taking stock of the estate's value, figuring what the poor kids actually possessed. I gathered all their belongings—house, store, horse, cow, this that and the other thing—and converted everything to cash.

It wasn't too easy, you know, for Menashe, may he rest in peace, was a rich, well-established chap—loaded, as they say. No matter how much the townspeople thought he had, he had more. But he kept no records. I hope he forgives me for saying this, but he was totally illiterate. New assets kept turning up constantly. He had lent money all over; everyone was in debt to him. So—no choice—I had to shoulder the entire burden and try to collect all the money due him. And I did everything myself. For his wife—my stewardess, that is—was good only for pots and pans. She was as naïve as they come. She couldn't tell a good or a bad IOU from a hole in the wall. Didn't have a head for business or this that and the other thing.

To make a long story short, I gathered up the few rubles, which came to quite a neat bundle. Having collected the money with heartache and woe, I now had to decide what to do with it. Merely living off the capital would be absolutely senseless. The kids, alas, always needed new shirts, shoes, this that and the other thing. Food—that goes without saying. If we didn't put the money to good use, they'd just keep on eating until everything would be devoured. What would happen then? An honest man—get me?—must look to the future. So I racked my brains, debating what to do with the money. Open up a business? Then who would run it, if the mother was a ninny and the poor kids were little tots? Put it out on loan and get interest for it? Suppose the other fellow went bankrupt? Who'd be responsible? The steward or his ship?

So I decided there was no business better than mine. Right? And certainly no business was sounder or more secure than mine. Right? Thank God, I have credit all over, even at all the fairs. I also have a good name—may my reputation never get any worse. Wasn't it a thousand times better for me to invest the few rubles in my own store? Right? Perk it up with a continual supply of the latest goods. Right? And if you buy merchandise for cash, you obviously get a better deal, for everyone loves to see cash on the line. Rubles, cash down, you know, is a rather rare sight nowadays. Wherever you look you only see notes, bills of exchange, IOU's, this that and the other thing.

To make a long story short, I put all the money into my business and things ran pretty smoothly. In fact, not bad at all. The capital increased, you know, for with plenty of merchandise sales are brisker. Like they say: Fishing's no problem in a well-stocked lake. Nevertheless, there was one drawback. The expenses! My expenses actually doubled. After all, I was now supporting two households, knock wood. About my own I won't even say a word. But the widow was always needing something or other, and so were the five kids, who were no kin of mine, you know. It wasn't peanuts providing them with shoes, clothes and a Jewish education. Add to this an occasional tip to the village clerk, a trip, a snack, this that and the other thing. But—no choice—that was the only way. For what would people say? What a captain that stewardship has! He grabbed all the money and begrudged the orphans a kopeck for candy.

But the fact that I slaved, broke my head over the business, went abroad on buying trips, had a ledger full of debts hanging over me, as well as ulcers, plagues, this that and the other thing—that was nobody's business! My widow, she didn't offer me a fifty-fifty partnership, you know. You say she put in money? Well, first of all, the money was tied up in merchandise, and secondly, it wasn't just lying around doing nothing. I was paying interest on it. And wasn't the tumult and turmoil I was in day and night with this that and other thing worth anything? Go step into a stewed ship, I mean a stewardship. Care for another man's kids, poor things, and see that they get an education whether they want it or not; that they go where they're supposed to, and not where they're not supposed to; that they do this that and the other thing. What am I, their father? Must I watch and see that they stay out of mischief? Nowadays, you know, one can't even properly keep an eye on one's *own* children, especially, heaven help you, if one of them is a wild brat.

Menashe, may he forgive me, was a simple fellow, but at least he was honest. And—dear God—what a batch of kids he left behind! One worse than the other. At least the older ones were tolerable. One lad was deaf. Always despondent and completely crestfallen. So I made a workingman out of him. Another was a perfect idiot, a quiet boy who didn't pester a soul and didn't need a thing. A third was bright and capable as a child, but when he grew up he palled around with all sorts of riffraff and developed into a first-rate scoundrel, God save us. He stormed and ranted, fussed and fumed, did this that and the other thing until I finally had to give him a few rubles—and Godspeed your way to America, a place which he'd been attracted to ever since childhood. So that's how we got rid of *him*.

The girl I married off. I gave her a dowry of about a thousand rubles, dressed her from top to toe, arranged a fine wedding with musicians and with this that and the other thing, just as it should be. Almost as if she were my own daughter. What else? That's the way it had to be. She had no father, poor thing, and her mother was a ninny. So who would knock his head against the wall if not me?

"You dumbbell, you driveling idiot," my wife would holler. "Sure you have to sacrifice yourself for another man's children! Just wait and see the stony thanks you'll get for stewing their estate."

So said my old lady and, believe me, she hit the nail right on the head. Stones are all I get for thanks. And what stones they are! Just listen to the pack of troubles I carry on my back. I tell you, I must be made of steel to put up with all this.

To make a long story short, among all of Menashe's orphans there was one clever lad, thank heaven. The smallest, called Dani. Really something. Literally a gift of God. From childhood on he was no more and no less than a perfect nuisance. At the age of five his idea of fun was smacking his mother in the mouth with the leg of a boot. And of all days, on Sabbath mornings before services. Ripping off his mother's headdress when a stranger sat in the house was one of his daily stunts. Believe me, she must have been made of steel to put up with him. Day and night she had her hands full with Dani. Whenever I came there I found her—the widow, I mean—sitting and sniveling. Why had God punished her with such a child? she always complained. Why hadn't she miscarried with him before he came into the world?

I can't even begin to catalogue all his tricks. He snatched every single piece of jewelry she had—rings, earrings, a string of pearls. He took an old pair of glasses, a silk kerchief, a lamp, a knife, a this that and the other thing. Everything was fair game for him. He carted everything out of the house, sold it and spent the money on candy, nuts, watermelons and good tobacco for himself and his pals. And you can imagine what a fine bunch of pals he had. Beggars, thieves and drunkards—the deuce knows where he met that rabble. Whatever he had he gave away to his friends: a new pair of boots, a cap, the shirt off his back.

"Dani, what've you done? Given away a brand-new pair of boots?"

"I don't give a damn!" he said. "I feel sorry seeing some poor guy going barefoot."

Well, what do you say to such a compassionate creature? I'm not even talking about money. Whenever he laid his hands on a bit of cash he gave it to his sidekicks.

"For goodness sake, Dani, why are you doing this?"

"I don't give a damn," he said. "The next fellow's also human. He's got to eat, too."

Well, how do you like that sweet philosopher? So hospitable! There's a rare and gifted soul for you. An exceptional creature. And do you think that he was a fool, or an ugly boy? God forbid! He was shrewd, handsome, sound as an apple. He was jolly, he sang and danced, but—the devil take it—there was a bad streak in him.

What didn't we try to do with him? We tried both the kind and the harsh approach. We locked him in his room for three days and three nights. We whipped him. We broke a good bamboo cane over him. Cost me three rubles, too, that cane of mine. But it was no use. Like lashing the waves or beating air. So I wanted to teach him a trade. Wanted to make him a watchmaker, a goldsmith, a carpenter, a musician, a blacksmith, a this that and the other thing. But it was impossible. Though you cut him in two, he didn't want to work.

"What's going to be with you, Dani?"

"I'm gonna be a free bird," he laughed.

"A free bird? A jailbird is what you'll be. A thief."

"I don't give a damn," he said, and before you knew it, he slipped away and disappeared.

To make a long story short, we didn't give a damn about *him*. We let him grow up and, as you can imagine, he developed into a prize jewel. At least he stopped stealing. For there was hardly anything left to steal. So, it was just his behavior, his fine pals, his gestures and his clothes that bothered us. You should have seen the way he dressed: a red shirt over his trousers which were tucked into a pair of high boots. He wore his hair long and wild like an artist and, what's more, he shaved the beard right off his chin. In other words, he was a little sweetie pie. But he never had the gall to come near *me*. If he needed anything, he fired his requests through her—his mother, I mean. And his mother, that ninny, loved that precious gem of hers. As far as she was concerned he could do no wrong.

One morning I came to the store. I give a look and there he was waiting for me, the rascal.

"A hearty welcome, Dani," I said. "What's the good word?"

"I've come to tell you that I'm getting married."

"Congratulations and lots of luck," I said. "Who's the lucky girl?"

"Asna," he said.

"Which Asna?"

"Our Asna. The girl who used to keep house for us."

"Thunderations," I said. "You're marrying a domestic?"

"I don't give a damn," he said. "What's the matter, isn't a maid a human being?"

"I just pity your poor mother. In other words, you've come to invite me to the wedding?"

"Nope," he said. "I've come to you for clothes. I want to get dressed up for the wedding. Me and Asna figured out what we need. Here it is: one worsted suit, one cotton summer suit, half a dozen shirts and a dozen undershirts. And Asna needs calico and wool for a couple of dresses, some of the best silk for blouses, fur for a hood, two shawls, half a dozen handkerchiefs and a bit of this that and the other thing."

"And nothing else?" I said, trying hard to keep a straight face.

"No, nothing else."

To make a long story short, I couldn't hold it back any longer and suddenly burst out in such a fit of laughter that I almost fell off the chair. Looking at me, all my salesmen began laughing, too. Our laughter almost brought the walls down. When the spell was over, I called to the groom:

"Just tell me one thing if you will, dear Dani—have you invested so much cash in my store that you feel at liberty to barge in on me like a bolt from the blue with such a shopping list?"

"I'm not quite sure," he said, "exactly how much of it is my share, but if you'd split the money my father left me into five equal shares, it would certainly cover the cost of the wedding outfits; in fact, I have a feeling that there'd be something left over for after the wedding, too."

To make a long story short, what could I do? When he uttered these words I felt as though someone had either fired a pistol into my heart, cast me into flames, thrown hot water over me, or done me some other terrible thing. I tell you, I saw stars. You understand? Not enough that I broke my back for so many years by supporting a poor widow with five children, taking care of their weddings, doing this that and the other thing, but the upshot was that I had a son of a bitch like that on my back who talked of equal shares!

"Well, what did I tell you?" said my wife. "My very words. Didn't I warn you about the stony thanks you'd get from them?"

To make a long story short, it was no use. I gave him everything he wanted. I didn't want to start up with a scoundrel like that. It was beneath my dignity. Here you are! Go to the blazes. Choke on it. Burn in hell in a slow fire for all I care. Anything, so long as I could get rid of that pest. But do you think that that was the last I saw of him? Wait, there's plenty more to tell. About a month after his wedding he came to me, this fine young man, and said:

"For God's sakes, give me two hundred and twenty-three rubles quick."

"What sort of bill is it that comes to exactly two hundred and twenty-three rubles?"

"That's what it comes to," he said nonchalantly, "for the beerhouse with the pool tables."

"What beer? What pool?"

"I'm in business," he exclaimed. "Took over a beerhouse with pool tables. Asna will sell beer and I'll watch the pool tables. We can make a pretty penny with it."

"Some pretty penny," I said to my breadwinner. "That sort of business is right up your alley—a tavern and pool tables."

"I don't give a damn," he said, "so long as I don't take it gratis from anyone. I don't mind a dry crust twice a day so long as it isn't someone else's."

Well, how do you like Dani's philosophizing?

"Lots of luck," I said. "Sell beer and play pool all you want. But what's it got to do with me?"

"It's got plenty to do with you," he said, "for it's you who has to give me money to the tune of two hundred and twenty-three rubles."

"What do you mean I *have* to give you?" I said. "Just tell me whose money I'm going to use?"

"My father's," he said, not even batting an eyelash.

Would you believe it? As he spoke I felt like taking him by the seat of the pants and booting him the hell out of the store. But then I thought the better of it. Blast him to perdition! Should I dirty my hands with such a lowlife? So never mind my money.

"Tell me, Dani," I said to him, "do you at least know how much money your father left?"

"No," he said, "what do I care? I'll have time to find out a year from now, God willing, when I'll be twenty-one. That's when I'll come to you for a complete accounting. Meanwhile, just give me two hundred and twenty-three rubles and let me go."

Hearing this, my head swam. Why? Not because I was afraid of anyone, God forbid, for what have I got to be afraid of? Didn't I spend enough on them? No trifle, you know, supporting a poor widow and her five kids so many years, taking care of them all and marrying them off, doing this that and the other thing, and along comes this punk and wants me to give him an accounting.

To make a long story short, I took out the money and gave him two hundred and twenty-three rubles and prayed to God that he'd leave me alone. In fact, I didn't see his face for a long time. But one day I came home and there he was. Seeing him, my heart sank. But I didn't let on that I was annoyed. So I played dumb and said:

"Look who's here! Greetings! How come we don't see you, Dani? How's your health? How's your business?"

"About health I don't give a damn. But the business could be better."

Congratulations, I thought. May you live to tell us better news. This smacks of another handout.

"Namely?" I said aloud. "What's up? Aren't you making any money?"

"What money? Who's talking about money? About money I don't give a damn. I no longer have a beerhouse, I no longer have pool tables, I no longer have a wife. She threw me over, Asna did. But the devil take her, I don't give a damn. I'm leaving—off to America. My brother's been asking me to come for ever so long."

Hearing that he was leaving for America, a stone rolled off my heart. All of a sudden he seemed like such a likable chap. Embarrassment aside, I could have jumped up and kissed him.

"To America," I said. "Wonderful! They say that America is a free country. They say that people find happiness in America. They rake in the money. Especially if you've got kin there, then it's really grand. In other words, I gather you've come to say good-bye. Well, that's very nice of you. Just don't forget to drop us a line once in a while. After all, we're pals, like they say. By the way, Dani, do you perhaps need something for expenses? If so, I can help you out."

"That's exactly what I've come to see you about," he said. "I need three hundred rubles, so give them to me."

"Three hundred rubles?" I said. "Isn't that a bit too much? Perhaps one hundred and fifty will do?"

"What sense is there in bargaining with me? Don't I know that if I asked you for four hundred you'd give me four hundred, five hundred, even six hundred? But I don't need money, so I don't give a damn. I just need three hundred rubles for expenses."

So said Dani to me and looked me straight in the eye. May three hundred blisters break out on my enemies' skin! I thought. If I could only be sure that this was the last time he'd be coming to me and asking for this that and the other thing.

To make a long story short, I took out the money and counted out three hundred-ruble bills, one by one, and even bought a present for his older brother: a full pound of Wissotsky's tea, one thousand of the best cigarettes, a few bottles of Carmel wine. Besides all this, my wife roasted a duck for him, gave him rolls and oranges—plagues and heartaches, dear Lord!—as well as this that and the other thing for the journey. We accompanied him to the railroad station, bade him a fond farewell, kissed him as though he were our own child. So help me God, we even shed some tears.

After all, he grew up on our laps. He wasn't a bad boy, so why deny it? Just a bit unruly. Aside from that I swear he had a good heart. But I'll tell you the unvarnished truth. I was rather happy to see him go. I was now rid of a parasite. But my heart pained me, too. He was a young lad, setting out on a long journey. Who knows where he would land and what would become of him? If he would only write once in a while. On the other hand, perhaps it would be better if he didn't write at all. Let him live there happily for one hundred and twenty years. As I live and breathe, I prayed to God for him as I would for my own child.

But here's what happened. Just about two years after his departure for America, the door opened up one day and in walked a queer bird rigged out in a high hat. And this handsome, happy-go-lucky, strapping, and broad-shouldered young man threw his arms around me and kissed me.

"What's the matter?" he said. "Don't you recognize me, or are you just pretending?"

"Confound it! Is it really you, Dani?" I forced a laugh. But in my heart a fire burned and I thought: Dammit, why didn't you get killed by a train or drown in the sea? "When did you arrive, Dani, and what are you doing here?"

"I just came this morning. What am I doing here? I've come to settle the accounts with you."

The latter phrase sent an arrow through my heart. What sort of accounts did that charlatan have to settle with me? But I braced myself and said:

"So why did you have to go to the trouble of coming all the way over here? My goodness, if you wanted to settle up, you could just as well have written me how much you owe me."

"How much I owe *you?*" he laughed. "If anyone owes anything around here, I'm afraid it's *you*. And *you're* the one who's going to have to pay."

"Pay who?" I said. "*You,* by any chance?"

"Right you are. Me and my brothers and my sister. All of us. I purposely came from America to settle the accounts for all of us. I want an exact accounting of my father's money. What's coming to you, you'll deduct. What's coming to us, you'll pay us. And if there's any little snag, I don't give a damn. We'll surely come to terms. There'll be no fights, God forbid. . . . And now, how are *you* doing? How are the kids? Here, I've brought each of them a present."

Another minute and I would either have fainted, or picked up a chair and smashed it over his head. But I restrained myself and asked him to come back after the Sabbath and then we'd settle accounts. As for me, I went straight to the lawyers asking them what to do, how to get rid of this millstone on my neck. But the lawyers, God bless 'em, either didn't know or pretended not to. One said that since more than ten years had passed it was a closed affair. Another said, No! Since I was in a stew—a stewardship, that is—it made no difference if one hundred years passed; I still had to render a complete accounting.

"But how can I give an accounting," I asked, "if I didn't keep any books or any bills?"

"Then you're in a bad fix," replied the lawyer.

"That I know myself. You better give a suggestion as to what I ought to do."

But there was no answer. I had to be made of steel to bear up under the strain. I ask you, what purpose did it all serve, all the bargaining, the bother, the this that and the other thing? What ill wind was it that made me agree to a stewed ship—a stewardship, that is—over another man's children? It would have been a thousand times better if at that time I had succumbed to a delirious fever, or broken a leg, or fallen victim to some other disaster—anything, so long as I could have avoided that millstone on my neck, that stew involving a widow and her poor orphans, and Dani, books, accounts and this that and the other thing.

A WHITE BIRD

I don't know how you feel about it, but come hell or high water, I simply *must* have a white bird for the atonement ceremony on the Eve of Yom Kippur. To tell the truth, I don't know how I'd managed to go through the sacrificial ceremony without a white bird. Without it I'd worry all year long about dropping dead. That's the habit I've gotten into ever since I've been a child. Everything's a matter of habit. My mother, I'll have you know, isn't such a saint either, but things like that she believes in. For example, for Passover there must be a borscht; for Shevuos, greens; for the Yom Kippur atonement, a white bird; for Hanuka, pancakes; for Purim, a platter of sweets. Sacred precepts such as these she observes like a rabbi's wife. The apple of her eye is the Yizkor Memorial Service. And if, God forbid, she misses hearing the ram's horn on Rosh Hashana, she considers it a greater calamity than if I miss—forgive the comparison—a Chaliapin concert.

Nevertheless, if you'd get to know her you'd surely think that she was an amazingly well-educated woman. Unto this very day she hasn't stopped talking about Goethe and Schiller; she can't fall asleep until she's read something by Chekhov. Yet a month before Rosh Hashana, at the beginning of the month of Elul, you ought to see her covering her head with a white kerchief and going out to the marketplace to deal with the common gossips. I have a feeling that she even haggles with them for memorial candles. And when the weeping days of Elul are over, she casts off her kerchief and returns once more to Goethe, Schiller and Chekhov. That's the sort of Jewish woman my mother is.

And she's brought up her daughters in this same Jewish fashion. There were five of us, and we all married for love. What I mean is, we were all pretty, educated, of course, and even had a dowry of fifteen thousand apiece set aside for us at the bank. So was there any reason to hate us? We were famous, I'll have you know, not so much for our learning and beauty, but for our good upbringing. A good upbringing, you see, is a very great thing. For instance, when it came to other matters, our mother brought us up free and easy. We were at perfect liberty to talk to *any*one, go *any*where, and do *any*thing. But yet when it came to matters Jewish, we went overboard.

For instance, though you chop my head off, you won't catch me talking about my kids without knocking wood. But my Vladimir laughs and makes fun of me and my Jewish customs. But if I'd use him as a criterion, then my Passover would be pure unadulterated Easter, with colored Easter eggs to the bargain, and without even so much as a crumb of matza. When it comes to Judaism, my Vladimir is a bit—well, how shall I put it?—perverse. Of course, he respects a Jew. When he hears that Jews are suffering somewhere, or when he learns of a pogrom, he walks about like a chicken without a head. After all, he's a Jew—Jewish blood runs through his veins. He only hates Jewish gestures and Jewish manners. A Jew, says he, is an insolent creature, a cheeky smart aleck. But just let a stranger try and say something bad about the Jews and he'll tear him limb from limb.

Vladimir is a funny sort. I've often heard him brag to the noblemen who occasionally came to our house to play cards that we have our own Jewish diplomat, Herzl, who frequents the palace of the Sultan of Turkey. And yet when the Zionists came to him for a contribution some time ago, he had a long argument with them. He tried to convince them that they were backing a pipe dream and building castles in the sky. But what about the money? Don't you think he contributed? Sure he did. That's the sort of creature my Vladimir is.

You should see the arguments I have with him over the children. My kids, may the evil eye not harm them, are beautiful, healthy, neat and lively, knock wood. Can one hope for anything more? But Vladimir wants them to know everything. You want them to know everything? With pleasure! I too want them to know everything. Who doesn't want educated children? But I'm more concerned about their health. I'm not such a dandy mama, but still in all I'm a mother, so I know the value of health. Ah me, what I went through before I finally saw my Sasha and Sonke grown up. So Vladimir comes along and badgers them to know everything under the sun; he even wants them to know Yiddish. As if they haven't got enough to handle, what with high school, music lessons, dancing masters, and other plagues—so they have to have another pest on their back, Yiddish. If they would at least teach Yiddish like they teach German, French or English, for example. Or if the Yiddish tutor would at least be a qualified teacher, like all the others. But he's—oh Lord forgive me—I myself don't know what he is. Vladimir himself can't stand the Yiddish tutor's smell. After he's gone Vladimir always throws open the windows.

"What good is he?" I protested.

"Today Yiddish is the fad," he said, "so the kids have to learn Yiddish."

Get the picture? It's the fad! It's smart to be fashionable. Cards too are the fashion. My Vladimir once knew a few card games—preference, pinochle and sixty-six. Yet nowadays he can sit down and play forty-eight hours straight. He practically can't live without cards. But as long as he played at home, it didn't bother me. I myself go for a game of preference, and I don't mind a round of sixty-six, either. We even used to play sixty-six quite often in our mother's house. What galls me is that he plays in the club.

Oh, that club. That awful club. May all the clubs in the world go up in smoke. First of all, it's a waste of money. Naturally, he plays to win, but he always loses a fortune. I can tell when he loses and when he wins. If he comes home nervous and jittery, that is, stark raving mad, takes out all his rancor on me and constantly seeks fault—well that's a sign that he's lost. And second of all, think of the time that's wasted. Oh the nights, the nights. At first, before I found out where he disappeared to each night, I was beside myself, almost went out of my mind. He invented a new alibi every time. Once he told me it was an arbitration meeting which lasted three nights in a row. Another time a pal of his had simply dragged him home for a game of preference. But what's the rub? I know my Vladimir. I know when he's lying and when he's telling the truth. If he swears to high heaven while in a fit of anger, that's a sign he's lying. So of course I began asking questions, snooping here and there, until I finally discovered that he was going to the club. Believe me, a stone rolled off my heart. Thank heaven, at least it wasn't to some other place.

"Vladimir," I pleaded, "can't you get your fill of cards at home?"

"At the club," he replied, "you meet this fellow and the next. You get to know what's going on in the world."

Fiddlesticks! That's a lot of nonsense.

"Vladimir," I continued, "just think what you're doing by leaving me all alone nights on end. You don't ever lay eyes on your children, you wretch. Have you no fear of God?"

His answer was that he hated scenes and couldn't stand me bringing God into the conversation. So I began to cry. He stalked out, banged the door and returned the next morning in a huff. Get the picture? And *he* feels he's been unjustly wronged.

I took a good look at my Vladimir and recalled the time he was running after me, aiming to get married. He used up loads of shoe leather following me. He was my shadow; hung on to my skirts. But it wasn't easy going for him. First of all, he had to see to it that he would appeal to my mother. He listened to her reciting pieces from memory by Goethe, Schiller and Chekhov. Then he read to her from romantic novels, especially the sort that can soften a heart of stone. He held his hands out as she spooled yarn on them. He helped her boil jam during the summer; he played cards with her during the winter. He really suffered, and all for my sake. He was just dying to marry me. He worshipped the ground I walked on. He wore his knees to the bone before I finally accepted his proposal, for at that time I had three suitors, all fine young chaps like him. One of them—he's a doctor today— loved me to distraction. That is, they were *all* head over heels in love with me.

And today? You think if the fancy takes me I'd find it hard

to make someone's head spin? For example, take Burnholtz, the pharmacist, who's fluttering about me. The stories he's been telling me! He wants to convince me that I'm ten years younger than I actually am. And why does he come just when Vladimir is out? Because, to tell the truth, I lead him on a bit. In fact, I *want* Vladimir to know, and I want it to gall him.

I myself tell Vladimir afterward. "You know who's been here?" I say.

"Burnholtz?" he says. You'd expect him to grimace at least.

"Tomorrow," I tell him, "we're going to hear Chaliapin. Just the two of us."

"Who are you going with?" he asks. "Burnholtz?"

At this I look at him and think: Just you wait, I'm going to start getting under your skin. And out loud I say:

"Vladimir, do you think it would be a bad idea to rent a summer cottage with Burnholtz?"

"Not a bad idea at all," he says.

"Burnholtz wants to go to Marienbad with me this year," I say.

"Have a good trip."

Have a good trip? If that's the case, then nothing doing. Just because you want me to, I won't go. Now I ask you, what's come over my Vladimir? His clique at the club has surely sunk their claws into him. And boy, do they know how! Nothing good can come of the clubs. Every night after the club they go—I know right well where they go. I've asked around. Every night after the club they go to the Parnassus, to the Olympia, to the Arcadia, and to other such lively night spots where they pass the time quite merrily.

To the blazes with the club. May all cards burn to a crisp. To hell with his companions. There used to be a time when Vladimir and I used to sit up night after night just talking, never at a loss for words. And now we can't even sit together for half an hour. We've got nothing to talk about. That's why the pharmacist and I have something in common. We talk about everything under the sun. Idle chatter, jokes, songs, anecdotes. My oh my, does he have a store of anecdotes, that Burnholtz, may he burn in hell! And Jewish anecdotes at that, ha-ha—as well as other kinds. I love a fine story. I

never get bored listening to a good story. So he sits here,
nights on end—Burnholtz, that is—and tells me stories.

I know that the entire town is talking about me. I know
quite well what they're saying, but it doesn't bother me a bit.
The only thing that bothers me is that it doesn't bother
Vladimir.

Oh woe is me! In the good old days if Vladimir were told
that a pharmacist was sitting up nights on end with me and
telling me stories—ha-ha-ha, brother watch out! And today?
Absolutely nothing. Sometimes he comes home late at night
and finds Burnholtz sitting on the veranda with me, but he
says nothing.

"Well, what's new, Mister Burnholtz?" he says.

So Mister Burnholtz tells him what's new. Vladimir smokes
a cigar and pretends that he's paying attention, but actually
he's thinking of—the devil knows what he's thinking of—for
his thoughts are over *there*. You want to know where? Ah! If
I only knew where this place was, I'd be much better off. I've
been wanting to know for a long time—in fact I'm on the
proper trail. Don't breathe a word of it, but just recently I
shook a little letter out of Vladimir's pocket. A very fine
letter, soaked in perfume and signed "Masha."

Masha? Who can this Masha be? I've been breaking my
head over this problem for two weeks, but I still can't make
heads or tails of it.

Oh, just let me find out for sure, and he'll get a right good
dose of Masha from me! I'm going to raise such a storm that
his head will be mashed right off.

Wait up. It seems that I've been sidetracked. What did I
start with? Oh yes, the sacrificial fowl. I don't know how you
feel about it, but come hell or high water, I simply *must* have
a white bird for the atonement ceremony on the Eve of Yom
Kippur.

"As the bird is white and clean, so am I white and cleansed
of sin." That's what my mother taught me. And I follow my
mother's footsteps. That's why I must have a white bird. Not
only for me, but one for Vladimir, too, and one for each of
the children. Even for my little Lyolitchka—may all harm
destined for her come to me instead—I buy a small white
chicken, a little white sacrificial fowl. And I twirl the bird

about my head in the traditional manner. I do this for all of
them. Woe is me, but I'm the only Jew in the house who
understands a Jewish law and observes the Jewish precepts. I
take the prayerbook and, as I recite the Atonement Service, I
twirl the chicken about my head three times.

"This chicken is offered in exchange for us. This is our
ransom. This is our atonement." Having said this, I immediately feel better, for it's a white, a pure white bird, the very
sort that God Himself has ordained.

STICKS AND STONES MAY BREAK
MY BONES

You want to know why I'm laughing? I just reminded myself of an incident where I pulled the wool over the eyes of Yehupetz. Ha-ha-ha. Yes, sir! It was me, all right, none other than Moishe-Nakhman from Kenele, a man with a chronic cough and asthma. How did I manage it, you want to know? Well, I pulled a fast one in Yehupetz, ha-ha, the sort of stunt they'll remember a long long time. Just give me a few minutes until my coughing fit passes—what a cough I got! I wish it on that anti-Semite Purishkevitch—and you'll hear the sort of thing a chap is capable of doing.

One bright day I arrived in Yehupetz. Why was a Jew like me with a chronic cough and asthma traveling to Yehupetz? Naturally, to a specialist, a famous professor. As you can well imagine, what with my chronic cough and asthma I'm a frequent visitor to Yehupetz. Actually, I'm not such a welcome guest there, for after all what am I, Moishe-Nakhman from Kenele, doing in Yehupetz if I don't have a residence permit? But if among other things you've got a chronic cough and asthma, there's just no way out. So you come to Yehupetz. And you hide. And worry yourself to death. You arrive early in the morning and run away at night. If you don't run, you get kicked out, but then you come again. You don't care so long as you're not sent home tramping the road with the transported convicts.

If, God forbid, I were sentenced to one of those marching convoys, I'm afraid I wouldn't live through it. I think I'd drop dead three times over just from shame alone. For, thank God, you're looking at a respected householder who has a bit of an estate in Kenele. I've got my own apartment, a goat and two daughters, one already married off and the other still waiting. But what's one thing got to do with the other?

In brief, I came to Yehupetz to see the professor. Actually, not the professor but the professors. That is, for a consultation with no less than three famous professors. I wanted to find out once and for all whether these specialists considered me kosher or not. That I had asthma they all agreed. But what was to be *done* to the asthma to get *rid* of it—well, that, you see, was an entirely different matter. Those doctors tormented themselves, poor souls. They tried their best. But they ran up against a stone wall.

For instance, when I came to my old professor—Stritzel is his name, a gem of a man—he prescribed "pulverized sugar and codeine." It wasn't expensive and was sweet to the palate. Yet when I went to see the second specialist, *he* prescribed "tincture of opium." Awful-tasting little drops. So I picked myself up and went to the third specialist. He prescribed similar-tasting drops. They weren't called "tincture of opium," but "tincture of tobacco." Think that's the end of it? I went to yet another specialist and he too prescribed a bitter medicine called "morphium aqua amigdalarium." You surprised at my knowledge of Latin? I know Latin like you know Turkish. But if among other things a man has a chronic cough, asthma and tuberculosis, he also manages to learn Latin.

In brief, I came to Yehupetz one day for a consultation. Now where does a Jew like me lodge when he comes to Yehupetz? Naturally, neither in a hotel nor in an inn. First of all, they fleece you there. Furthermore, how can I stay in a hotel if I don't have a residence permit? So I always stay with my brother-in-law. My brother-in-law, I'll have you know, is a blunderhead; he's a teacher and a pauper and may all his other ills seep into that anti-Semite Purishkevitch's skull! And, Lord preserve us, you ought to see the bevy of children he has to support!

But on the other hand God had blessed him with a hundred percent kosher residence permit. How did he get one? Leave it to the sugar king Brodsky who employed him, as it were. My brother-in-law wasn't the factory manager, heaven forbid. But in the tailor's basement prayer-room annex to Brodsky's synagogue he read the Torah. Which in the eyes of the authorities made him a bona fide "ecclesiastical personage," or, as they called him there, a "caretaker." Being a "caretaker" he could get permission to live on Malovasilkovsky Street, where the ex-chief of police once resided. So there my brother-in-law lived and struggled and just about managed to make ends meet. Naturally, I was their only hope. Ah me, I was considered the rich man of the family.

When I came to Yehupetz I always stopped at their place, ate lunch and supper and sent my brother-in-law out on errands of one sort or another for which he managed to make a ruble or two. Such profits I wish on Purishkevitch!

But when I came to them that day I saw that they were crestfallen. They walked around gloomy and glum.

"What's up?"

"Things are bad."

"To wit?"

"There's been a raid."

"Blast it! Is that all? I thought God-knows-what happened. A raid? That's an old plague. As old as the hills."

"No," they said, "raid is not the word for it. Nowadays not a night goes by without a raid. And if they catch a Jew, come what may, they straightaway pack him off with the next shipment of transported convicts."

"Well, what about a payoff?"

"Nothing doing!"

"Not even a ruble?"

"Out of the question."

"How about three?"

"Not even a million!"

"In that case, we're in trouble."

"Trouble's not the word for it," they said. "First of all, you get slapped with a fine. And then comes the long walk home with the transported convicts. Not to mention the scandal for Brodsky."

"Look," I said, "you can talk Brodsky from today till tomorrow. But for the sake of Brodsky I'm not going to speculate with my health. I came for a consultation with some famous specialists and I can't turn back now and run away."

In short, we argued back and forth, but time did not stand still. I had to see the professors about my consultation. But the upshot was, what consultations? Where, how and when? One doctor could first come Wednesday morning, the other one, the following Monday afternoon. The third, no earlier than a week from Thursday. What to do? The appointments were stretched out for three weeks and a doomsday. For what did they care that Moishe-Nakhman from Kenele had a chronic cough and asthma and couldn't sleep nights—may that anti-Semite Purishkevitch wheeze and toss and turn like me! Meanwhile, night fell. We ate supper and went to sleep. I had just dozed off when I heard—bang boom bang! I tore my eyes open.

"Who is it?"

"We're done for," said my brother-in-law, the blunderhead, standing over me like a cadaver and shaking like a palm branch.

"What do we do now?" I asked.

"Why don't *you* tell *me* what to do?"

"What should we do?" I said. "We're in a bitter fix."

"Bitter is not the word for it. Our position is as bitter as gall."

Meanwhile, the noise at the door continued: bang boom bang! The poor kids woke up in a fright, crying: "Mama, Mama!" So the mother gagged them with her hands; she practically strangled them to keep them still. A fine turn of events.

Well, I said to myself, Moishe-Nakhman from Kenele, now you're in a pickle. May Purishkevitch be pickled like me. But then all of a sudden I had a brainstorm.

"Listen, David," I told my brother-in-law. "You know what? You be me and I'll be you."

So he gaped at me like a dunce and said, "What do you mean?"

"I mean we're going to switch personalities. You give me your identity card and I'll give you mine. Then you'll be Moishe-Nakhman and I'll be David."

But that half-wit just stared at me openmouthed. As though he didn't catch the drift of my words.

"You ass. Don't you get it? It's such a simple plan a child can understand it. You'll show them my identity card and I'll show them yours. And so on and so forth. Get it? Or do I have to chop it up and spoon-feed you?"

Apparently he caught on, for we proceeded to switch identity cards. He gave me his, I gave him mine. By now they were practically breaking the door down: bang boom bang!

"What's the matter?" I said. "What's the rush? The river's not on fire!"

Then turning to my brother-in-law, I said, "Remember, David, you're no longer David, but Moishe-Nakhman."

I went to the door, opened it and said: "Welcome, friends!" And in traipsed an entire mob of officials, accompanied by an assortment of lackeys and underlings. So help me, the place looked festive.

Naturally, they made a beeline for my brother-in-law, the blunderhead. Why to him? Because I bore myself with poise and self-assurance, of course. You know, you stand up straight and fake a blasé smile. But you should have seen the jittery look on my brother-in-law's face. I wish it on Purishkevitch! So they grabbed him and said:

"Where are you from, Mister Jew?"

But the cat got his tongue. So I stood up as his advocate and told him in Hebrew:

"Hey, tongue-tied! Look sharp! Speak up, for goodness sake! Talk. Talk to them. Tell them that you're Moishe-Nakhman from Kenele."

And I turned to the police and begged them: "So on and so forth. Your Excellencies! Most Honorable Residence Permits! He's a poor relative. Haven't seen each other in a long time. Came visiting from Kenele."

But deep down, I was in stitches. I couldn't keep a straight face. Any minute, I felt, I was going to explode in laughter. Do you understand? I, Moishe-Nakhman from Kenele, was begging for Moishe-Nakhman—for myself, actually. The only trouble was that all my pleading did as much good as last year's snow. They took hold of him and with all due ceremony very neatly cooped him up behind bars. They also wanted to take me away. That is, I was already under arrest. But they let me go immediately. In any case, I couldn't care less. For I had a residence permit, black on white, which explicitly listed me as a "caretaker" in the tailor's basement prayer-room annex to Brodsky's synagogue! Of course a ruble on the sly didn't hurt either—you get the picture—and so on and so forth.

"Fine, Mister Caretaker," they said to me. "You can go home now and nibble noodle pudding. A little later we'll teach you a lesson not to conceal contraband on Malavasil-kovsky Street."

Well, there was another pickle thrown right at my face. Ha-ha!

You want to hear more? I didn't even think about the consultations. Who had a mind for consultations, when my uppermost thought was saving my brother-in-law? Saving him from what? From the walking tour with the transported convicts? Are you kidding? Naturally, nothing helped. He tramped right along them. And how he tramped! I wish it on Purishkevitch! Before we finally saw that blunderhead in Kenele our nerves almost gave out. And when they finally brought him to Kenele a new misfortune had befallen him. Charged with possessing someone else's identity card, assuming someone else's name, and so on and so forth. Don't ask! I had my hands full with him. Too bad I don't earn every three months what that identity card pickle cost me.

Besides my own load of troubles I now have to support him and his family, too. Because he claims that I'm responsible for his miserable state of affairs. He claims that because of me he lost his residence permit and his position in Brodsky's synagogue. Now there's just a slight chance he's not entirely wrong.

But that's not the best part of it, ha-ha-ha. The best part of it was the brainstorm I had, the scheme I dreamt up. Get me? You'd never think it could come to pass. I'm just a plain Jew from Kenele with a chronic cough and asthma and tuberculosis to the bargain, which I wish on Purishkevitch, and without a residence permit, mind you! Yet despite all this, when Moishe-Nakhman has to come to town, he comes to Yehupetz without a worry in the world and sleeps over on Malavasilovsky Street, practically under the nose of the ex-chief of police. And I don't give a hoot what you call me—for sticks and stones may break my bones and so on and so forth.

NO LUCK!

So you're both talking about thieves, huh? When it comes to
thieves, gentlemen, let *me* do the talking. Where in the
world do you have as much swiping as in our line? Diamonds
aren't peanuts, you know! The passion for gems is so great
that there are even crooks among the customers themselves.
And the men aren't half as bad as the women. Oh, those
women customers! We scrutinize each lady we don't know
with seventy-seven pairs of eyes. Stealing merchandise from a
jeweler is no cinch. I can proudly boast that in my entire
career as a merchant and jewelry dealer I've never been
robbed. Because I guard this suitcase I'm holding on to like
the apple of my eye. But if you're destined for a calamity—
well, just listen and you'll hear what can happen.

I myself am not actually a jeweler. What I mean is, I *am* a
jeweler, but that's not my main occupation. I'm simply a
merchant who handles diamonds. I buy and sell them, mostly
wholesale, and mostly abroad at the fairs. But if I happen to
find a retail customer, I pick up my suitcase—this one right
here—and take a train to my destination.

Once I found out that a wealthy Yehupetz grandee was
marrying off his daughter. No doubt he needed diamonds.
But on the other hand, there were enough jewelers in Yehupetz, perhaps more than necessary. But one thing's got nothing to do with the other. I don't care if there are eighteen
thousand jewelers. Just show me a customer and I'll show you
who's going to make a sale, me or them. When it comes to
selling jewels you've got to know your business. One has to
know *what* to show, *how* to show it and *whom* to show it to. I
don't have to brag—in fact, I hate all sorts of boastfulness—

but if you mention my name among jewelers, they'll all tell you that it's not easy to compete with me. Where someone else would make a hundred, I'd clear three hundred. I know my business.

In a word, I boarded the train to Yehupetz. As you can imagine, I took quite a bit of merchandise with me. I wish all three of us would earn half of what they cost. Yet it all fitted into this very suitcase. I sat down in my seat—naturally, right next to my suitcase—and didn't budge from my place. Sleeping was out of the question. When you travel with diamonds you don't sleep. Every time a new passenger entered the car, I felt my heart in my mouth: perhaps this one's a thief. It's not written on anyone's face, you know.

I traveled one full day and night, neither eating nor sleeping. I came to the Yehupetz grandee, opened up my portable shop, talked myself blue in the face and, as usual, ended up with an ulcer instead of a sale.

I don't want to say anything nasty about rich men, but nevertheless I wish them a pack of plagues. They suck the blood out of you. They eye each item, run their fingers over it, try it on, look in the mirror, revel in it—yet when it comes down to making a deal, nothing doing! Well, that's life! Whether you make a sale or no, you have to keep moving on. For who knows what opportunities are liable to be missed? So you keep scurrying about. Naturally, I forthwith hopped into a droshky and rode to the station to catch a train. Meanwhile, I heard someone shouting behind me:

"Hey, mister, mister!"

I turned around. Lo and behold, there was a young man running after me, waving a suitcase exactly like my own.

"Here, you almost lost it," he said.

Plagues and damnation! It *was* my suitcase. But how? When? Where? Well, it was destined, I tell you. It had slipped out of my hand and that young man had picked it up. And that was that. I turned to my young man, squeezed his hands and expressed my gratitude.

"Thanks a lot! May God grant you good health and good fortune. Thanks again and again."

"Don't mention it," he said.

"What do you mean, don't mention it?" I said. "You've

just saved my life. You've just performed such a good deed that there isn't a reward large enough for you either in this world or the next. Just tell me how much you want. Go ahead. Tell me. Don't be shy."

As I put my hand into my pocket, he said to me: "Since you yourself say it's such a good deed, why should I sell it for cash?"

Hearing such talk from my young friend, I grabbed him and began to kiss him.

"Well, then let God himself repay you for what you've done for me. Will you at least join me for a bite and a glass of wine?"

"A glass of wine? Certainly. With greatest of pleasure!"

So both of us sat down in the droshky—I had forgotten all about the train—and we headed for a café to have a snack.

In the café I requested a private compartment, ordered the best of everything, and began to chat with the young man. I tell you, he took my fancy, did this young fellow whom you might very well have called my lifesaver. He was a likable chap, with a likable face and deep-set black and thoughtful eyes. In a word, a gem of a man, and terribly shy to boot. I told him not to be bashful, but to order anything his heart desired, the best and the finest of everything. Of course, no matter what he chose, I gave him double. So we ate and drank and lived it up like lords. But not to the point of intoxication, God forbid. A Jew is not a drunkard. But just to *eat, drink and be merry,* like the Bible says.

"Do you at least appreciate what you've done for me?" I said to the young man. "I'm not even talking about the fortune you've saved me. I wish me and you both earned what I owe on this merchandise. It's not even mine, you know. It belongs to someone else. You've simply saved my honor and my life, for if I had come home without this suitcase, my creditors would surely have thought it was a trick, the likes of which are often pulled by our jewelers. They get rid of their bit of merchandise and then let fly a rumor that they've been robbed. The only thing left for me to do would have been to buy a length of rope and hang myself from the first tree. Well, here's to long life! May God give you everything you wish for yourself. Be hale and hearty—and now let's kiss good-bye, for the time has come to move on."

I bade him good-bye, paid my bill at the café, turned to take my suitcase—what suitcase? There wasn't even a hint of either the suitcase or the young man. Not a trace remained.

And I fell into a dead faint.

After I passed out, someone revived me. I took one look around me and fainted once more. Then, when I was brought to again, I really raised the roof, called out the entire Yehupetz police force, promised a fat reward, followed them to the dingiest dives, searched out every rat hole, got to know the world's biggest thieves—but my fine young man had vanished into thin air. All my strength was drained. Life was no longer worthwhile. And I bedded down in a hotel room near the station and pondered the best way to commit suicide. Should I slit my throat? Hang myself? Or throw myself into the Dnieper River? And as I lay immersed in such gloomy thoughts, I heard a knock on the door. Who was it? Someone had come to take me to the police station. The bird had been caught. With the suitcase. With all the merchandise intact.

Do I have to tell you how I felt when I saw my valise and my diamonds? I passed out again. I have a funny habit: I keep fainting. When I came to, I approached the young man and said to him:

"There's something I don't understand. Would you mind explaining? For I'm at my wit's end. What's the logic behind it? You found the suitcase, you ran after me, you handed it back, and you didn't even want to be rewarded for the good deed that you'd done. But just as soon as I turned my back, you immediately made off with my merchandise, my treasure, my life. You almost ruined me. Another minute and I'd have taken my own life."

So this young man with the deep-set black and thoughtful eyes replied quite calmly: "What's one thing got to do with another? A good deed is a good deed—but stealing is my trade."

"Young man," I said to him, "who are you?"

"Who am I supposed to be?" he said. "I'm a poor Jewish

thief, alas, a family man with loads of kids and I'm a great bungler to the bargain. My trade's not a hard one, knock wood, but I can't make a go of it. Actually, I can't complain. The stealing is coming along pretty well, thank God. But the only drawback is that I don't always succeed. I've got no luck."

Only when I sat in the train did I realize that I'm a perfect ass. I could have had him freed for next to nothing. Then again, why should *I* have been his redeemer? Let somebody else take care of him.

By the way, would you gentlemen perhaps care to take a look at a pair of diamond earrings at a reasonable price? If so, I've got just the thing for you. You've never ever dreamed of such diamonds. First-class goods!

IT DOESN'T PAY TO DO FAVORS

I tell you, it doesn't pay to do favors. You hear me, Mister Sholom Aleichem. It just doesn't pay to do favors. Being that I'm good-natured and terribly softhearted I got myself into a real mess and spawned a tragedy, actually two tragedies, in my own house. Just listen. You won't be sorry if you hear me out. By the way, can you spare a cigarette? Thanks.

The good Lord wanted to give me the opportunity to do a good deed so he sent me a pair of orphans, a boy and a girl. He didn't bless me with any children of my own, so I went and got myself some. I got someone else's children, plied them with kindness, made decent human beings out of them, for which they're now thanking me with bouquets of heartaches.

First of all, let me tell you about the little orphan girl. How did I happen to get hold of an orphan girl? Here's the story. My wife had a younger sister named Pearl. I tell you, this Pearl was an extraordinary creature, second to none. All the sisters were beautiful. In fact, my wife is good-looking even now. They were so beautiful that men were willing to give a king's ransom for their hand. But that's not what I'm driving at.

My sister-in-law's marriage was described as a once-in-a-lifetime stroke of good fortune. She'd fallen into a bed of clover. Her husband was the son of a rich man, the heir not only of his father, but also of his grandfather and his childless uncle, both loaded. Wherever you looked there was money. What luck! But that's not what I'm driving at.

The only trouble was that the young man himself was an out-and-out loafer. Actually, he was quite a fine fellow.

Neither foolish nor smart-alecky. On the contrary, kind, friendly and cheerful. But what was the rub? Begging his pardon—for he's already gone to the next world—but he was a bit dissolute. He liked cards. What am I saying *liked?* He loved them heart and soul. For a card game he would have walked a hundred miles. At first he merely played sixty-six, poker, pinochle and turtle-myrtle once a month with close friends to while away the long winter nights. Then he began playing more and more with the young riffraff, with any hoodlum, scamp, lazy bum, or ne'er-do-well that came along. No need telling you that the card habit opened the door to a variety of other vices. Forgotten was the Afternoon Service. Not to mention going bareheaded or desecrating the Sabbath. Or other matters relating to Jewish tradition.

But as if on spite, my sister-in-law, Pearl, happened to be a devout woman, pious as can be. So, naturally, she couldn't stand all his whims and ways. Day and night she lay pressed into her pillow bewailing her lot until finally her health began to fail. At first little by little, then with leaps and bounds. Well, what more can I say, Pearl died. But that's not what I'm driving at.

Pearl left a child, a girl of six or seven. The father was the devil-knows-where in Odessa. He had sunk so deep into the quagmire of cardplaying that he squandered all his money, his father's money and his grandfather's inheritance. He was utterly ruined. People said that he was probably clapped into jail to the bargain. Then he tramped about somewhere, developed some outlandish disease and died in borrowed shrouds. There in a nutshell is the life story of a wastrel.

That's how their young daughter, a poor little orphan named Reyzl, came under my care. I took her when she was still a child. I myself wasn't blessed with any of my own children, you know. Consequently, I considered her mine. Everything would have been dandy, but the trouble was that too good is no good. With any other uncle a child like that would have grown up in the kitchen and been a help to the household—heating up the samovar, running errands and the like. But at my place, you understand, she was regarded as one of the family, and was treated as well as my wife when it came to clothes, shoes and food. I can't express it any better than to say she was one of us. But that's not what I'm driving at.

Later, when Reyzl grew up, I apprenticed her to a public scribe. And to tell the truth she was a bright, capable girl—quiet, honest, kind and clever, and as pretty as can be. I loved her like a daughter. Children, you know, grow like mushrooms. Before you look around—oho—you've got to start thinking of a wedding.

And as if on spite, my niece grew like a yeast cake. She was tall, healthy and beautiful. A flower of a girl—a rose. Little by little my wife prepared a trousseau for her—blouses, sheets, pillowcases. As for my part, I even planned on presenting her with a dowry of a few hundred rubles, too.

Then the matchmakers began coming around. But who could an orphan girl like that be matched up with? After all, she had no parents. Her father, begging his pardon, wasn't the finest chap in the world and, what's more, I couldn't offer a few thousand rubles dowry, either. So we had to find someone equal to her means, a young man who could support her. But where could we get a suitable match, if to a householder *she* wasn't acceptable and if a plain workingman wasn't acceptable to *me*? After all, she was my flesh and blood, my wife's sister's daughter!

So God sent a young salesman my way, a chap of about twenty or so who made a nice ruble and already had a neat little bundle of rubles put away. To make a long story short, I had a talk with that young fellow and, so help me, things worked out. He liked the idea. Then I approached her. But nothing doing. It was like talking to the wall. What was up? She didn't want him and didn't need him and that was that.

"So who else will take you?" I asked her. "Baron Hirsch's grandson?"

But go talk to the wall. She looked down at the floor and didn't say a word. But that's not what I'm driving at.

Now I have to interrupt my story in the middle and tell you a new story, which actually is part of the other story. That is, this story and the other story are really one story.

I had a sum total of one younger brother. His name was Moishe-Hershel and here's the story with him. As you can see, this story's full of such little side stories. I hope to God that what happened to him never happens to you or anyone we know. He was in the bathhouse one Friday and wanted to rinse himself with cold water. But instead he picked up a bucket of boiling water, poured it over his head and scalded himself. After suffering for eight days he died, leaving a wife and one child, a six-year-old boy named Peysi. But within six months the matchmakers were already knocking on the door proposing matches to the widow. This vexed me to the quick and I went to my sister-in-law and told her:

"If you want to get married, give me the boy."

At first, she refused. She pretended that she wouldn't hear of it. But the long and short of it was that I finally convinced her. She brought the boy to me, went off to Poland and married there. Word has it that she's not too badly off. But that's not what I'm driving at.

And so the Almighty blessed me with a son, too. I say "son" because I adopted him as my own. It so happened he was a bright lad, as bright as they come. Actually, since he's my brother's son, it really isn't right for me to praise him. But take my word for it that you won't find another such Peysi—I won't say in the entire world, but you certainly won't find his equal in our town or in the surrounding provinces.

You name it and he knew it. Reading, writing and reckoning. French, you say? He knew that, too. The fiddle? Yes, he could also play the fiddle. And to top it off, he was a strapping lad, knock wood, handsome and quick-tongued. Calling him bright would have been an understatement. What's more, I promised him a few thousand rubbles as a dowry, too, for after all he was my adopted son, practically my own flesh and blood and, glory to God, not of low birth, either. So he deserved a fine bride, right? Don't you agree? Of course, they tried offering him the best, the most illustrious matches in the world. And, naturally, I was very picky. What else? Think one can part with such a prize so readily? But that's not what I'm driving at.

To make a long story short, they offered me matches from all over: from Kamenitz, Yelisavet and Homel; from Luben and Mohliv in Lithuania; from Berditchev, Kaminke and Brod. They bathed me in gold. Dowries of ten thousand, twelve thousand, fifteen thousand, eighteen thousand! I didn't know where to turn first. So I decided it was no use crawling to far-off places. Who knows where and what I'd get myself into? Like they say: A local shoemaker is better than a distant rabbi.

In our town there was a rich man who had an only daughter. He offered a dowry of several thousand rubles. The girl herself was a fine young lady and her father wanted the match. Was there any reason, then, not to conclude it? Right? Especially since we had two matchmakers, thank God, who scurried back and forth between me and him, urging us on to go through with the match. They were in a rush, you understand, for they themselves had daughters to marry off and grown ones to boot. But that's not what I'm driving at.

To make a long story short, the upshot was that we agreed to get together for the formal engagement. But today's times aren't like those of yesterday. In olden times you arranged a match without the children knowing a thing. You came home, congratulated them and that was that. Lately the fashion has been to first have a talk with the children, to get them to meet and see whether or not they appeal to each other. Some don't even need the invitation to get together—they've already done so on their own. Which makes it all the better. So I went up to my boy and asked him:

"Peysi, darling, does so-and-so appeal to you?"

His face became red as a beet, but he didn't say a word. Silence is also a reply, I thought. No answer is an answer, too. But then why did he blush so furiously? He was probably embarrassed. So we decided that we'd get together the following night, first at the bride's house, of course, and then at my place. Well, what more was needed? So cakes were baked and dinner preparations made, as usual. But that's not what I'm driving at.

The next morning when I got up I was given a letter. Where was the letter from? Some drayman brought it. I took the letter, opened it and began reading. My head swam—I saw stars. What news did I get? You'll hear in a minute. My Peysi wrote saying that I shouldn't be angry at him for eloping with Reyzl—can you beat that?—without our knowing it. He told me not to even try to look for them, for they were far, far away. And when, God willing, they would be duly married, they would return.

Well, what do you say to a letter like that? No need telling you how my wife took the news. She fainted three times, for the whole scandal was *her* fault. Reyzl was *her* niece, not mine.

"There you have it," I told her, "you've raised a snake on your bosom."

And, as usual, I brought down upon her all the bitterness in my heart, and gave her the royal raking down she deserved. But that's not what I'm driving at.

As you can imagine, I was beside myself with rage. After all, you take a strange kid, a poor and naked little orphan girl, you raise her and want to make her happy, and she goes and pulls a stunt like that and entices my brother's son from the straight and narrow path. I yelled blue murder, stamped my feet, tore the hair from my head—I almost went out of my mind.

But then I said to myself. Will my anger help me any? What good will stamping my feet do? I have to start *doing* something. For chances were I'd still be able to catch the two of them and frustrate their plans. So first of all I turned to the authorities, greased some palms, and announced that I had a niece named so-and-so who stole my money and enticed my son—my legally adopted son—into running away with her to God-knows-where. Then I started scattering money around, sent telegrams to the four corners of the earth, to all the towns and villages in the region until, thank God, they were finally caught. Where were they caught? Not far from here. In a little village. All right. Congratulations and lots of luck!

When the glad tidings reached me that they had been nabbed, the authorities and I drove right out to that little village. Don't ask me about that trip! Words can't describe what I went through. I was on pins and needles. I was shivering with fright. Who knows? Perhaps they were already married. In that case, then it was too late. Like locking the stable door after the horse is stolen.

With God's help we came into town and discovered that they hadn't as yet seen a rabbi. But what then? There was a

new misfortune. Since I had formally declared that I had
been robbed, the local authorities had them jailed until
matters were cleared up. *Them,* mind you! *Both* of them. So
I got sick to my stomach and yelled blue murder: that it was
her fault, my niece's, that is, but that the young man, my son
I mean—for after all he *was* legally my son—was completely
innocent. But when they finally wanted to free him—Peysi, I
mean—he told me:

"Look! If you've been robbed, then both of us did it."

Can you beat that? That's what the vile vixen had enticed
him into saying. Leave it to a strumpet! Well, does it pay to
do favors? Should one have pity on a poor little orphan girl?
I'm asking you, is it worth it? Well, in any case, it cost me
plenty till I got both of them out, for on account of him I
had to drop charges against her, too. And so we came home.
But that's not what I'm driving at.

Naturally, I didn't let Reyzl set foot in my house again. I
provided her with room and board in a little village by a
relative of hers, a simple villager named Moishe-Meyer, and I
took my Peysi home and had a long talk with him.

"After all, is it right? I adopted you, I intend to give you a
few thousand rubles dowry and make you my sole heir—and
yet you go and play a dirty trick like that on me and cause
such a big scandal."

"What's the big scandal?" he said. "She's your niece, I'm
your nephew. And both of us stem from the same fine family
tree."

"How can you compare yourself with her?" I said. "Your
father was my own brother, a decent, respectable man, and
her father, begging his pardon, was a charlatan, a cardsharp."

I give a look—my wife had passed out. Pandemonium
broke loose. What was up? She couldn't bear listening to such
talk about her sister's husband.

"They're both in the true world," she said, "and we have
to leave them alone."

"Be that as it may," I said, "he was still a scoundrel."

So she fainted again. What a plague, what disaster! One
couldn't even say a word in one's own house. But that's not
what I'm driving at.

To make a long story short, I took Peysi under my wing. I

watched him like a hawk so that he shouldn't give me a
repeat performance of his disappearing act. And, God be
praised, he took to the straight and narrow path and let
himself be talked into becoming engaged. She wasn't anything special, but she did come from a fairly well-to-do home.
Her father had a good name, there was a dowry, and so forth
and so on, as befits my dignity. I was in seventh heaven. So
everything was fine and dandy, right? But just wait and you'll
hear a nifty little tale.

One day I came home from my store to have lunch. I
washed, sat down to the table, said the blessing over bread,
looked around—no Peysi. The first thought that flashed
through my head was: Perhaps he's flown the coop once
more? I turned to my wife.

"Where's Peysi?"

"I don't know," she said.

I finished eating, rushed back to town, asked around, but
no one knew anything. So I sent a messenger to her village
relative, Moishe-Meyer, to find out how Reyzl was doing. I
got a note in reply stating that Reyzl had gone away the
previous day. She said she was going to town to pay a visit to
her dear ones in the cemetery. Naturally, I got all worked up
at my wife, brought down upon her all the bitterness in my
heart, because this entire misfortune was her fault—Reyzl was
her niece, not mine.

I ran to the police, sent telegrams everywhere, scattered
money left and right. But nothing doing. Vanished without a
trace. I got busy, I yelled my head off, I grew frantic. Still
nothing doing. Anyway, three weeks passed and I almost
went out of my mind. Then suddenly I got a letter from
them which began with: "Congratulations!" They were already married, thank God, in an auspicious hour, and were
no longer in fear of me. Can you beat that? Now they would
no longer be pursued, no longer would false accusations be
hurled at them. They said they had loved each other ever
since they were children; thank heaven, they had now
achieved everything they wanted. But what would they live
on? Don't worry, they said. He was studying for the medical
school entrance exams and she was studying to be a midwife.
Meanwhile, both of them were giving private lessons and

were earning fifteen rubles a month, praise the Lord. Rent came to six and a half, food to eight, and as for the rest, why there was a God in heaven, wasn't there?

All right, I said to myself. Just wait. First let your stomach growl with hunger, then when you come knocking at my door I'll show you who's boss.

"Now you see what I mean by a rotten root begetting rotten fruit? Can something good come of a blackguard cardsharp?" I said to my wife, throwing that and similar jabs her way. But do you think that she so much as opened her mouth?

"What's the matter?" I said. "You used to pass out as soon as I said boo about your sweet brother-in-law. Why don't you faint now?"

But go talk to the wall.

"You think I don't know that you're in cahoots with those two, working hand in glove with them, and that the whole thing was your idea?"

Still she kept quiet. Didn't say a word. What *could* she say, for instance, when she realized I was right? And she knew that it rankled me. What did I do to deserve this? Was it the favors I did, which were now being repaid me? But that's not what I'm driving at.

Don't think that this was the end of the matter. Just listen and you'll hear a finer tale.

To make a long story short, a full year went by. They wrote letters, but didn't say a word about money. Then one day I suddenly got a note of congratulations. Reyzl had given birth to a boy and I was invited to the circumcision.

"Congratulations," I said to my wife. "I see your sweetie pie has brought you joy. A welcome celebration! And he's being named after your dandy brother-in-law."

She didn't say a word, but became white as a sheet. She turned on her heels, got dressed and left the house. She'll be back in a minute, I thought. I waited one hour, two, three, four—twilight came, so did nighttime, but she still hadn't returned. A pretty kettle of fish, huh? The long and the short of it was—she had left my house for theirs. Since then two years have passed and she still hasn't returned. Doesn't even intend to. Did you ever hear such a thing? First I waited awhile, hoping to get a letter from her. Seeing that I didn't hear from her, I sat down and wrote her a letter.

"Can it be?" I wrote. "How does it look for the world at large?"

Her reply was that her world was there with the children. That her grandson—it turned out that they had named him Hershele, after my brother Hershel—was dearer to her than eighteen worlds. To find another Hershele like that, she said, you'd have to travel the length and breadth of the entire world. And she wished me a prosperous and respectable old age—alone, without her.

So I wrote to my wife again and again and told her in no uncertain terms that she won't get a kopeck from me. Her reply was that she didn't need my money. I wrote her another letter to inform them that I was disinheriting all of them and would bequeath all my money to charity. She didn't sit on her hands, but wrote back that she had no cause for complaint. She said she was living quite decently; in fact, she hoped it would never be any worse, for Peysi was enrolled in the university and Reyzl was almost a midwife. They were already earning seventy rubles per month. And regarding the disinheritance, she said I could take all my money and give it away to anyone I wished. Even to a cloister! Can you beat that? And she concluded by saying that I was stark raving mad. She said everyone was ready to tar and feather me for what I'd done.

"What's the great tragedy?" she wrote. "That your brother's son married my sister's daughter? Why do you consider it beneath your dignity, you dumb oaf?

"If you would only be here and look at the way little Hershele points to his grandfather's picture and says 'gyanpa,' you'd kick yourself thirty-three times."

That's what she wrote me from their house. But that's not what I'm driving at.

Well, I ask you, mustn't a man be tougher than iron? Don't you think it burns me up to come home and roam about all by myself in an empty house? I try to figure it out. I ask you, what do I have out of life? What did I do to deserve such a bitter end? Why has such a lonely old age befallen me? Why and what for? For the favors I've done? Because I'm

terribly softhearted? Please forgive me, Mister Sholom Aleichem, but when I start talking about all this, the aggravation
brings tears to my eyes and I choke up and c . . . c . . .
can't talk!

Ah me, it doesn't pay to do favors. You listening? It just
doesn't pay to do favors!

Railroad Yarns

One of the most delightful of Sholom Aleichem's books is the one called Railroad Yarns. Subtitled "The Writings of a Traveling Salesman," the preface by a persona (an idea which Sholom Aleichem undoubtedly took from Swift, one of his favorite authors) asserts that the author is simply a businessman with absolutely no pretensions to the craft of writing. For his own amusement he has merely jotted down in a notebook the various stories he has heard on his journey.

An amazing versatility is evident in the railroad stories. In some, the train is an integal part of the plot: both the teller and event must necessarily compete with the end of the trip or the oncoming station; in others, it is just a catalyst between the narrator and his audience: the train merely provides the storyteller with the means to tell his tale.

THE STATION AT BARANOVITCH

Since no more than twenty of us occupied the third-class compartment that day, we were all quite comfortable. That is, only those of us who had managed to grab seats in time were comfortable. The rest stood. But nevertheless the standees chatted amiably with those seated. The conversation was in full swing. Everyone spoke. All at once. As usual. It was morning. Everyone had had a good night's sleep, recited his morning prayers, eaten some sort of breakfast and had a few smokes. And then everyone was in an excellent mood for talking.

About what? About anything under the sun. Everyone wanted to relate something new, lively and different, something which would make fellow passengers sit up and take notice. But nobody succeeded in arousing enthusiasm for any one topic. Every minute the subject was switched. First the talk was about the good wheat and oat crops and then—some connection!—it moved to war. The war was bandied about for no more than five minutes and then the subject was the revolution.* From the revolution it jumped quickly to the constitution and from there, naturally, to the pogroms, murders, persecutions, new decrees against Jews, the exile of entire Jewish communities from the villages, the scramble for America, as well as all the other plagues, riots and disasters which made the news during those beautiful times: bankruptcies, expropriations, martial law, hangings, starvation, cholera, the anti-Semite Purishkevitch, Azev. . . .**

---

* The revolution of 1905. [Tr.]

** Yevno Azev was an informer who simultaneously masterminded acts of terror against the Czarist regime and betrayed most of these conspirators

"A-Z-E-V!" said one man. Another repeated it. And a storm broke out in the car. Again and again the name Azev rang out from one end of the car to the other.

"No offense meant, gentlemen, but you're all a bunch of asses. What a tumult—Azhev! Foo! Great big hullabaloo—Azhev! Who is Azhev? A scroundrel, a scurvy bastard, an informer, a rat, a good-for-nothing, a worthless scamp. But if you ask me, I'll tell you a story about a real informer—one of our own Jews from Kaminke—and then you'd say that Azhev was a mere pup compared to him."

These words were spoken by one of the standees, a fleshy individual who was leaning against the side of a seat. I craned my neck and looked up to the speaker and saw beneath his Sabbath hat a red, freckled face, twinkling eyes and gap teeth, which apparently caused him to pronounce the "z" like a "zh" and to whistle "Azhev" instead of "Azev."

I took a fancy to this man right away. His exuberance, his manner of speaking and his labeling us asses apppealed to me. That's the sort of man I like and envy.

At first the Kaminke Jew's unexpected compliment momentarily stunned the crowd. As though they'd been doused with a pitcher of ice water. But they quickly recovered, exchanged glances and said to him:

"You want us to ask you—well, we're asking you. Come on, tell us what happened in Kaminke. But why are you standing? Why don't you sit down? No room, you say? Come on, friends, move over. That's it. Make room for the gentleman."

And the already crowded passengers squeezed together some more and cleared a space for the Kaminke Jew. The latter spread himself out right comfortably (like a godfather at a circumcision when the sexton shouts for the baby to be brought in), pushed his hat to the back of his head, rolled up his sleeves and began talking in his exuberant manner:

Listen carefully, my dear fellow Jews. What I'm going to tell you now is no farfetched romance that you read in cheap pamphlets and no fantasy from *A Thousand and One Nights*.

---

to his paymasters in the Czar's secret police. His double-dealing was not discovered until 1909. [Tr.]

Please understand that this story really and truly happened in our own town of Kaminke. My father himself, may he rest in peace, told me the story, and he heard it from *his* father dozens of times. Opinion has it that the story was written down somewhere in our communal book of records which was destroyed in a fire a long time ago. Laugh if you like, but I tell you it's too bad that that book went up in smoke. Folks say that the many fine stories recorded there were far better than those published nowadays in books and newspapers.

In short, this incident took place during the days of Nicholas the First, during the times of grace. Why are you smiling? Do you know what grace means? Grace means that they used to grace you by making you run the gantlet. What's the gantlet? Don't you know that either? Well, then I guess I have to clear it up for you. Imagine two lines of soldiers holding iron rods. You parade back and forth between the lines, let's say twenty times or so, and—begging your pardon— you're as naked as the day you were born. And they do what your Talmud Torah teacher used to do to you when you didn't want to study. Now you know what running the gantlet means? All right, now we can continue.

Here's the story. An order came from the governor—Vasiltchikov was governor then—to grace a certain Jew named Kivke. Who this Kivke was and what his crime was I can't say for sure. It is believed that he was a tavernkeeper by trade, a run-of-the-mill chap and an old bachelor to boot. So one Sunday the spirit moved him to get into a long theological discussion concerning "your God and my God" with a group of peasants in the tavern. One word led to another and soon the village chief and the constable were brought down and they swore out a warrant against him. So why don't you take a barrel of whiskey, you clunk, set it before them and thus make the warrant disappear?

But he said: "No! Kivke doesn't go back on his word."

So he was an obstinate mule to the bargain. You see, he thought they would simply slap him with a three-ruble fine and bid him good day. Whoever expected such a severe sentence? Making a man run the gantlet for one foolish remark. In short, they nabbed the old bachelor and clapped

him into jail until he would get his twenty-five round trips
through the gantlet, as God has ordered it.

No need telling you, of course, how the people of Kaminke
reacted to this misfortune, the news of which we received on
a Friday night. The next morning everyone gathered in the
synagogue and raised a clamor.

"Kivke's been arrested."

"He's been given the gantlet!"

"Gantlet?"

"Why? What for?"

"For nothing, for a word."

"A trumped-up charge."

"What do you mean trumped-up? He's got a big mouth."

"I don't care if he's got a dozen big mouths. Why the
gantlet? Is that fair?"

"What do they mean they're going to make a Jew run the
gantlet? One of our Kaminke Jews?"

The town seethed like a boiling cauldron all during Sabbath until after sundown. After the Prayer of Separation
everyone rushed in tumultuously to my grandfather, Reb
Nissel Shapiro.

"Is that what they call justice, Reb Nissel? Why don't you
speak up? How can you permit one of our own Kaminke
Jews to be beaten like this?"

You'll probably ask why they came running straight to my
grandfather. Well, for your information, my grandfather
(may a bright Paradise be his!) happened to be—and I'm not
saying this to boast or brag—the finest, richest, most prominent householder in town, a sensible, intelligent man who
was respected by the authorities. When the tumult subsided,
Grandpa slowly paced back and forth through the rooms of
the house (my father—may he rest in peace—told me of
Grandpa's habit: whenever Grandpa contemplated anything,
he loved to pace back and forth). Then Grandpa stopped
and exclaimed:

"Children! Return to your homes. Don't be apprehensive
at all. God willing, everything will work out. Up till now, the
Lord be thanked, no one has ever *been* beaten in Kaminke
and with God's help no one *will* be beaten."

Those were Grandfather's words. And it was common

knowledge that Reb Nissel Shapiro's word was as good as gold. But he hated questions such as: how, what and when. A man of wealth, you understand, sensible and intelligent, with influence among the authorities—a man like that was respected and held in awe. And don't you think that Grandfather's words came true? What happened? Wait and you'll soon find out.

Seeing that the crowd in the car was in suspense and wanted to hear the rest of the story, the Kaminke Jew stopped, removed a large tobacco pouch from his pocket and leisurely rolled a cigarette. So esteemed had he become in the car that several people rushed to give him a light. After he had smoked and inhaled to his heart's content, he returned to his story with renewed energy:

Now you'll hear how enterprising a wise and clever Jew can be. I'm referring to my saintly grandfather, of blessed memory. He decided upon a relatively simple ruse. To wit: he suggested to the authorities that the prisoner Kivke should drop dead for a minute or two right in jail. . . . What are you people staring at me like that for? Don't you understand? Or are you afraid that they poisoned him, God forbid? Have no fear. We don't poison people. But what *did* we do? Things were worked out in a much subtler fashion. Arrangements were made for the prisoner to go to bed in the pink of health but wake up the following morning stone-dead. Get it now? Or do I have to chew it up for you and spoon-feed you?

And that's just what happened. In the morning a messenger from the prison came and brought Grandpa a note:

"Whereas during this past night the Jewish prisoner Kivke met his demise, and whereas you are the chief trustee of the Burial Brotherhood, be it noted herewith that the remains of said deceased are to be removed and given proper Jewish burial."

What do you say to that scheme? Neat trick, huh? But wait! Restrain your joy. The plan was easier said than done. Don't forget that it wasn't just any Jew who had died. Mixed up here were soldiers . . . the governor . . . the gantlet. . . . No trifle, you know! First of all we had to be careful that there be no autopsy. So, naturally, we had to approach the doctor and ask him to sign an official paper stating that he had examined the deceased immediately after his death and found that he had died of a heart attack—a form of apoplexy, God spare us! Various other officials were contacted to sign that very paper. And that was that. No more Kivke. Defunct.

May each and every one of you earn every month the sum that that scheme cost our community. In fact, I wish *I'd* earn that much a *year*. Who accomplished all this? Grandpa, may he rest in peace. You could depend upon Grandfather. He considered all the angles, then worked out the plan neatly and cleverly, smoothly and deftly. And that very evening the sextons of the Burial Brotherhood came with the coffin. The fine corpse was ceremoniously taken from the prison and brought to the cemetery with all due honor. That is, two soldiers followed the coffin and behind them came the entire town. I tell you, Kivke never dreamt of such a grand funeral. And when they reached the gate of the cemetery, the two soldiers were given a liberal dose of whiskey and the corpse was brought inside. And there waiting with four fiery steeds was Shimon the wagoner—I'm relating the name just as I heard it from my father, may he rest in peace. And before the cock could crow our corpse was being transported beyond the cemetery fence, and in an auspicious and fortunate hour he was brought to Radivil and from there to the other side of the border—giddy-yap!—to Brod.

It goes without saying that no one slept in Kaminke until Shimon the wagoner came back from Radivil. Meanwhile, we all walked around in a dither. And more restless than the others was my grandfather, may he rest in peace. For, who knows, if he were caught at the border, that fine corpse named Kivke, and brought back alive, hale and hearty, the whole town would be packed off to Siberia.

But with God's help Shimon the wagoner returned from Radivil with his fiery steeds, bringing a letter written in Kivke's own hand:

"I herewith beg to inform you that I have arrived in Brod."

The town was ecstatic with joy. A banquet was prepared in Grandpa's house. The prison warden, the police inspector, the doctor and the rest of the officials were all invited and they lived it up. Musicians played and the guests got so drunk that the prison warden kissed my grandfather and everyone else in the family perhaps a dozen times. Toward dawn the police inspector even did a jig on the roof of the house, wearing—begging your pardon—nary a stitch of clothing. No trifle, you know, ransoming a captive. Saving a Jew from a beating. A good thing, huh? But just wait, my dear friends— for now the real to-do began. And if you want to hear some more, I'll have to ask you to bear with me for a while. At this station I must step out for a minute and ask the stationmaster to tell me exactly when we're supposed to arrive at Baranovitch. Actually, I'm going beyond that station, but at Baranovitch I have to get off and catch another train.

What could we do? We had to wait. While the Kaminke storyteller went to talk to the stationmaster about Baranovitch, the passengers discussed the Kaminke Jew and his story.
"How do you like that chap?"
"Nice fellow."
"Nice and meaty."
"Some talker."
"Glib tongue."
"Fine story."
"Too short though."
And some of the passengers recalled, by the by, that such an incident had happened in their home towns. That is, not exactly the same incident, but something like it. And since everyone wanted to tell his story, pandemonium broke loose in the car. Until the Kaminke Jew returned. When he came back, everyone fell silent, pressed together like bricks in a wall and paid close attention to his story:

Where were we? Have we already laid Kivke to rest? Yes? Is that what you think? Well, then you're mistaken, my dear friends. Six months or a year later, I can't say for sure, a certain Jew named Kivke decided to send a letter addressed to my grandfather, Reb Nissel Shapiro:
"First of all, I herewith beg to inform you that I am in the

best of health, praised be the Lord, and hope to God that I
shall hear the same from you.

"Secondly, I have no more money and no means of support, living as I do among Germans in a strange land. They
don't understand me and I don't understand them. I can
knock my brains out, but I still can't find a way to make a
living. Consequently, I am asking you to send . . ."

How do you like that wise guy? In other words, send
money. Naturally, we had a good laugh. We tore the letter
into tiny pieces and forgot about the matter. Three weeks
later another letter—this one full of complaints—came from
the corpse, one Kivke by name, again addressed to my grandfather:

"I herewith beg to inform you that I have already asked
you once to send me money. After all, what have you got
against me? Perhaps it would have been better to be beaten.
The wounds would have healed a long time ago and I would
have been able to ply my trade once more and not be
roaming around among the Germans totally idle and swollen
with hunger."

After having received such a letter, my grandfather summoned the town's leaders to his house.

"What can we do?" Grandpa said. "The man's dying of
hunger. We must send him something."

And if Reb Nissel Shapiro made a request, one could not
be a hog and refuse. So they asked for donations—it goes
without saying that Grandpa gave the biggest one—and they
sent the corpse some money and once again forgot that there
existed a Jew named Kivke.

But Kivke, you see, did not forget that there existed a town
named Kaminke. Six months or a year later, I can't say for
sure, don't you think we got another letter from him? Addressed to Grandpa in the same old style. But now there was
an added note of congratulations:

"I herewith beg to inform you that I have recently become
engaged to a fine woman from a respectable family. Consequently, I am asking you to send two hundred rubles which I
have pledged as a dowry, or else the match is off."

Well, what do you say to a plague like that? There were
chances that Kivke might remain without a bride, God for-

bid. Like some rare treasure, the letter made the rounds in Kaminke. Everyone had a good laugh over it. People were actually in stitches. And the jibes flew around town:

"Oho, congratulations! Wish us luck!"

"Well what do you know? Kivke's gonna be a groom."

"Have you heard? A two-hundred-ruble dowry."

"And a respectable bride to boot!"

"Ha-ha-ha."

This joke, however, did not have a very long life-span, for a fortnight later Grandpa received another letter; however, this time Kivke's customary opening salutation was missing:

"I'm rather surprised that I haven't as yet received the two hundred rubles which I have pledged as a dowry. Consequently, if the stated sum is not immediately dispatched the match will be called off, and out of sheer humiliation I shall either have to drown myself in the river or be forced to return with just the shirt on my back to Kaminke."

The latter phrase was like a blow in the breadbasket and the townspeople stopped laughing. That very night the most prominent householders had a meeting at Grandpa's house. The decision was that Grandpa along with some of the town's foremost citizens, begging their honors' pardon, should betake themselves from door to door with a large kerchief and collect money for Kivke's dowry. Was there any choice? And to add insult to injury, we even had to write him a congratulatory letter wishing him loads of good fortune upon this auspicious occasion and hoping that he and his wife would be blessed with many years of wealth and honor and live to see grandchildren growing up et cetera and so forth.

The strategy behind this was that after his marriage Kivke would be in such a dither that he would forget that Kaminke ever existed. But the upshot was exactly the reverse. Six months or a year later, I can't say for sure, don't you think we got another letter from him? What now?

"I herewith beg to inform you that I am now married, thanks be to God, having had the good luck to find a fine Jewish woman, may all Jewish men be blessed with her like. Yet one cannot have all the good virtues. For my wife's got a father—may he be the atonement for us all. He's a liar, a finagler, a swindler, an honest-to-goodness crook. He bamboozled the two hundred rubles out of my hands, then kicked my wife and me out on the street. Consequently, I am asking you to send me two hundred additional rubles immediately. If not, my only other alternative is to jump into the river or come directly home with just the shirt on my back."

Now this really vexed the town, and no joking either. A double dowry? That already smacked of knavery. The decision was to ignore his letter completely. But Kivke made his own decision. He waited two or three weeks and then sent another letter, addressed as usual, to my grandfather:

"I herewith beg to inform you that I have not yet received the money. Why the delay? Why don't you send out the two hundred rubles? The most I'll wait is ten days. If the stated sum does not arrive by then, Kaminke will in due course have me as a guest, God willing, and let us say—Amen!"

There's a wily scoundrel for you!

There's no need telling you how this infuriated and rankled everyone. But what could be done? Another meeting in Grandpa's house and once more a committee made up of our foremost citizens marched from door to door with a large kerchief. The townspeople hesitated. They weren't overly anxious to send that crook any more money. But the committee would not take no for an answer. Especially if Reb Nissel Shapiro asked them to contribute, no one could be a hog and refuse. But everyone gave with the express condition that this was absolutely the last time. Grandfather himself echoed their sentiments. And thus they wrote Kivke, stating explicitly that this was positively the last time any money would be sent to him, and that he should not even dare mention the word money again.

Of course, this remark scared the wits out of that thief! That's what you think! So one fine morning, just before a holiday, we get another letter from that crook (addressed to Grandpa, of course). What did he want now?

"I herewith beg to inform you that I have met a German Jew in Brod, a very decent and honest fellow, and have gone into partnership with him in a porcelain and china shop. This is a good, sound business from which one can derive an excellent living. Consequently, I herewith request that in the name of God you send me four hundred and fifty rubles. And immediately, too—so don't dillydally in sending it out, for my partner is impatient. He's got other prospective partners, dozens of them and if, God forbid, I don't take this business, I'll remain without a business. And if I'm without a business there's only one thing for me to do—jump into the river or come home with just the shirt on my back."

His usual style. But he concluded it with a threat that if he would not receive the four hundred and fifty rubles in two weeks it would cost them more, for they would have to reimburse him for the round trip from Brod to Kaminke.

The nerve of that sponger!

I don't have to tell you what sort of miserable holiday we had. Especially, Grandfather. Grandfather, may he rest in peace, alas, had the worst part of it. For at the meeting after the holiday the community began to complain and protest:

"Enough! There's a limit! How much longer does he expect to extort money from us? Everything in moderation, knishes included! Your Kivke is going to make beggars of us all."

So agreed the townspeople.

"Since when is he *my* Kivke?" Grandfather retorted.

"Whose then? Whose idea was it that that bastard should suddenly get apoplexy in prison?"

Hearing this, Grandfather understood (he was quite a clever man) that his efforts would be in vain—the townspeople would give no more money. So he turned to the authorities. After all, they were in the same boat along with everyone else. Perhaps they would contribute something, too. Fiddlesticks! A gentile's not a Jew, you know. A gentile doesn't give a damn. What concern of theirs was it that Grandfather, begging his honor's pardon, had to dig into his own pocket and send some money to that murderer, may he fry in hell. Grandfather also sent Kivke the letter he deserved. My grandfather, may he rest in peace, could show his colors if he wanted to.

In that letter Grandpa gave him a verbal tongue-lashing. He called him a scoundrel, a crook, a rogue, a boor, a sinner, a bloodsucker, a leech, an evil monster, a spiteful apostate and so on. He told him once and for all not to dare write any more and never again mention money. He reminded him that there was a God in heaven who saw all, knew all and repaid everything with interest. And Grandpa concluded the letter (he had a Jewish heart, after all) with a plea to Kivke to have mercy on an old man and not to bring misfortune upon an entire community. And by virtue of this the good Lord would help him succeed in all his undertakings.

That's the sort of letter my grandfather, may he rest in peace, wrote Kivke. And Grandpa signed it with his full name: Nissel Shapiro. But that was—may he forgive me—a great piece of folly on his part, as you shall soon hear when I continue the story.

Here the Kaminke Jew stopped again, took out the tobacco pouch, leisurely rolled a cigarette, inhaled deeply once, twice, three times—unmindful of the fact that everyone was burning with curiosity, dying to know the crux of the story. After he had smoked and coughed to his heart's content, he blew his nose, rolled up his sleeves and proceeded in his usual fashion:

You probably think, my dear friends, that my grandfather's letter frightened that son of a bitch? Not in the least! Six months or a year later that scoundrel sent us another letter: "I herewith beg to inform you that my partner, the German, may all my nightmares seep into his skull, swindled all my money, stripped me from top to toe and threw me out of the store. I even wanted to swear out a warrant against him and start proceedings, but I saw that it would be a wild-goose chase. For if you bring suit against a German you might as well kiss your life good-bye. They are such bastards that one dare not come within earshot of them. So I thought I'd be better off renting a store next to his, right next door, in fact. And I plan to open up a new store, in which I'll also sell porcelain and china, and with the help of God I'm going to bury that German so quickly he'll be groveling in the dirt before I'm through with him. There's only one thing—for all this I'll need cash, one thousand rubles at the very least. Consequently, I am asking you to send . . ." So wrote Kivke, concluding with these words: "And if you don't send me the thousand rubles within eight days, I will immediately send your last letter, signed with your own signature, 'Nissel

Shapiro,' to the governor's office and tell them the entire story from A to Z: my apoplexy in the prison, my resurrection at the cemetery, my safe trip to Brod with Shimon the wagoner and my receipt of the several installments of hush money you sent me. I will tell them everything. Let them know that we have a mighty God and that Kivke did not die."

How is that for a greeting? As soon as Grandpa read that sweet letter he became sick to his stomach. Ready to pass out. God save us, he became para— Oh my goodness, the train stopped! Where are we?

"Baranovitch . . . Baranovitch . . ." cried the conductors running by the windows of our car.

Hearing the name Baranovitch, the Kaminke Jew jumped up from his seat, snatched his bundle—some sort of nondescript sack stuffed with God-knows-what—and dragged it to the door. A moment later he was already on the platform, sweating and pulling the sack through the crowd and asking everyone:

"Baranovitch?"

"Baranovitch!"

It sounded like some sort of exotic greeting.

"Baranovitch?"

"Baranovitch!"

Many in our car (including me) dashed out and grabbed the Kaminke Jew by the shoulders.

"Hold your horses, uncle! You're not going to get away that easily. You're going to have to tell us the end of the story."

"What end? That's just the beginning. Leave me alone! Do you want me to miss my train on account of you? What a strange bunch of Jews! Don't you hear what the conductors are saying? We're at Baranovitch."

And before we had a chance to turn around there wasn't even a trace of the Jew from Kaminke.

Blast that station at Baranovitch!

TWO ANTI-SEMITES

Max Berliyant was a shrewd chap who traveled back and forth from Lodz to Moscow several times a year. He knew the buffet proprietors in every station and was on good terms with all the conductors. He traveled into the distant provinces where a Jew was forbidden to remain more than twenty-four hours, sweated it out in dozens of police stations, suffered a host of humiliations, was often upset and ate his heart out—and all because of Jews. That is, not because of the existence of Jews, but because he himself—don't breathe a word of it!—was Jewish. And not so much because he himself was Jewish as the fact that he, alas and alack, *looked* Jewish. It was his face, oh that Jewish face: gleaming black eyes and glossy, black, honest-to-goodness Semitic hair. His pronunciation, with its gargled r's, was sheer murder, Jewish to the core. And he had a nose to the bargain—and what a nose it was!

Moreover, as if on spite, our hero was punished with the sort of occupation (he was a traveling salesman) wherein he had to follow—and display—his nose over the length and breadth of the entire world and talk, talk without letup. In other words, he had to be seen *and* heard. In a nutshell, he was a pitiful creature.

In retaliation, our hero took revenge upon his beard—he sliced it right off. He was always spruced up in the finest clothes, including a most extraordinary tie, which his grandfather, I assure you, would have used to tie bundles. His moustaches were curled and he cultivated a long nail on his little finger. He grew accustomed to the foods served at the buffets, and poured out his bitter heart to pork chops. May all swine succumb to half the plagues that Max wished them the first time he tasted pig meat! Soon—there was no helping it—he risked life and limb and began eating lobsters.

Why do I say risked life and limb? I'll tell you why. May your enemies know as much about good health as Max Berliyant knew about lobsters. He didn't even have the faintest notion of how to deal with one. Do you cut it with a knife, stick it with a fork, or swallow it whole?

But despite all these concessions on his part, Max still could not conceal his Jewishness, either from his own people or from strangers. He was spotted as quickly as a false coin, just like the accursed Cain; and wheresoever he went he was given to understand *who* he was and *what* he was. In a nutshell, he was a pitiful creature.

2

But if Max Berliyant was unhappy before the Kishinev pogrom, after it he was certainly the most miserable man in the world. The hell of suffering and simultaneously being ashamed of heartfelt anguish could be appreciated only by one who underwent such torture. Max was ashamed of Kishinev as though it were *his* town. And as if on spite, his firm sent him to Bessarabia right after the Kishinev pogrom. On his way to that notorious region he felt that another period of hellish agony was beginning for him. Hadn't he had his fill of those hair-raising reports back home? Wasn't his heart full of sorrow, anger and woe over those murders, the likes of which the world had never seen? Would he ever forget that moment in the synagogue when old men wept and women fainted as the Memorial Prayer was recited for the martyrs of Kishinev?

No doubt your train has passed a place where a catastrophe had once occurred. Yet you sit at ease, confident that such a disaster cannot happen twice at the same place. But still you remember that not too long ago several cars had gone off the tracks at this very spot and tumbled down the slope. Here people were decapitated, bones were crushed, blood and marrow spilled—and you breathe a sigh of relief when you pass that place unharmed.

Max knew that in and about Bessarabia he would surely

hear plaintive and doleful stories about the Kishinev pogrom from the Jews—and insults and sarcastic jibes from the non-Jews. And the closer he came to that region the more he sought a means of escape and a way of hiding from himself.

When he first approached his destination he wanted to remain secluded in his car. Then he reconsidered and along with some other passengers jumped down to the station platform and marched up to the buffet with an air of spirited self-confidence. He drank a tumbler of whiskey, ate an assortment of forbidden snacks, had a glass of beer as a chaser and lit a cigar. Jauntily puffing away, he strolled to the newsstand, where he spotted *The Bessarabian,* the notorious anti-Semetic gazette of the infamous Jew-hater, Krushevan.*

For your information, in the very regions where that despicable paper was baked fresh daily, it did not even move from the counter of the newsstand. No one so much as picked it up. The local Jews considered it contemptible filth; even the non-Jews were thoroughly disgusted with it. Consequently, it lay placidly on the counter, merely reminding the world of the existence of a certain Krushevan who neither rested nor slumbered, but sought means to make the world safe and secure from that dangerous disease known as Judaism.

Max Berliyant was the only passenger who approached the newsstand and requested an issue of *The Bessarabian.* Why? Perhaps for the same reason he ordered lobsters. Or perhaps he wanted to see what a son of a bitch like Krushevan wrote about Jews. According to some people, most of the anti-Semitic papers are read by Semites—that is, if you'll pardon me for saying so, by the Jews themselves. The publishers realize this, but their view is that though the Jew is a swine, his money is absolutely kosher.

In a nutshell, our Max bought a copy of *The Bessarabian,* took it into the train, stretched himself out on the seat and covered himself with the paper, just as one would with a blanket or a quilt. And while so doing, a thought flew through his mind:

---

* P. A. Krushevan bore heavy responsibility for the Kishinev pogrom of 1903. [Tr.]

Let's see. What would a Jew think if he came up and saw someone stretched out and covered with *The Bessarabian?* He'd never suspect that there was another Jew underneath it. So help me, that's a great way of getting rid of any Jew entering the car. No one will disturb me and I'll be able to stretch out like a lord all night long and have the entire length of the bench to myself.

And in order that no mortal know who slept there, our hero covered his nose, his eyes, his hair—in fact, his entire Jewish countenance—with *The Bessarabian* and imagined the following scene:

A Jew laden with packages scrambles into the car during the night, looking for a seat, alas, and sees someone stretched out and covered with an issue of *The Bessarabian.* The Jew no doubt assumes that the man before him is a nobleman, an evilhearted man and an anti-Semite—perhaps even Krushevan himself. The poor Jew with the packages jumps back and spits three times, while he, Max, remains undisturbed, occupying the entire row like a lord.

Ha-ha-ha, so help me, that's a great way of getting privacy. It's better than suddenly breaking out with a case of cholera in the middle of a journey. . . .

Max was so pleased with his plan that he began to laugh underneath his copy of *The Bessarabian.* And for your information, a man who has had a snack, a glass of beer and a cigar, and lay stretched out at night like a lord on an entire row of seats—a man like that had all the reason in the world to laugh.

But ssh! Let's be still while our hero, Max Berliyant, the traveling salesman who covered the Lodz-Moscow route, lay asleep on a bench, covered with an issue of *The Bessarabian.*

So let's not disturb his sweet dreams.

3

Max Berliyant was indeed a clever man, but this time his plan was not successful. For soon a husky, strapping man entered the compartment completely out of breath. He carried several suitcases, approached the stretched-out Max, looked him over and noted that he was covered with an issue of *The Bessarabian*. But he did *not* spit three times and did *not* jump back. He just stood there, contemplating the creature before him, that anti-Semite with the Semitic nose. (During Max's snooze the paper had slid down a bit, exposing his stigma—his nose, that is—which now revealed itself in all its might and glory.)

Our newcomer stood for a few minutes with a smile on his lips; then he set his suitcases on the bench opposite Max, slipped out to the station for a while and also returned with an issue of *The Bessarabian*. He opened one suitcase, removed a pillow, a blanket, a pair of slippers and a bottle of eau de cologne. He made himself quite at home, stretched himself out on his bench and, like Max Berliyant, covered himself with his copy of *The Bessarabian*. He lay there smoking, looking at Max and smiling. First he closed one eye, then the other and gradually fell asleep.

Now that our two Bessarabians were asleep on opposite benches, we can tell our readers all about the newcomer.

He was a general. . . . Not a general in the military and not a governor-general, but an inspector-general for an insurance company. Although his family name was Nyemtchik and his surname Khaim, he signed himself Albert and was called Peti.

At first glance it would seem a bit wild. For Albert to blossom into Khaim is no problem, but how in heaven's name did Khaim turn into Peti? A profound question indeed. But after some serious linguistic research we can now give a logical reply: First of all, from Khaim we remove the "Kh"; then, with all due respect, we evict, respectively, the "i" and "m"—leaving the "a" all alone. To the latter letter we then attach "l," "b," "e," "r" and "t"—now doesn't that add up to Albert? Albert them simply becomes Alberti, Berti, Beti, Peti. *Sic transit gloria mundi*—that's how a sick duckling makes the glorious transition into a swan.

In a nutshell, our newcomer, Peti Nyemtchik, was an inspector-general and traveled about just like Max Berliyant. But Peti was altogether a different sort. He was jolly, high-spirited and talkative. And although he was called Peti and held the rank of inspector-general, he was nevertheless a plain, ordinary chap who liked his own people and adored telling stories and anecdotes about them.

Peti Nyemtchik's anecdotes had won far-flung fame. The only drawback was that he swore upon everything that's holy that each anecdote had happened to him personally. But since he forgot from one telling to the next, the locale of the anecdote always changed. Apparently, Inspector-General Peti Nyemtchik loved to exaggerate and lay it on thick. Back home he would have been called—and I hope you'll excuse the brusque expression—a liar. Perhaps I should merely have said that he was an insurance agent—since you all know an agent's penchant for tall tales.

Upon entering the car and seeing our Max stretched out on the bench and covered with an issue of *The Bessarabian*— Peti realized from the looks of Max's nose that Max was no crony of Krushevan nor of his fine gazette—the first thought that flashed through Peti's mind was: Here's an anecdote, a brand-new anecdote. With God's help he would now have something to talk about. So he dashed out to the station, armed himself with a copy of *The Bessarabian* and lay down opposite Max to see what would happen. And soon he was fast asleep.

Now we leave our second Bessarabian, Inspector-General Peti Nyemtchik and we return to our first Bessarabian, Traveling Salesman Max Berliyant.

4

Max Berliyant had a rough night. . . . Apparently the various snacks he had consumed at the station disagreed with him, for he had the most fantastic nightmares. For instance, he dreamt that he was not Max Berliyant but Krushevan, the editor of *The Bessarabian;* that he was not riding on a train, but on a pig; and that a bright red, boiled lobster was beckoning to him with its antennae. From somewhere came the sound of weeping: "Ki-shi-nev!" A wind blew into his ears and he heard the rustling of leaves or women's dresses. He wanted to open his eyes but could not. He groped for his nose but no trace of it remained. Instead of a nose he found an issue of *The Bessarabian*. He didn't know where he was;

he wanted to move but could not. He realized that he was
dreaming but could not break the web of sleep; he had
absolutely no control over his own will. He lay there in
helpless lethargy suffering great anguish. Sensing his energy
being sapped away, he plucked up his last ounce of strength
and let out a soft moan, audible only to himself. He opened
one eye just wide enough to be able to see and discerned a ray
of light and the form of a person lying stretched out opposite
him; he, too, occupied an entire bench; he, too, was covered
with an issue of *The Bessarabian*. Our Max was flabbergasted
and thunderstruck. He imagined that it was he himself he
saw stretched out on the other bench. Max could not understand what in the world he was doing on the other bench, and
how anyone could possibly see his own reflection without a
mirror. Max felt his hairs bristling, standing up one by one.

But gradually Max regained his composure and began to
realize that the other man stretched out on the bench was not
Max, but someone else. The problem was how did that
individual get here, especially on that bench, and with *The
Bessarabian* to boot?

Our Max had no patience to wait for morning. He wanted
a quick solution to the enigma; in fact, he wanted it forthwith. So he stirred and began to rattle the newspaper. He
heard that his opposite on the other bench also moved and
began to rattle *his* newspaper. Then Max stopped, took a
good look and saw the other man gazing at him with a half-
smile. And thus our two Bessarabians each lay on their
respective benches silently staring at each other. Both anti-
Semites were itching, dying to know who the other was. But
each restrained himself with all his might and remained
silent. Then Peti had a brainstorm; he softly began whistling
the well-known refrain from a famous Yiddish folk song:

> In the fireplace
> the wood is burning . . .

At which Max began to accompany him, softly whistling,
too:

> And the house is hot . . .

Our two anti-Semites slowly assumed a sitting position and cast away *The Bessarabian*. Now both joined in the next line of the famous Yiddish folk song, whistling no longer, but indeed singing the words out loud:

> And the *rebbi* teaches
> little children
> the *alef-beys* . . .

SIXTY-SIX

This story was told to me by a fellow passenger, an apparently respectable sixty-year-old Jew who was a traveling salesman like myself and perhaps even a merchant. As has been my custom of late, I am relating the story to you word for word as he told it to me:

If getting acquainted with some passengers and having someone to chat with is all you have to look forward to while traveling—why you can go out of your mind.

First of all, not all passengers are the same. There are some who love to chatter on without end. They leave you with your head spinning and your ears ringing. Then there are those who remain silent. Absolutely tongue-tied. Why they don't want to talk, I don't know. Perhaps they're in a bad mood. Perhaps they're silently suffering from stomach ulcers, depression or toothache. Perhaps they've slipped out to take a breather from a hell-ridden house, a nagging wife, bad children, nasty neighbors, rotten business—who knows what in the world can be troubling the next fellow?

Find some other pastime, you say. If there's no one to talk to—leaf through a newspaper or read a book. Oho, a newspaper! But traveling is not like being at home. At home I have *my* paper. I'm as used to my paper as I am to my slippers. Your slippers may be brand-new, but mine are old and tattered and—pardon my image—they look like pancakes. Yet my slippers have one advantage which yours do not: they are *mine*.

Forgive the comparison, but what's true for slippers is true for newspapers. Take my next-door neighbor. He subscribed to one paper and I to another.

"Look, why do we both have to have two separate subscriptions?" I once told him. "How about splitting the cost of my paper and we'll only have to pay for one?"

So he heard me out and said, "With pleasure. Great idea. We'll split the cost of *my* paper."

"But your paper is a rag," I said, "while mine is a first-class journal."

"Who told you that *my* paper is a rag?" he said. "Perhaps it's just the other way around?"

"Since when are you a connoisseur of newspapers?" I asked him.

"Who says *you're* a connoisseur?"

"Well," I said, "if you're just a common smart aleck, I have nothing else to say to you."

To make a long story short, he stayed with his paper and I with mine. And so it remained for a long time.

One day during the Odessa cholera epidemic, which I don't wish on anyone, the following happened. Both my neighbor and I had business in Odessa. He had his business and I had mine. Once we both went down the stairs and met the newspaper delivery boy. Having taken the newspapers, he his and I mine, we both strolled on the sidewalk, scanning the pages. He his and I mine. What does one read first? The late bulletins. So I looked and saw that the first bulletin was datelined Odessa.

"Yesterday 230 people fell victim to cholera and 160 died. . . . Tolmatshov has summoned the trustees of all the synagogues, and so on and so forth."

Ah, well, never mind that anti-Semite Tolmatshov and all the synagogue trustees. That's no news for me. If he wouldn't keep himself busy with synagogues, his name wouldn't be Tolmatshov. What interested me was the Odessa cholera epidemic. So I called to my neighbor—after all, I couldn't be rude; he shared the sidewalk with me:

"What do you say to the news from Odessa? Another cholera epidemic."

"Impossible," he exclaimed.

This made me mad. "What do you mean, impossible?"
And I began reading the bulletin from my paper:

"Yesterday 230 people fell victim to cholera and 160 died.
. . . Tolmatshov has summoned the trustees of all the synagogues, and so on and so forth."

So my neighbor heard me out and said: "We'll see in a
minute." And he stuck his nose into his paper. Which made
me madder than ever, so I said:

"You mean to tell me that your paper has different late
bulletins?"

"One can never tell," he mumbled.

Which made me even more furious.

"Or do you think that your paper is referring to another
Odessa, another cholera epidemic and another Tolmatshov?"

He didn't answer, but kept scanning the late bulletins for
news of Odessa. Well, that's what one gets for talking to an
uncivilized boor.

That's why I say no to newspapers. While traveling in a
train there is a much better pastime—cards. A game of sixty-
six.

Generally speaking, cards are an evil passion. You know
that yourself. But on a trip cards are a blessing. If you set up
a game in the car, you don't even notice the time flying by.
Of course you have to have the right partners. Because sometimes, and I don't wish this on anyone, you can fall into a
terrible trap. You always have to be on the lookout not to
cross the path of those cardsharps who make martyrs of
innocent bystanders.

Of course it's hard to tell a gentleman from a gambler. In
fact, most of these rascals look like pitiful creatures, innocent
as babes. They pose as milksops, play fixed games among
themselves and pretend to get excited over small losses. They
keep this up until they inveigle you into their setup. They let
you win the first game, the second, even the third, until
finally the cards do a somersault and you begin to lose. And
then you're a cooked goose. You can be sure that you won't
get away until you've lost your watch, chain and every other
valuable. You sense that you've fallen into the hands of a
pack of crooks, yet you still creep like a little lamb right into
the jaws of the wolf. Boy, do I know these characters! They

taught me a lesson, and the tuition was sky-high! I can tell you so many stories about them it would fill a book. For when you travel by train, you get to hear plenty.

For instance, there's a story about a cashier who was traveling with a huge sum of his firm's money. He played cards with those scoundrels and lost so much money—every last kopeck, in fact—that he wanted to jump out the window.

Then there's one about a young man who had just completed his tenure of free board at his father-in-law's house in Warsaw. He carried a huge dowry with him, gambled away every kopeck of it and passed out on the spot.

I can tell you another story about a student who was going home to Tchernigov for the High Holy Days. He had a few rubles with him which he had sweated and slaved for by tutoring during the summer. At home a poor old mother and a sick sister were waiting for him. . . .

As you see, these stories have the same beginning and the same ending. And no one knows these stories as well as I do. I assure you, *I* won't be enticed so quickly any more. No, sir! I got burned once. And that's enough. I can spot those crooks a mile away and tell you who's a swindler and who isn't. And that's why I observe the following hard-and-fast rule: I never play cards with a stranger. Shower me with gold, but during a train trip I just never play cards. Except, of course, for a twosome of sixty-six. That I'll play without a moment's hesitation. I ask you, is there any danger in a twosome of sixty-six? Espcially with my own cards? So who's there to be afraid of? I always travel with my own deck of cards. Like a Jew—forgive the comparison—with his own prayer shawl and phylacteries.

I must confess, I love a game of sixty-six. Sixty-six is a Jewish game. I don't know how *you* play it, but I play it the old way. When you have a king and queen of any suit it's 20; if it's trumps, it's 40. The nines can be exchanged for another card. When you have a trick, you can cover it; if not, you can't. Decent enough, right? That's how all the Jews play it, that's how we play it at home, and that's how I play it on a trip. You're looking at a man who can sit down—only while on a train, of course—to a game of sixty-six and play day and

night without a break. There's only one thing I can't stand.
Someone standing behind me and looking into my hand, or
kibitzing and telling me when to cover and when not to. But
the truth is—God forgive me—Jews are an obnoxious bunch.
It's impossible to play sixty-six when there are other Jews
around, for you're immediately surrounded by onlookers,
each of them is a top-notch cardplayer and an expert at sixty-
six. There's no escaping them. There's no chasing them away.
They're like summer flies. Shoo them away, insult them as
much as you will, it doesn't do any good.

"Say, pal, who asked for your advice?"

"Mister, who sent for you?"

"If you don't mind, sir, how about not slouching over my
shoulder. Your breath isn't perfume, you know!"

But it's like talking to a stone wall.

One such kibitzer once got us into a real fix—I tell you, we
were glad to escape with our skins. This story's just too good
to keep to myself. I've simply got to tell it to you.

It happened during the winter. On a train. The car was
crowded. Hot as a Turkish bath. Hardly any seats, Jews, God
bless 'em, a-plenty. Like stars in the sky. Shoulder to shoulder. So tight there wasn't even room for a pin to squeeze
through. And that's where the good Lord sent me a partner
for a game of sixty-six. A quiet, unpretentious Jew, dying for
a round of sixty-six, just like me. We looked for a spot to lay
our deck of cards. Not to be had for love or money. So what
does the good Lord do? On the bench opposite ours a monk,
wrapped in a lambskin coat, was stretched out face down and
fast asleep. His healthy snores, knock wood, trumpeted
through the length and breadth of the car. My partner and I
exchanged glances. We understood each other at once. A fat,
sleek, well-fed monk with a soft fur coat—him God had
destined for our game of sixty-six. So without wasting a
moment we placed our deck of cards on the monk's whatcha-
macallit and began to play.

I remember it as clearly as though it had happened yesterday. Spades were trumps. I had the queen, the ten and the
king of trumps, the ace of clubs, and the king of diamonds.
The sixth card was . . . let me see. . . . It slips my mind
now. Either a jack or a queen of hearts. I think it was a jack.

But it could have been the queen. But it makes no difference now, anyway. The main thing was that I had a beauty of a hand, a godsend. The king and queen of trumps gave me a sure 40, and I was all set to rack up three full points. The only question was what would my partner open with? If he would lead with clubs I'd consider him an angel. Boy would I love him for that!

And that's just what happened. My partner thought and pondered at great length (God Almighty, I said to myself, what will he think up?), and finally opened with a ten of clubs. I practically jumped up and kissed him. And I want you to know I'm the sort of person who hates to see others getting excited when I play sixty-six. My motto is: Take it easy, take it slow. I've got plenty of time. In fact, I like to play a slow game. So I rubbed my forehead and faked a worried look. What do I care? Let my partner have a moment of pleasure. Let him think I was in trouble. But go be a prophet and know that behind your shoulders there stood a kibitzer, may he stand on his head, and eyed my cards, may his eyes run out. Seeing the ten of clubs, the kibitzer pulled the ace of clubs out of my hand, covered the ten, and slammed the palm of his hands down on the deck of cards resting on the monk's fur-coated rear end and shouted:

"Covered!"

Ten baths couldn't have washed away all the filthy insults that monk hurled at me. May all the curses which he spewed at me bounce right back at him. He threatened to get off at the first stop and send a telegram to that notorious anti-Semite, Purishkevitch. Well, I ask you? Isn't that the last straw?

But all this isn't the main point of the story. I just wanted you to get an idea of what an ardent fan of sixty-six like me goes through for the sake of a game. Actually, I still haven't even begun the story I wanted to tell you. Just listen.

This incident also took place during a winter train ride. At this time of the year. On Hanuka. I was traveling to Odessa and carrying a small fortune with me—may we both earn as much every month. I observe the following hard-and-fast rule when I carry money with me: I never sleep. Actually I'm not afraid of thieves, for when I carry money I keep it right over here, see, in my breast pocket, in a good wallet tied with two lengths of cord. A thief couldn't touch it with a ten-foot pole. But just the same, you know how it is today—hooligans and expropriations! One can never tell! So I sat all alone. That is, not exactly alone. There *were* other passengers, but no Jews. What good were they? There was no one to join me in a game of sixty-six.

Meanwhile, as I sat there, worried and longing for a fellow Jew, the door of our car opened up—we were still several stations away from Odessa—and in walked two passengers. And Jews to boot. I can spot a Jew immediately, even though he's dressed like a dozen Russian noblemen. He can even talk Turkish! One was an old man, the other rather young. Both wore fine fur coats and elegant hats. Elegant isn't even the word for it! They put away their suitcases, took off their fur coats and hats, smoked some cigarettes, even offered me one, and exchanged a few words. At first, of course, we spoke Russian, then we switched to Yiddish.

"Where are you from? Where are you going?"

"Where are *you* headed for?"

"Odessa."

"Odessa? That's where I'm headed for."

"In other words, all three of us are headed for Odessa."

One word led to another and we soon got to talking.

"Do you know what holiday we're celebrating today?"

"Which one?"

"Have you forgotten? Hanuka!"

"My goodness, Hanuka. On Hanuka it's a pious duty to play cards. Sixty-six!"

"Right you are!"

At which the younger of the two jumped up and pulled a deck of cards out of his companion's pocket and said to him:

"Papa? How about a game of sixty-six in honor of Hanuka?"

Which meant they were father and son. I thought it would be fun to see how a father and son played sixty-six. I myself was rather anxious to play. But like they say, I didn't give in to temptation and contented myself by watching them.

They turned a suitcase on its side, set it between their legs, and after drawing for the deal, which the father won, they proceeded to play. I sat at the old man's side and looked at his cards. While playing, the old man casually asked me if I was familiar with this game. Naturally, I burst out laughing. Some question! Asking the inventor of sixty-six himself if he knew the game. So I sat on the side and watched the father and son playing.

I had to be made of iron to restrain myself, for that old fox was making such idiotic moves it killed me. Imagine, the man held two trump cards, plus an exchangeable nine, the two high spades—the ten and the king—and one club. So why don't you play your club and perhaps you'll buy another trump and get 40 points? You might even be able to take a trick. But no! *He* played the king, the lesser spade, and was left like a dumbbell holding a strong ten of spades. So, leading with trumps, the son neatly won two tricks in a row. Then he took his father's ten of spades, showed a king and a queen for 20, and good-bye and good luck. And since the son got sixty-six before the father had won one trick, he scored three full points.

That was one game.

During another game it was even worse. It was sheer murder. Listen to this. The old man already had six points. All he needed was a seventh to win the game. His opponent— that is, his son—only had two. That old libertine had three trumps as well as a clear 20 in his hand. So he covers without drawing for trumps. Can you imagine? That fool would rather declare his 20. So his opponent—his son, that is—went and took away the 20, plus the trump card and another card, declared 20 himself and scored three full points. Now this infuriated me. What a miserable Hanuka this turned out to be. I just couldn't stand it any longer.

"Pardon me," I said to the old lecher. "I observe a hard-and-fast rule of not kibitzing. But for curiosity's sake, I wish you'd explain your reason for covering just a moment ago. I beg you, please tell me the logic behind it. If your partner has a lousy hand, why then you're in the clear. But even supposing he had a great hand, what's the difference? What have you got to lose? Only one full point! After all, you've already racked up six points to his two. It's an out-and-out crime to play that way."

That old dog kept mum, but his son and heir smiled.

"Papa is a very poor player. Papa can't play sixty-six at all."

"Your papa shouldn't be *allowed* to play sixty-six. When it comes to sixty-six let *me* do the playing."

But the old hound wouldn't step down under any circumstances. He continued making such bad moves that I felt an apoplectic fit coming on. Finally, after much pleading on my part, the old axle-greaser gave me the cards for no more than two or three games.

"In honor of Hanuka," I said, "let me, too, be worthy of a pious deed."

"What stakes?" said the son.

"Name them?" I said.

"A ruble a point."

"All right," I said, joking, "but on condition that your papa doesn't kibitz and give you any advice, God forbid."

They burst out laughing. We began to play. One game, a second, a third. Thank heaven, everything went smoothly for me. My partner became excited. He wanted to double the stakes. Agreed, I said. Let's double them. So naturally he lost twice as much and became doubly excited. Now he wanted to quadruple the stakes. Fine with me. Let's quadruple them. Still he kept losing. Then he became really mad. Now he wanted to play for twenty-five rubles a point. But the old saint—the father, I mean—intervened and wouldn't let him. But his darling son paid him no mind and we brought the stakes up to twenty-five per point. And he kept losing. So the old dunce became angry, jumped up, then sat down again immediately and looked at my hand, humming to himself and snorting. And his son fumed and foamed at the mouth. The more he lost the madder he got. The madder he got the more he lost. And the old bird was beside himself. He muttered and mumbled and cursed and looked at my cards, humming to himself and snorting. And his precious son, burning like a house afire, kept losing one game after another.

"May a foul disease come over me," the father exclaimed, "if you play another hand."

"Papa," the son pleaded. "Just one more hand. If I play more than that may I drop dead right here."

"Just one more hand," I said to the old geezer.

In short, he dealt out another hand and, thank God, he won. I myself was happy that he won. But now he wanted another game. What a question! How can one be so rude and refuse a man who has lost so much money? So we played one game after another until finally the wheel turned completely the other way.

"Well?" I said to the old Haman. "How come you're not mad at your sonny boy now?"

"He'll get it right and proper when we come home," he said. "He'll remember it the rest of his life."

That's what the old crook said, constantly looking at my cards, humming to himself and coughing and snorting. From the very beginning his looking at my cards and his humming, coughing and snorting didn't appeal to me. But so long as I was winning I figured: Hum, cough and snort all you like. Now that things were going badly, I thought: Should I tolerate his humming, coughing and snorting, or is there some intrigue going on? Meanwhile, the cards were dealt out. And I kept losing. One game after another. Bad business! Each time I stepped aside, untied the wallet in my breast pocket and took out one hundred-ruble bill after another. There were very few left. Dawn was breaking. Suddenly the old gangster took hold of my hand.

"May an ill wind take me," he said, "if I let you play any more. Look, you've reached your last hundred-ruble bill."

Naturally, I blew my top.

"How do you know that I'm up to my last hundred-ruble bill?"

And to spite him I slapped the hundred-ruble bill on the suitcase.

Only when I was flat broke, cleaned-out, and naked as the day I was born, when I could no longer throw anything into the pot, and when I saw my opponent, his cheeks flushed, buttoning up his jacket—only then did I begin to comprehend my situation. Somehow, my heart told me that I had fallen into a trap, that I'd been hoodwinked. It dawned on me that the father was no father and the son no son. I didn't like the way they exchanged glances nor the way the son stood up and stepped aside, followed by his father. It seemed to me that the old man said something to the young one, and I could have sworn that the young man slipped something into the old man's hand.

My first thought was to jump out the window. Then I said to myself: No, slitting both their throats, or shooting them through the heart, or just simply grabbing them by their windpipes and keep on choking and choking would be better. But what could I do if the odds were two against one? Meanwhile the train was speeding on. The wheels clattered. My head spun. A fire raged in my heart. What now? Before I knew it we'd be in Odessa. What would I do then? Where would I go? What would I say? I looked around and noticed that my two scoundrels were picking up their suitcases.

"Where are we now?" I asked.

"In a town known as Odessa," they replied. I searched my pockets—I didn't even have a coin to tip the porter. I broke out in a cold sweat. Tears started to my eyes. My hands began to tremble. I approached the old butcher.

"I have a little favor to ask you," I said. "Can you at least spare twenty-five rubles?"

"Don't ask me! Ask him." The old heathen pointed to the young man. But the young rogue twirled his moustache, pretending not to hear. The locomotive whistle blew. The train stopped. We were in Odessa. The first one to jump off the train, as you can well imagine, was me. And it was yours truly who raised a storm. With the last bit of strength in me I shouted:

"Police! Police!"

A moment later a constable appeared, then another, then two and three more. But meanwhile the young blackguard had disappeared, leaving only old skin-and-bones behind—for I had grabbed him and held him fast to keep him from stealing away. People gathered from all over the station. There was a veritable stampede. And both of us were invited into a special room. There I told my entire story from A to Z. I didn't spare a tear; I poured out my embittered heart. Apparently my story touched the police deeply, for they immediately turned to the old sorcerer and told him to tell the whole truth. The upshot was—he didn't know where to begin, for he didn't know a thing. Might as well ask him about noodles. What sixty-six? Which cards? What son? He didn't have a son. Never had one.

"This man is nuts," said the old bastard pointing to his head, indicating that I was demented.

"Is that so?" I said to the police. "Why don't you search him up and down?"

So they took him and, begging your pardon, stripped him to his undershirt. But there were neither cards nor money. All told he had twenty rubles and seventy kopecks. He looked like such a pitiful, innocent creature that I began to have second thoughts about my sanity. Perhaps I *was* out of my mind. Perhaps I *had* dreamed that I had seen a father and son and played sixty-six with them and lost a fortune. How did it all end? Don't ask! Let's you and me drive cares away by playing a twosome of sixty-six in honor of Hanuka.

Thus concluded the apparently respectable man who like myself was a traveling salesman and perhaps even a merchant. A deck of cards sprang out of his hands and he drew a card for first deal and said, "What are the stakes?"

I looked at the man and noted that his manner of dealing cards was too deft, too artful and too quick. His hands were too white. Far too white and soft. And a wicked thought flew through my mind.

"I'd gladly play sixty-six with you in honor of Hanuka," I said, "but I haven't the faintest notion of what that game is all about. What actually do you mean by sixty-six?"

As the man looked me in the eye a hint of a smile played on his lips, and with a light sigh, he silently replaced the cards in his pocket.

At the very first station he disappeared. Out of curiosity, I walked back and forth twice through all the cars, but not a trace of him remained.

RITUAL FRINGES

Speaking of catastrophes and the recent rash of fires—would you like to hear how we got a hundred rubles for the fire victims out of a rich miser, a stingy swine who had never ever opened up his purse for charity? You would? Well, then, let's have a smoke. Here. Take one of mine.

During the trip I've already described some of our town's characters. Well, now I've got a new one for you—a chap called Yoel Tashker. There was a Jew you wouldn't give a wooden kopeck for. He was small, thin and dried-out. His beard was wispy. When he walked, he ran. And his clothing—you'd wish it on your worst enemy. Yet he was well-to-do. What am I saying well-to-do? He was wealthy, he was loaded, he was a millionaire. Of course, I haven't counted his millions. Perhaps he had a million, perhaps he was far short of half a million. But no matter what he had, he didn't deserve it. Because he was a swine. Wrenching a donation out of him was like splitting the Red Sea. Try to find the beggar who remembers Yoel Tashker giving so much as a dry crust to a poor man. Yoel Tashker's reputation in town was such that when a poor man complained about a handout he was told: "All right, now go to Yoel Tashker and see how much more you'll get." That's the sort of rich man Tashker was.

But do you think that he was a robber, God forbid, or a coarse brute, or a low-class boor? Absolutely not. Yoel Tashker came from a respectable family. He was well versed in the sacred texts and was quite an honest man. What belonged to the next fellow he would not touch. So long as his possessions were left alone he was content. What's mine is mine, what's yours is yours. Get the picture?

226

What did he do for a living? He was a moneylender. He owned houses and did business with the landed nobility. He was in a tumult day and night. He traveled and ran about constantly, neither ate nor slept, begrudged himself assistants, did everything single-handedly, had neither kith nor kin.

Actually, he did have some children but, blast it, he kicked them out of the house—rumor has it they're in America—after his wife's death. People are saying that Tashker starved her to death. But that's probably a lie. On the other hand, maybe it is true. For his second wife divorced him two weeks after their wedding. Guess why? Over a glass of milk. Ha-ha, that's the God's honest truth. He once caught her drinking a glass of milk.

"Either way it's bad," he told her. "If you're drinking milk because you've got consumption, I don't need you. And if you're just guzzling milk for no good reason, higgledy-piggledy, why then you're a self-indulgent waster."

But yet Yoel Tashker had one redeeming virtue—after all, no one is all bad. He was pious. A fanatic! Look, if you want to be pious, go right ahead, who cares? But no, not him. He insisted that the whole world match his piety. The Lord's advocate. He couldn't stand seeing a Jew bareheaded. Young married women who did not exchange their own hair for marriage wigs made his blood boil. He wrangled with parents for sending their children to secular high schools. And so on.

So God saw to it that he had a tenant in his house, one of those self-educated, self-styled attorneys of the old school. And not so God-fearing either. Walked around without a hat. Was beardless. Smoked on Sabbath. Everything as it should be. Accuse him of what you will. Kompanyevitch was his name, a tall, broad-shouldered chap, slightly stooped, with sunken cheeks and shrewd eyes. Although quiet and taciturn, he was a libertine on the sly. He made more money at cards than at law. All the fine young men who fancied cards, pork sausages and like treats came to him.

Well, it's the old story. What do you care if your tenant's no saint? I'm referring to Yoel Tashker, of course. So you won't arrange a match with him. Big deal! But no! There were a number of things which Tashker couldn't tolerate.

Why did they heat up the samovar on Sabbath at Kompan-yevitch's place? And why did they serve a meat dinner on the Tisha B'Av fast? And why weren't the new Passover utensils ritually immersed? And so on. Tashker was incensed at his tenant, spread all sorts of slanderous reports about him, shouted each of these accusations from the rooftops:

"Did you ever? The nerve of that heathen! Lives next door to me and heats the samovar on Sabbath!"

Hearing this, the following Sabbath Kompanyevitch heated up two samovars. Which made Yoel froth at the mouth. Imagine, he nearly got a stroke. You idiot! Evict him from the house and you'll be rid of a plague! Nothing doing, Tashker said, he's a good tenant. Paid the best rent. Ha-ha!

All right. I've introduced you to two characters. Now I must bring in a third—Froike the Scamp, who also plays a role in this story. That is, the entire story actually revolves about him.

This is the sort of character Froike was: He was a young man whom folks call a hail-fellow-well-met. Imagine, half Hasid, half French. Rigged out in a long gaberdine—but a modern beret. White shirt, red tie—yet he wore a pair of ritual fringes under his shirt and one of the four fringes was always visible. What's more, there were rumors in town about him and a young married woman—yet he always made a beeline for the synagogue. In a word, he was the sort of character we call a pious fraud. He was a money broker, a middleman for ready cash, loans and signed notes. Thousands upon thousands of rubles went through Froike's hands. There was no one whom Tashker trusted as much as Froike. When it came to a loan, Tashker was scared to let a hundred rubles out of his hands. But as soon as Froike approved the loan no more questions were asked. But do you think that Froike was such a saint in money matters? That I won't guarantee. He was a shrewd little bastard, cunning and wily, and an impudent brat to boot. Falling victim to his barbed tongue was like falling headlong into hell. Now you know why he was nicknamed Froike the Scamp although his real name was Efroim Katz.

Now you've got a sum total of three characters. So listen to what happened. The summer conflagrations began and, God save us, an entire town, Drazhne, was burned to the ground. Then began the outcries, letters and telegrams asking everyone to quickly send whatever help they could—for an entire community of Jews was starving and homeless. Naturally, a storm broke out in our village:

"Fellow Jews! Goodhearted people! Why are we silent? Why don't we do something?"

In short, we sent a delegation around town to collect contributions. Who were the delegates? The foremost citizens of town. Me, of course, and two-three other reputable householders, including Froike the Scamp—because for such matters you had to have someone with lots of cheek. So we took a kerchief and went collecting from door to door. Where first? Naturally, to the rich men. So we came to Yoel Tashker.

"Good morning, Reb Yoel!"

"Good morning and good day. What's the good word? Have a seat."

Very fine reception. Couldn't be any finer. Tashker, for your information, was a very hospitable person. If you came to his house, he'd welcome you as his guest, order a chair to be brought for you and ask you to be seated. He'd even chat pleasantly with you—so long as you didn't talk of money. Mention money and his face changed color, one eye developed a sudden tic and his left cheek contracted as though he'd had a stroke. It was a pity to look at him then, I tell you.

All right, where are we? Oh yes, so the delegation came to Tashker.

"Good morning, Reb Yoel."

"Good morning and good day. Have a seat. What's the good word?"

"We came to ask you for a donation."

One eye promptly began to twitch and his cheek—God save me!—contracted.

"A donation? Suddenly, out of the blue, a donation?"

At which glib-tongued Froike said:

"It's a very special donation, Reb Yoel, quite an urgent matter. You probably heard about it. An entire town—Drazhne—burned down to the ground."

"Really? Drazhne burned down? Ah me, I'm woebegone.

I've got so much money invested there. Oh, I'm ruined!"

So Froike told him that none of his mortgagees were involved; the fire affected only the poor people. But go talk when the next fellow refused to listen. He wrung his hands, ran around the house like a madman, screaming:

"I'm ruined. Impoverished. Don't even talk to me now. You've taken a sword and chopped my head off. I won't survive this."

We sat awhile and then stood up to leave. We bade Reb Yoel good-bye, kissed the *mezuza* and moved on. A moment later Froike shouted to us:

"Listen here. If I don't wheedle one hundred rubles out of that son of a bitch for the Drazhne fire victims my name isn't Efroim Katz."

"What are you talking about, Froike? Are you crazy?"

"What do you care? If I tell you I'll get the money, you can depend on it—for my name *is* Efroim Katz."

Now listen to what happened next. A few days later Reb Yoel Tashker took the train to the Toltchin fair. Riding with him was his tenant, Kompanyevitch, as well as other Jews from Toltchin and Uman. The car was packed and as usual everyone was talking and jabbering at once. Reb Yoel Tashker sat by himself in a corner studying, as was his wont, a sacred text called *The Law of Israel*. After all, he had nothing in common with all these other Jews. Especially with that libertine, Kompanyevitch, whose shaven face he could not stand.

However, as though on spite, Kompanyevitch sat himself down smack opposite Yoel Tashker. God Almighty, how do I get rid of this heretic? thought Yoel. If I transfer to a second-class compartment I'll be throwing money out the window. If I remain here I'll have to suffer his shaven chin and devilishly shrewd eyes. But to make a long story short, God performed a miracle and at the very first station Yoel met a friend—none other than Froike the Scamp. Seeing Froike, our man Tashker got a fresh lease on life. New spirit came into him. At least now there would be someone to talk to.

"Well, where are you bound to?"

"Where are *you* going?"

And so they began talking at random about last year's snow, noodles, attics, onions, pie in the sky. Soon they hit upon a subject quite to Tashker's taste: modern children, idle young men, dissolute daughters, an immoral world. Froike jumbled together an old story about some young wife from Uman who ran off with an officer, an incident of a man who had married in two towns, and a third tale of a youngster who had struck his father when the latter beat him for refusing to don phylacteries.

"Struck his *father?* His own father?"

This caused a hullabaloo in the car. Everyone became excited, most of all Yoel Tashker.

"Just what I've been saying all along. It's an immoral world, I tell you," said Yoel. "Jewish children refuse to pray. Refuse to put on *tfillin.*"

"*Tfillin* I can overlook," the hitherto silent Kompanyevitch suddenly exclaimed. "It's all the same whether you put them on or not. That doesn't bother me. What bothers me more is ritual fringes. What burns me up is the fact that nowadays youngsters don't wear ritual fringes. *Tfillin,* well, they're somewhat of a task. They have to be put on, they have to be taken off. But wearing a pair of ritual fringes under a shirt—who'd even notice?"

Thus sermonized the free-thinker Kompanyevitch, in a soft, deliberate and serious manner. Tashker couldn't have been more surprised if a thunderbolt had struck the train and overturned it.

What's up? he thought. Has the Messiah arrived? This pork-glutter talking about ritual fringes? Then he said aloud —not to Kompanyevitch but to Froike:

"Well, what do you say to this plaster saint? Ha-ha. Him talking about ritual fringes."

"Why not?" said Froike, faking complete naïveté. "Isn't the gentleman Jewish, too?"

This last remark was more than Tashker could bear.

"First of all, what do you mean by calling him 'gentleman'? And second of all, what sort of Jew is Kompanyevitch? Ha-ha. Some Jew! A Jew who heats up a samovar on Sabbath. A Jew who gorges upon meat during the Tisha B'Av fast. A

Jew who doesn't even immerse his utensils for Passover. Is that the sort of Jew who's preaching to us about ritual fringes?"

"So what?" said Froike, once again faking naïveté. "What's one thing got to do with another, Reb Yoel? A Jew like Kompanyevitch may be as irreligious as you imagine, but if he wears ritual fringes under his shirt I see no wrong in it."

"Who? That beardless one?" poor Tashker screamed. "That libertine? That sinner against the God of Israel?"

Everyone fell silent and stared at Kompanyevitch. The latter did not say a word. Neither did Froike the Scamp. Then Froike jumped up like a man determined to risk his neck.

"You know what, Reb Yoel? My view is that we simply cannot assess the moral value of a Jewish soul. If a Jew talks about ritual fringes, he's probably wearing them. Look. I'm willing to put up a hundred rubles for the Drazhne fire victims. Put up a hundred yourself and let's beg the gentleman's pardon—it's your tenant, Kompanyevitch, I'm talking about—and ask him to unbutton his gaberdine and shirt and show us if he's wearing ritual fringes or not."

"Right! Right!" cried the passengers, excitedly discussing the turn of events. Soon there was quite a merry to-do in the car. Only one man was unperturbed by it all—Kompanyevitch. He sat there like a perfect stranger. As though he weren't the subject of the fuss at all.

And what about our man Tashker? Sweat poured out of him. He looked like a corpse. He had never even bet a kopeck in his life. Now he was suddenly being asked to put up a hundred rubles. What would happen, thought Tashker, if, God forbid and heaven forfend, that rascal actually *did* wear a pair of ritual fringes? But on the other hand, could it be that Kompanyevitch . . .? That apostate? May I get a good solid migraine if he wears ritual fringes.

So Yoel screwed up his courage, unbuckled his moneybag and withdrew a hundred-ruble note. Two reputable Jews were then chosen to hold the money. Now everyone turned to Kompanyevitch to ask him to remove—but where? What? When? Fiddlesticks!

"Who am I, a little schoolboy?" Kompanyevitch said. "Or

a traveling clown? What are you talking about? Expect me to undress all of a sudden here in the train in the middle of the day and show my naked chest to a host of Jews?"

Hearing such talk, our man Yoel Tashker began to swell with pride.

"Aha!" he said to Froike, beaming. "Who's right? Me or you? Boy, do I know these characters. And that Jew's got the nerve to talk about ritual fringes! Ha-ha-ha."

We were in a pickle. So the crowd began berating Kompanyevitch.

"It's not fair. After all, it's an important matter. It's got to be one way or another. Consider it. In either case it's a hundred rubles for the unfortunate fire victims."

"The unfortunate fire victims," Yoel Tashker echoed, without looking at Kompanyevitch.

"Men, women and children, poor souls, are sleeping under open skies," they pleaded with Kompanyevitch.

"Poor souls, under open skies," Yoel Tashker repeated.

"How can a Jew be so heartless?"

"So heartless," echoed Yoel Tashker.

To make a long story short, they finally managed to convince Kompanyevitch to unbutton his gaberdine, jacket and shirt. Just imagine what they saw! That character Kompanyevitch actually wore a pair of ritual fringes underneath his shirt. And what a pair it was. Large and one hundred percent traditional, it was made of blue wool, with oversize, finely twined rabbinic fringes. A pair of ritual fringes to remember!

Only such a rascal as Froike the Scamp could have pulled a stunt like that. True, he lost Yoel Tashker as a customer. Unto this very day Froike dare not show his face to him. But nevertheless Froike squeezed one hundred rubles out of Tashker for the Drazhne fire victims. Believe it or not, one hundred rubles! And do you know who from? From a rich miser, a swine who had never ever opened up his purse for charity. Had never even given a dry crust to a poor man. Now doesn't he deserve to die a miserable death? I mean Froike, of course.

Mottel the Cantor's Son

Sholom Aleichem was happiest when he was portraying the freewheeling spirit of childhood, which is embodied in the fun-loving Mottel. Mottel, whom Sholom Aleichem described as his favorite character, is the sort of boy who squeezes laughter out of sadness. This proximity of tears and laughter, typically a Sholom Aleichem trait, is exploited to the full in the novel-length series episodes which carry Mottel from Kasrilevke to America. A child in an adult's world, Mottel's magic glass sees sunshine and laughter where other denizens of a workaday world see only gloom, discomfort and mourning. In "A Job as Easy as Pie," too, the potential hair-raising incident is lightly treated: as usual, Mottel remembers only what is comic and good. The adventures of Mottel were begun in 1907, but they remain unfinished. Even on his deathbed, Sholom Aleichem's turbulent imagination was at work: the last lines the Yiddish humorist ever wrote were the start of a new story for his beloved young hero.

A JOB AS EASY AS PIE

Mama just told me a good piece of news—I've got a job. And not at a plain workingman's shop, either, God forbid. Mama said that her enemies won't live to see the day when Mottel, the son of the late Peissi the Cantor, becomes a common workingman. My job, she said, was simply grand and easy as pie. All day long I'd be in school—that is, in the Talmud Torah—and at night I'd sleep over at Old Man Lurie's house.

"Old Man Lurie is a wealthy man," Mama said. "The only trouble is that he's not a healthy man. I mean generally he feels quite well—he eats, drinks, and sleeps. Except at night. That's when he can't sleep a wink. Lies awake all night long. So his children are afraid of leaving him alone at night. They just need another human being in the room with him. Even a youngster would do, as long as he's human. Putting another old man into the room doesn't seem proper. But a child doesn't matter. It's just like having a little cat around. They're offering five rubles per week and supper when you come back from Talmud Torah. And the supper's going to be first-class, as befits a rich house. What they throw away there would be enough for all of us. Now off to school, Mottel, and when you come home this evening, I'll bring you over to Old Man Lurie's. You won't have to do a bit of work. You'll have a royal dinner and a fine place to sleep. Plus five rubles a week. That will buy you some new clothes and a pair of boots."

Sounds good, huh? So why the tears? But with Mama it can't be helped. She's simply got to have a good cry.

2

At Talmud Torah I only take up space. I don't learn a thing. There's no grade for my age level. So I help the teacher's wife around the house and play with the pussycat. Working for the teacher's wife isn't hard at all. I sweep the house, bring in the firewood, do anything she tells me to. It's a snap. You can't even call it work. Just so long as I don't have to study. Studying—there's nothing worse!

But best of all is the pussycat. People say a cat is an unclean beast. I say that's a lie. A cat is a clean animal. People say a cat is a mischievous little devil. I say that's a lie, too. A cat is a kind, cuddly creature. A dog is a tail-wagging cringer. A cat plays up to you. When you pat her head, she shuts her eyes and begins to purr. I love cats—but so what? Talk to my pals and they'll tell you thousands of fairy tales. That when you touch a cat you have to wash your hands. That touching a cat affects your memory. They don't know what else to dream up.

They've got a funny habit—if a cat comes up to them, they give it a swift kick in the ribs. Me, I can't bear to see a cat beaten. But my friends laugh at me. They don't feel sorry for animals at all. I'm talking about the kids who go to Talmud Torah with me. They're a bunch of murderers. They make fun of me. On account of my stiff, coarse pants they call me "Wooden Pantaloony," and my mother "Mrs. Sniffles," because she's always crying.

"Here comes your ma, Mrs. Sniffles," they yelled. She had come to call for me and take me to my job—a job as easy as pie.

3

On the way, Mama complained about her sad and bitter lot (sad alone was not enough). God had given her two children, but now she was widowed and alone.

"Knock wood," she said, "at least your brother Eli made a good marriage. He fell into a bed of clover. The only trouble is that his father-in-law is a boor. Ah me, a baker, alas! What can you expect of a baker?" Mama complained as we made our way to the Lurie house.

"Old Man Lurie's room is like a royal palace," Mama whispered. Which was just the place I was dying to see. But meanwhile we were still in the kitchen, Mama and I. But the kitchen wasn't half bad, either. The oven was gleaming and white. The pots shone. Everything sparkled. We were asked to be seated. A lady appeared, dressed like a rich noblewoman. She talked to Mama and pointed at me. Mama nodded in agreement, continually wiped her lips, and refused to sit down. But me, I took a seat. As Mama was leaving, she told me to mind my manners and be a good boy, and managed to sniffle a bit and wipe her eyes. Tomorrow she would call for me and take me to school.

They gave me supper. Soup and white-loaf (imagine, white bread in the middle of the week!). And meat, heaps of it. After supper, they told me to go upstairs. Since I didn't know what they meant by "upstairs," Khana the cook, a swarthy woman with a long nose, took me by the hand and showed me. I followed her. It was a pleasure to walk barefoot up the carpeted stairs. It wasn't quite dark yet, but already the lamps were lit. Dozens of them. There were all sort of designs and pictures pasted on the walls. The chairs were covered with leather. Even the ceiling was painted like— forgive the comparison—the one in the synagogue. Even nicer.

I was brought into a large room. It was so huge that had I been alone, I would have raced from one wall to another, or even rolled around on the velvet quilt spread over the entire floor. Turning somersaults on such a quilt must be loads of fun. Even sleeping on it wouldn't be half bad, either.

4

Old Man Lurie was a tall, handsome man with a gray beard and a broad forehead. He wore a skullcap made of pure velvet; his slippers, stitched with heavy thread, were of velvet, too. He sat poring over a huge thick book. He didn't say a word as he studied, but merely chewed the tip of his beard, jiggling his leg and grumbling softly to himself.

Old Man Lurie was a queer duck. I stared at him and asked myself: Does he see me or doesn't he? Apparently he didn't see me, for he didn't even look my way, and no one said anything to him about me. They just placed me in the room and locked the door behind me. Suddenly Old Man Lurie, still not looking at me, began to speak:

"Come here, sir, and I'll show you what Rambam* has to say."

Who was he addressing? Me? Calling *me* sir? I looked around. There was no one else in the room.

"Come here, sir," Old Man Lurie bellowed once again in his gruff voice, "and you'll see what Rambam says."

By now I was afraid to approach.

"Are you calling me?"

"Yes, you, sir, who else?" said Old Man Lurie, gazing into the book.

He took me by the hand, pointed out the passage, and explained what Rambam had to say. As he proceeded, his voice grew shriller and he became increasingly wrought up. Finally, he worked himself into such a dither that he turned beet-red. He kept gesticulating with his thumb and frequently treated me to an elbow jab in the ribs.

"Well, sir, what do you say to that? That was good, huh?"

Even if it were top-notch, I couldn't make heads or tails of it. So I kept quiet. I was silent and he seethed. He seethed and I was silent. Then I heard the jangle of keys on the other side of the door.

The door opened and in came the lady dressed like a rich noblewoman. She approached Old Man Lurie and shouted right into his ear. Apparently he was deaf. If not, why did she have to shout? She told him to leave me alone, for it was time for me to go to sleep. She took me away from the old man and bedded me down on a cot with springs. The linen was white as snow. The silken quilt was soft. I was in Paradise. The nobly dressed lady covered me and left the room, locking the door.

Hands behind his back, Old Man Lurie began pacing in the room, looking down at his fine slippers. He muttered and grumbled to himself, moving his eyebrows most peculiarly. But I was so drowsy I couldn't keep my eyes open any longer.

---

* Rambam stands for *Rabbi Moses ben Maimon*, or Maimonides, the famous Jewish philosopher (1135–1204). [Tr.]

Suddenly Old Man Lurie came up to me and said: "You know what? I'm going to eat you up."

I stared at him. I didn't know what he was driving at.

"Get up. I'm going to eat you up."

"Who? Me?"

"Yes, you. I have to eat you up. And no ifs and buts about it."

Old Man Lurie kept talking and pacing in the room, his head down, his hands at his side, his forehead wrinkled. But little by little he lowered his voice. Soon he was whispering to himself. I followed every word, scarcely able to catch my breath. He asked himself questions and then answered them.

"Rambam states that the universe is not eternal. How is that inferred? By the fact that every effect must have a cause. How can I demonstrate this? By asserting my own will. How? If I want to eat him up, I eat him up. But what about compassion? Compassion has nothing to do with it. I assert my will. The will is the ultimate purpose. I eat him up. I want to eat him up. I must eat him up."

5

That Old Man Lurie certainly brought me a fine piece of news. He must eat me up. What would Mama say? Suddenly I became scared. A shiver ran over me. The cot I was lying on was not quite up to the wall. Little by little I moved closer to the wall and slipped to the floor. My teeth began to chatter. I listened, waiting for him to come and eat me up. How did I pass the time? I quietly called to Mama and felt the wet drops rolling down my cheeks into my mouth. The drops were salty. Never before did I long for Mama as I did then. I also longed for my brother Eli, but not that much. And I also recalled my father, after whom I am saying the Mourner's Prayer. Who would say the Mourner's Prayer after me if Old Man Lurie gobbled me up?

Apparently I had fallen asleep. For when I suddenly woke up, I looked around, anxious to know where I was. I touched the wall and the cot. I raised my head and saw a huge, bright room. Velvet quilts were on the floor. Pictures were pasted on the walls. The ceiling like—forgive the comparison—the one in the synagogue. Old Man Lurie was still sitting over his huge book which he called "Rambam." I liked the name "Rambam" because it sounded like "Bimbam." Suddenly I recalled that only last night Old Man Lurie had wanted to eat me up. I was afraid that if he saw me he'd try the same trick again. So once more I hid between the cot and the wall and remained absolutely still.

The door opened up with a clatter. The nobly dressed lady entered, followed by Khana carrying a big tray filled with pitchers of coffee and hot milk, and a platter of freshly baked butter rolls.

"Where's the lad?" said Khana. She looked around and spotted me in my hiding place.

"You're some little devil, aren't you? What are you doing down there? Come down to the kitchen with me. Your mother's waiting for you."

I jumped up and dashed barefoot down the padded stairs, singing rhythmically, "Rambam, Bimbam. Bimbam, Rambam," until I came to the kitchen.

"What's the rush?" Khana said to Mama. "Let him at least have a cup of coffee and a butter roll. You also ought to have a cup of coffee. It's no skin off their back. They got plenty."

Mama thanked her and sat down. Khana served coffee and fresh butter rolls.

Did you ever eat sugar cakes made with fresh eggs? Well, that's what a rich man's butter rolls taste like. They're even better than cake. I can't even begin to describe the taste of the coffee. It was sheer delight. Mama held the cup and sipped the coffee, enjoying every drop. She gave me most of her butter roll. Seeing this, Khana raised a fuss, as though we had insulted her.

"What are you doing? Eat. Eat. There's plenty."

Khana gave me another butter roll. That made two and a half. I listened to their conversation, one I was already familiar with. Mama complained about her bad fortune. A widow left with two children, one in a bed of clover, the other, poor fellow, not. I would like to know just what a bed of clover really is. Is it a bed filled with clover leaves? Always green and grassy?

Khana listened to Mama and shook her head. Then Khana began to talk and complain about *her* bad fortune. She stemmed from a fine, respectable family, yet now she had to cater to others. Her father had been a well-to-do householder, but a fire ruined him. Then he fell sick. After that he died. If her father were to get up and see his Khana standing in front of someone else's oven . . . ! But thank God she had no cause for complaint. She had a good job. The only trouble was that the old man was a bit . . .

A bit what? I didn't know. Khana made little circles around her ear with her finger. Mama listened to Khana and shook her head. Then Mama began to talk again. Now Khana listened and shook *her* head. As we left Khana gave me another butter roll and I showed it to the kids in Talmud Torah. They crowded around me, gaping at me as I ate it. Apparently it was a rare delicacy for them. I gave each of them a little piece. They licked their fingers.

"Where'd you get a treat like that?"

I puffed out both my cheeks and stood before them with my hands deep in the pockets of my stiff, coarse pants. I chewed slowly, swallowed and did a silent little jig with my bare feet, as though to say: "Tsk, tsk, you poor beggars. Some treat, butter rolls! Ha, ha. You ought to try it with coffee, and then you'd know what heaven is really like."

Jewish Soldiers

Russian Jews had a deep-rooted antipathy to serving the autocratic and basically anti-Jewish regime of the Czar. A Jewish soldier was usually reviled, mistreated and almost certain to be removed from contact with the traditional ways of his people's life. The relatively few who came through unscathed after many years of obligatory service were heroes in their home towns. Given all these difficulties, then, parents did all they could to have their sons avoid conscription. This concern with one of the harsh realities of shtetl life is reflected in several stories that Sholom Aleichem wrote about Jews and (rather: versus) the army. The ill luck of one hapless father is described in "Back from the Draft"; but in contrast to this story is "The First Passover Night of the War," where, as if to put the lie to the draft-dodger stereotype, Sholom Aleichem creates a Jewish soldier who is proud of his uniform and wants to show the gentile soldiers that a Jew, too, can loyally serve and even die for the land where his forefathers lived.

BACK FROM THE DRAFT

You want to know which station I'm coming from? Just wait till I put my prayer shawl and phylacteries away and I'll tell you. Now. You asked where I'm coming from. Ah me, from Yehupetz is where I'm coming from. We're on our way back from the draft board, me and my son—this young fellow stretched out here on the bench. We went to get advice from some lawyers and while there we stopped to consult some specialists to see what *they* would say. The good Lord has blessed me with a draft call. My boy has already presented himself four times and still the end is not in sight. And to the bargain he's a one-and-only son with an honest-to-goodness, officially attested-to first-class exemption. Why are you staring at me like that? Are you surprised? Just keep your ears open and hear me out.

Here's the background to the story. I happen to be from Mezeretch, but actually my home town, to coin a phrase, is Mazepevke and I'm registered in Vorotilevke. That is, once upon a time I lived in that blasted Vorotilevke, but I now live in Mezeretch. I don't think it should make much of a difference to you who I am and what my name is. But I must tell you my son's name, for it's absolutely essential to the story at hand.

His name is Itzik, that is Avrohom-Yitzhok, but he's known as Alter—a nickname my old woman gave to our one-and-only son. Actually, we had another son, about a year and a half younger than Itzik. This other boy was called Ayzik. But once when he was a little boy he was left all alone—I'm talking about Ayzik—and he had an accident. (In those days I still lived in that blasted Vorotilevke.) So the child—Ayzik,

that is—got it into his head to crawl right up to the samovar
and upset it. And the boiling water scalded him to death,
God spare you a like fate. Since then Itzik—Avrohom-
Yitzhok, that is—has remained an only son. My wife, may she
live and be well, pampered him and named him Alter.

Now you may well ask—how can it be? If he's an only son, a
one-and-only boy, why should he be subject to a draft call?
Well, that's exactly what's eating me. Wait. Perhaps you're
thinking, God forbid, that he's one of those robust youngsters
that grow up in the lap of luxury. If so, you're mistaken. You
wouldn't even give two broken kopecks for him. He's not
much for looks and he's a sick boy to boot. What am I saying
sick? He's not *sick*, God forbid, but he's certainly not well.
Too bad he's sleeping now. But I don't want to wake him.
Wait till he gets up and then you'll lay eyes on a walking
skeleton, all skin and bones, long lean and lanky as a bean-
pole with a face the size of a dried fig; the spitting image of
his mother, may she live and be well, who is also tall and
skinny—I mean, frail and delicate. Being that he's so tall and
skinny and unfit for the draft and has a first-class exemption
besides, do you think I ever had to worry about a draft call?

But when the draft call came, the exemption went out the
window. Completely forgotten. What happened? Quite
simple. They had apparently forgotten to strike my other
boy, Ayzik, the one who was scalded to death by a hot
samovar, from the registry. So I ran to that idiot, the crown-
rabbi,* screaming:

"Justice, you robber, you murderer! What have you got
against me? Why didn't you remove my Ayzik's name?"

So that ass asked me, "And just who is this Ayzik, pray
tell?"

"What do you mean?" I shouted. "Don't you know Ayzik?
My son Ayzik, the one who upset the hot samovar."

"What samovar?" he said.

"Welcome, stranger," I said. "You must be a long way
from home. Some head you've got on your shoulders! A head
like yours should be used as a nutcracker. Who doesn't

---

* One who would represent the community vis-à-vis the state—not the
town's spiritual leader.

remember the story of how my Ayzik scalded himself to death with a samovar of boiling water! I don't understand what sort of crown-rabbi you are. Questions pertaining to religious affairs you don't answer, because for that we have our rabbi, long life to him. So it would only be fair to assume that you'd at least take proper care of the deceased. And if not, what do we need you and your meat tax for?"

But the tongue-lashing I gave that fine crown-rabbi was all in vain, for it turned out that the samovar incident had taken place not here in Mezeretch, but in Vorotilevke, blast it. Get the picture? I had completely forgotten that we were still living there at the time. To make a long story short—what's the use of long-winded histories and twice-told tales?—till I made a move, sent papers and affidavits here and there, my Avrohom-Yitzhok—that is, Itzik—otherwise called Alter, lost his exemption privilege. In other words, he was no longer exempt. If so, we were in a fine pickle. There was an outcry, an uproar. What? How can it be? A one-and-only only son with an honest-to-goodness, officially attested-to first-class exemption and now he had lost his nondraftable status? But go knock your head against the wall. It was completely futile.

But we've got a great and mighty God. So my Alter—Itzik, that is—went and pulled the highest number, 699. There was a big to-do in the council chamber. The chairman of the draft board himself slapped him on the back.

"Bravo, Itzko, there's a fine lad."

The entire village envied me. Number 699. What luck! Congratulations. All the best. Best wishes for a happy life. As though we had won first prize in the national lottery, all 200,000 rubles.

But you know our Jews. When it came to the draft and the board began rejecting them, they rejected them left and right. Everyone suddenly became a helpless, hopeless cripple. This one had this, that one had that.

To make a long story short—what's the use of long-winded histories and twice-told tales?—they finally reached number 699, and my Itzik—that is, Alter—had to go, alas, and personally present himself to the draft board with all the tailors and shoemakers. And what a weeping at home! What am I saying weeping? There was mournful wailing and sobbing. My wife,

bless her, raised the roof; my daughter-in-law passed out.
After all, has it ever been heard of that an only son, a one-and-
only only boy who has an honest-to-goodness, officially
attested-to first-class exemption is denied the privilege of his
nondraftable status? And my son, he's as cool as a cucumber,
as though the whole mess didn't concern him at all.

"Whatever happens to all will happen to Alter," he
quipped, feigning nonchalance. But don't you think he was
shivering in his boots all the while?

But we've got a great and mighty God. They stripped my
Itzik, if you'll pardon the expression, stark naked for the
physical. The doctor looked Itzik—Alter, that is—over,
measuring him up, down and across, searching, tapping,
touching, tormenting him. But, alas, what's the use, if the
rascal is unfit?—What am I saying unfit? He's fit all right, but
not for military duty. Why, for goodness sakes, your fingers
can span his chest. So he was disqualified and got a white
rejection slip. So once again there was joy in the house. A
celebration. Congratulations and lots of luck. The family got
together. We had some drinks, toasted each other's health.
Thank the good Lord, we had gotten rid of the draft.

But you know our Jews. . . . Don't you think there was a
rat who was just dying to inform the provincial government
that I had greased someone's palms? At any rate, two months
after the physical I got an official letter inviting Itzik—that is,
Alter—to take the trouble to present himself once more
before the province's central draft board for another physical.
Well, how's that for good news? Some pickle! My wife, bless
her, raised the roof; my daughter-in-law passed out. Unfair!
What a shame! Twice to the draft board, an only son, a one-
and-only only boy with an honest-to-goodness, officially
attested-to first-class exemption!

To make a long story short—what's the use of long-winded
histories and twice-told tales?—when the authorities summon
you, you can't be a pig and refuse. When I arrived, I began
running about, hoping that perhaps some pull here, or a
good word there, would help. But even if you tell them
you're King Solomon and that you have a one-and-only son
who's sick to boot—why they only laugh right in your face.
And what about my boy? He looked so poorly—I tell you,

they bury healthier specimens. Not on account of the draft, mind you! That went in one ear and out the other. If military service was in the cards, he said, he'd serve. He just simply couldn't bear *our* anguish—that is, the way the women suffered. After all, an examination in presence of all the members of the central draft board itself! Who could tell what would happen? Like they say, it's all a matter of luck. It's all one big lottery.

But we've got a great and mighty God. My Itzik—Alter, that is—was led into the examination room, if you'll excuse the expression, as naked as the day he was born. They started again from scratch, measuring him up, down and across, once more searching, tapping, touching, tormenting him. But, alas, what's the use if the rascal is unfit?—What am I saying unfit? He's fit all right, but not for military duty. One council member even stood up and tried to say: "He's fit," whereupon the doctor cut him off with: "Unfit." This one said, "Fit," the other said, "Unfit." They kept shouting "Fit, unfit" at each other until the governor in all his glory stood up from his chair, approached Itzik, looked him over and said:

"Absolutely unfit!"

Meaning that the only thing he's fit for was nine and ninety plagues. So I immediately wired home, in code, naturally:

"Congratulations. The goods have been categorically rejected."

Well, listen to this. As luck would have it, my telegram was not delivered to my house but to my cousin's. We've got the same names, but he's a wealthy man and, if you'll excuse the expression, a great big swine. And it's no surprise, either, since he deals with oxen. To the very province where my son and I had gone he had sent a shipment of oxen. He was so impatient for a telegram that his eyes nearly popped out of his head. So you can imagine how he felt when he received a telegram stating: "The goods have been categorically rejected." I thought that he would eat me up alive when I came home. Picture a swinish rich man who deals with oxen and you'll know how his mind works. It's not enough that he accepts other people's telegrams, but he insists that he's in the right, too.

Now let's turn the clock back to the time when I still lived in that blasted Vorotilevke and my Itzik—Alter, that is—was still a little child. One day the census takers were in town and they went around from door to door listing young and old, and asking everyone his name, age, the number of children he had and their sex and names. When it came to writing down Itzik's name, my wife, bless her, said, "Alter." What did the census taker care! If they tell me Alter, he probably thought, that's their business. So he wrote down "Alter."

Guess what happened? Exactly one year after the last draft call I got a new piece of news. They were looking for my son Alter and asking him to present himself to the draft board at Vorotilevke. May all my nightmares seep into my enemies' skulls! There's a glad bit of tidings! We've got another son! So how do you do, Reb Alter!

To make a long story short—what's the use of long-winded histories and twice-told tales?—they were summoning my Itzik—Alter, that is—to the draft board once again. My wife, bless her, raised the roof; my daughter-in-law passed out. It was perfectly disgraceful. Travel the length and breadth of the entire world and see if you'd find one instance where an only son, a one-and-only boy with an honest-to-goodness, officially attested-to first-class exemption should be called to the draft board three times. But go talk Turkish or Tatar—there was nothing to be done. So I ran to our communal leaders and shouted blue murder. I just about succeeded in getting ten people to swear out an affidavit saying that they were positive that Itzik is Avrohom-Yitzhok and that Avrohom-Yizhok was Alter and that Alter and Itzik and Avrohom-Yitzhok were all one and the same person.

I took the affidavit and brought it to Vorotilevke. I came to Vorotilevke and the welcome mat was spread out for me.

"Oh, Reb Yossel, how are you? What's new? What are you doing here?"

Naturally, I didn't want to tell them. What in the world for? The less a Jew knows the better.

"Nothing, really. I have some business with a landed nobleman."

"About what?"

"About some millet," I said. "I bought some millet from him, I did, and gave him a down payment. But now there's no millet and no down payment. I lost everything—both the cow and the clapper."

And I went straight to the council chamber of the draft board. There I met one of the old-time clerks and handed him the affidavit. After reading the affidavit he flared up and flung it back at my face with such a fury that I hope to God you never see the like.

"Beat it," he said. "Go to hell with all your names and with all your Jewish tricks. You want to squirm out of the draft, you Yid finagler. You change Avrohom to Yitzhok, and Yitzhok to Itzik, and Itzik to Alter. Such shenanigans don't go with us, you double-dealing swindlers."

Oho, thought I. If it's come to finagler and swindler, he's no doubt throwing out a hint for a ruble. So I took out a coin with the intent to slip it into his hand.

"Excuse me, your Eminent Draftboardship!"

And don't you think he jumped a foot off the ground with a yelp: "Bribe?"

Other clerks came a-running and within a minute they showed me the door. What a disaster! My luck, I had to meet up with an official with scruples and clean hands. But imagine, his honesty was only for show. Among Jews, you know, you always find your way. So I found a Jew who served as his middleman. But it helped as much as leeches help a corpse. And the upshot was that I now had another son named Alter. So with all due respect he was ordered to present himself at the Vorotilevke draft board. Some kettle of fish, eh?

How I managed to live through that year I'll never know. I must have been made of iron. But on the other hand, what have I, dumbbell that I am, got to be afraid of? Draft him *ten* times, what do I care if the rascal's unfit—what am I saying unfit? He's fit all right, but not for military duty. And especially since he's been rejected two times. But then again, who knows, it's a strange town. None of its officials were bribable.

But we've got a great and mighty God. My Alter—Itzik, that is—once again drew a high number and presented himself for the physical. But God performed a miracle and the Vorotilevke council also disqualified him and gave him a white rejection slip. So now, praised be God, we had two of those white slips.

We came home and there was great joy. We threw a party, invited almost everyone in town, and danced and lived it up until dawn. Now I was riding high. Was anyone my equal? I was King.

Now we have to turn back to my Ayzik, may he rest in peace, the one who was scalded to death by a boiling samovar when he was a child. Here's where the story gets interesting. Listen. Go be a prophet and know that the fine crown-rabbi of Vorotilevke would forget to remove him from the registry —the dead child, that is—and that I'd still have a debt outstanding, a son named Ayzik who would have to present himself to the draft board this year. There's a bomb out of the blue.

"What sort of calamities am I blessed with?" I protested to the crown-rabbi. "What Ayzik? Ayzik has been dead and buried for ages. What am I supposed to do now?"

"It's no good," he said.

"Why is it no good? Why?" I said.

"Because Itzik and Ayzik are one name."

"Can you tell me how Itzik and Ayzik are one name, wise guy?"

"Itzik is Yitzhok," he said, "Yitzhok is Isak, Isak is Izak, and Izak is Ayzik."

Some logic!

To make a long story short—what's the use of long-winded histories and twice-told tales?—they were looking for my Ayzik. They were pulling me to pieces, telling me to bring him to the draft board. Once again the weeping began in the house. What am I saying weeping? It was the Destruction of the Holy Temple all over again! First of all my wife, bless her, reminded herself of the dead child and it reopened old wounds.

"I'd rather have him alive and go to the draft board than lie in the earth with his bones rotting. What's more, I'm afraid that perhaps the crown-rabbi is right, may it never come to pass, and that Itzik is Yitzhok, Yitzhok is Isak, Isak is Izak, and Izak is Ayzik. If that's so then we're in a pickle."

So said my wife, bless her, raising the roof, while my daughter-in-law, as usual, passed out. No trifle, you know, an only son, a one-and-only only boy with an honest-to-goodness officially attested-to first-class exemption who's presented himself three times to the draft board, has two white rejection slips and is still not through.

So I picked myself up and took a train to Yehupetz in order to consult a good lawyer. I also took my son along to visit a specialist and hear what he would say concerning his fitness, even though I knew right well that the rascal is unfit—what am I saying, unfit? He's fit all right, but not for military duty. And after hearing the opinion of both lawyer and the specialist, why then I'd be able to sleep well and this runaround with the draft would stop. But what do you think the upshot was? The upshot was that lawyers and the specialists didn't know a damn thing. This one said this, that one said that. If one said white, the other insisted on black. They can drive you stark raving mad. Just listen.

The first lawyer I met was a thick, dull-witted dunderhead, despite his high forehead and a skull so bald and smooth you could have used it as a sliding pond. That smart aleck could not comprehend who was Alter and who was Itzik and who was Avrohom-Yitzhok and who Ayzik had been. So I told him the whole story over and over again—that Alter and Itzik and Avrohom-Yitzhok were one and the same person, and that Ayzik was the one who had upset a samovar of boiling water while I was still living in Vorotilevke.

So I thought that I had gotten through to him. But when I was done he asked me again:

"Wait a minute, if you please. Who's the oldest one? Itzik, Alter or Avrohom-Yitzhok?"

"There you go again," I said. "I thought I already told you fifteen times that Itzik and Avrohom-Yitzhok and Alter are all one person. In other words, his real name is Itzik—that is, Avrohom-Yitzhok—but he's called Alter, a nickname given to him by his mother. Now Ayzik is the one who knocked a samovar of boiling water over himself when I was still a Vorotilevker living in Vorotilevke."

"Then which year was it," he said, "that Avrohom-Alter, I mean Yitzhok-Ayzik, presented himself to the draft board?"

"What are you mumbling about?" I said. "Why are you mixing moonbeams and borscht? This is the first time in my life that I've met a Jew who is both pigheaded and featherbrained. I'm trying to tell you that Yitzhok and Avrohom-Yitzhok and Itzik and Ayzik and Alter are all one person. One person!"

"Pipe down," he said. "Stop screaming. What are you screaming for?"

Did you ever? And he's got the nerve to think he's right.

To make a long story short, I spat in disgust and left for another lawyer. This one happened to have a keen Talmudic mind, a bit too keen perhaps. He rubbed his brow, sought out the facts, split hairs, wrangled with the laws and concluded that on the basis of such and such a statute the Mezeretch draft board had no right to register him. But what then? There was a law that if one draft board *did* register him, then the other one had to remove him from its lists. Then there was another law, he said, that stated if the first board had registered him and the second did not remove him, then the first one was obliged to remove him. Moreover, there was a statute on the books which stated that if the first board refused to remove his name, then—

To make a long story short, this law, that law, this statute, that statute—he stuffed my head so full of those legal terms that I simply had to go to a third lawyer. There I encountered a new bungler, a young attorney still wet behind the ears—that is, he had just finished law school. Quite a friendly chap. A tongue like a bell—and it kept on ringing. Apparently he was still practicing public speaking, for when he talked one could see the great pleasure the sound of his own voice gave him. He rambled on, became hot under the collar, delivered a full-fledged sermon, which I had to cut short in the middle.

"Very nice," I told him. "No doubt you're right, but what good is your bewailing my lot going to do me? I'd rather you gave me some advice concerning the steps I should take if they call him, God forbid."

To make a long story short—what's the use of long-winded histories and twice-told tales?—I finally got hold of the right lawyer. This one was a lawyer of the old school, one who immediately grasped the heart of a matter. I told him the whole story from A to Z. While I spoke he sat with eyes closed and paid close attention. When I had finished he said:

"Is that it? Are you through? Go home. It's nothing. You won't have to pay more than a three-hundred-ruble fine."

"Is that all?" I said. "Tut-tut. If I could be sure that it was merely a matter of a three-hundred-ruble fine! But it's my son I'm worried about."

"What son?"

"What do you mean what son?" I said. "Alter! That is, Itzik."

"What has Itzik got to do with it?" he said.

"What do you mean, what's Itzik got to do with it? What if he's dragged out to the draft board again, God forbid?"

"But you yourself have said that he has a white rejection slip?"

"He's got *two* of them!"

"So what do you want?" said the lawyer.

"What should I want? Actually I don't want anything. I'm just afraid that since they're looking for Ayzik, and Ayzik is not here any more, and since Alter—that is Itzik—is registered as Avrohom-Yitzhok, and since according to that noodle-headed crown-rabbi, Yitzhok is Isak and Isak is Izak and Izak is Ayzik, they're liable to say, God forbid, that Itzik or Avrohom-Yitzhok—that is, Alter—is Ayzik."

"So what?" the lawyer said. "On the contrary, you'll be better off. If Itzik is Ayzik then you'll save yourself the fine. He's got a white rejection slip, you say."

"*Two* white rejection slips. But Itzik has got them, not Ayzik."

"But you just said that Itzik is Ayzik."

"Who said that Itzik is Ayzik?"

"You just said that Itzik is Ayzik," he said.

"Me? How could I say such a thing if Itzik is Alter, and Ayzik is the one who upset the boiling samovar while I was still a Vorotilevker living in Vorotilevke?"

So he flew off the handle and told me to get out.

"Beat it," he said. "You're pestering me to death, you pesky Jew!"

In other words, this meant that I was a pesky pest. Fancy that! Me, a pesky pest! Me!

THE FIRST PASSOVER NIGHT
OF THE WAR

A thin black ribbon consisting of two threads stretched over a broad white field in ancient Manchuria: the great Siberian railway wending its way downhill over the wild expanse of Asia toward Kwantung, Port Arthur and the sea.

Day and night locomotives traversed the endless rails. One after another they came, whistling and clattering, carrying wagonloads of soldiers, weapons and horses, as well as provisions for man and beast.

Night had fallen. The first night of Passover.

One of the train's coaches was crowded to capacity with soldiers. Exhausted from the long journey and the day's activity, the soldiers were quiet. One sat cross-legged and puffed on a piece of paper, pretending it was a cigarette. Another lay stretched out on his back; he whistled softly and sent a melancholy greeting to his far-off village home, where surely the snow had long since melted and spring's fragrance was already being felt. In turn, the soldier seemed to hear from afar the peasant girls straining their vocal cords and singing their beautiful sweet songs. Imagining that he heard their melodies quite clearly, he whistled along with them.

Off to a side, two soldiers sat alone on a bench beneath the lantern. One was an older man with a clipped black beard, the other a youngster whose light beard was short and yellow. And though both wore huge Siberian lambskin hats, one could immediately tell by their pale faces, white hands and black eyes that they were our brethren, fellow Jews.

Both looked intently into one prayerbook, swaying and

chanting softly. Every once in a while they ceased chanting to converse softly, after which they resumed their melodic recitation of the prayers.

They were celebrating the Seder aboard the train, reading the Passover Hagada with the traditional tunes which were sung at home. But they sang so softly their words were barely audible:

"*What does the matza that we eat symbolize?*"

"If only we would have a piece of matza," the young soldier sighed.

"Silly oaf!" said the older man. "During wartime we're excused. Excused from everything."

"Then why are we saying the Hagada?"

"Just so we remember that back home it's Passover."

The young soldier thought for a while about the sweet, endearing words: "Passover . . . back home." They coursed into his heart and pervaded his body, filling him with sad nostalgia and increased homesickness. His soul momentarily wrenched itself from his body and soared to a small village in Bessarabia called Holoneshti. The village was no bigger than a yawn; the mud was waist-high, and its poor—oh, those Holoneshti paupers—were legion. The stench and the stifling air of the overcrowded village were unbearable. Yet how he loved this poor little muddy, smelly, and stuffy Holoneshti. If ever there was an earthly Paradise, it was surely his village.

And no wonder, for there he was born and bred. There he grew up and there were his parents, sisters and brothers, friends and acquaintances. What were they doing now? Probably celebrating their Seder and thinking of him. Undoubtedly of him. "Alas," they would say, "God alone knows where our Leibke is, poor boy."

"Come on, let's continue. Why aren't you reciting, lad?" The older soldier encouraged Leibke with a jab in the side and proceeded with the familiar tune: "*What do the bitter herbs that we eat symbolize?*"

"If only we had some bitter herbs." Leibke smiled sadly and threw a glance at his older friend, Yerakhmiel.

"Nonsense!" replied Yerakhmiel. "What do you need bitter herbs for?" And he returned forthwith to the Hagada, saying: *"Because the Egyptians embittered the lives of our forefathers in Egypt."*

However, Yerakhmiel's thoughts were not in Egypt at that moment, but back home with his wife and children, in the village of Malopereshtchepeneh, in the Malorosye province. He re-created the scene of his departure, when he had tried to console everyone. First of all, he sought to convince them that they were just scared. That war was not so dangerous, because it was as easy to kill as get killed. Secondly, he told them that now that the enemy had attacked his land, as a true-blue soldier who had already faithfully served the Czar for five years, he had no alternative but to go fight till his last drop of blood.

However, during leave-taking Yerakhmiel's brave front collapsed. As he kissed the children good-bye, they burst into tears. When little Itsikl clasped him like a snake and cried, "Papa, no go war," and his wife fainted, Yerakhmiel could no longer contain himself. He just managed to tear himself away from them in one piece and flee.

But as soon as he entered the car he dismissed from his mind all thoughts of wife and children. For he was going to war. "For Czar and Fatherland."

So Yerakhmiel said proudly, his black shining eyes ablaze with an odd light which Leibke liked to see. He liked this pride, but did not understand it. Yerakhmiel was an experienced man, a soldier who had completed his required term of service, while Leibke from Holoneshti was a raw recruit. He had been sent hither a long time ago with an entire group of draftees, but during his journey he had fallen ill and spent a month in the hospital. Upon recuperating, he was placed on this train. Here the two Jews met, became friends, and poured out their bitter hearts to each other—in short, they became one soul. Leibke had proudly told Yerakhmiel that at home he had been given a little prayerbook and a pair of small *tfillin*. Yerakhmiel had gazed at the prayerbook and the *tfillin* and said that the prayerbook would come in handy for Passover, for it contained the Hagada. But, above all, Yerakhmiel envied Leibke for his *tfillin*. He said that if Leibke were shot he would at least be buried like a Jew. Yerakhmiel had been given everything: clothes, underwear, warm woolen boots—but not *this*. He envied Leibke for his small *tfillin*.

Leibke's pale face became white as chalk and his huge eyes grew larger as he asked his older, more experienced friend, Yerakhmiel:

"Wh-what do you m-mean b-b-buried like a J-J-Jew?"

Yerakhmiel explained that during wartime hundreds of slain soldiers, all in uniform, were buried in one mass grave. And as long as a Jew had *tfillin* with him, it was as though he had been properly buried in a Jewish cemetery.

Leibke stared at his friend Yerakhmiel, astonished at how calmly he talked of death. Young Leibke, a poor and simple workingman, could not understand why his friend Yerakhmiel went to battle with such joy. Yerakhmiel tried to reason with Leibke, but the latter could not grasp the line of thought. His brain refused to accept one fact.

"Well," said Leibke, "I can understand your point that it's every man's duty. But why the great joy? What's so glorious about it?"

"You ass!" snapped Yerakhmiel, then tried to make Leibke understand. "Just three things are enough to make me happy. That a Jew like me is equal with everyone else; that a Jew like me is one of the Czar's men; and that a Jew like me can show his loyalty to the entire world. Let our enemies see that a Jew too can serve faithfully and well, and that a Jew can also hold his head high in honor of the land where his ancestors' bones lie buried and where his bones too will lie."

Leibke stared at his friend and thought: What queer fish these Malorosye Jews are.

The other soldiers, in turn, stared at the Jews, eager to know what sort of outlandish language they were talking. Although the other soldiers referred to the two as "our Yids," they got along well with them. Everyone slept together, ate together, and everyone smoked everyone else's cigarettes, like true buddies.

Perhaps the friendship stemmed from the fact that in the entire train there was only one man who knew how to read and write Russian—Yerakhmiel.

Yerakhmiel had in his possession a Russian newspaper which reported the progress of the war and printed a map showing the position of the Russian fleet, Manchuria, Port Arthur, Korea, and Japan—a wretched, shriveled-up bit of land, the goal of all these soldiers. And along with Yerakhmiel they could hardly wait to reach their destination, so eager were they to settle accounts with the enemy. Yerakhmiel read the paper to the entire group and pointed out the enemy's land on the map.

"Japan! That's no land. It's a joke," said the soldiers.

"Some pipsqueak Jap-land that is!"

"One nip and Nippon is licked!"

"What a pushover! We'll squash 'em like bedbugs!"

Since the wrinkled gazette was read to tatters, it was now ready to be converted to cigarette paper. Too bad, since from it Yerakhmiel read such interesting stories of old-time Russian soldier-heroes, and tales of the Battle of Sevastapol describing how the Russians attacked and cast themselves into the heart of the fire. And in like manner would all the soldiers, including Yerakhmiel, cast themselves into the fire, fighting the Japanese.

Yerakhmiel also read them a story about a mountain called Malkhov Kurgan, where tens of thousands of Russian soldiers had perished.

"They all died at once, one atop the other." Yerakhmiel provided his own commentary. "All fell into one tinderbox. Sergeant majors along with privates first-class and plain foot soldiers."

"Jews, too?" Leibke asked with a frightened look.

"Jews, too. Along with all the others," said Yerakhmiel with the assurance of one who knew everything.

"You're lying," cried a pimply-faced young soldier.

"No, it's the truth." A few soldiers came to Yerakhmiel's defense and asked him to continue. "Read on, little brother."

But Yerakhmiel, seething, felt his Jewish blood rising. He did not want to let the pimply-faced soldier escape unscathed.

"You blockhead." Yerakhmiel flared up. "You don't understand a thing. After death and during battle everyone's equal. The Angel of Death doesn't recognize Jews or non-Jews. They're all human beings before God."

"You're lying," the pimply-faced soldier repeated. "I once heard someone reading from a book that when the Antichrist comes all the Christians will rise from the dead, but you Yids will rot in the earth like dogs."

"You nincompoop, you thick-witted dunderhead," Yerakhmiel said, infuriated, "What are you talking about? Do you know what you're talking about?"

The pimply-faced soldier raised his hand to Yerakhmiel, but the other soldiers, unwilling to have Yerakhmiel insulted, came to the Jew's defense. Nevertheless, Yerakhmiel refused to calm down.

"He's still jabbering, that imbecile," he raged. "That loony numbskull doesn't know that all men are equal before Czar and God; that both of us, both me and him, are going to fight one common enemy; he doesn't know that a bullet isn't choosy. Whoever it hits, it finishes off. If the enemy's bullet hits me, I'll know that I fell for the same Czar and for the same land that you did."

Such were the warm sentiments that Yerakhmiel expressed, ever fierce and fiery. All the onlookers respected this Jew and took a fancy to him for his clever remarks. Although they were not fond of Leibke because of his cowering, rabbitlike look, out of respect for Yerakhmiel they also respected his friend; and they let the two Jews sit by themselves on a bench beneath the lantern, so that they might say what they had to say.

"How come the Jews are swaying back and forth?" a soldier asked.

"Let 'em sway," another replied. "It's their holiday."

"Sabesh?"

"No, not Sabbath, but a holiday."

"What kind of holiday?"

"Shush, let's ask Rakhmiel himself. Rakhmiel?"

"Leave him alone," the other soldier called out. "The Jews are praying now. Let 'em pray."

Yerakhmiel and Leibke swayed with greater fervor. They were already up to the Hallel, the Psalms of Praise, which they chanted melodiously:

"Hallelujah! Praise ye, servants of the Lord. Praise the name of the Lord . . ." For the conclusion of each psalm, one of them, usually Yerakhmiel, assumed the role of the cantor. He broke into song and quavered in tremolo:

"He who makes the barren wo-m-an to dwell in her house as a joyful m-m-oth-er of chil-dren. Ha-l-le-lu-jah!"

The thoughts of both Leibke and Yerakhmiel sprouted wings and removed them from the railroad car. One was taken to Holoneshti, to his parents, sisters and brothers, perhaps even to his fiancée, a young girl with black braids, apple cheeks, and white teeth; the other to Malopereshtchepeneh, to his wife and children.

In Holoneshti, Leibke mused, they're also having a Seder, but there all of them are sitting around a table which is set with matzas, cups filled with raisin wine or mead, as well as bitter herbs and the symbolic mortar, made of chopped apples, nuts, and wine. Soon they'll be serving fresh, peppered fish which makes your mouth water. What ecstasy! Indeed, Leibke's nostrils flared, and it seemed to him that he could detect the fragrance of freshly cooked peppered fish. . . .

Yerakhmiel's thoughts were also at home, in Malopereshtchepeneh, with his young, pretty wife, Feige, who was probably celebrating the Seder at this very moment in her parents' house. He imagined them talking kindly to her, trying to console her by saying that although Yerakhmiel was far away, he'd rush home, God willing, as soon as the war was over. . . . They want to convince her that talk of peace was in the air. But his wife Feige refuses to listen. She cannot be comforted because of the children, especially little Itsikl who, upon being asked where his papa is, raises his little hand, points and replies: "Papa, far 'way."

And to prevent Leibke from noticing, Yerakhmiel, the hero of Malopereshtchepeneh, turned aside, pretending to blow his nose, and hastily wiped away a tear.

Holiday Tales

In the dozens of holiday tales that Sholom Aleichem wrote throughout his literary career, he introduced a variety of plots, locales and moods—from the Chekhovian still life of "Purim Sweet-Platters" and the tender character sketch of "David, King of Israel," to the imaginative political satire of "The Malicious Matza." Whether realistic or fantastic, his holiday tales give artistic expression to his own frequently stated love for the Jewish festivals and his desire to honor each one with a special story.

PURIM SWEET-PLATTERS

Wearing a silk kerchief and a plain apron—a combination of holiday and weekday attire—Mama stood by the table, practically at her wit's end. It was no trifle, you know, receiving almost a hundred Purim sweet-platters and sending out a like number. Mama had to be careful not to omit anyone or make any mistakes, God forbid; she also had to remember what sort of platter to send to whom. For instance, if someone favored you with a fruit-cut, two jam-filled pastries, a poppy-seed square, two tarts, a honey bun and two sugar cookies, it was customary to give in return two fruit-cuts, one jam-filled pastry, two poppy-seed squares, one tart, two honey buns, and three sugar cookies.

One had to have the brains of a prime minister not to create the sort of first-class muddle which once took place, alas, in our village. What happened was that one certain Rivke-Beyle mistakenly shipped back to one of the rich matrons the very same platter of Purim goodies that the rich matron had sent her. You should have seen the scandal it caused. The squabble that broke out between the husbands blossomed into a full-blown feud—smacks, denunciations and unending strife, as usual.

Besides worrying about what to send to whom, you also had to tip those who delivered the Purim sweet-platters. And you had to know whether to give them one kopeck, or two or three.

The door opened up and in came my teacher's daughter, a freckled girl with bright red hair. She went about from house to house collecting the Purim sweet-platters for the teacher. She carried a saucer covered with a cloth napkin which already contained one honey bun, dotted with a solitary raisin and a silver coin. Mama lifted the napkin and placed another coin alongside the first. She also slipped something into the girl's hand. The redhead blushed furiously and rattled off the traditional blessing:

"May you enjoy Purim a year from now, you, your husband, and your children."

Following the girl came a chubby lad with a swollen cheek bound with a blue kerchief and eyes of unequal size. In his hand he held a little brass tray on which lay a fruit-cut. This small cake was impressed with the shape of a tiny fish filled with honeyed dough crumbs. Next to it lay several silver coins and a few paper rubles. The chubby lad went right up to Mama and in one breath rattled off his greeting as though it had been memorized by rote:

"Happy holiday the rabbi sent you this Purimsweetplatter may you enjoy Purim ayearfromnow you 'n' your husband 'n' your children."

The chubby lad palmed his tip and took off without a farewell, because by mistake he had dashed it off upon entering.

More people kept coming by. They brought various treats from the rabbinic judge, the cantor, the *shokhtim,* the scribe, the Talmud Torah teacher, the man who blew the ram's horn, the butcher who specialized in removing thigh veins, the Scroll of Esther reader, and the water-carrier and the bathhouse keeper (the latter two also fancied themselves religious functionaries). After them came Velvel the sexton himself, hoarse and ailing—he was asthmatic, poor man. He stood awhile at the door and, hand to his chest, coughed his heart out.

"Well, what's the good word?" Mama asked him, exhausted by now from the day's work.

"You've been sent a Purim sweet-platter," said Velvel, displaying a honey cake he had in his hand. "May you enjoy Purim a year from now, you and . . ."

"Who's it from?" asked Mama and stuck her hand beneath her apron, looking for a coin.

"Well, it's actually from me. May you enjoy Purim, you . . ." and he began coughing. "Pardon me . . . for coming myself . . . got no one to send . . . had a daughter but, alas, God preserve you . . . you remember Freydel, may she rest in peace . . ."

Velvel the sexton coughed for an entire minute and Mama quickly dug into her pocket and removed a few coins which she put into his hand. She also offered him some cake and a couple of fruit-cuts. Velvel stuffed the cake and the fruit-cuts into his breast pocket, thanked her and said: "May you enjoy Purim a year from now, you and your husband . . ." and once again began coughing. I looked at Mama and noticed a tear standing in each of her beautiful eyes.

Velvel and his Purim treat cast a momentary gloom over the holiday mood. But it did not last long. Immediately after Velvel's departure others arrived with more Purim sweet-platters, and Mama kept on doling out the coins, here one, there two or three. Everyone received a piece of cake, a fruit-cut or a honey bun. For a poor man, too, should feel the joy of the holiday.

"May you enjoy Purim a year from now, you and your . . ."

"The same to you and many more to you and yours!"

DAVID, KING OF ISRAEL

Old Dodi had snow-white hair and curly sidelocks, which he covered with an old-fashioned Napoleon-style hat. He was always seen holding a long thick staff with a carved ivory handle and carrying a sack on his bent back. On Friday afternoons and the eves of holidays he always went from house to house collecting Sabbath loaves for the poor Jewish prisoners.

Old Dodi, who was almost one hundred years old, was a town celebrity better known as David, King of Israel. Since everyone knew that he merely wanted bread for his poor prisoners, no one argued with him. There were those who had bread and the will to share, as well as those who had neither. But Old Dodi did not take it amiss if he was turned away empty-handed. If everyone had bread and the will to share, he asked, what would happen to the takers? And without givers and takers what would become of compassion, righteousness and good deeds? Then what need would there be for the World-to-Come and Paradise? And if there would be neither World-to-Come nor Paradise where would the righteous souls go?

Such were the questions that ran through Old Dodi's mind. His view was that whatever God did was right; there had to be takers and givers, haves and have-nots, prisoners and free men who cared for the prisoners by collecting white-loaf on Friday afternoons and on the eves of holidays.

2

Who was Old Dodi—David, King of Israel? What did he do during his first hundred years and before he began collecting bread for the poor Jewish prisoners?

No one knew.

What means of support did old David have? How did he earn his living? Exactly how old was he? Where were his children and grandchildren?

No one knew that either. The answers were a well-kept secret. There simply wasn't a man who could remember. And if you asked Dodi himself he wouldn't reply. In fact, you'd be much better off if you didn't even try to find out. If you got to talking with him he'd ask you to contribute something for his poor prisoners. For he always managed to steer any conversation to his favorite subject:

"Reb Dodi! Where did you sleep last night?"

"God be praised, at least it wasn't in the prison. Do you perchance have some old clothing for my prisoners?"

"Reb Dodi! Where have all your children and grandchildren gone to?"

"God be praised, they're scattered all over. One here, the other there, spread over seven seas. Some have died, some are alive. Some are well off, others not. So long as they're not in prison, God forbid. Do you perchance have—excuse the expression—some underwear for my prisoners?"

"Reb Dodi! May you live to be one hundred and twenty, exactly how old are you?"

"God be praised, I'm no youngster. May the good Lord grant that you too reach my old age. But I wish you better luck. And most of all, may you never know of prison as long as you live. Do you perchance have a pair of tattered boots lying around for my prisoners?"

Such a man was Old Dodi—David, King of Israel.

3

Why was he called David, King of Israel?

Because once a year during Simkhas Torah he became a king, the King of the Jewish children.

At Simkhas Torah you would not recognize Old Dodi. His bent back was straight, his beard and sidecurls were combed. His Napoleon-style hat was turned inside out. His broad white collar was smooth and neat. And he no longer carried his staff and sack. Old Dodi was transformed. His face shone, his eyes sparkled. Having taken a drop of liquor in honor of the holiday, Old Dodi became spirited and gay—he became a new man with a reanimated soul.

He gathered all the small fry from all the synagogues, lined them up in circles around him, then walked about in the midst of the circle, stretched his hands heavenward and sang:

"Holy little lambs!"

"Baa-baa," replied the youngsters.

"Tell me now, who's leading you?"

"Our King David, baa-baa."

"What's his full name?"

"David, King of Israel, baa-baa."

"Then shout it out, Jewish children, with a pretty melody: David, King of Israel, is still alive!"

"David . . . King . . . of Israel . . . is still . . . alive!"

"Once again. Holy little lambs!"

"Baa-baa."

"Tell me now, who's leading you?"

"Our King David, baa-baa."

"What's his full name?"

"David, King of Israel, baa-baa."

"Then shout it out, Jewish children, with a pretty melody: David . . . King . . . of Israel . . . is still . . . alive!"

"David . . . King . . . of Israel . . . is still . . . alive!"

More children joined the troupe. The cavalcade grew. The onlookers kept increasing. The sound of tumultuous voices surrounded the village. David, King of Israel, stopped at every Sukkos booth, where he was given a drink by the householders and a piece of cake by their wives. He drank the whiskey and distributed the cake among the children, singing:

"Holy little lambs!"

"Baa-baa."

"What have I got in my hand?"

"Honey cake, baa-baa."

"What blessing is said over it?"

"Blessed is he who creates various kinds of foods. Baa-baa."

"Tell me now, who's leading you?"

"Our King David, baa-baa."

"What's his full name?"

"David, King of Israel, baa-baa."

"Then shout it out, Jewish children, with a pretty melody: David . . . King . . . of Israel . . . is still . . . alive!"

"David . . . King . . . of Israel . . . is still . . . alive!"

4

You might wonder what harm was there in a poor old centenarian's taking a drop of liquor once a year on Simkhas Torah, becoming cheerful and gay and posing as a king, while young merrymakers trailed after him bleating "Baa-baa"?

But here's what happened.

Just before Rosh Hashana, during the season of the Penitential Prayers, a new police chief was sent to our village (the old one had dropped dead). As usual, the new police chief, sporting a personality all his own, instituted brand-new procedures. First of all, it was said that he was a scrupulously conscientious man—too conscientious, in fact. Meeting a Jew he would straightaway ask him: "What's your name and where are you from? Got a passport?" Secondly, his palms were absolutely ungreasable. He took nothing. Neither cash nor goods. Talk of being ethical! He was clean as a whistle. The news spread like wildfire through town. Bad business! A rat! A Haman!

The next morning he was already strolling through the village. He ran through the marketplace, inspected all the stores and butcher shops, poked his nose into the synagogue courtyard, sniffed here and there. . . . But, poor fellow, what illicit business could he have found during the holiday season? The Hebrew teachers had already released the schoolchildren, and counterfeit money was not our stock in trade. So we dismissed the police chief from our thoughts.

But God provided him with grist for the mill. The holiday of Sukkos! Just listen. He didn't like the way the Jews built their booths. Said they were a fire hazard, dangerous to life and limb. Get the picture? For thousands of years Jews have lived in these booths and feared absolutely nothing. Now all of a sudden there was a fire to worry about!

"Well, your lordship, what exactly is it you want?"

"I don't want you to build your booths this way, but in the following manner."

Of course they paid as much attention to him as Haman does to the Purim rattle-clacker. And they began building their Sukkos booths in the age-old traditional way. So the police chief got wind of this and had them torn down.

A delegation was sent to him. "Your lordship," they said, "how can we celebrate Sukkos without our booths?"

"Nothing doing," he said.

So go knock your head against the wall. For if you really insisted he'd demand to see your passport and take down your name.

To make a long story short, we were in hot water. We went into hiding. Several families shared one booth, scared to death lest—I don't have to spell it out for you! But the good Lord had mercy on us and most of the holiday passed by without incident. All our fears had been in vain. But then came the final day of the holiday, Simkhas Torah.

5

On the last day, Simkhas Torah, Old Dodi and his troupe of merrymakers came into the synagogue courtyard.

"Holy little lambs!" he called out in his usual fashion.

"Baa-baa," replied the holy little lambs.

Suddenly the police chief materialized as though out of nowhere. He gazed at the scene in utter amazement, apparently seeing such a show for the first time. Since Old Dodi had no reason to fear the new police chief, he continued:

"Tell me now, Jewish children, who's leading you?"

"Our King David!"

"What's his full name?"

"David, King of Israel."

"Then shout it out, Jewish children, with a pretty melody: David . . . King . . . of Israel . . . is still . . . alive!"

"David . . . King . . . of Israel . . . is still . . . alive!"

The police chief then demanded an explanation. What did all this mean? Who was the old man? And what were the youngsters singing?

Reb Shepsl the teacher, who had a reputation for his knowledge of Russian, stepped forth. He brushed his side-curls behind his ears and volunteered to be the interpreter.

"He is David the Jewish Czar and the children are his serfs," said Reb Shepsl in Russian.

At this the police chief slapped his hands in glee and began to laugh. But do you think he just chuckled? He held his sides and laughed so hysterically he almost went into convulsions. David, King of Israel, did not stop singing, "Holy little lambs!" and the holy little lambs did not stop shouting, "Baa-baa." After a while the police chief got sick of the performance. He chased the troupe of children and, in his usual fashion, took David, King of Israel, to task.

"Where are you from?" he demanded. "Got a passport?"

It turned out that the old man himself did not know where he was from. And so, alas, he was sent to jail, where he joined his poor prisoners.

"He'll sober up there," said the police chief, "that old sot!"

A year later, Jews dwelled in their Sukkos booths, as usual. They made merry at Simkhas Torah as they did every year. But one element was missing. David, King of Israel, was gone. And his little song, "Holy little lambs," which elicited the reply, "Baa-baa," was heard no more.

THE MALICIOUS MATZA

Once upon a time there was a great and mighty king who did not like Jews. And so, like the Pharaoh of Egypt, he would occasionally issue severe decrees against them.

During one Passover all his ministers gathered in the council chamber to cook up a new decree with which to burden the Jews. But they had a problem, since declarations limiting Jews' rights of residence, forbidding them to be officers and their children to attend the high schools had already been formally decreed.

Then some minister got the bright idea to come out against the matza:

"Before Passover Your Majesty's Jews bake an eight-day supply of a sort of crisp round cracker known as matza," he informed the king. "God knows what sort of concoction it is! In my opinion, it would be perfectly just to forbid them to eat this matza."

The king reflected awhile and then ordered a matza to be brought to him. So the king's men scattered all over the capital looking for Jews, but none could be found. When they finally did find a Jew and demanded of him a matza for His Majesty, the Jew swore that he didn't even know what a matza looked like. (The Jews had immediately sensed a new decree in the wind.)

After a great deal of effort and trouble the king's men finally found a Jew who wasn't afraid to admit that he ate matza. So they helped themselves to one and brought it to the king's council chamber.

As soon as the king saw the matza he took a fancy to it.

After the first bite he slowly kept on nibbling until there was not a crumb left.

A moment later he began to feel ill. By and by he felt worse and worse. Finally, when he felt absolutely sick to his royal stomach, the greatest doctors and specialists in the land were called in. They discovered that something inside the king's stomach was pestering him to death.

When the most renowned specialist pressed his ear to the king's belly in order to investigate, he heard someone singing in there.

"Your Majesty," he called out. "With your permission, I would like to converse with whatever is in your stomach."

"Speak," said the king.

The specialist addressed the creature in the king's stomach. "Tell me, who are you?"

"I'm a Jew," came the reply.

"What are you doing there?"

"Nothing."

"Would you perchance like to leave?"

"Not at all, thank you."

"Whatever for?"

"That's my business."

"If you come out, you'll receive a fine present."

"I'm quite familiar with the fine present you have in mind. Twenty-four hours to pack up and leave town."

"Why?"

"Because I'm Jewish and Jews aren't allowed to live here in the capital."

"What if they promise you that you can live here."

"I don't care a fig about myself. I want all the Jews to have permission to live here."

This exchange made the king feel worse than ever. The Jew spoke with his hands and feet, gesticulating to beat the band. The king felt that he was about to give up the ghost. He asked the specialists to conclude the interview.

Then the most venerable of the specialists addressed the Jew in the king's stomach:

"His Majesty promises you that you may remain in the city as long as you wish."

"I've already told you that I'm not after personal favors. I want this permission for all the Jews."

"Splendid. All the Jews may remain. Just hurry up and come out."

"Who's speaking to me?"

"It's us, the king's royal physicians. But we're conveying His Majesty's will to you."

"How do I know?"

"Haven't you heard it from the king himself?"

"The king's word isn't enough for me. Now that he's in pain, he'll promise anything. Later, when the pain stops, he'll change his mind. Just like the Pharaoh of Egypt."

"All right, what is it you wish?"

"I want him to put it on paper, and I want it signed and sealed and approved by his Council of Ministers."

And the Jew in the king's stomach began thrashing about so furiously that the king couldn't bear the pain. He assembled the ministers and ordered them to decree a new law signed and sealed by the king and approved by the entire Council that Jews were to be perfectly free to live in the capital city and anywhere else in the land.

And so it came to pass.

No sooner had the Jew heard this than with one bound he squeezed himself out of the little finger of the king's left hand, bowed to the entire council, and rushed off to his brethren looking for a spot of business.

Village Stories

⚛

The shtetls described in "One Hundred and One," "Burnt Out," and "The Village of Habne"—they too, in addition to the renowned Kasrilevke, make up the geography of Sholom Aleichem's world—in a sense become supporting characters through the personal force they generate in the stories.

"The Village of Habne" offers a good example of how Sholom Aleichem handled a theme whose source is a popular Hasidic story.

Following is the core of the oral tale:

After a newly chosen Hasidic rabbi (about whom some of the townspeople had their doubts) assumed his duties, an out-of-town merchant deposited some money with one of the rich men of the community. When the merchant came to call for his money, the rich man denied receiving it. The merchant complained to the rabbi, who forthwith summoned the rich man. When the rabbi's messenger was ignominiously thrown out of the rich man's house, the rabbi wrote another summons wherein he warned the rich man that he would publicize his disrespect for the authority of the rabbinical court, and would be excluded from the Jewish community. The rich man then appeared before the rabbi, returned to the merchant not only his money but also an additional sum for damages and admitted to the rabbi that he had purposely done all this to see if the rabbi would give him, the rich man, special consideration because of his prominence.

Although Sholom Aleichem of course changed the details and artistically enhanced the plot, the basic elements of the folk tale remain: a new man in a strange town, money deposited by a rich communal leader who denies receiving it, and the test that the rich man imposes upon his fellow villagers.

ONE HUNDRED AND ONE

Although Holte and Bohopolye were separated by the beautiful Bug River, these two Jewish villages—actually one community cut in half by the water—were reunited by a bridge which could be spanned in five minutes.

For many years Bohopolye considered itself a small town, whereas Holte considered itself a village. Hence, owing to the latter's self-declared status, it fell victim to the decree of May 3, 1882, which stated that no new Jews would be permitted to settle there.

Subsequent to that May decree Holte, quite naturally, became a very desirable place for the Bohopolye Jews, all of whom suddenly got the urge to pick themselves up and live in that forbidden village. And so, after May 3, the Bohopolye Jews clandestinely began moving to Holte. But they didn't succeed. At the bridge they were asked, with all due deference, to about-face and march right back:

"Mister Itzko, kindly take a walk to the Bohopolye rabbi."

At other times the officials simply turned the Jewish wagons around without so much as a word and jeered:

"Why don't you hit the trail for Berditchev?"

"It's unfair," cried a poor Jew in his halting vernacular. "I've been a Holter for years. I've got my own seat in the synagogue. I've even got relatives in the cemetery."

But all these entreaties were as efficacious as yesteryear's snow. For the constant reply was: "Document! Papers!"

Soon there began a run on documents and papers, for which Jews paid lots of money. Go-betweens made money hand over fist. The informers also were kept busy. Some were successful, some not. Many Jews ruined others' chances by tattling. And several families had to pick up their bedding, alas, and head back over the bridge from Holte to Bohopolye. And so a new crop of beggars arrived in Bohopolye, new boarders whose only nourishment was eating each other's hearts out.

But since the Jews didn't want to surrender so easily, they waged (a paper) war. Jews fought the police as well as each other. Documents, affidavits and depositions dispatched to the police were sent up to the regional governor's office and then to the Senate; from there they were returned to the regional governor's office and then back to the police. This paper battle lasted twenty years. I'm afraid that the future historian of these two villages will have to call that era the Twenty Years' War, a reference which the Jews of Holte and Bohopolye will certainly understand.

Among the leading warriors were two men: Yerakhmiel-Moishe Bohopolsky of Holte, and his bitter enemy, Nakhman-Leyb Holtiansky of Bohopolye.

2

Don't be surprised at the fact that Yerakhmiel-Moishe from Holte was called Bohopolsky and that Nakhman-Leyb from Boholpolye was called Holtiansky. Don't even ask why! Why, I know a Tcherkasy from Byelotcherkov and a Byelotcherkovsky from Tcherkas! What's more, I know a Tarashtchasky from Krementchug, and a Krementchusky from Tarashtche. Would it be so terrible if Tcherkasy, who no doubt stemmed from Tcherkas, would live in Tcherkas, Byelotcherkovsky in Byelotcherkov, Tarashtchasky in Tarashtche and Krementchusky in Krementchug? The answer to this question is quite simple—if each man would have to be bound to his home town the world would go to pieces!

But let's get back to May 3, 1882.

By pure coincidence, on the May 2nd prior to that May 3rd, Nakhman-Leyb Holtiansky, a lifelong resident of Bohopolye, had to be in Holte in connection with some official matter. And since he had to sleep there, he registered with the police, which served as sufficient proof that he was a resident of Holte. Which is how one man's luck can be another's misfortune.

Understandably enough, this got under Yerakhmiel-Moishe's skin. He pecked away at Nakhman-Leyb with great zeal until he miraculously succeeded in showing black on white that Nakhman-Leyb was a Bohopolyer. Naturally, Nakhman-Leyb wasn't asleep either, and provided documented proof that on the May 2nd prior to that May 3rd he was registered in the village constable's books. His name alone, Holtiansky, showed that he, Nakhman-Leyb, was a Holter, and that Yerakhmiel-Moishe was a Bohopolyer, just as his name suggested: Bohopolsky of Bohopolye.

So wrote Nakhman-Leyb to the regional governor's office concerning Yerakhmiel-Moishe. The latter did not sit on *his* hands, either; he forthwith filed affidavits and brought witnesses to show that Nakhman-Leyb was actually a Bohopolyer, despite the fact that he called himself Holtiansky. The most convincing evidence was that he had his own apartment and a seat in the Preacher's Synagogue in Bohopolye. Why did a resident of Holte need an apartment in Bohopolye and a seat in a Bohopolyer synagogue?

In a nutshell, the two pestered each other and filed so many affidavits and counter-affidavits in the regional governor's office that finally an official order was issued. Both were to be shipped out of Holte at once, and special precautions were to be taken to prevent them from ever again setting foot in town, except during daylight hours.

3

"Why don't you speak up, you ass!" said Yerakhmiel-Moishe's friend.

"What do you think I'll gain by shouting?"

"There's a Senate in this land. Appeal to them," said the friend.

"What's the use of appealing to them if the regional governor's office declared that I'm a Bohopolyer?"

At which Yerakhmiel-Moishe's wife butted in. "No need to apply to the Senate. You need the Senate like a hole in the head. You want us to be kicked out of Bohopolye, too?"

Usually Yerakhmiel-Moishe's wife won out. But here her
hands were tied. Yerakhmiel-Moishe was a stubborn mule
and submitted his appeal to the Senate.

And guess what happened?

A long time passed. Twenty years, I'm afraid. One early
summer day Yerakhmiel-Moishe was sitting in his shop. The
furthest thing from his thoughts was the Senate. In fact, he'd
forgotten that such an institution existed. And then suddenly
a policeman appeared and summoned him to headquarters.

"What now?" said Yerakhmiel-Moishe's wife. "Another
meeting of the Holy Synod? You and your petitions!"

"I don't know the first blasted thing about it," said
Yerakhmiel-Moishe. "Look, if the police call you, you can't
be a pig about it and refuse to go."

"Just see to it that they don't lock you up," was his wife's
parting blessing as she accompanied him out of the store.

About twenty minutes later Yerakhmiel-Moishe dashed
into the store, completely out of breath. "Con-gra-tu-la-
tions," he puffed. "From the Senate . . . a letter . . . stating . . . I'm a Bohopolyer. . . . Got . . . permission . . .
to live . . . in Bohopolye."

Yerakhmiel-Moishe's wife clapped her hands. "Well isn't
that just one big deal! What do you say to luck like that?
Finally he's permitted to live in Bohopolye!"

"Tfu," he spat. "What am I saying? I mean Holte. That's
what I mean."

"Holte? Now you're talking! Well, Yerakhmiel-Moishe,
what did I tell you?"

"What did you tell me?"

"Didn't I tell you to appeal to the Senate?"

The overjoyed Yerakhmiel-Moishe was in such an ecstatic
state of bliss that he ran out trumpeting the good news from
one end of town to the other: Official word had come down
from the Senate that he could live in Holte, whither, God
willing, he would soon pack up and move.

That day Yerakhmiel-Moishe neither ate nor rested. He
ran from one friend to another. He felt like sprouting wings
and taking off. He stopped everyone he met and said:

"Have you heard?"

"About what? The Senate? Sure I heard. What do you think? Congratulations and lots of good luck."

"Same to you and more."

"When do you plan to move?"

"God willing, after Shevuos."

"I wish you all the best."

"Thanks."

4

Although success is sweet, success plus revenge is sweeter yet. That unbeatable combination prompts indescribable joy. A man who sees the next fellow turn green with envy and watches him simmer slowly and die a thousand deaths is filled with such a sense of well-being, power and viciousness that he forgets himself in his hour of triumph and begins to act like a fool.

There wasn't a place that was safe from Yerakhmiel-Moishe's chattering about the Senate—a topic which soon thoroughly disgusted and bored the townspeople. They reacted to it as they would to pork. They felt their bile rising whenever they heard Yerakhmiel-Moishe telling his incessant story about the Senate.

But if the townspeople had their fill of the story, don't you think poor Nakhman-Leyb was burned up and fuming? Yet, alas, he had to hear the story over and over again from none other than Yerakhmiel-Moishe, who constantly sought out Nakhman-Leyb in a crowd and then went up to him and said:

"Well, it seems that there are some good chaps in the Senate after all."

Nakhman-Leyb stepped aside and tried to hide, but Yerakhmiel-Moishe followed him, talking not to Nakhman-Leyb but to the others, yet loud enough for him to hear.

"Last night I purposely went to sleep over in Holte. I was dying to have the constable come to me. But just to spite me he didn't even show up."

Yerakhmiel-Moishe and his wife had such a good life together and got along so swimmingly, praised be God, that whenever she possibly could she double-crossed him. However, with Nakhman-Leyb's defeat, she came to Yerakhmiel-Moishe's aid and helped him spread the news over town. She was so instrumental in tormenting Nakhman-Leyb and his wife that the latter prayed to God for a quicker advent of Shevuos so that Yerakhmiel-Moishe and his wife would already pick themselves up and go to the blazes.

"I can't even look anyone in the eye," Nakhman-Leyb's wife said.

The good Lord took pity and Shevuos came. But Yerakhmiel-Moishe and his wife were in no rush to move out to Holte. What's the big hurry? What would they miss if they came a week later? The main thing was that, thank God, permission was granted.

And so they procrastinated until one Sunday, the 25th of May, when the newspapers (who ever dreamed up newspapers, anyway?) published a list of one hundred and one villages wherein Jews could reside, build houses, buy land and plant gardens. One hundred and one villages! Including Holte! It was unheard of! Yerakhmiel-Moishe refused to believe anyone.

"It's impossible. It's a lie," he screamed. "For twenty years in a row we've been forbidden to remain overnight in Holte —and now all of a sudden we can build houses, buy land and plant gardens? And now it's no more and no less than one hundred and one of these villages, including Holte in the bargain? I tell you, my enemies have concocted this. It probably sprang right out of Nakhman-Leyb's head, may he roast in hell. When hair sprouts from the palm of my hand, that's when Jews will be able to live in Holte."

So screamed Yerakhmiel-Moishe, as his wife nodded and agreed. For she, too, had heard something in the marketplace concerning one hundred and one villages, including Holte.

"If that report is true," she said, spitting fire like a frying pan aflame, "then you and your Senate can both pack up and go to hell."

Suddenly the door opened and in came the sexton of the Preacher's Synagogue holding a Yiddish newspaper.

"Here you are, Reb Yerakhmiel-Moishe. No offense, but it's been sent so's you can glance at it and see for yourself what it has to say. There's some news in it, folks say, about

Bohopolye and Holte and one hundred and one villages. See where the page is folded and where number 94 is underlined?"

Yerakhmiel-Moishe understood who had taken the trouble to send him the newspaper. He took the paper and put on his glasses. The first thing that struck his eye was item number 94 and the word "Holte." He didn't even want to read any further. Realizing that the report was true, he approached his wife.

"Well," she laughed bitterly, knowing why he had come to her. "There's your Senate for you."

"Since when is it *mine?*"

"Then whose *is* it? Senate-shmenate, that's all he's ever wanted. May you all burn to a crisp, dear sweet God!"

5

That day was a black one for Yerakhmiel-Moishe and his wife. She set the table silently. Didn't even say a word. She slapped the dishes down and clanged the silverware.

"Go wash up," she told her husband. "He has to be invited twenty-two times."

"Twenty-two? If memory serves me, I don't think you even called me once!" sighed Yerakhmiel-Moishe. Having washed, he recited the benediction and thought: One hundred and one villages . . . perfectly free . . . including Holte. He sat down, said the blessing over bread, looked for something on the table but couldn't find it. Since he was not allowed to talk prior to eating the bread, he waved his hands about and spoke in Hebrew: "Um—er—ah—salt!"

"Salt-shmalt. It's right under your nose. What are you mumbling about?"

Yerakhmiel-Moishe just about managed to swallow the piece of bread; he felt it gagging him. He mistook a spoon for a knife, and a fork for a spoon. Throughout the entire meal neither husband nor wife exchanged a word. The only sounds were those of sipping, smacking, crunching and the noisy clatter of dishes.

Only once did Yerakhmiel-Moishe's wife speak up.

"Cat's got your tongue?"

Yerakhmiel-Moishe did not reply. The entire lunch passed so silently they could have heard a pin drop. After the meal, Yerakhmiel-Moishe picked his teeth with the fork and addressed the ceiling.

"The fingerbowl," he said.

His wife looked him straight in the eye and, tilting her head to a side, said: "Say, Yerakhmiel-Moishe, on which side of the bed did you get up today?"

Yerakhmiel-Moishe did not say a word. He dipped his fingers into the bowl of water, then flung the plates aside and quietly began to say the Grace After Meals.

Now, during his prayer, when he could not answer back, was the opportune time for his wife to get even with him—to get under his skin, gnaw at him like a worm and eat his heart out; she'd teach him not to be a lunatic, nor play the boss, nor fling dishes around.

"Just look at him still acting up. Spreading happiness and joy. Just because he's a man he thinks he can do what he wants. A man and a big shot in the Senate. He's really something! Tsk, tsk, tsk!"

His head down, his eyes closed, swaying to and fro, Yerakhmiel-Moishe said grace softly: "He who sustains all and does good to all . . ."

But his wife continued gnawing at him in her own sweet way: "I'll bet if you ask him what he's mad about he won't even know. Actually, why *are* you sore as hell? It's your Senate, not mine."

Yerakhmiel-Moishe continued his grace in a slightly louder voice:

"As it is written—you shall eat and have your fill . . ." and concluded with a high-pitched quaver: "Blessed are you, O Lord, for the land and for the sus-tenance."

His wife waited a minute, then continued:

"What a hot temper. He's got murder in his eye. All burned up, huh? God protect us, I'd better take cover."

Yerakhmiel-Moishe raised his voice. "You continuously bestow upon us kindness and mercy, relief and deliverance, prosperity and blessing . . ."

"So how come none of it comes our way?" said his wife. "In our case just the opposite seems to be true."

Yerakhmiel-Moishe raised his voice some more.

"Salvation and consolation, livelihood and sustenance, mercy and life, peace and all goodness."

But Yerakhmiel-Moishe's wife refused to remain silent:

"Ask him what he's so concerned about? What's he got to lose? So Nakhman-Leyb *will* be able to live in Holte? So what? Let him live there with a pack of plagues! I don't give a damn. He can burst for all I care."

Yerakhmiel-Moishe seethed like a samovar, but contained his rage as far as he was able and continued chanting in an even louder, more plaintive voice.

But man is not made of stone. Yerakhmiel-Moishe's wife persisted in her relentless gnawing until he finally grated his teeth and roared:

"Grr, may the All-merciful bless my wife and my children and my grandchildren, blast it . . ." and he ran out of the house like a lunatic.

Nakhman-Leyb and his wife moved to Holte and Yerakhmiel-Moishe and his wife have remained in Bohopolye unto this very day.

BURNT OUT

Just between you and me, my dear fellow passengers, the Jews—God forgive me for saying so—the Jews are a rash, impetuous people. The only things one can safely share with a Jew are a noodle pudding, a prayerbook and a cemetery—the devil take them one and all, for I couldn't care less.

You may ask why I'm so wrought up and why I'm smearing the Jews. Well, if you'd be in my shoes and have my pack of troubles on your back, and if Jews had treated *you* the way they treated *me*, then you'd grab perfect strangers on the street and either choke them or beat them black and blue. But never mind. I'm the sort of man who hates to fight the world. I always say, so what if I'm the loser. But like the Talmud says: People never change. So let God get even with them and let the devil take them one and all, for I couldn't care less.

Listen to this. I happen to be from Bohslev, may God spare you that fate. Well, actually, from a small village near Bohslev. Small but nice. The sort of village which, like the proverb has it, should be thickly sown but sparsely grown. You know what sort of village it is? The sort that if you *really* want to punish someone, don't exile him to Siberia—no sir!— just exile him to us in Bohslev. Give him a shop and just enough credit to go bankrupt. Let him have a fire and be burnt out lock stock and barrel and not save so much as a shoelace, so that Bohslever Jews should say that he himself lit the match in order to—

I suppose you realize by now the sort of things the Bohslever Jews are capable of. They concoct stories, spread them around town and even address insinuating letters to the proper places—the devil take them one and all, for I couldn't care less.

By now you've got some inkling into the man you're looking at. You're looking at a crestfallen man, a man triply wretched, a man who bears a threefold pack of troubles on his back. First of all, I'm a Jew; second of all I'm a Bohslever Jew; and third of all I'm a burnt-out Bohslever Jew. Boy am I burnt out! I'm one of those honest-to-goodness burnt offerings mentioned in the prayerbook.

I had a fire this year. What sort? A conflagration! I burned like a thatched roof. Like they say: I just escaped by the skin of my teeth. In other words, I came out of it as naked as the day I was born. And—wouldn't you expect it?—it just so happened that on that very night I was not at home. Where was I? Actually, not too far from home. In Tarashtche, at my sister's for an engagement party. It was a beautiful affair: a banquet, fine guests, none of your lousy Bohslever riffraff. And as you can imagine, they drank up one and a half barrels of whiskey, not counting beer and wine. In brief, it was a festive occasion and we lived it up. Then all of a sudden I got a telegram addressed to me, Moishe-Mordecai.

"Wife sick. Children sick. Mother-in-law sick. Very critical."

So naturally Moishe-Mordecai kicked up his heels and rushed home helter-skelter.

When I arrived, I found that pandemonium had broken loose. No house, no shop, no merchandise—not even a pillow, not even a shirt to warm my back. Like the Book says: *Solitary hath he come and solitary departed.* In other words, he came poor and left broke.

The wife was weeping, poor thing, and seeing her crying, my kids too burst into tears. They had no place to put their heads. Luckily, I was insured—and for plenty, too. And there's where the dog lies buried. The fire itself wouldn't have been half bad. The real trouble was that this wasn't the first time it happened, Lord preserve us. This wasn't my first fire, you see. The first one also broke out at night when I was out of town. But at that time, thank God, everything went off smoothly. The adjuster came, made a list of the scorched rags, estimated the amount of the damage, settled up nicely and neatly—give or take a ruble—the devil take them one and all, for I couldn't care less!

That's story number one. But this time they sent me an adjuster, the likes of which I don't wish on any Jew! A black-hearted monster! And—my luck!—he was clean as a whistle to boot. His palms simply wouldn't be greased. Imagine! He refused to take money and go knock your head against the wall. So he looked and rummaged, grubbed and burrowed. He investigated here and there and wanted me to explain how and where the fire started. And how much was burned. And how come not a scrap of anything remained. Not even a piece of thread.

"You took the question right out of my mouth," I said. "My very words. Why don't you ask God Almighty?"

"Something's fishy here," he said. "Don't think that it's so easy to get money from us."

How do you like that wise guy? Scaring the scarecrow! He was just like the police investigator in our village who wanted to catch me contradicting myself. He thought he was matching wits with a first-grader.

"Tell me, Moshke," that policeman asked me, "tell me, pal, how come you're always burning to the ground?"

"Because of fire, Your Excellency," I told him. "That's what keeps me burning."

"And how come you insured yourself only two weeks before the fire?"

"My dear sir, what do you expect me to do," I said, "take out insurance two weeks *after?*"

"And how come at the very moment when your place is on fire you're not at home?"

"And if I *would* have been at home during the time of the fire, sir, would you feel any better?"

"And how come they wired you that your wife and kids were sick, and that your mother-in-law was near death?"

"To get me to rush home on the double."

"Why didn't they tell you the truth?"

"So I shouldn't panic."

"In that case," he said, "I now know what's what with you. For your information you're under arrest!"

"Why and what for?" I asked. "What have I done? You're

making an absolutely innocent man wretched. Killing someone is no trick, you know. You want to kill me—go right ahead. Don't you know that there are laws and that there's a God?"

"You have the gall to talk about God?" he fumed. "You so-and-so!"

But since I was perfectly innocent, innocent as a lamb, it didn't bother me a bit. Like they say: Silence is golden. In other words, if you don't eat garlic, no one will get wind of it—the devil take them one and all, for I couldn't care less.

Things would have worked out—if not for Bohslev. A Boshlev Jew can't bear to see his fellow villager getting money for nothing. So they got busy and sent out affidavits. In other words, they tattled on me. Some wrote letters, others took the trouble of presenting themselves in person at the offices of the insurance company. They went in and blabbed that I myself had started the fire. Those intriguing scoundrels! They said I purposely left home that night in order to— Get the picture? Those scheming riffraff! They insisted that I never had as much merchandise as I claimed to have, that the accounts and the books I presented were a bunch of lies, and that they would prove black on white that—those Hamans! The devil take them one and all, for I couldn't care less.

I turned a deaf ear to them, I assure you, for I was perfectly innocent, innocent as a lamb. Their claim that I had started the fire was utter nonsense. Even a baby knows that if someone really wants to do an underhanded thing like that he doesn't have to strike the match himself. Certain individuals, representatives of the Brotherhood of Fly-by-night-fireflies, can be hired for three rubles, right? Isn't that so? What's the system like in your town?

As for their claim that I purposely left home—that's absolute drivel. It so happened that there *was* an engagement party at my sister's. I have a one-and-only sister in Tarashtche and she was marrying off her middle daughter. So would you expect me to stay home? Would that be right? I ask you: What would you do if you had a one-and-only sister and she was marrying off her middle daughter? Would you sit home and miss the engagement party? Well, why don't you speak up? Or would you expect me to be a prophet and predict that on the very evening when my sister was marrying off her middle daughter I would have a fire in Bohslev? Lucky for me, I was insured at least. Actually, I insured myself on account of all the recent fires. Come summertime and all the little villages go up in smoke. It's perfectly maddening. There's one fire after another. There's either a fire in Mir, or in Bobroisk, or in Retchitse, or in Bialistok. The world's ablaze!

So I made up my mind. Like the expression has it: All Israelites are pals. In other words, if all Jews are burning, where does that leave me? If I can go and insure myself, why should I, lummox ibn blockhead, take chances with my store and depend on miracles? And since I was already insuring myself, why don't I insure myself to the hilt, as is right and proper? Like they say, if you're already eating pork, might as well lick the platter clean. The devil won't run off with the insurance company, and the few rubles they'd give me won't make them any poorer—the devil take them one and all, for I couldn't care less.

So I went to my insurance agent and told him:

"Listen Zaynvel, here's the story. Everyone's been having fires. Why should I take chances? I want you to insure my store."

"Really?" he said, looking at me with an outlandish smirk on his face.

"How come you're grinning like an unwashed corpse?"

"I'm both glad and sorry," he said.

"What do you mean you're both glad and sorry?"

"I'm sorry I insured you once before," he said. "And I'm glad I'm not going to insure you a second time!"

"Why?" I asked.

"Because you fooled me once."

"When did I fool you?"

"When you had the fire."

"At least say: 'God spare us the same,' you impudent brat."

"God spare us and all Jews the same, now and forever more," he said, laughing right into my face.

Some smart aleck! As you can imagine, I immediately went looking for another agent. Big deal! Like the Book says:

Aren't there enough graves in Egypt? In other words, aren't
there plenty of insurance companies here? Dear Lord in
heaven, there were as many agents as flies! So I got hold of a
young man who had just finished his year of free board at his
father-in-law's. He had become an insurance agent and was
looking for business. Well, naturally, he insured 'me. And for
ten thousand rubles, too. Why not? Don't you think it befits
me to have more than ten thousand rubles' worth of stock on
hand? Like they say: The turnover is stupendous. In other
words, what we're out of today we'll have tomorrow. And
what about the villagers' remark that I'd never had that
much merchandise? Who cares about their remarks? Let
them go prove it! Let them talk, let them mumble, let them
howl, let the devil take them one and all, for I couldn't care
less.

It was my good luck that when I insured myself, no one in
Bohslev knew about it. And that's why the transaction came
off smoothly. Only after the catastrophe, when I was burned
to the ground a second time, did our good brethren and
fellow Israelites immediately scamper to the agents. Who was
he insured by, they wanted to know, when and for how
much? And when they found out it was for ten thousand
there was an uproar—they kicked up a full-fledged storm.
What? Ten thousand? Moishe-Mordecai is going to get ten
thousand rubles?

Ten thousand plagues upon you Bohslevers! What do you
care if Moishe-Mordecai will get ten thousand rubles? Is it
any skin off your back if Moishe-Mordecai earns a ruble or
two, God forbid? And what would happen if the situation
were reversed and Moishe-Mordecai happened to lose money
in the fire? Would you have reimbursed him?

I tell you, Bohslev is some town. Don't trifle with Bohslev!
It's a city of absolutely honest people. Perfect saints! Can't
stand iniquity. You'd think people would have some pity.
They witness such a tragedy, a man's family escapes by a hair,
suffers incalculable damage. And suppose his damage were
not *that* great? I wish a plague on them for every ruble over—
I mean *under* ten thousand I'm going to make on the deal.
Well, what of it? Suppose I'd even get the entire ten thousand? So what? Why should anyone lose sleep over it? If the

next fellow's on fire—let him burn. In fact, why don't *you* burn, to the blazes with you Bohslevers!

Poking your nose into another man's affairs has become a pious deed, right? Suppose he's a father of children? Suppose he has to marry off a daughter, a lovely girl with a heart of gold? Suppose he can finally have some joy but doesn't even have enough to pay the matchmaker? Suppose he has a brilliant son who desperately wants to study, poor thing, but doesn't have the means? Suppose he suffered, spit blood for the sake of his wife and children? That no one thinks of even! They just think of *getting* even. Like the Book says: *Perhaps the Lord will be compassionate.* In other words, perhaps with God's help I'll end up flat broke. For after all, they say, why *should* I get anything—the devil take them one and all, for I couldn't care less.

And yet? I'll tell you the truth. The fact that the shop-keepers begrudge me the money and the poor are green with envy doesn't bother me a bit. But how come the wealthy folk are butting in? Our rich man's son, Moishe the Brain, burns me up more than anyone. He's kind and warmhearted, clever and gentle. An impeccably honest chap. Generous to a fault. Despises usury. Philanthropic. Simply an excellent young man.

"What's new with your pack of troubles?" this saint would ask me each time he saw me. "Tsk, tsk. I heard all about your great damage. How unfortunate!"

And while saying this he would slide his hands into his pockets, stick out his stomach and gaze at me with his asinine eyes. The smirk on his face made me itch to smack him. And what an itch that was! But you have to bite your tongue. What can I do? Like the books say: *Forbearance is a virtue.* In other words, grin and bear it.

I just hope the police investigation will soon end. I'm under investigation, you see. I'm always being called to the police station. Each time they ask me another question. But I couldn't care less. It's like water off a duck's back. For, alas, why should I worry if I'm perfectly innocent, innocent as a lamb? But in the interim, till things clear up they made me sign a paper which forbids me to leave town; but to spite the Bohslever Jews, that's just what I *do* do—and as you see, I travel around day and night. Like the Hagada says: *All who wish may enter and eat.* In other words, whoever feels like following me can, and let's see if they can do anything to me—the devil take them one and all, for I couldn't care less.

You'd think that on account of my pack of troubles the insurance company wouldn't want to settle with me. Nonsense! May a thousand boils and blisters break out on Moishe the Brain's idiotic face for every thousand rubles I could get from them. The obvious question is—then why don't I take it? Eh! But you don't know me! I want you to know that I'm a tough Jew, I got the soul of a gangster! I'm not any easy bite. I go my own sweet way. Like the books say: Since your fall has begun, keep right on falling! In other words, so long as things have gone this far, let them take their own course. And what about the investigation? Well, that's just what it is, an investigation and no more. Why should I worry, if I'm perfectly innocent, innocent as a lamb?

Things are only bad now while I can't make use of my money and while I'm in such a tight squeeze that I'm gasping for breath. That's the worst part of it. Yet I swear it's still enough to make your blood boil. The money which is due me I most certainly will get. Nothing will stop me. So why do they make it a long-dragged-out affair? Just give me my money, I demand. My money is what I want. Murderers! What have you got against my children? I shouted. Am I asking for the moon? Just give me ten thousand rubles, my children's money, and leave me alone and let's put an end to it—the devil take you one and all, for I couldn't care less.

But neither demands nor shouts did any good. Meanwhile, things were so bad with me they couldn't get any worse. I neglected my business, canceled marriage arrangements—no money for dowry—and tuition was costing me plenty. Every day, God be praised, money was being squandered. We were going broke. Not to mention the anguish. Think I slept nights? I didn't even so much as shut an eye. Of course I wasn't scared. What's there to be scared about if I was perfectly innocent, innocent as a lamb? But, you know, one is only human and all sorts of thoughts and ideas run through your mind. There was an investigation and a prosecutor and Bohslever Jews who were only too ready to testify and swear that they saw me walking around in the attic with a lit candle. Don't toy with the Bohslever Jews! Believe me, there's a certain David-Hersh in town! May me and you both earn every week what this David-Hersh is costing me in hush money. And he's a pal, I want you to know, a scion of a fine family. And it's all done with a friendly smile, with pious expressions like "God willing" and "The good Lord will help"—the devil take them one and all, for I couldn't care less.

Now have you got an inkling into what sort of town Bohslev is? Am I not justified in being incensed at our Jews? Just wait, once I get my hands on those few rubles, God willing, I'll settle accounts with them. First of all I'll pledge some money to the town's communal coffers—I can't tell you exactly how much, but I assure you I won't be outdone by our rich men's contributions. You can take my word for it that I will play the part of the most illustrious man of wealth: the finest synagogue honors, the most generous donations, publicly proclaimed from the pulpit, and loudly too, so that all who hear it will burst, then turn green with envy. Of course that doesn't include the Talmud Torah and the Visit-the-Sick Society. To the latter I'll present half a dozen calico shirts for the sick, and to the Talmud Torah, brand-new ritual fringes for all the kids.

And only *then* will I marry off my daughters. But lavishly, and with style. You probably think that I'd simply marry off my daughters like other Jews do. If that's what you think, then you don't know me at all. No sir! When I marry off a daughter I'll do it like it's never been done before. Folks will never see a wedding like that again. A tent covering the entire synagogue courtyard. A first-class orchestra from Kiev. The pauper's table with setting for three hundred poor, an excellent meal, the best white-loaves, the finest whiskey, and lots of charity—a couple of kopecks for every beggar.

As for the wedding feast—I'll invite the entire village and I mean *every*one from one end of town to the other. And especially my enemies—they'll be seated at the dais and I'll drink to their health and dance with them, again and again and yet again. Play on, you fiddlers, for all you're worth, and let's keep on dancing!

That's the sort of man I am. But you don't know me. Are you listening? You don't know me at all. When I begin to celebrate, I treat money like dirt. One quart of whiskey after another. Like the Book says: *May my soul perish with the Philistines.* In other words, I don't give a damn for myself. Drink till you burst and begone!—The devil take you one and all, for I couldn't care less.

THE VILLAGE OF HABNE

It happened in Odessa. A group of intellectuals sat around a table at an outdoor café. Among them were writers and readers, young and old, and a couple of students, one of them a beautiful, wholesome-looking, apple-cheeked young girl. Also present were a group of plain, unpretentious Jews who didn't belong to our circle, but seeing other Jews talking, they merely pricked up their ears at first, and then gradually moved closer and closer to the table. By and by, our small circle became one big party. Glasses were exchanged on the table, and feet under the table, in line with the proverb: All Israelites are brothers. . . .

Now it wasn't the Sabbath, but a weekday. We weren't even talking about the Sabbath, but about other matters. If I'm not mistaken, we were arguing Zionism, territorialism and related topics. The furthest thought from our minds were such matters as money, the Sabbath, or a village called Habne. In light of all this, then, I haven't the faintest idea why a sallow young man with white eyebrows suddenly rose—he was one of the newcomers to our table—waved his hand and began to speak:

Shh! Enough said! What's the use of all this chatter? Hold on and I'll soon tell you a better story, one that happened to me in Habne—that is, in a village known as Habne. It had everything a village needed: a post office, a rabbi and a crown-rabbi, a river, a telegraph office, a cemetery, a police station, a Talmud Torah, Hasidim, two synagogues, a host of paupers and a handful of rich men. In brief, it was a typical little village.

It so happened that the winds of fortune once blew me into Habne for the Sabbath. Now listen carefully, for this is an excellent story. It's short and sweet and you might be able to put it to good use. I don't have to tell you that when you come to a small town for Sabbath you simply must become provincial. You've got no other choice. Just forget about traveling farther on the Sabbath. Habne is not the big city of Odessa, you know. Since time immemorial no Jew has ever desecrated the Sabbath in Habne. And if you stay in Habne, that is, if you become a Habner for the Sabbath, you must straightaway beat a path to the bathhouse. You've got no other choice! What else could you do? Sit down and write a novel? Attending services is taken for granted. I'd just like to see you come to Habne for the Sabbath and *not* go to the synagogue. Do you think they'd harm you in some way, God forbid? Not at all. They wouldn't *do* a thing *to* you. They'd just stare *at* you. The entire village would simply assemble to stare at the man who had come to Habne for the Sabbath and refused to go to the synagogue.

Anyway, what would your host think of you? How would the food, served in the privacy of your room, taste? That is, if they would deign to give you a meal in private! Who do you think you are, a big shot—eating alone and neither joining your host at the Sabbath table to chant Kiddush nor helping him sing the Sabbath table-hymns? If you really were some rich nobleman—why that's a horse of another color! Then you'd get everything in your room: food, drinks, a smoke, even—but don't breathe a word of it!—a samovar on Sabbath.

Where do I get my information from? Don't ask. There's where I draw the line. For if you start asking questions—why this, why that—why then there'd be no end to the matter. In a word—when in Habne, do as the Habners do.

But an extraordinary thing befell me there. I happened to be on my way to a certain rich nobleman who lived not far from Habne. I carried so much money with me—several thousands in cash—that my pockets were literally bulging. I suppose it should have been obvious to anyone who didn't even know I was carrying money, for a man who has so much cash on him looks different. Even his walk, his stance, his

manner of speaking change radically. Money has a certain
power—after all, it's money.

Well then, what should I do with so much cash? First of all,
it was Sabbath. Since Habne is not Odessa, you know, I
couldn't carry money with me on Sabbath. And secondly, I
must admit that I was somewhat apprehensive of sleeping at
an inn while carrying so much cash, knock wood. Not that I
was afraid of the innkeeper, God forbid. He was a pious,
upright Jew, wearing an elegant begirded gaberdine. I wasn't
even concerned about robbers. Habne isn't known for its
thieves or robbers. In fact, there has never even been one
single case of murder or robbery in Habne.

Ah me, if Habne once experienced a bit of a pogrom, why
then the murders took place during the pogrom. Anyway,
can you find a place nowadays which hasn't had a pogrom? I
swear you can go about all alone in Habne at midnight and,
so help me, nothing will happen to you. In that case, what
was I afraid of? I was afraid of only one thing: it was such a
huge sum of cash, knock wood, another man's money, not my
own. What if, God forbid—well, you know the sort of thing
that can happen. I turned this way and that—in short I was
in a fix. So what did I do? I spoke to the innkeeper and asked
him:

"Tell me, who are the most prominent and respected men
of means in town?"

"Why do you ask?" he said. "Want to make a little business, huh?"

Should I tell him what's eating me? I thought. It's true
that he was a fine Jew with an elegant begirded gaberdine,
and that Habne wasn't known for its thieves or robbers; but
the truth of the matter was that it was money after all, a huge
sum of cash, knock wood, another man's money, not my own.

To make a long story short, I asked him this and he asked
me that. I said, "man of means"; he said, "business." We beat
around the bush until I finally managed to squeeze out the
information I wanted: that Habne was a village made up
entirely of paupers. That is, they did have some prosperous
men, but they were few and far between.

There was only one man who could in all honesty be
considered somewhat well-to-do, perhaps even downright rich

—well, not only downright rich, but absolutely loaded. True, no one had ever counted his money, but money he had, perhaps even lots of it. He owned several houses, a market-place full of shops, some woods—you might even say an entire forest; two forests, in fact.

To top it off, he wasn't a bad sort, not at all an ill-natured man. One might even say he was quite kindly: he had a good heart and a generous hand. He liked to show off with a dona-tion, a free loan, a little favor. He never refused anyone who came to him. Naturally, he did it for honor, he loved honor, a rich man is crazy for honor. Yet he pretended to be modest, considered himself one of the common people, and sup-posedly despised honor.

It could even be said that he was quite an upright man. Of course, he was no great saint, but he would never violate a precept publicly. What he did in the privacy of his home, amid his own four walls, no one knew. After all, that's none of our business. But concerning his honesty there wasn't the slightest question. And he didn't expect any gratitude for this, either. For if a man like him weren't honest, who then *would* be?

In brief, I gathered from this description that I could entrust my entire bundle to this man. So on that Friday afternoon, before Jews began to go to the bathhouse, I left for his house. I found him at home, poring over a book. He was a handsome man, I saw, and as he sat in his chair I noted that his bearing was lordly and placid, the typical demeanor of a provincial man of wealth. After greeting him, I told him the entire story—that I was going to a rich landowner, had lots of cash in my possession and was obliged to spend the Sabbath here in town. And so, naturally enough, I was apprehensive. Habne indeed was not known for its thieves or robbers, and my innkeeper was truly a fine man wearing an elegant begirded gaberdine. Nevertheless, it still was a huge sum of cash, knock wood, another man's money, not my own.

"Then what's on your mind, young man?" he replied with a smile.

I asked him if he could possibly put my money into his safe until after the Sabbath. If so, I could rest assured. I wanted to make it clear that I didn't suspect anyone, God forbid. After

all, I said, Habne was not known for its thieves or robbers.
Nevertheless, it still was a huge sum of cash, knock wood,
another man's money, not my own.

He heard me out and smiled. "My dear young man," he
said. "You've never met me before. You don't even know me.
Why then are you entrusting me with such a vast amount of
money?"

"A man's name is his reputation," I told him. "But in any
case, I suppose you probably won't mind giving me a little
receipt."

So he smiled again and said, "In my entire lifetime I have
never given anyone a receipt."

"All right, so there won't be a receipt."

"No," he said. "Nothing doing."

"Then what's to be done?" I said.

"Do as you see fit."

"How about witnesses?"

"Fine with me."

"Who shall I bring?"

"Whoever you wish," he said.

"Can you recommend a couple of upstanding villagers?"

"In this village they're all upstanding."

"If so, then I'll just run out for a minute and bring back
two householders."

"Run and bring whoever you like," he said.

Seeing that this entire affair vexed him, I tried to justify
myself by saying:

"I would never have done such a thing if it were my own
money. I wish I had a kopeck for every thousand rubles I
would have trusted you with. But since it's not my money but
someone else's, I have to be careful. Well? Don't you agree?
Don't I have to be careful?"

He heard me out, gave me that enigmatic smile of his and
remained silent. I noticed that he was not too pleased. But
since I had already said that I'd run out and bring back two
householders—why, I had to run out and bring back two
householders. So I returned to the inn and approached the
innkeeper once again in order to ferret out who were the
finest Jews in town. But it was impossible to squeeze a word
out of him. There was only one thing he wanted to know.

"It's one thing if it concerns a match," said he, "but it's quite another if it concerns credit. In any case, even if it's nothing special, I'd like to know what's going on."

We bandied back and forth until I finally wrested out of him the news that all the Habner householders were fine men.

"But on the other hand," he said, "may the good Lord grant them the virtues they're still lacking. For what actually is fineness? Taken individually, each one of the Habner householders could be considered a fine man. But you could also say, if you wish, that ideal fineness is nonexistent. It also depends on what aspects of fineness you're looking for in the next person. Money? Family? Torah? Good breeding? Perhaps all of these. But since all of these cannot be found in one person, hence everyone in Habne is a fine man. However, if you want the cream of the crop, there are only two fine men in Habne: Reb Leyzer and Reb Yossi. Of them it may truly be said: These are the finest of men."

"If you don't mind, please tell me just who are Reb Leyzer and Reb Yossi?"

"What do you care?" he said. "If I tell you, will you be any the wiser?"

"Of course! After all, every man is known by his character."

"You're a strange chap," he said. "You have to know everything. Reb Leyzer is a Jew who goes by the name of Leyzer, and Reb Yossi is a Jew whom everybody calls Yossi. Feel better now?"

To make a long story short, I went over to Reb Leyzer who goes by the name of Leyzer and to Reb Yossi whom everybody calls Yossi, and I introduced myself. They were handsome Jews with comely beards and we had a pleasant chat concerning this and that, talking about anything that struck our fancy. Finally we got to the heart of the matter and I quite simply told them the entire story—that I was on my way to a rich nobleman and carried money with me. I was afraid, lest—Habne indeed was not known for its thieves or robbers, but after all it was a huge sum of cash, knock wood, another man's money, not my own. Which is why I was asking them to favor me by coming to the rich man's house for a minute and merely be present when I give him the money for safekeeping until after the Sabbath.

Well, they heard me out, did Reb Leyzer who goes by the name Leyzer and Reb Yossi whom everybody calls Yossi. They listened judiciously, stroked their beards and asked again and again: whence and whither, what and how. But it didn't take them long to agree, whereupon all three of us promptly set out for the rich man of Habne. There, after begging his pardon and stating that Habne indeed was not known for its thieves or robbers, I emptied all my pockets, removed the money, counted out that parcel of poverty, wrapped it in a piece of paper and handed it over to the rich man of Habne for safekeeping until after the Sabbath. Once more I apologized for imposing upon him. Beyond doubt Habne was not known for its thieves or robbers, God forbid; but after all, it was a huge sum of cash, knock wood, another man's money, not my own.

The rich man very adroitly took over the little bundle—it went from my hand to his like a circumcised infant passed from the godmother to the godfather. Meanwhile my two witnesses did their part as witnesses, stroking their beards and licking their lips, like a cat who had spotted a crock of butter. Then I bade them good-bye, begged their pardon for imposing on them—Habne indeed was not known for its thieves or robbers, God forbid, but—and so I bade them a good Sabbath and that was that.

Having emptied my pockets, I now felt as if I'd gotten rid of a heavy burden. My mind at ease, I now went to a synagogue and heard a fine cantor, who trilled and tremoloed a bit too much; a variety of phenomenal sounds came out of his throat. He warbled the "Come My Beloved" hymn like a nightingale, but rendered the Psalm for the Sabbath like— forgive the comparison—a music hall performer. Yet his "Grant Peace" was so sweetly Jewish in style and pious in intonation, I could have heard it again and again. It was ages since I had heard a cantor like the one in Habne; it was ages since I had heard such a Kiddush and such Sabbath table-hymns or eaten such peppered fish, delicious noodles and a roast with honeyed carrots. It was ages since I had had such a sound, delectable night's sleep as I did that Friday night; and like a lord I even napped most of the next day.

Having had enough sleep, I picked myself up and went out for a stroll to take a look at the men and women and the boys and girls of Habne who paraded up and down, decked out in the latest fashions. Toward evening I had myself quite a pleasant Sabbath supper which was graced by lovely table-hymns. Then I went to the synagogue for the evening service, returned home, recited the Prayer of Separation, and, after knocking off the customary two or three rubles from the bill, settled my account with the innkeeper's wife. And then, with the same sense of calm and equanimity, I meandered over to the rich man's house.

When I entered, I found him walking about leisurely in his living room. He wore a beautiful silk gaberdine adorned with silk tassels, which he twisted as he hummed and sang in a fine voice:

> Elijah the Prophet,
> Elijah the Tishbite,
> Elijah the Gileadite,
> May he come,
> Speedily in our days.

As long as he's singing, said I to myself, let him sing on. Once he stops singing, I'll say my piece. But my rich man did not stop singing or humming or twisting the tassels from one finger to another. I began to feel as if I were sitting on hot coals. I kept jumping up in order to settle the matter, but interrupting him was impossible. He sang and hummed, twisted the tassels, and his voice kept rising:

> Elijah the Prophet,
> Elijah the Tishbite,
> Elijah the Gileadite,
> Ay-ay-ay-ay,
> Ay-ay-ay-ay,
> May he come,
> Speedily in our days.
> Elijah the Prophet,
> Elijah the Tishbite,
> Elijah the Gileadite,

Well, here goes, thought I, and braced myself. I rose, approached him and said:

"Since I'm planning to leave, God willing, this very evening—immediately, in fact—and continue on my journey, I wanted to ask you about the m—"

But he raised his tasseled finger quite high and sang into my face:

> Elijah the Prophet,
> Elijah the Tishbite,
> Elijah the Gileadite,
>
> Ay-ay-ay-ay . . .

My goodness, it's like the dream I had last night, the night before and throughout the week! I thought. This man's fallen in love with Elijah. We can't tear him away.

To make a long story short, the man hummed and sang until he had hummed and sung himself dry.

"Now that the Sabbath is over," he said to me, "let me wish you a good week. Please be seated."

We both sat down at a table. He offered me a cigarette, ordered a glass of tea for each of us and then asked:

"Well, my dear young man, what's the good word?"

"What is there for me to say? Since I'm leaving tonight—that is, immediately—I wanted to ask you to give me the few coins—"

"What coins?"

"Those few rubles."

"What rubles?"

"The money," I said. "My money!"

"What money?"

"What do you mean, what money? Don't you know what I'm talking about? I mean the money I gave you for safe-keeping until after the Sabbath."

"You mean to tell me that you gave me money?" he said, pulling a face as though I had just told him that his nose wasn't his at all, but mine.

You can imagine how I felt at that moment. Who knows? Habne indeed was not known for its thieves or robbers, God forbid. But then I thought—perhaps he's playing a joke on me. So I began to laugh.

"Ha, ha, you're really a clown," I said. "You certainly know your business."

"What business?" he said with a perfectly straight face.

"The joke you're playing on me."

"My dear young man," he said, quite seriously, "I am not your equal and I am not playing any jokes on you. Now please tell me what it is you wish?"

At this point I felt a nervous tic on my face. My eyes blinked, my knees trembled. In another minute I'd keel over. But still I didn't bat an eyelash. I took it all as a huge joke and said:

"All right now, enough kidding around. For goodness sake, give me my money and let me go."

But my rich man of Habne sat opposite me and looked me right in the eye. You would have at least expected his nostrils to flare or his eyes to blink. But there was absolutely no reaction. As if I'd been talking nonsense, God forbid, or spouting drivel.

"My dear young man," he said calmly, "you must have made a mistake. You've got the wrong party."

This last remark enraged me and I called out:

"If you're not joking, then I don't understand what sort of game you're playing. I've given you some money for safe-keeping, a huge sum of cash, knock wood, another man's money, not my own . . ."

I felt my tongue becoming thick, a choking sensation enveloped my throat. My left ear hummed. Another minute and I'd pass out.

"I haven't got the faintest notion of what you're talking about."

"Haven't you taken any money from me?" I asked.

"*Me?* from *you?*" he said. "Well, prove it. Have you got something black on white?"

At this point I felt absolutely sick. Now I understood why he said he never signed receipts.

"My God!" I said. "What about the witnesses who were here?"

"Witnesses? What witnesses?"

"Weren't Reb Leyzer and Reb Yossi here?"

"What Leyzer and which Yossi?"

"God Almighty! So help me, I'm going to run out and bring them over here."

"Run wherever you like," he said, "but leave me alone. For I don't think you're quite right in the head, my dear young man."

While running for my witnesses I thought that perhaps I was *not* quite right in the head. Perhaps I *was* imagining things. Perhaps it was all a dream. Perhaps I wasn't even in Habne. I ran and my thoughts tagged along. My head nearly split wide open. What an ill wind had blown me into Habne for the Sabbath! Woe is me. What shall I do? Blast it, I've been ruined.

To make a long story short, I came to Reb Leyzer and to Reb Yossi and set forth my calamity.

"Come along, merciful Jews. Hurry! Have pity. It's a huge sum of cash, knock wood, another man's money, not my own. Save me!"

All three of us came running to the rich man's house. He greeted us with a peculiar smile and said to my two witnesses:

"Well, what do you say to this scoundrel? This young fellow has been building castles in the sky. He claims to have given me a huge sum of money for safekeeping, as it were, and points to you as witnesses. Now what do you say to such a troublemaker?"

My two witnesses, the two fine Jews with the comely beards, stood there gaping at the rich man, at me, and at each other.

"Well, why don't you speak up?" the rich man told them. "Did you ever hear such a trumped-up charge?"

My two witnesses, the two fine Jews with the comely beards, exchanged glances and declared:

"May the Almighty and blessed God protect us from the likes of him."

"He claims that it was a vast amount of money," the rich man continued, "some umpteen thousand rubles, and that you yourselves saw him giving me the money for safekeeping until after the Sabbath. How do you like that? I'm afraid that the young man, alas, is a bit off."

"Exactly. Alas, he's . . . a bit off," said my two witnesses, looking at the rich man and at each other as they stroked their comely beards.

I felt like saying something, like screaming—but I could not. I saw stars. My tongue stuck to the roof of my mouth. I felt an odd sensation in my throat, as though a bone were stuck there.

My two fine witnesses, Reb Leyzer and Reb Yossi, looked at the rich man, exchanged confused glances, and slipped silently out of the house. Despite their drawn, pallid faces, their eyes had glowed and beamed like those of a man into whose lap the Almighty and blessed God had thrown a neat little bundle for the coming week.

Are you listening? God knows what would have happened to me had not the rich man approached me, thrown his arm around my shoulders and then opened his iron safe, saying:

"My dear young man! Don't eat your heart out. Here's your money. I merely wanted to show you the true colors of Habne and of its fine, upstanding citizens."

Ever since then I steer clear of Habne. If I must go there, I arrive with empty pockets. If I must bring money, I don't stay there for the Sabbath. If I must spend the Sabbath there, why you can be sure I know what to do.

As soon as the sallow young man with the white eyebrows finished telling his tale, he pushed his chair back a bit and began to look each of us in the eye to see what sort of an impression his story had made. We all sat thunderstruck. Our discussion had been stopped dead in its tracks, severed, as it were, by the blow of an ax.

One of us (I don't recall who it was—perhaps me) got up and asked the sallow young man with the white eyebrows:

"In reference to what in our discussion did you tell us this story?"

"In reference to what?" he exclaimed in surprise. "What do you mean, in reference to what? In reference to nothing at all. It's just a story, out of the blue. I just happened to think of it, so I told it."

GLOSSARY

Afternoon Service: one of the three weekday services. The other two are the Morning Service and the Evening Service.

alef-beys: the Hebrew word for alphabet; specifically, the first two letters.

bagel: a doughnut-shaped hard roll, whose dough is first boiled, then baked.

borscht: a soup made of beets or cabbage, of Russian origin.

Elul: the last month of the Jewish year (August-September); the month preceding the season of the High Holy Days.

eruv: a line of wire or even string around the community which permitted Jews to carry personal articles on the Sabbath; a legal device for converting public into private domain.

Ethics of the Fathers: one of the tractates of the Mishna (the body of oral law redacted c. 200 C.E. by Rabbi Judah). The tractate deals with the ethical principles formulated, often in epigrammatic form, by the fathers of Jewish rabbinic tradition. The Ethics of the Fathers is included in the Prayerbook and has become the most popular book in the Mishna.

Hagada (lit "the telling"): the book of the Passover home service which through narrative and song recounts the story of Jewish slavery in Egypt and the liberation. The Hagada is read during the first two nights of Passover.

Hallel (lit. "praise"): Psalms 113–118, recited during the morning service on Sukkos, Passover, Shevuos, Hanuka and the New Moon.

Hanuka (lit. "dedication"): the Festival of Lights celebrated for eight days, starting the twenty-fifth of Kislev (November-December). Hanuka marks the struggle for religious freedom

and the successful revolt of poorly armed Jews against the
forces of Antiochus Epiphanes, who proscribed the practice
of Judaism. In 165 B.C.E., the Jewish fighters, led by Judah
Maccabeus, routed the Hellenistic Syrians and rededicated
the Temple. Hanuka is a time when card games, usually
forbidden, are permitted.

Hasidism: founded by Israel Baal Shem Tov, the Master of the
Good Name (1700–1760). The Hasidic movement, a revolt
against rabbinism and its accent on talmudic accomplish-
ment, stressed good deeds and piety through joy of worship,
songs, legends and dance. It had a wide appeal to the masses
and its followers were, and still are, called Hasidim.

Havdala (lit. "separation" or "distinction"): the Prayer of Separation is recited at the conclusion of the Sabbath, about
one hour after sundown; it marks the separation between the
Sabbath and a weekday, or between the Sabbath and a festival which immediately follows. The Havdala is also said at
the conclusion of a festival.

High Holy Days: Rosh Hashana and Yom Kippur.

Kabala: a body of mystical lore and scriptural interpretation developed by the Kabalists, who through study and meditative
speculation sought communion with God.

Kaddish (lit. "sanctification"): a prayer which marks the conclusion of a unit in the service and which is also recited as a
mourner's prayer. The Kaddish, which makes no reference
at all to death, is actually a doxology.

Kiddush (lit. "sanctification"): blessing recited over wine at the
beginning of the Sabbath or holiday evening meal.

Lag B'Omer: a day of festivity, especially for Jewish children,
who are released from their studies and taken into the fields
and woods. Tradition says that on this day the plague which
beset the disciples of Rabbi Akiba, who fought and died, in
the last, and unsuccessful, Jewish revolt against Rome (132
C.E.) came to an end.

mezuza (pl. mezuzos): a rolled piece of parchment containing the
verses from Deuteronomy 6:4–9 and 11:13–17, and inserted
in a wooden or metal case. It is affixed on the right-hand
doorposts of Jewish homes and synagogues.

Midrash (lit. "explanation" or "interpretation"): rabbinic commentary and explanatory notes, homilies and stories on scriptural passages.

Misnagdim (lit. "opponents"): the group which opposed the Hasidim and their *rebbes.*

Mourner's Prayer: See Kaddish.

Passover: the eight-day festival starting the fifteenth of Nissan (March-April) and commemorating the Jews' freedom from Egyptian bondage. It was also an agricultural feast during which the Israelites offered up the first fruits of the winter barley.

Prayer of Separation: see Havdala.

Purim: the festival celebrating the Jews' deliverance from Haman's plan to exterminate them, as described in the biblical Book of Esther. It is celebrated on the fourteenth of Adar (March), and is noted for its gaiety, especially its Purim plays and festive meal. In the synagogues, where the Book of Esther is read from scrolls, children twirl the rattle-clackers each time Haman's name is mentioned. Purim, too, is a time for sending sweet-platters to neighbors and charity to the poor.

ram's horn: known in Hebrew as *shofar,* it is blown several times during Rosh Hashana and once at the conclusion of the Yom Kippur service. The awesome sounds of the ram's horn are supposed to arouse the people to repentance. According to tradition every Jew must hear the *shofar.*

Rashi: Rabbi *Shlomo ben Itzhak* (1040–1105), of Troyes, France, whose commentaries on the Bible and the Talmud almost immediately became classics. No Talmud and hardly a Pentateuch is printed without the popular commentary by Rashi.

Reb: mister.

Rebbe: the spiritual leader of a group of Hasidim, not necessarily the rabbi of a community. It was quite common for Jews to travel distances great and small to visit their *rebbe.*

rebbi: a Hebrew teacher, not ordained as a rabbi.

ritual fringes: known in Hebrew as *tsitsis* or *talis-kotn,* it is a four-cornered, fringed garment worn underneath the shirt by male Jews who observe the biblical commandment to wear a garment with fringes (Numbers 15:37–41).

Rosh Hashana (lit. "head of the year"): the Jewish New Year, celebrated the first and second days of Tishri (September). Next to Yom Kippur, these are the most solemn days of the year.

Sacrificial Ceremony: performed the day before Yom Kippur, this is a ceremony wherein a person's guilt is symbolically transferred to the fowl, which is waved around the head three times. Many rabbinic authorities have decried the pagan nature of the ceremony and stated that it lacked authentic Jewish content. Hence, the irony in "A White Bird" of a woman who "religiously" follows a folk custom of dubious Jewish value.

Seder: the festive home ritual of the first and second nights of Passover, at which the Hagada is recited.

Shemini Atzeres: the eighth day of the festival of Sukkos.

Shevuos (lit. "weeks"): the Feast of Weeks celebrated on the sixth and seventh of Sivan (May-June), seven weeks after Passover. Shevuos marks the day on which the Torah was given to Israel on Mount Sinai, and also the day on which the first fruits of the wheat harvest were offered to God.

shokhet (pl. shokhtim): the man ritually qualified to slaughter cattle and fowl for those who observe the Jewish dietary laws.

Silent Devotion: the prayer silently recited during each of the Services by the congregation in a standing position.

Simkhas Torah: the festival immediately following Shemini Atzeres, on which the reading of the Torah is completed and begun anew. This joyous holiday is traditionally celebrated with singing and dancing around the synagogue with the Torah.

Sukkos: the Feast of Booths celebrated for seven days (nine, including Shemini Atzeres and Simkhas Torah), starting the fifteenth of Tishri. Sukkos commemorates the Jews' living in booths (sukkos) during their wandering in the desert, and is, in addition, the harvest festival.

Tisha B'Av: a day of mourning and fasting (August). Tradition tells us that both the First Temple (586 B.C.E.) and the Second (70 C.E.) were destroyed on that day by Nebuchadnezzar and

Titus, respectively. On Tisha B'Av the biblical book of Lamentations is chanted.

Talmud Torah: the school where children were taught Hebrew, the prayers and the Pentateuch.

tfillin: known in English as phylacteries, these are square leather boxes containing scriptural passages worn on the arm and head during morning prayers daily, except Sabbath and holidays, by male Jews over thirteen.

Ten Days of Repentance: the ten-day period commencing with Rosh Hashana and ending with Yom Kippur; a time when the Jew is supposed to examine his moral and religious state of being and begin to pursue the path of good deeds which he will follow throughout the year.

tsimess: vegetables simmered in honey or sugar; usually with carrots, or potatoes and prunes.

Yiddish: the language of the Jews of Eastern Europe, and now spoken by their descendants in various parts of the world. An outgrowth of Middle High German, Yiddish, which contains Hebrew and Slavic words, is written in Hebraic characters and is read from right to left. It has been spoken by Jews for nearly 1,000 years.

Yizkor: the Memorial Service, recited on the last days of the three major festivals, Sukkos, Passover, Shevuos, and on Yom Kippur, in memory of parents, children, wives or husbands, and martyrs.

Yom Kippur: the Day of Atonement, the tenth day of Tishri. This is the most solemn day of the year, wherein the Jews pray and fast all day long and publicly confess their sins directly to their Creator and beg for forgiveness.